FRANKLIN KANE

MORE WILDSIDE CLASSICS

FRANKLIN KANE

ANNE DOUGLAS SEDGWICK

WILDSIDE PRESS

FRANKLIN KANE

This edition published in 2006 by Wildside Press, LLC.
www.wildsidepress.com

CHAPTER I.

Miss Althea Jakes was tired after her long journey from Basle. It was a brilliant summer afternoon, and though the shutters were half closed on the beating Parisian sunlight, the hotel sitting-room looked, in its brightness, hardly shadowed. Unpinning her hat, laying it on the table beside her, passing her hands over the undisordered folds of her hair, Miss Jakes looked about her at the old-gold brocade of the furniture, the many mirrors in ornate gold frames, the photographs from Bougereau, the long, crisp lace curtains. It was the same sitting-room that she had had last year, the same that she had had the year before last — the same, indeed, to which she had been conducted on her first stay at the Hôtel Talleyrand, eight years ago. The brocade looked as new, the gilded frames as glittering, the lace curtains as snowy as ever. Everything was as she had always seen it, from the ugly Satsuma vases flanking the ugly bronze clock on the mantelpiece, to the sheaf of pink roses lying beside her in their white paper wrappings. Even Miss Harriet Robinson's choice of welcoming flowers was the same. So it had always been, and so, no doubt, it would continue to be for many years to come; and she, no doubt, for many summers, would arrive from Basle to sit, jadedly, looking at it.

Amélie, her maid, was unpacking in the next room; the door was ajar, and Miss Jakes could hear the creaking of lifted trays and the rustling of multitudinous tissue-paper layers. The sounds suggested an answer to a dim question that had begun to hover in her travel-worn mind. One came back every summer to the Hôtel Talleyrand for the purpose of getting clothes; that, perhaps, was a sufficient answer. Yet, today, it did not seem sufficient. She was not really so very much interested in her clothes; not nearly enough interested to make them a compensation for such fatigue and loneliness as she was now feeling. And as she realised this, a further question followed: in what was she particularly interested? What was a sufficient motive for all the European journeyings with which her life, for the past ten or twelve years, had been filled? In a less jaded mood, in her usual mood of mild, if rather wistful, assurance, she would have answered at once that she was interested in everything — in everything that was of the best — pictures, music, places, and people. These surely were her objects.

She was that peculiarly civilised being, the American woman of independent means and discriminating tastes, whose cosmopolitan studies and acquaintances give, in their multiplicity, the impression of a full, if not a completed, life. But today the gloomy question hovered: was not the very pilgrimage to Bayreuth, the study of archæology in Rome, and of pictures in Florence, of much the same nature as the yearly visit to Paris for clothes? What was attained by it all? Was it not something merely superficial, to be put on and worn, as it were, not to be lived for with a growing satisfaction? Miss Jakes did not answer this question; she dismissed it with some indignation, and she got up and rang rather sharply for tea, which was late; and after asking the garçon, with a smile that in its gentleness contrasted with the sharpness of the pull, that it might be brought at once, she paused near the table to lean over and smell her sheaf of roses, and to read again, listlessly, Miss Harriet Robinson's words of affectionate greeting. Miss Robinson was a middle-aged American lady who lived in Paris, and had long urged Althea to settle there near her. Ten years ago, when she had first met Miss Robinson in Boston, Althea had thought her a brilliant and significant figure; but she had by now met too many of her kind — in Rome, in Florence, in Dresden — to feel any wish for a more intimate relationship. She was fond of Miss Robinson, but she prayed that fate did not reserve for her a withering to the like brisk, colourless spinsterhood. This hope, the necessity for such hope, was the final depth of her gloomy mood, and she found herself looking at something very dark as she stood holding Miss Robinson's expensive roses. For, after all, what was going to become of her? The final depth shaped itself today in more grimly realistic fashion than ever before: what was she going to do with herself, in the last resort, unless something happened? Her mind dwelt upon all the visible alternatives. There was philanthropic lunch-going and lunch-giving spinsterhood in Boston; there was spinsterhood in Europe, semi-social, semi-intellectual, and monotonous in its very variety, for Althea had come to feel change as monotonous; or there was spinsterhood in England established near her friend, Miss Buckston, who raised poultry in the country, and went up to London for Bach choir practices and Woman's Suffrage meetings. Althea couldn't see herself as taking an interest in poultry or in Woman's Suffrage, nor did she feel herself fitted for patriotic duties in Boston. There was nothing for it, then, but to continue her present nomadic life. After seeing herself shut in to this conclusion, it was a real relief to her to hear the tea-tray chink outside, and to see it enter, high on the garçon's shoulder, as if with a trivial but cheerful reply to her dreary questionings. Tea, at all events, would always happen and always be pleasant. Althea smiled sadly as she made the reflection, for she was not of an Epicurean temperament. After she had drunk her tea she felt strengthened to go in and ask Amélie about her clothes. She might have to get a great many new ones, especially if she went home for the autumn and winter, as she half intended to do. She took up the roses, as she passed them, to show to Amélie. Amélie was a bony, efficient Frenchwoman, with high cheek-bones and sleek black hair. She had come to Althea first, many years ago, as a courier-maid, to take her back to America. Althea's mother had died in Dresden, and Althea had been equipped by anxious friends with this competent attendant for her sad return journey. Amélie had proved intelligent and reliable in the highest degree, and though she had made herself rather disagreeable during her first year in Boston, she had stayed on ever since. She still made herself disagreeable from time to time, and Althea had sometimes lacked only the courage to dismiss her; but she could hardly imagine herself existing without Amélie, and in Europe Amélie was seldom disagreeable. In Europe, at the worst, she was gruff and ungracious, and Althea was fond enough of her to ignore these failings, although they frightened her a little; but though an easily intimidated person, and much at a loss in meeting opposition or rudeness, she was also tenacious. She might be frightened, but people could never make her do what she didn't want to do, not even Amélie. Her relations with Amélie were slightly strained just now, for she had not taken her advice as to their return journey from Venice. Amélie had insisted on Mont Cenis, and Althea had chosen the St. Gothard; so that it was as a measure of propitiation that she selected three of the roses for Amélie as she went into the bedroom. Amélie, who was kneeling before one of the larger boxes and carefully lifting skirts from its trays, paused to sniff at the flowers, and to express a terse thanks and admiration. 'Ah, bien merci, mademoiselle,' she said, laying her share on the table beside her.

She was not very encouraging about the condition of Althea's wardrobe.

'Elles sont défraîchies — démodées — en vérité, mademoiselle,' she replied, when Althea asked if many new purchases were necessary.

Althea sighed. 'All the fittings!'

'Il faut souffrir pour être belle,' said Amélie unsympathetically.

Althea had not dared yet to tell her that she might be going back to America that winter. The thought of Amélie's gloom cast a shadow over the project, and she could not yet quite face it. She wandered back to the sitting-room, and, thinking of Amélie's last words, she stood for some time and looked at herself in the large mirror which rose from mantelpiece to cornice, enclosed in cascades of gilt. One of the things that Althea, in her mild assurance, was really secure of — for, as we have intimated, her assurance often covered a certain insecurity — was her own appearance. She didn't know about 'belle,' that seemed rather a trivial term, and the English equivalent better to express the distinctive character-istic of her face. She had so often been told she was nobly beautiful that she did not see herself critically, and she now leaned her elbow on the mantelpiece and gazed at herself with sad approba-tion. The mirror reflected only her head and shoulders, and Miss Jakes's figure could not, even by a partisan, have been described as beautiful; she was short, and though immature in outline, her form was neither slender nor graceful. Althea did not feel these defects, and was well satisfied with her figure, especially with her carriage, which was full of dignity; but it was her head that best pleased her, and her head, indeed, had aspects of great benignity and sweetness. It was a large head, crowned with coils of dull gold hair; her clothing followed the fashions obediently, but her fashion of dressing her hair did not vary, and the smooth parting, the carved ripples along her brow became her, though they did not become her stiffly conventional attire. Her face, though almost classic in its spaces and modelling, lacked in feature the classic decision and amplitude, so that the effect was rather that of a dignified room meagrely furnished. For these deficiencies, how-ever, Miss Jakes's eyes might well be accepted as atonement. They were large, dark, and innocent; they lay far apart, heavily lidded and with wistful eyebrows above them; their expression varied easily from lucid serenity to a stricken, expectant look, like that of a threatened doe, and slight causes could make Miss Jakes's eyes look stricken. They did not look stricken now, but they looked profoundly melancholy.

Here she stood, in the heartless little French sitting-room, meaning so well, so desirous of the best, yet alone, uncertain of any aim, and very weary of everything.

CHAPTER II.

Althea, though a cosmopolitan wanderer, had seldom stayed in an hotel unaccompanied. She did not like, now, going down to the *table d'hôte* dinner alone, and was rather glad that her Aunt Julia and Aunt Julia's two daughters were to arrive in Paris next week. It was really almost the only reason she had for being glad of Aunt Julia's arrival, and she could imagine no reason for being glad of the girls'. Tiresome as it was to think of going to tea with Miss Harriet Robinson, to think of hearing from her all the latest gossip, and all the latest opinions of the latest books and pictures — alert, mechanical appreciations with which Miss Robinson was but too ready — it was yet more tiresome to look forward to Aunt Julia's appreciations, which were dogmatic and often belated, and to foresee that she must run once more the gauntlet of Aunt Julia's disapproval of expatriated Americans. Althea was accustomed to these assaults and met them with weary dignity, at times expostulating: 'It is all very well for you, Aunt Julia, who have Uncle Tom and the girls; I have nobody, and all my friends are married.' But this brought upon her an invariable retort: 'Well, why don't you get married then? Franklin Winslow Kane asks nothing better.' This retort angered Althea, but she was too fond of Franklin Winslow Kane to reply that perhaps she, herself, did ask something better. So that it was as a convenience, and not as a comfort, that she looked forward to Aunt Julia; and to the girls she did not look forward at all. They were young, ebullient, slangy; they belonged to a later generation than her own, strange to her in that it seemed weighted with none of the responsibilities and reverences that she had grown up among. It was a generation that had no respect for and no anxiety concerning Europe; that played violent outdoor games, and went without hats in summer.

The dining-room was full when she went down to dinner, her inward tremor of shyness sustained by the consciousness of the perfect fit and cut of her elaborate little dress. People sat at small tables, and the general impression was one of circumspection and withdrawal. Most of the occupants were of Althea's type — richly dressed, quiet-voiced Americans, careful of their own dignity and quick at assessing other people's. A French family loudly chattered and frankly stared in one corner; for the rest, all seemed to be compatriots.

But after Althea had taken her seat at her own table near the pleasantly open window, and had consulted the menu and ordered a half-bottle of white wine, another young woman entered and went to the last vacant table left in the room, the table next Althea's — so near, indeed, that the waiter found some difficulty in squeezing himself between them when he presented the *carte des vins* to the newcomer.

She was not an American, Althea felt sure of this at once, and the mere negation was so emphatic that it almost constituted, for the first startled glance, a complete definition. But, glancing again and again, while she ate her soup, Althea realised there were so many familiar things the newcomer was not, that she seemed made up of differences. The fact that she was English — she spoke to the waiter absent-mindedly in that tongue — did not make her less different, for she was like no English person that Althea had ever seen. She engaged at once the whole of her attention, but at first Althea could not have said whether this attention were admiring; her main impression was of oddity, of something curiously arresting and noticeable.

The newcomer sat in profile to Althea, her back to the room, facing the open window, out of which she gazed vaguely and unseeingly. She was dressed in black, a thin dress, rather frayed along the edges — an evening dress; though, as a concession to Continental custom, she had a wide black scarf over her bare shoulders. She sat, leaning forward, her elbows on the table, and once, when she glanced round and found Althea's eyes fixed on her, she looked back for a moment, but with something of the same vagueness and unseeingness with which she looked out of the window.

She was very odd. An enemy might say that she had Chinese eyes and a beak-like nose. The beak was small, as were all the features — delicately, decisively placed in the pale, narrow face — yet it jutted over prominently, and the long eyes were updrawn at the outer corners and only opened widely with an effect of effort. She had quantities of hair, dense and dark, arranged with an ordered carelessness, and widely framing her face and throat. She was very thin, and she seemed very tired; and fatigue, which made Althea look wistful, made this young lady look bored and bitter. Her grey eyes, perhaps it was the strangeness of their straight-drawn upper lids, were dazed and dim in expression. She ate little, leaned limply on her elbows, and sometimes rubbed her hands over her face, and sat so, her fingers in her hair, for a languid moment. Dinner was only half over when she rose and went away, her black dress trailing behind her, and a moon-like space of neck visible between her heavily-clustered hair and the gauze scarf.

Althea could not have said why, but for the rest of the meal, and after she had gone back to her sitting-room, the thought of the young lady in black remained almost oppressively with her.

She had felt empty and aimless before seeing her; since seeing her she felt more empty, more aimless than ever. It was an absurd impression, and she tried to shake it off with the help of a recent volume of literary criticism, but it coloured her mind as though a drop of some potent chemical had been tipped into her uncomfortable yet indefinable mood, and had suddenly made visible in it all sorts of latent elements.

It was curious to feel, as a deep conviction about a perfect stranger, that though the young lady in black might often know moods, they would never be undefined ones; to be sure that, however little she had, she would always accurately know what she wanted. The effect of seeing some one so hard, so clear, so alien, was much as if, a gracefully moulded but fragile earthenware pot, she had suddenly, while floating down the stream, found herself crashing against the bronze vessel of the fable.

A corrective to this morbid state of mind came to her with the evening post, and in the form of a thick letter bearing the Boston postmark. Franklin Winslow Kane had not occurred to Althea as an alternative to the various forms of dignified extinction with which her imagination had been occupied that afternoon. Franklin often occurred to her as a solace, but he never occurred to her as an escape.

He was a young man of very homespun extraction, who hovered in Boston on the ambiguous verge between the social and the scholastic worlds; the sort of young man whom one asked to tea rather than to dinner. He was an earnest student, and was attached to the university by an official, though unimportant, tie. A physicist, and, in his own sober way, with something of a reputation, he was profoundly involved in theories that dealt with the smallest things and the largest — molecules and the formation of universes.

He had first proposed to Althea when she was eighteen. She was now thirty-three, and for all these years Franklin had proposed to her on every occasion that offered itself. He was deeply, yet calmly, determinedly, yet ever so patiently, in love with her; and while other more eligible and more easily consoled aspirants had drifted away and got married and become absorbed in their growing families, Franklin alone remained admirably faithful. She had never given him any grounds for expecting that she might some day marry him, yet he evidently found it impossible to marry anybody else. This was the touching fact about Franklin, the one bright point, as it were, in his singularly colourless personality. His fidelity was like a fleck of orange on the wing of some grey, unobtrusive moth; it made him visible.

Althea's compassionate friendship seemed to sustain him sufficiently on his way; he did not pine or protest, though he punctually requested. He frequently appeared and he indefatigably wrote, and his long constancy, the unemotional trust and closeness of their intimacy, made him seem less a lover than the American husband of tradition, devoted and uncomplaining, who had given up hoping that his wife would ever come home and live with him.

Althea rather resented this aspect of their relation; she was well aware of its comicality; but though Franklin's devotion was at times something of a burden, though she could expect from him none of the glamour of courtship, she could ill have dispensed with his absorption in her. Franklin's absorption in her was part of her own personality; she would hardly have known herself without it; and her relation to him, irksome, even absurd as she sometimes found it, was perhaps the one thing in her life that most nearly linked her to reality; it was a mirage, at all events, of the responsible affections that her life lacked.

And now, in her mood of positive morbidity, the sight of Franklin's handwriting on the thick envelope brought her the keenest sense she had ever had of his value. One might have no aim oneself, yet to be some one else's aim saved one from that engulfing consciousness of nonentity; one might be uncertain and indefinite, but a devotion like Franklin's really defined one. She must be significant, after all, since this very admirable person — admirable, though ineligible — had found her so for so many years. It was with a warming sense of restoration, almost of reconstruction, that she opened the letter, drew out the thickly-folded sheets of thin paper and began to read the neat, familiar writing. He told her everything that he was doing and thinking, and about everything that interested him. He wrote to her of kinetics and atoms as if she had been a fellow-student. It was as if, helplessly, he felt the whole bulk of his outlook to be his only chance of interesting her, since no detail was likely to do so. Unfortunately it didn't interest her much. Franklin's eagerness about some local election, or admiration for some talented pupil, or enthusiasm in regard to a new theory that delved deeper and circled wider than any before, left her imagination inert, as did he. But tonight all these things were transformed by the greatness of her own need and of her own relief. And when she read that Franklin was to be in Europe in six weeks' time, and that he intended to spend some months there, and, if she would allow it, as near her as was possible, a sudden hope rose in her and seemed almost a joy.

Was it so impossible, after all, as an alternative? Equipped with her own outlooks, with her wider experience, and with her ample means, might not dear Franklin be eligible? To sink back on Franklin, after all these years, would be, of course, to confess to failure; but even in failure there were choices, and wasn't this the best form of failure? Franklin was not, could never be, the lover she had dreamed of; she had never met that lover, and she had always dreamed of him. Franklin was dun-coloured; the lover of her dreams a Perseus-like flash of purple and gold, ardent, graceful, compelling, some one who would open doors to large, bright vistas, and lead her into a life of beauty. But this was a dream and Franklin was the fact, and tonight he seemed the only fact worth looking at. Wasn't dun-colour, after all, preferable to the trivial kaleidoscope of shifting tints which was all that the future, apart from Franklin, seemed to offer her? Might not dun-colour, even, illuminated by joy, turn to gold, like highway dust when the sun shines upon it? Althea wondered, leaning back in her chair and gazing before her; she wondered deeply.

If only Franklin would come in now with the right look. If only he would come in with the right word, or, if not with the word, with an even more compelling silence! Compulsion was needed, and could Franklin compel? Could he make her fall in love with him? So she wondered, sitting alone in the Paris hotel, the open letter in her hand.

CHAPTER III.

When Althea went in to lunch next day, after an arduous morning of shopping, she observed, with mingled relief and disappointment, that the young lady in black was not in her place. She might very probably have gone away, and it was odd to think that an impression so strong was probably to remain an impression merely. On the whole, she was sorry to think that it might be so, though the impression had not been altogether happy.

After lunch she lay down and read reviews for a lazy hour, and then dressed to receive Miss Harriet Robinson, who, voluble and beaming, arrived punctually at four.

Miss Robinson looked almost exactly as she had looked for the last ten years. She changed as little as the hotel drawing-room, but that the pictures on the wall, the vases on the shelf of her mental decoration varied with every season. She was always passionately interested in something, and it was surprising to note how completely in the new she forgot last year's passion. This year it was eugenics and Strauss; the welfare of the race had suddenly engaged her attention, and the menaced future of music. She was slender, erect, and beautifully dressed. Her hands were small, and she constantly but inexpressively gesticulated with them; her elaborately undulated hair looked like polished, fluted silver; her eyes were small, dark, and intent; she smiled as constantly and as inexpressively as she gesticulated.

'And so you really think of going back for the winter?' she asked Althea finally, when the responsibilities of parenthood and the impermanency of modern musical artifices had been demonstrated. 'Why, my dear? You see everybody here. Everybody comes here, sooner or later.'

'I don't like getting out of touch with home,' said Althea.

'I confess that I feel this home,' said Miss Robinson. 'America is so horribly changed, so vulgarised. The people they accept socially! And the cost of things! My dear, the last time I went to the States I had to pay five hundred francs — one hundred dollars — for my winter hat! *Je vous demande!* If they will drive us out they must take the consequences.'

Althea felt tempted to inquire what these might be. Miss Robinson sometimes roused a slight irony in her; but she received the expostulation with a dim smile.

'Why won't you settle here?' Miss Robinson continued, 'or in Rome — there is quite a delightful society in Rome — or Florence, or London. Not that I could endure the English winter.'

'I've sometimes thought of England,' said Althea.

'Well, do think of it. I'm perfectly disinterested. Rather than have you unsettled, I would like to have you settled there. You have interesting friends, I know.'

'Yes, very interesting,' said Althea, with some satisfaction.

'You would probably make quite a place for yourself in London, if you went at it carefully and consideringly, and didn't allow the wrong sort of people to *accaparer* you. We always count, when we want to, we American women of the good type,' said Miss Robinson, with frank complacency; 'and I don't see why, with your gifts and charm, you shouldn't have a salon, political or artistic.'

Althea was again tempted to wonder what it was Miss Robinson counted for; but since she had often been told that her gifts and charm demanded a salon, she was inclined to believe it. 'It's only,' she demurred, 'that I have so many friends, in so many places; it is hard to decide on settling.'

'One never does make a real life for oneself until one does settle. I've found that out for myself,' said Miss Robinson.

It did not enter into her mind that Althea might still settle, in a different sense. She was of that vast army of rootless Europeanised Americans, who may almost be said to belong to a celibate order, so little does the question of matrimony and family life affect their existence. For a younger, more frivolous type, Europe might have a merely matrimonial significance; but to Miss Robinson, and to thousands of her kind, it meant an escape from displeasing circumstance and a preoccupation almost monastic with the abstract and the æsthetic. To Althea it had never meant merely that. Her own people in America were fastidious and exclusive; from choice, they considered, but, in reality, partly from necessity; they had never been rich enough or fashionable enough to be exposed to the temptation of great European alliances. Althea would have scorned such ambitions as basely vulgar; she had never thought of Europe as an arena for social triumphs; but it had assuredly been coloured for her with the colour of romance. It was in Europe, rather than in America, that she expected to find, if ever, her ardent, compelling wooer. And it irritated her a little that Miss Robinson should not seem to consider such a possibility for her.

She did not accept her friend's invitation to go with her to the Français that evening; the weariness of the morning of shopping was her excuse. She wanted to study a little; she never neglected to keep her mind in training; and after dinner she sat down with a stout tome on political economy. She had only got through half a chapter when Amélie came to her and asked her if she could suggest a remedy for a young lady next door who, the *femme de chambre* said, was quite alone, and had evidently succumbed to a violent attack of influenza.

'C'est une dame anglaise,' said Amélie, 'et une bien gentille.'

Althea sprang up, strangely excited. Was it the lady in black? Had she then not gone yet? 'Next door, you say?' she asked. Yes; the stranger's bedroom was next her own, and she had no *salon*.

'I will go in myself and see her,' said Althea, after a moment of reflection.

She was not at all given to such impulses, and, under any other circumstances, would have sent Amélie with the offer of assistance. But she suddenly felt it an opportunity, for what she could not have said. It was like seeing a curious-looking book opened before one; one wanted to read in it, if only a snatched paragraph here and there.

Amélie protested as to infection, but Althea was a resourceful traveller and had disinfectants for every occasion. She drenched her handkerchief, gargled her throat, and, armed with her little case of remedies, knocked at the door near by. A languid voice answered her and she entered.

The room was lighted by two candles that stood on the mantelpiece, and the bed in its alcove was dim. Tossed clothes lay on the chairs; a battered box stood open, its tray lying on the floor; the dressing-table was in confusion, and the scent of cigarette smoke mingled with that of a tall white lily that was placed in a vase on a little table beside the bed. To the well-maided Althea the disorder was appalling, yet it expressed, too, something of charm. The invalid lay plunged in her pillows, her dark hair tossed above her head, and, as Althea approached, she did not unclose her eyes.

'Oh, I beg your pardon,' said Althea, feeling some trepidation. 'My maid told me that you were ill — that you had influenza, and I know just what to do for it. May I give you some medicine? I do hope I have not waked you up,' for the invalid was now looking at her with some astonishment.

'No; I wasn't asleep. How very kind of you. I thought it was the chambermaid,' she said. 'Forgive me for seeming so rude.'

Her eyes were more dazed than ever, and she more mysterious, with her unbound hair.

'You oughtn't to lie with your arms outside the covers like that,' said Althea. 'It's most important not to get chilled. I'm afraid you don't know how to take care of yourself.' She smiled a little, gentle and assured, though inwardly with still a tremor; and she drew the clothes about the invalid, who had relapsed passively on to her pillows.

'I'm afraid I don't. How very kind of you!' she murmured again.

Althea brought a glass of water and, selecting her little bottle, poured out the proper number of drops. 'You were feeling ill last night, weren't you?' she said, after the dose had been swallowed. 'I thought that you looked ill.'

'Last night?'

'Yes, don't you remember? I sat next you in the dining-room.'

'Oh yes; of course, of course! I remember now. You had this dress on; I noticed all the little silver tassels. Yes, I've been feeling wretched for several days; I've done hardly anything — no shopping, no sight-seeing, and I ought to be back in London tomorrow; but I suppose I'll have to stay in bed for a week; it's very tiresome.' She spoke wearily, yet in decisive little sentences, and her voice, its hardness and its liquid intonations, made Althea think of wet pebbles softly shaken together.

'You haven't sent for a doctor?' she inquired, while she took out her small clinical thermometer.

'No, indeed; I never send for doctors. Can't afford 'em,' said the young lady, with a wan grimace. 'Must I put that into my mouth?'

'Yes, please; I must take your temperature. I think, if you let me prescribe for you, I can see after you as well as a doctor,' Althea assured her. 'I'm used to taking care of people who are ill. The friend I've just been staying with in Venice had influenza very badly while I was with her.'

She rather hoped, after the thermometer was removed, that the young lady would ask her some question about Venice and her present destination; but, though so amiable and so grateful, she did not seem to feel any curiosity about the good Samaritan who thus succoured her.

Althea found her patient less feverish next morning when she went in early to see her, and though she said that her body felt as though it were being beaten with red-hot hammers, she smiled in saying it, and Althea then, administering her dose, asked her what her name might be.

It was Helen Buchanan, she learned.

'And mine is Althea Jakes. You are English, aren't you?'

'Oh no, I'm Scotch,' said Miss Buchanan.

'And I am American. Do you know any Americans?'

'Oh yes, quite a lot. One of them is a Mrs. Harrison, and lives in Chicago,' said Miss Buchanan, who seemed in a more communicative mood. 'I met her in Nice one winter; a very nice, kind woman, who gives most sumptuous parties. Her husband is a millionaire; one never sees him. Do you come from Chicago? Do you know her?'

Althea, with some emphasis, said that she came from Boston.

'Another,' Miss Buchanan pursued, 'lives in New York, though she is usually over here; she is immensely rich, too. She hunts every winter in England, and is great fun and is frightfully well up in everything — pictures, books, music, you know: Americans usually are well up, aren't they? She wants me to stay with her some day in New York; perhaps I shall, if I can manage to afford the voyage. Her name is Bigham; perhaps you know her.'

'No. I know of her, though; she is very well known,' said Althea rather coldly; for Mrs. Bigham was an excessively fashionable and reputedly reckless lady who had divorced one husband and married another, and whose doings filled more scrupulous circles with indignation and unwilling interest.

'Then I met a dear little woman in Oxford once,' said Miss Buchanan. 'She was studying there — she had come from a college in America. She was so nice and clever, and charming, too; quaint and full of flavour. She was going to teach in a college when she went back. She was very poor, quite different from the others. Her father, she told me, kept a shop, but didn't get on at all; and her brother, to whom she was devoted, sold harmoniums. It was just like an American novel. Wayman was her name — Miss Carrie Wayman; perhaps you know her. I forget the name of the town she came from, but it was somewhere in the western part of America.'

No, Althea said, she did not know Miss Wayman, and she felt some little severity for the confusion that Miss Buchanan's remarks indicated. With greater emphasis than before, she said that she did not know the West at all.

'It must be rather nice — plains and cowboys and Rocky Mountains,' Miss Buchanan said. 'I've a cousin on a ranch in Dakota, and I've often thought I'd like to go out there for a season; he says the riding is wonderful, and the scenery and flowers. Oh, my wretched head; it feels as if it were stuffed with incandescent cotton-wool.'

'You must remember to keep your arms under the covers,' said Althea, as Miss Buchanan lifted her hands and pressed them to her brows. 'And let me plait your hair for you; it must be so hot and uncomfortable.'

And now again, looking up at her while the friendly office was performed, Miss Buchanan said, 'How kind you are! too kind for words. I can't think what I should have done without you.'

CHAPTER IV.

It became easy after this for Althea to carry into effect all her beneficent wishes. The friends who had taken Miss Buchanan to the Riviera had gone on to London, leaving her alone in Paris for a week's shopping, and there was no one else to look after her. She brought her fruit and flowers and sat with her in all her spare moments. The feeling of anxiety that had oppressed her on the evening of gloom when she had first seen her was transformed into a soft and delightful perturbation. As the unknown lady in black Miss Buchanan had indeed charmed as well as oppressed her, and the charm grew while the oppression, though it still hovered, was felt more as a sense of alluring mystery. She had never in her life met any one in the least like Miss Buchanan. She was at once so open and so impenetrable. She replied to all questions with complete unreserve, but she had never, with all her candour, the air of making confidences. It hurt Althea a little, and yet was part of the allurement, to see that she was, probably, too indifferent to be reticent. Lying on her pillows, a cigarette — all too frequently, Althea considered — between her lips, and her hair wound in a heavy wreath upon her head, she would listen pleasantly, and as pleasantly reply; and Althea could not tell whether it was because she really found it pleasant to talk and be talked to, or whether, since she had nothing better to do, she merely showed good manners. Althea was sensitive to every shade in manners, and was sure that Miss Buchanan, however great her tact might be, did not find her a bore; yet she could not be at all sure that she found her interesting, and this disconcerted her. Sometimes the suspicion of it made her feel humble, and sometimes it made her feel a little angry, for she was not accustomed to being found uninteresting. She herself, however, was interested; and it was when she most frankly owned to this, laying both anger and humility aside, that she was happiest in the presence of her new acquaintance. She liked to talk to her, and she liked to make her talk. From these conversations she was soon able to build up a picture of Miss Buchanan's life. She came of an old Scotch family, and she had spent her childhood and girlhood in an old Scotch house. This house, Althea was sure, she really did enjoy talking about. She described it to Althea: the way the rooms lay, and the passages ran, and the queer old stairs climbed up and down. She described the ghost that she herself had seen once — her matter-of-fact acceptance of the ghost startled Althea — and the hills and moors that one looked out on from the windows. Led by Althea's absorbed inquiries, she drifted on to detailed reminiscence — the dogs she had cared for, the flowers she had grown, and the dear red lacquer mirror that she had broken. 'Papa did die that year,' she added, after mentioning the incident.

'Surely you don't connect the two things,' said Althea, who felt some remonstrance necessary. Miss Buchanan said no, she supposed not; it was silly to be superstitious; yet she didn't like breaking mirrors.

Her brother lived in the house now. He had married some one she didn't much care about, though she did not enlarge on this dislike. 'Nigel had to marry money,' was all she said. 'He couldn't have kept the place going if he hadn't. Jessie isn't at all a bad sort, and they get on very well and have three nice little boys; but I don't much take to her nor she to me, so that I'm not much there any more.'

'And your mother?' Althea questioned, 'where does she live? Don't you stay with her ever?' She had gathered that the widowed Mrs. Buchanan was very pretty and very selfish, but she was hardly prepared for the frankness with which Miss Buchanan defined her own attitude towards her.

'Oh, I can't stand Mamma,' she said; 'we don't get on at all. I'm not fond of rowdy people, and Mamma knows such dreadful bounders. So long as people have plenty of money and make things amusing for her, she'll put up with anything.'

Althea had all the American reverence for the sanctities and loyalties of the family, and these ruthless explanations filled her with uneasy surprise. Miss Buchanan was ruthless about all her relatives; there were few of them, apparently, that she cared for except the English cousins with whom she had spent many years of girlhood, and the Aunt Grizel who made a home for her in London. To her she alluded with affectionate emphasis: 'Oh, Aunt Grizel is very different from the rest of them.'

Aunt Grizel was not well off, but it was she who made Helen the little allowance that enabled her to go about; and she had insured her life, so that at her death, when her annuity lapsed, Helen should be sure of the same modest sum. 'Owing to Aunt Grizel I'll just not starve,' said Helen, with the faint grimace, half bitter, half comic, that sometimes made her strange face still stranger. 'One hundred and fifty pounds a year: think of it! Isn't it damnable? Yet it's better than nothing, as Aunt Grizel and I often say after groaning together.'

Althea, safely niched in her annual three thousand, was indeed horrified.

'One hundred and fifty,' she repeated helplessly. 'Do you mean that you manage to dress on that now?'

'Dress on it, my dear! I pay all my travelling expenses, my cabs, my stamps, my Christmas presents — everything out of it, as well as buy my clothes. And it will have to pay for my rent and food besides, when Aunt Grizel dies — when I'm not being taken in somewhere. Of course, she still counts on my marrying, poor dear.'

'Oh, but, of course you *will* marry,' said Althea, with conviction.

Miss Buchanan, who was getting much better, was propped high on her pillows today, and was attired in a most becoming flow of lace and silk. Nothing less exposed to the gross chances of the world could be imagined. She did not turn her eyes on her companion as the confident assertion was made, and she kept silence for a moment. Then she answered placidly:

'Of course, if I'm to live — and not merely exist — I must try to, I suppose.'

Althea was taken aback and pained by the wording of this speech. Her national susceptibilities were again wounded by the implication that a rare and beautiful woman — for so she termed Helen Buchanan — might be forced, not only to hope for marriage, but to seek it; the implication that urgency lay rather in the woman's state than in the man's. She had all the romantic American confidence in the power of the rare and beautiful woman to marry when and whom she chose.

'I am sure you need never try,' she said with warmth. 'I'm sure you have dozens of delightful people in love with you.'

Miss Buchanan turned her eyes on her and laughed as though she found this idea amusing. 'Why, in heaven's name, should I have dozens of delightful people in love with me?'

'You are so lovely, so charming, so distinguished.'

'Am I? Thanks, my dear. I'm afraid you see things *en couleur de rose.*' And, still smiling, her eyes dwelling on Althea with their indifferent kindness, she went on: 'Have you delightful dozens in love with you?'

Althea did not desert her guns. She felt that the very honour of their sex — hers and Helen's — was on trial in her person. She might not be as lovely as her friend — though she might be; that wasn't a matter for her to inquire into; but as woman — as well-bred, highly educated, refined and gentle woman — she, too, was chooser, and not seeker.

'Only one delightful person is in love with me at this moment, I'm sorry to say,' she answered, smiling back; 'but I've had very nearly my proper share in the past.' It had been necessary thus to deck poor Franklin out if her standpoint were to be maintained; and, indeed, could not one deem him delightful, in some senses — in moral senses; he surely was delightfully good. The little effort to see dear Franklin's goodness as delightful rather discomposed her, and as Miss Buchanan asked no further question as to the one delightful suitor, the little confusion mounted to her eyes and cheeks. She wondered if she had spoken tastelessly, and hastened away from this personal aspect of the question.

'You don't really mean — I'm sure you don't mean that you would marry just for money.'

Miss Buchanan kept her ambiguous eyes half merrily, half pensively upon her. 'Of course, if he were very nice. I wouldn't marry a man who wasn't nice for money.'

'Surely you couldn't marry a man unless you were in love with him?'

'Certainly I could. Money lasts, and love so often doesn't.' Helen continued to smile as she spoke.

There was now a tremor of pain in Althea's protest. 'Dear Miss Buchanan, I can't bear to hear you speak like that. I can't bear to think of any one so lovely doing anything so sordid, so miserable, as making a *mariage de convenance.*' Tears rose to her eyes.

Miss Buchanan was again silent for a moment, and it was now her turn to look slightly confused. 'It's very nice of you to mind,' she said; and she added, as if to help Althea not to mind, 'But, you see, I am sordid; I am miserable.'

'Sordid? Miserable? Do you mean unhappy?' Poor Althea gazed, full of her most genuine distress.

'Oh no; I mean in your sense. I'm a poor creature, quite ordinary and grubby; that's all,' said Miss Buchanan.

They said nothing more of it then, beyond Althea's murmur of now inarticulate protest; but the episode probably remained in Miss Buchanan's memory as something rather puzzling as well as rather pitiful, this demonstration of a feeling so entirely unexpected that she had not known what to do with it.

If, in these graver matters, she distressed Althea, in lesser ones she was continually, if not distressing her, at all events calling upon her, in complete unconsciousness, for readjustments of focus that were sometimes, in their lesser way, painful too. When she asserted that she was not musical, Althea almost suspected her of saying it in order to evade her own descriptions of experiences at Bayreuth. Pleasantly as she might listen, it was sometimes, Althea had discovered, with a restive air masked by a pervasive vagueness; this vagueness usually drifted over her when Althea described experiences of an intellectual or æsthetic nature. It could be no question of evasion, however, when, in answer to a question of Althea's, she said that she hated Paris. Since girlhood Althea had accepted Paris as the final stage in a civilised being's education: the Théâtre Français, the lectures at the Sorbonne, the

Louvre and the Cluny, and, for a later age, Anatole France — it seemed almost barbarous to say that one hated the splendid city that clothed, as did no other place in the world, one's body and one's mind. 'How can you hate it?' she inquired. 'It means so much that is intellectual, so much that is beautiful.'

'I suppose so,' said Miss Buchanan. 'I do like to look at it sometimes; the spaces and colour are so nice.'

'The spaces, and what's in them, surely. What is it that you don't like? The French haven't our standards of morality, of course, but don't you think it's rather narrow to judge them by our standards?'

Althea was pleased to set forth thus clearly her own liberality of standard. She sometimes suspected Miss Buchanan of thinking her naïve. But Miss Buchanan now looked a little puzzled, as if it were not this at all that she had meant, and said presently that perhaps it was the women's faces — the well-dressed women. 'I don't mind the poor ones so much; they often look too sharp, but they often look kind and frightfully tired. It is the well-dressed ones I can't put up with. And the men are even more horrid. I always want to spend a week in walking over the moors when I've been here. It leaves a hot taste in my mouth, like some horrid liqueur.'

'But the beauty — the intelligence,' Althea urged. 'Surely you are a little intolerant, to see only people's faces in Paris. Think of the Salon Carrée and the Cluny; they take away the taste of the liqueur. How can one have enough of them?'

Miss Buchanan again demurred. 'Oh, I think I can have enough of them.'

'But you care for pictures, for beautiful things,' said Althea, half vexed and half disturbed. But Miss Buchanan said that she liked having them about her, not having to go and look at them. 'It is so stuffy in museums, too; they always give me a headache. However, I don't believe I really do care about pictures. You see, altogether I've had no education.'

Her education, indeed, contrasted with Althea's well-ordered and elaborate progression, had been lamentable — a mere succession of incompetent governesses. Yet, on pressing her researches, Althea, though finding almost unbelievable voids, felt, more than anything else, tastes sharp and fine that seemed to cut into her own tastes and show her suddenly that she did not really like what she had thought she liked, or that she liked what she had hardly before been aware of. All that Helen could be brought to define was that she liked looking at things in the country: at birds, clouds, and flowers; but though striking Althea as a creature strangely untouched and unmoulded, she struck her yet more strongly as beautifully definite. She marvelled at her indifference to her own shortcomings, and she marvelled at the strength of personality that could so dispense with other people's furnishings.

Among the things that Helen made her see, freshly and perturbingly, was the sheaf of friends in England of whom she had thought with such security when Miss Robinson had spoken of the London *salon*.

Althea had been trained in a school of severe social caution. Social caution was personified to her in her memory of her mother — a slender, black-garbed lady, with parted grey hair, neatly waved along her brow, and a tortoiseshell lorgnette that she used to raise, mildly yet alarmingly, at foreign *tables d'hôtes*, for an appraising survey of the company. The memory of this lorgnette operated with Althea as a sort of social standard; it typified delicacy, dignity, deliberation, a scrupulous regard for the claims of heredity, and a scrupulous avoidance of uncertain or all too certain types. Althea felt that she had carried on the tradition worthily. The lorgnette would have passed all her more recent friends — those made with only its inspiration as a guide. She was as careful as her mother as to whom she admitted to her acquaintanceship, eschewing in particular those of her compatriots whose accents or demeanour betrayed them to her trained discrimination as outside the radius of acceptance. But Althea's kindness of heart was even deeper than her caution, and much as she dreaded becoming involved with the wrong sort of people, she dreaded even more hurting anybody's feelings, with the result that once or twice she had made mistakes, and had had, under the direction of Lady Blair, to withdraw in a manner as painful to her feelings as to her pride. 'Oh no, my dear,' Lady Blair had said of some English acquaintances whom Althea had met in Rome, and who had asked her to come and see them in England. 'Quite impossible; most worthy people, I am sure, and no doubt the daughter took honours at Girton — the middle classes are highly educated nowadays; but one doesn't know that sort of people.'

Lady Blair was the widow of a judge, and, in her large velvet drawing-room, a thick fog outside and a number of elderly legal ladies drinking tea about her, Althea had always felt herself to be in the very heart of British social safety. Lady Blair was an old friend of her mother's, and, with Miss Buckston, was her nearest English friend. She also felt safe on the lawn under the mulberry-tree at Grimshaw Rectory, and when ensconced for her long visit in Colonel and Mrs. Colling's little house in Devonshire, where hydrangeas grew against a blue background of sea, and a small white yacht rocked in the bay at the foot of the garden.

It was therefore with some perplexity that, here too, she

brought from her interviews with Helen an impression of new standards. They were not drastic and relegating, like those of Lady Blair's; they did not make her feel unsafe as Lady Blair's had done; they merely made her feel that her world was very narrow and she herself rather ingenuous.

Helen herself seemed unaware of standards, and had certainly never experienced any of Althea's anxieties. She had always been safe, partly, Althea had perceived, because she had been born safe, but, in the main, because she was quite indifferent to safety. And with this indifference and this security went the further fact that she had, probably, never been ingenuous. With all her admiration, her affection for her new friend, this sense of the change that she was working in her life sometimes made Althea a little afraid of her, and sometimes a little indignant. She, herself, was perfectly safe in America, and when she felt indignant she asked herself what Helen Buchanan would have done had she been turned into a strange continent with hardly any other guides than the memory of a lorgnette and a Baedeker.

It was when she was bound to answer this question, and to recognise that in such circumstances Miss Buchanan would have gone her way, entirely unperturbed, and entirely sure of her own preferences, that Althea felt afraid of her. In all circumstances, she more and more clearly saw it, Miss Buchanan would impose her own standards, and be oppressed or enlightened by none. Althea had always thought of herself as very calm and strong; it was as calm and strong that Franklin Winslow Kane so worshipped her; but when she talked to Miss Buchanan she had sharp shoots of suspicion that she was, in reality, weak and wavering.

Althea's accounts of her friends in England seemed to interest Miss Buchanan even less than her accounts of Bayreuth. She had met Miss Buckston, but had only a vague and, evidently, not a pleasant impression of her. Lady Blair she had never heard of, nor the inmates of Grimshaw Rectory. The Collings were also blanks, except that Mrs. Colling had an uncle, an old Lord Taunton; and when Althea put forward this identifying fact, Helen said that she knew him and liked him very much.

'I suppose you know a great many people,' said Althea.

Yes, Miss Buchanan replied, she supposed she did. 'Too many, sometimes. One gets sick of them, don't you think? But perhaps your people are more interesting than mine; you travel so much, and seem to know such heaps of them all over the world.'

But Althea, from these interviews, took a growing impression that though Miss Buchanan might be sick of her own people, she would be far more sick of hers.

CHAPTER V.

Miss Buchanan was well on the way to complete recovery, was able to have tea every afternoon with Althea, and to be taken for long drives in the Bois, when Aunt Julia and the girls arrived at the Hôtel Talleyrand.

Mrs. Pepperell was a sister of Althea's mother, and lived soberly and solidly in New York, disapproving as much of millionaires and their manners as of expatriated Americans. She was large and dressed with immaculate precision and simplicity, and had it not been for a homespun quality of mingled benevolence and shrewdness, she might have passed as stately. But Mrs. Pepperell had no wish to appear stately, and was rather intolerant of the pretension in others. Her sharp tongue had indulged itself in a good many sallies on this score at her sister Bessie's expense; Bessie being the lady of the lorgnette, Althea's deceased mother.

Althea, remembering that dear mother so well, all dignified elegance as she had been — too dignified, too elegant, perhaps, to be either so shrewd or so benevolent as her sister — always thought of Aunt Julia as rather commonplace in comparison. Yet, as she followed in her wake on the evening of her arrival, she felt that Aunt Julia was obviously and eminently 'nice.' The one old-fashioned diamond ornament at her throat, the ruffles at her wrist, the gloss of her silver-brown hair, reminded her of her own mother's preferences.

The girls were 'nice,' too, as far as their appearance and breeding went, but Althea found their manners very bad. They were not strident and they were not arrogant, but so much noisiness and so much innocent assurance might, to unsympathetic eyes, seem so. They were handsome girls, fresh-skinned, athletic, tall and slender. They wore beautifully simple white lawn dresses, and their shining fair hair was brushed off their foreheads and tied at the back with black bows in a very becoming fashion, though Althea thought the bows too large and the fashion too obviously local.

Helen was in her old place that night, and she smiled at Althea as she and her party took their places at a table larger and at a little distance. She was to come in for coffee after dinner, so that Althea adjourned introductions. Aunt Julia looked sharply and appraisingly at the black figure, and the girls did not look at all. They were filled with young delight and excitement at the prospect of a three weeks' romp in Paris, among dressmakers, tea-parties, and the opera. 'And Herbert Vaughan is here. I've just had a letter from him, forwarded from London,' Dorothy announced, to which Mildred, with glad emphasis, cried 'Bully!'

Althea sighed, crumbled her bread, and looked out of the window resignedly.

'You mustn't talk slang before Cousin Althea,' said Dorothy.

'What Cousin Althea needs is slang,' said Mildred.

'I shan't lack it with you, shall I, Mildred?' Althea returned, with, a rather chilly smile. She knew that Dorothy and Mildred considered her, as they would have put it, 'A back number'; they liked to draw her out and to shock her. She wanted to make it clear that she wasn't shocked, but that she was wearied. At the same time it was true that Mildred and Dorothy made her uncomfortable in subtler ways; she was, perhaps, a little afraid of them, too. They, too, imposed their own standards, and were oppressed and enlightened by none.

Aunt Julia smiled indulgently at her children, and asked Althea if she did not think that they were looking very well. They certainly were, and Althea had to own it. 'But don't let them overdo their athletics, Aunt Julia,' she said. 'It is such a pity when girls get brawny.'

'I'm brawny; feel my muscle,' said Mildred, stretching a hard young arm across the table. Althea shook her head. She did not like being made conspicuous, and already the girls' loud voices had drawn attention; the French family were all staring.

'Who is the lady in black, Althea?' Mrs. Pepperell asked. 'A friend of yours?'

'Yes, a most charming friend,' said Althea. 'Helen Buchanan is her name; she is Scotch — a very old family — and she is one of the most interesting people I've ever known. You will meet her after dinner. She is coming in to spend the evening.'

'Where did you meet her? How long have you known her?' asked Aunt Julia, evidently unimpressed.

Althea said that she had met her here, but that they had mutual friends, thinking of Miss Buckston in what she felt to be an emergency.

Aunt Julia, with her air of general scepticism as to what she could find so worth while in Europe, often made her embark on definitions and declarations. She could certainly tolerate no uncertainty on the subject of Helen's worth.

'Very odd looking,' said Aunt Julia, while the girls glanced round indifferently at the subject of discussion.

'And peculiarly distinguished looking,' said Althea. 'She makes most people look so half-baked and insignificant.'

'I think it a rather sinister face,' said Aunt Julia. 'And how she slouches! Sit up, Mildred. I don't want you to catch European tricks.'

But, after dinner, Althea felt that Helen made her impression.

She was still wan and weak; she said very little, though she smiled very pleasantly, and she sat — as Aunt Julia had said, 'slouched,' yet so gracefully — in a corner of the sofa. The charm worked. The girls felt it, Aunt Julia felt it, though Aunt Julia held aloof from it. Althea saw that Aunt Julia, most certainly, did not interest Helen, but the girls amused her; she liked them. They sat near her and made her laugh by their accounts of their journey, the funny people on the steamer, their plans for the summer, and life in America, as they lived it. Dorothy assured her that she didn't know what fun was till she came to America, and Mildred cried: 'Oh, do come! We'll give you the time of your life!' Helen declared that she hoped some day to experience this climax.

Before going to bed, and attired in her dressing-gown, Althea went to Helen's room to ask her how she felt, but also to see what impression her relatives had made. Helen was languidly brushing her hair, and Althea took the brush from her and brushed it for her.

'Isn't it lamentable,' she said, 'that Aunt Julia, who is full of a certain sort of wise perception about other things, doesn't seem to see at all how bad the children's manners are. She lets them monopolise everybody's attention with the utmost complacency.'

Helen, while her hair was being brushed, put out her hand for her watch and was winding it. 'Have they bad manners?' she said. 'But they are nice girls.'

'Yes, they are nice. But surely you don't like their slang?'

Helen smiled at the recollection of it. 'More fun than a goat,' she quoted. 'Why shouldn't they talk slang?'

'Dear Helen,' — they had come quite happily to Christian names — 'surely you care for keeping the language pure. Surely you think it regrettable that the younger generation should defile and mangle it like that.'

But Helen only laughed, and confessed that she really didn't care what happened to the language. 'There'll always be plenty of people to talk it too well,' she said.

Mrs. Pepperell, on her side, had her verdict, and she gave it some days later when she and her niece were driving to the dress-maker's.

'She is a very nice girl, Miss Buchanan, and clever, too, in her quiet English way, though startlingly ignorant. Dorothy actually told me that she had never read any Browning, and thought that Sophocles was Diogenes, and lived in a tub. But frankly, Althea, I can't say that I take to her very much.'

Aunt Julia, often irritating to Althea, was never more so than when, as now, she assumed that her verdicts and opinions were of importance to her niece. Althea shrank from open combat with anybody, yet she could, under cover of gentle candour, plant her shafts. She planted one now in answering: 'I don't think that you would, either of you, take to one another. Helen's flavour is rather recondite.'

'Recondite, my dear,' said Aunt Julia, who never pretended not to know when a shaft had been planted. 'I think, everyday *mère de famille* as I am, that I am quite capable of appreciating the recondite. Miss Buchanan's appearance is striking, and she is an independent creature; but, essentially, she is the most common-place type of English girl — well-bred, poor, idle, uneducated, and with no object in life except to amuse herself and find a husband with money. And under that air of sleepy indifference she has a very sharp eye to the main chance, you may take my word for it.'

Althea was very angry, the more so for the distorted truth this judgment conveyed. 'I'm afraid I shouldn't take your word on any matter concerning my friend,' she returned; 'and I think, Aunt Julia, that you forget that it is my friend you are speaking of.'

'My dear, don't lose your temper. I only say it to put you on your guard. You are so given to idealisation, and you may find yourself disappointed if you trust to depths that are not there. As to friendship, don't forget that she is, as yet, the merest acquaintance.'

'One may feel nearer some people in a week than to others after years.'

'As to being near in a week — she doesn't feel near *you*; that is all I mean. Don't cast your pearls too lavishly.'

Althea made no reply, but under her air of unruffled calm, Aunt Julia's shaft rankled.

She found herself that afternoon, when she and Helen were alone at tea, sounding her, probing her, for reassuring symptoms of warmth or affection. 'I so hope that we may keep really in touch with one another,' she said. 'I couldn't bear not to keep in touch with you, Helen.'

Helen looked at her with the look, vague, kind, and a little puzzled, that seemed to plant Aunt Julia's shaft anew. 'Keep in touch,' she repeated. 'Of course. You'll be coming to England some day, and then you'll be sure to look me up, won't you?'

'But, until I do come, we will write? You will write to me a great deal?'

'Oh, my dear, I do so hate writing. I never have anything to say in a letter. Let us exchange postcards, when our doings require it.'

'Postcards!' Althea could not repress a disconsolate note. 'How can I tell from postcards what you are thinking and feeling?'

'You may always take it for granted that I'm doing very little of either,' said Helen, smiling.

Althea was silent for a moment, and then, with a distress apparent in voice and face, she said: 'I can't bear you to say that.'

Helen still smiled, but she was evidently at a loss. She added some milk to her tea and took a slice of bread and butter before saying, more kindly, yet more lightly than before: 'You mustn't judge me by yourself. I'm not a bit thoughtful, you know, or warm-hearted and intellectual, like you. I just rub along. I'm sure you'll not find it worth while keeping in touch with me.'

'It's merely that I care for you very much,' said Althea, in a slightly quivering voice. 'And I can't bear to think that I am nothing to you.'

There was again a little pause in which, because her eyes had suddenly filled with tears, Althea looked down and could not see her friend. Helen's voice, when she spoke, showed her that she was pained and disconcerted. 'You make me feel like such a clumsy brute when you say things like that,' she said. 'You are so kind, and I am so selfish and self-centred. But of course I care for you too.'

'Do you really?' said Althea, who, even if she would, could not have retained the appearance of lightness and independence. 'You really feel me as a friend, a true friend?'

'If you really think me worth your while, of course. I don't see how you can — an ill-tempered, ignorant, uninteresting woman, whom you've run across in a hotel and been good to.'

'I don't think of you like that, as you know. I think you a strangely lovely and strangely interesting person. From the first moment I saw you you appealed to me. I felt that you needed something — love and sympathy, perhaps. The fact that it's been a sort of chance — our meeting — makes it all the sweeter to me.'

Again Helen was silent for a moment, and again Althea, sitting with downcast eyes, knew that, though touched, she was uncomfortable. 'You are too nice and kind for words,' she then said. 'I can't tell you how kind I think it of you.'

'Then we are friends? You do feel me as a friend who will always be interested and always care?'

'Yes, indeed; and I do so thank you.'

Althea put out her hand, and Helen gave her hers, saying, 'You *are* a dear,' and adding, as though to take refuge from her own discomposure, 'much too dear for the likes of me.'

The bond was thus sealed, yet Aunt Julia's shaft still stuck. It was she who had felt near, and who had drawn Helen near. Helen, probably, would never have thought of keeping in touch. She was Helen's friend because she had appealed for friendship, and because Helen thought her a dear. The only comfort was to know that Helen's humility was real. She might have offered her friendship could she have realised that it was of value to anybody.

It was a few evenings after this, and perhaps as a result of their talk, that, as they sat in Althea's room over coffee, Helen said: 'Why don't you come to England this summer, Althea?'

Aunt Julia had proposed that Althea should go on to Bayreuth with her and the girls, and Althea was turning over the plan, thinking that perhaps she had had enough of Bayreuth, so that Helen's suggestion, especially as it was made in Aunt Julia's presence, was a welcome one. 'Perhaps I will,' she said. 'Will you be there?'

'I'll be in London, with Aunt Grizel, until the middle of July; after that, in the country till winter. You ought to take a house in the country and let me come to stay with you,' said Helen, smiling.

'Will you pay me a long visit?' Althea smiled back.

'As long as you'll ask me for.'

'Well, you are asked for as long as you will stay. Where shall I get a house? There are some nice ones near Miss Buckston's.'

'Oh, don't let us be too near Miss Buckston,' said Helen, laughing.

'But surely, Althea, you won't give up Bayreuth,' Aunt Julia interposed. 'It is going to be specially fine this year. And then you know so few people in England, you will be very lonely. Nothing is more lonely than the English country when you know nobody.'

'Helen is a host in herself,' said Althea; and though Helen did not realise the full force of the compliment, it was more than satisfactory to have her acquiesce with: 'Oh, as to people, I can bring you heaps of them, if you want them.'

'It is a lovely idea,' said Althea; 'and if I must miss Bayreuth, Aunt Julia, I needn't miss you and the girls. You will have to come and stay with me. Do you know of a nice house, Helen, in pretty country, and not too near Miss Buckston?' It was rather a shame of her, she felt, this proviso, but indeed she had never found Miss Buckston endearing, and since knowing Helen she had seen more clearly than before that she was in many ways oppressive.

Helen was reflecting. 'I do know of a house,' she said, 'in a very nice country, too. You might have a look at it. It's where I used to go, as a girl, you know, and stay with my cousins, the Digbys.'

'That would be perfect, Helen.'

'Oh, I don't know that you would find it perfect. It is a plain stone house, with a big, dilapidated garden, nice trees and lawns, miles from everything, and with old-fashioned, shabby furniture. Since Gerald came into the place, he's not been able to keep it up, and he has to let it. He hasn't been able to let it for the last year or so, and would be glad of the chance. If you like the place you'll only have to say the word.'

'I know I shall like it. Don't you like it?'

'Oh, I love it; but that's a different matter. It is more of a home to me than any place in the world.'

'I consider it settled. I don't need to see it.'

'No; it certainly isn't settled,' Helen replied, with her pleasant decisiveness. 'You certainly shan't take it till you see it. I will write to Gerald and tell him that no one else is to have it until you do.'

'I am quite determined to have that house,' said Althea. 'A place that you love must be lovely. Write if you like. But the matter is settled in my mind.'

'Don't be foolish, my dear,' said Aunt Julia. 'Miss Buchanan is quite right. You mustn't think of taking a house until you see it. How do you know that the drainage is in order, or even that the beds are comfortable. Miss Buchanan says that it is miles away from everything, too. You may find the situation very dismal and unsympathetic.'

'It's pretty country, I think,' said Helen, 'and I'm sure the drainage and the beds are all right. But Althea must certainly see it first.'

It was settled, however, quite settled in Althea's mind that she was to take Merriston House. She bade Helen farewell three days later, and they had arranged that they were, within a fortnight, to meet in London, and go together to look at it.

And Althea wrote to Franklin Winslow Kane, and informed him of her new plans, and that he must be her guest at Merriston House for as long as his own plans allowed him. Her mood in regard to Franklin had greatly altered since that evening of gloom a fortnight ago. Franklin, then, had seemed the only fact worth looking at; but now she seemed embarked on a voyage of discovery, where bright new planets swam above the horizon with every forward rock of her boat. Franklin was by no means dismissed; Franklin could never be dismissed; but he was relegated; and though, as far as her fondness went, he would always be firmly placed, she could hardly place him clearly in the new and significantly peopled environment that her new friendship opened to her.

CHAPTER VI.

Helen Buchanan was a person greatly in demand, and, in her migratory existence, her pauses at her Aunt Grizel's little house near Eaton Square were, though frequent, seldom long. When she did come, her bedroom and her sitting-room were always waiting for her, as was Aunt Grizel with her cheerful 'Well, my dear, glad to see you back again.' Their mutual respect and trust were deep; their affection, too, though it was seldom expressed. She knew Aunt Grizel to the ground, and Aunt Grizel knew her to the ground — almost; and they were always pleased to be together.

Helen's sitting-room, where she could see any one she liked and at any time she liked, was behind the dining-room on the ground floor, and from its window one saw a small neat garden with a plot of grass, bordering flower-beds, a row of little fruit-trees, black-branched but brightly foliaged, and high walls that looked as though they were built out of sooty plum cake. Aunt Grizel's cat, Pharaoh, sleek, black, and stalwart, often lay on the grass plot in the sunlight; he was lying there now, languidly turned upon his side, with outstretched feet and drowsily blinking eyes, when Helen and her cousin, Gerald Digby, talked together on the day after her return from Paris.

Gerald Digby stood before the fireplace looking with satisfaction at his companion. He enjoyed looking at Helen, for he admired her more than any woman he knew. It was always a pleasure to see her again; and, like Aunt Grizel, he trusted and respected her deeply, though again, like Aunt Grizel, he did not, perhaps, know her quite down to the ground. He thought, however, that he did; he knew that Helen was as intimate with nobody in the world as with him, not even with Aunt Grizel, and it was one of his most delightful experiences to saunter through all the chambers of Helen's mind, convinced that every door was open to him.

Gerald Digby was a tall and very slender man; he tilted forward when he walked, and often carried his hands in his pockets. He had thick, mouse-coloured hair, which in perplexed or meditative moments he often ruffled by rubbing his hand through it, and even when thus disordered it kept its air of fashionable grace. His large, long nose, his finely curved lips and eyelids, had a delicately carved look, as though the sculptor had taken great care over the details of his face. His brown eyes had thick, upturned lashes, and were often in expression absent and irresponsible, but when he looked at any one, intent and merry, like a gay dog's eyes. And of the many charming things about Gerald Digby the most charming was his smile, which was as infectious as a child's, and exposed a joyous array of large white teeth.

He was smiling at his cousin now, for she was telling him, dryly, yet with a mocking humour all her own, of her Paris fiasco that had delayed her return to London by a fortnight, and, by the expense it had entailed upon her, had deprived her of the new hat and dress that she had hoped in Paris to secure. Talking of Paris led to the letter she had sent him four or five days ago. 'About this rich American,' said Gerald; 'is she really going to take Merriston, do you think? It's awfully good of you, Helen, to try and get a tenant for me.'

'I don't know that you'd call her rich — not as Americans go; but I believe she will take Merriston. She wanted to take it at once, on faith; but I insisted that she must see it first.'

'You must have cried up the dear old place for her to be so eager.'

'I think she is eager about pleasing me,' said Helen. 'I told her that I loved the place and hadn't been there for years, and that moved her very much. She has taken a great fancy to me.'

'Really,' said Gerald. 'Why?'

'I'm sure I don't know. She is a dear little person, but rather funny.'

'Of course, there is no reason why any one shouldn't take a fancy to you,' said Gerald, smiling; 'only — to that extent — in so short a time.'

'I appealed to her pity, I think; she came in and took care of me, and was really unspeakably kind. And she seemed to get tremendously interested in me. But then, she seemed capable of getting tremendously interested in lots of things. I've noticed that Americans often take things very seriously.'

'And you became great pals?'

'Yes, I suppose we did.'

'She interested you?'

Helen smiled a little perplexedly, and lit a cigarette before answering. 'Well, no; I can't say that she did that; but that, probably, was my own fault.'

'Why didn't she interest you?' Gerald went on, taking a cigarette from the case she offered. He was fond of such desultory pursuit of a subject; he and Helen spent hours in idle exchanges of impression.

Helen's answer was hardly illuminating: 'She wasn't interesting.'

'It was rather interesting of her to take such an interest in you,' said Gerald subtly.

'No.' Helen warmed to the theme. It had indeed perplexed her, and she was glad to unravel her impressions to this understanding listener. 'No, that's just what it wasn't; it might have been if one hadn't felt her a person so easily affected. She had — how can I put it? — it seems brutal when she is such a dear — but she had so little stuff in her; it was as if she had to find it all the time in other things and people. She is like a glass of water that would like to be wine, and she has no wine in her; it could only be poured in, and there's not room for much. At best she can only be *eau rougie*.'

Gerald laughed. 'How you see things, and say them! Poor Miss Jakes! — that's her name, isn't it? She sounds tame.'

'She is tame.'

'Is she young, pretty?'

'Not young, about my age; not pretty, but it's a nice face; wistful, with large, quite lovely eyes. She knows a lot about everything, and has been everywhere, and has kept all her illusions intact — a queer mixture of information and innocence. It's difficult to keep one's mind on what she's saying; there is never any background to it. She wants something, but she doesn't know whether it's what other people want or whether it's what she wants, so that she can't want anything very definitely.'

Gerald still laughed. 'How you must have been taking her in!'

'I suppose I must have been, though I didn't know it. But I did like her, you know. I liked her very much. A glass of water is a nice thing sometimes.'

'Nicer than *eau rougie*; I'm afraid she's *eau rougie*.'

'*Eau rougie* may be nice, too, if one is tired and thirsty and needs mild refreshment, not altogether tasteless, and not at all intoxicating. She was certainly that to me. I was very much touched by her kindness.'

'I shall be touched if she'll take Merriston. I'm fearfully hard up. I suppose it would only be a little let; but that would be better than nothing.'

'She might stay for the winter if she liked it. I shan't try to make her like it, but I'll do my best to make her stay on if she does, and with a clear conscience, for I think that her staying will depend on her seeing me.'

'Wouldn't that mean that she'd be a great deal on your hands?'

'I shouldn't mind that; we get on very well. She will be here next week, you know. You must come to tea and meet her.'

'Well, I don't know. I don't think that I'm particularly eager to meet her,' Gerald confessed jocosely.

'You'll have to meet her a good deal if you are to see much of me,' said Helen; on which he owned that, with that compulsion put upon him, he and Miss Jakes might become intimates.

Gerald Digby was a young man who did very little work. He

had been vaguely intended, by an affectionate but haphazard family, for the diplomatic service, but it was found, after he had done himself some credit at Eton and Oxford, that the family resources didn't admit of this obviously suitable career for him; and an aged and wealthy uncle, who had been looked to confidently for succour, married at the moment, most unfeelingly, so that Gerald's career had to be definitely abandoned. Another relation found him a berth in the City, where he might hope to amass quite a fortune; but Gerald soon said that he far preferred poverty. He thought that he would like to paint and be an artist; he had a joyful eye for delicate, minute forms of beauty, and was most happily occupied when absorbed in Japanese-like studies of transient loveliness — a bird in flight, a verdant grasshopper on a wheat-blade, the tangled festoons of a wild convolvulus spray. His talent, however, though genuine, could hardly supply him with a livelihood, and he would have been seriously put to it had not his father's death left him a tiny income, while a half-informal secretaryship to a political friend, offered him propitiously at the same time, gave him leisure for his painting as well as for a good many other pleasant things. He had leisure, in especial, for going from country-house to country-house, where he was immensely in demand, and where he hunted, danced, and acted in private theatricals — usually in company with his cousin Helen. Helen's position in life was very much like his own, but that she hadn't even an informal secretaryship to depend upon. He had known Helen all his life, and she was almost like a sister, only nicer; for he associated sisters with his own brood, who were lean, hunting ladies, pleasant, but monotonous and inarticulate. Helen was very articulate and very various. He loved to look at her, as he loved to look at birds and flowers, and he loved to talk with her. He had many opportunities to look and talk. They stayed at the same houses in the country, and in London, when she was with old Miss Buchanan, he usually saw her every day. If he didn't drop in for a moment on his way to work at ten-thirty in the morning, he dropped in to tea; and if his or Helen's day were too full to admit of this, he managed to come in for a goodnight chat after a dinner or before a dance. He enjoyed Helen's talk and Helen's appearance most of all, he thought, at these late hours, when, a little weary and jaded, in evening dress and cloak, she lit her invariable cigarette, and mused with him over the events and people of the day. He liked Helen's way of talking about people; they knew an interminable array of them, many involved in enlivening complications, yet Helen never gossiped; the musing impersonality and impartiality with which she commented and surmised lifted her themes to a realm almost of art; she was pungent, yet never malicious, and the tolerant lucidity of her insight was almost benign.

Her narrow face, leaning back in its dark aureole of hair, her strange eyes and bitter-sweet lips — all dimmed, as it were, by drowsiness and smoke, and yet never more intelligently awake than at these nocturnal hours — remained with him as most typical of Helen's most significant and charming self. It was her aspect of mystery and that faint hint of bitterness that he found so charming; Helen herself he never thought of as mysterious. Mystery was a mere outward asset of her beauty, like the powdery surface of a moth's wing. He didn't think of Helen as mysterious, perhaps because he thought little about her at all; he only looked and listened while she made him think about everything but herself, and he felt always happy and altogether at ease in her presence. There seemed, indeed, no reason for thinking about a person whom one had known all one's life long.

And Helen was more than the best of company and the loveliest of objects; she was at once comrade and counsellor. He depended upon her more than upon any one. Comically helpless as he often found himself, he asked her advice about everything, and always received the wisest.

He had had often, though not so much in late years, to ask her advice about girls, for in spite of his financial ineligibility he was so engaging a person that he found himself continually drawn to the verge of decisive flirtations. His was rarely the initiative; he was responsive and affectionate and not at all susceptible, and Helen, who knew girls of her world to the bone, could accurately gauge the effect upon him of the pleading coquetry at which they were such adepts. She could gauge them the better, no doubt, from having herself no trace of coquetry. Men often liked her, but often found her cold and cynical, and even suspected her of conceit, especially since it was known that she had refused many excellent opportunities for establishing herself in life. She was also suspected by many of abysmal cleverness, and this reputation frightened admiring but uncomplicated young men more than anything else. Now, when her first youth was past, men more seldom fell in love with her and more frequently liked her; they had had time to find out that if she were cold she was also very kind, and that if abysmally clever, she could adapt her cleverness to pleasant, trivial uses.

Gerald, when he thought at all about her, thought of Helen as indeed cold, clever, and cynical; but these qualities never oppressed him, aware from the first, as he had been, of the others, and he found in them, moreover, veritable shields and bucklers for himself. It was to some one deeply experienced, yet quite unwarped by personal emotions, that he brought his recitals of distress and uncertainty. Lady Molly was a perfect little dear, but could he go on with it? How could he if he would? She hadn't any money, and her people would be furious; she herself, he felt sure, would be miserable in no time, if they did marry. They wouldn't even have enough — would they, did Helen think? — for love in a cottage, and Molly would hate love in a cottage. They would have to go about living on their relations and friends, as he now did, more or less; but with a wife and babies, how could one? Did Helen think one could? Gerald would finish dismally, standing before her with his hands thrust deeply into his pockets and a ruffled brow of inquiry. Or else it was the pretty Miss Oliver who had him — half alarmed, half enchanted — in her toils, and Gerald couldn't imagine what she was going to do with him. For such entanglements Helen's advice had always shown a way out, and for his uncertainties — though she never took the responsibility of actual guidance — her reflective questionings, her mere reflective silences, were illuminating. They made clear for him, as for her, that recklessness could only be worth while if one were really — off one's own bat, as it were — 'in love'; and that, this lacking, recklessness was folly sure to end in disaster. 'Wait, either until you care so much that you must, or else until you meet some one so nice, so rich, and so suitable that you may,' said Helen. 'If you are not careful you will find yourself married to some one who will bore you and quarrel with you on twopence a year.'

'You must be careful for me,' said Gerald. 'Please warn and protect.'

And Helen replied that she would always do her best for him.

It had never occurred to Gerald to turn the tables on Helen and tell her that she ought to marry. His imagination was not occupied with Helen's state, though once, after a conversation with old Miss Buchanan, he remarked to Helen, looking at her with a vague curiosity, that it was a pity she hadn't taken Lord Henry or Mr. Fergusson. 'Miss Buchanan tells me you might have been one of the first hostesses in London if you hadn't thrown away your chances.'

'I'm all right,' said Helen.

'Yes, you yourself are; but after she dies?'

Helen owned, with a smile, that she could certainly do with some few thousands a year; but that, in default of them, she could manage to scrape along.

'But you've never had any better chances, have you?' said Gerald rather tentatively. He might confide everything in Helen, but he realised, as a restraining influence, that she never made any confidences, even to him, who, he was convinced, knew her down to the ground.

Helen owned that she hadn't.

'Your aunt thinks it a dreadful pity. She's very much worried about you.'

'It's late in the day for the poor dear to worry. The chances were over long ago.'

'You didn't care enough?'

'I was young and foolish enough to want to be in love when I married,' said Helen, smiling at him with her half-closed eyes.

And Gerald said that, yes, he would have expected that from her; and with this dismissed the subject from his mind, taking it for granted that Helen's disengaged, sustaining, and enlivening spinsterhood would always be there for his solace and amusement.

CHAPTER VII.

Helen was on one side of her and Mr. Digby sat in an opposite corner of the railway carriage, and they were approaching the end of the journey to Merriston House on a bright July day soon after Althea's arrival in England. She had met Mr. Digby at Helen's the day before and had suggested that he should come with them. Gerald had remarked that it might be tiresome if she hated Merriston, and he were there to see that she hated it; but Althea was so sure of liking it that her conviction imposed itself.

Mr. Digby and Helen were both smoking; they had asked her very solicitously whether she minded, and she had said she didn't, although in fact she did not like the smell of tobacco, and Helen's constant cigarette distressed her quite unselfishly on the score of health. The windows were wide open, and though the gale that blew through ruffled her smooth hair and made her veil tickle disagreeably, these minor discomforts could not spoil her predominant sense of excitement and adventure. Mr. Digby's presence, particularly, roused it. He was so long, so limp, so graceful, lounging there in his corner. His socks and his tie were of such a charming shade of blue and his hair such a charming shade of light mouse-colour. He was vague and blithe, immersed in his own thoughts, which, apparently, were pleasant and superficial. When his eyes met Althea's, he smiled at her, and she thought his smile the most engaging she had ever seen. For the rest, he hardly spoke at all, and did not seem to consider it incumbent on him to make any conversational efforts, yet his mere presence lent festivity to the occasion.

Helen did not talk much either; she smoked her cigarette and looked out of the window with half-closed eyes. Her slender feet, encased in grey shoes, were propped on the opposite seat; her grey travelling-dress hung in smoke-like folds about her; in her little hat was a bright green wing.

Althea wondered if Mr. Digby appreciated his cousin's appearance, or if long brotherly familiarity had dimmed his perception of it. She wondered how her own appearance struck him. She knew that she was very trim and very elegant, and in mere beauty — quite apart from charm, which she didn't claim — she surely excelled Helen; Helen with her narrow eyes, odd projecting nose, and small, sulkily-moulded lips. Deeply though she felt the fascination of her friend's strange visage, she could but believe her own the lovelier. So many people — not only Franklin Winslow Kane — had thought her lovely. There was no disloyalty in recognising the fact for oneself, and an innocent satisfaction in the hope that Mr. Digby might recognise it too.

The day that flashed by on either side had also a festive quality: blue skies heaped with snowy clouds; fields brimmed with breeze-swept grain, green and silver, or streaked with the gold of butter-cups; swift streams and the curves of summer foliage. It was a country remote, wooded and pastoral, and Althea, a connoisseur in landscapes, was enchanted.

'Do you like it?' Helen asked her as they passed along the edge of a little wood, glimpses of bright meadow among its clearings. 'We are almost there now, and it's like this all about Merriston.'

'I've hardly seen any part of England I like so much,' said Althea. 'It has a sweet, untouched wildness rather rare in England.'

'I always think that it's a country to love and live in,' said Helen. 'Some countries seem made only to be looked at.'

Althea wondered, as she then went on looking at this country, whether she were thinking of her girlhood and of her many journeys to Merriston. She wondered if Mr. Digby were thinking of his boyhood. Ever since seeing those two together yesterday afternoon she had wondered about them. She had never encountered a relationship quite like theirs; it was so close, so confident, yet so untender. She could hardly make out that they liked each other; all that one saw was that they trusted, so that it had something of the businesslike quality of a partnership. Yet she found herself building up an absurd little romance about their past. It might be, who knew, that Mr. Digby had once been in love with Helen and that she had refused him; he was poor, and she had said that she must marry money. Althea's heart tightened a little with compassion for Mr. Digby. Only, if this ever had been, it was well over now; and more narrowly observing Mr. Digby's charming and irresponsible face, she reflected that he was hardly the sort of person to illustrate large themes of passion and fidelity.

A fly was waiting for them at the station, and as they jolted away Gerald remarked that she was now to see one of the worst features of Merriston; it was over an hour from the station, and if one hadn't a motor the drive was a great bore. Althea, however, didn't find it a bore. Her companions talked now, their heads at the windows; it had been years since they had traversed that country together; every inch of it was known to them and significant of weary waits, wonderful runs, feats and misadventures at gates and ditches; for their reminiscences were mainly sportsmanlike. Althea listened, absorbed, but distressed. It was Gerald who caught and interpreted the expression of her large, gentle eyes.

'I don't believe you like fox-hunting, Miss Jakes,' he said.

'No, indeed, I do not,' said Althea, shaking her head.

'You mean you think it cruel?'

'Very cruel.'

'Yet where would we be without it?' said Gerald. 'And where would the foxes be? After all, while they live, their lives are particularly pleasant.'

'With possible intervals of torture? Don't you think that, if they could choose, they would rather not live at all?'

'Oh, a canny old fox doesn't mind the run so much, you know — enjoys it after a fashion, no doubt.'

'Don't salve your conscience by that sophism, Gerald; the fox is canny because he has been terrified so often,' said Helen. 'Let us own that it is barbarous, but such glorious sport that one tries to forget the fox.'

It required some effort for Althea to testify against her and Mr. Digby, but she felt so strongly on the subject of animals, foxes in particular, that her courage did not fail her. 'I think it is when we forget, that the dreadful things in life, the sins and cruelties, happen,' she said.

Gerald's gay eyes were cogitatingly fixed on her, and Helen continued to look out of the window; but she thought that they both liked her the better for her frankness, and she felt in the little ensuing silence that it had brought them nearer — bright, alien creatures that they were.

Her first view of Merriston House hardly confirmed her hopes of it, though she would not have owned to herself that this was so. It was neither so beautiful nor so imposing as she had expected; it was even, perhaps, rather commonplace; but in a moment she was able to overcome this slight disloyalty and to love it the more for its unpretentiousness. A short, winding avenue of limes led to it, and it stood high among lawns that fell away to lower shrubberies and woods. It was a square stone house, covered with creepers, a white rose clustering over the doorway and a group of trees over-topping its chimneys.

Inside, where the housekeeper welcomed them and tea waited for them, was the same homely brightness. Hunting prints hung in the hall; rows of mediocre, though pleasing, family portraits in the dining-room. The long drawing-room at the back of the house, overlooking the lawns and a far prospect, was a much inhabited room, cheerful and shabby. There were old-fashioned water-colour landscapes, porcelain in cabinets and on shelves, and many tables crowded with ivory and silver bric-à-brac; things from India and things from China, that Digbys in the Army and Digbys in the Navy had brought home.

'What a Philistine room it is,' said Gerald, smiling as he looked around him; 'but I must say I like it just as it is. It has never made an æsthetic effort.'

Gerald's smile irradiated the whole house for Althea, and lit up, in especial, the big, sunny school-room where he and Helen found most memories of all. 'The same old table, Helen,' he said, 'and other children have spilled ink on it and scratched their initials just as we used to; here are yours and mine. Do you remember the day we did them under Fräulein's very nose? And here are all our old books, too. Look, Helen, the Roman history with your wicked drawings on the fly-leaves: Tullia driving over her poor old father, and Cornelia — ironic little wretch you were even then — what a prig she is with her jewels! And what splendid butter-scotch you used to make over the fire on winter evenings.'

Helen remembered everything, smiling as she followed Gerald about the room and looked at ruthless Tullia; and Althea, watching them, was touched — for them, and then, with a little counter-stroke of memory, for herself. She remembered her old home too — the dignified old house in steep Chestnut Street, and the little house on the blue Massachusetts coast where she had often passed long days playing by herself, for she had been an only child. She loved it here, for it was like a home, peaceful and sheltering; but where in all the world had she really a home? Where in all the world did she belong? The thought brought tears to her eyes as she looked out of the schoolroom window and listened to Gerald and Helen. It had ended, of course, for of course it had really begun, in Althea's decision to take Merriston House. It was quite fixed now, and on the way back she had made her new friends promise to be often together with her in the home of their youth. She had made them promise this so prettily and with such gentle warmth that it was very natural that Gerald, in talking over the event with Helen that evening, should say, strolling round Helen's little sitting-room, 'She's rather a dear, that little friend of yours.'

Helen was tired and lay extended on the divan in the grey dress she had not had time to change. She had doffed her hat and, thrusting its hatpins through it, had laid it on her knees, so that, as Gerald had remarked, she looked rather like Brünhilde on her rocky couch. But, unlike Brünhilde, her hands were clasped behind her neck, and she looked up at the ceiling. 'A perfect little dear,' she assented.

'Did you notice her eyes when she was talking about the foxes? They were as sorrowful and piteous as a Mater Dolorosa's. She is definite enough about some things, isn't she? Things like right and wrong, I mean, as she sees them.'

'Yes; she is clear about outside things, like right and wrong.'

'It's a good deal to be clear about, isn't it?'

'I suppose so,' Helen reflected. 'I don't feel that I really understand Althea. People who aren't clear about themselves are difficult to understand, I think.'

'It's that that really gives them a mystery. I feel that she really is a little mysterious,' said Gerald. 'One wonders what she would do in certain cases, and feel in certain situations, and one can't remotely imagine. She is a sealed book.'

'*She* wonders,' said Helen.

'And you suspect that her pages are empty?'

Helen reflected, but nothing seemed to come. She closed her eyes, smiling, and said, 'Be off, please. I'm getting too sleepy to have suspicions. We have plenty of time to find out whether anything is written on Althea's pages.'

CHAPTER VIII.

But, when Gerald was gone, Helen found that she was no longer sleepy. She lay, her eyes closed, straight and still, like an effigy on a tomb, and she thought, intently and quietly. It was more a series of pictures than a linking of ideas with which her mind was occupied — pictures of her childhood and girlhood in Scotland and at Merriston House. It was dispassionately that she watched the little figure, lonely, violent, walking over the moors, hiding in the thickets of the garden, choking with tears of fury, clenching teeth over fierce resentments. She almost smiled at the sight of her. What constant resentments, what frequent furies! They centred, of course, about the figure of her mother, lovely, vindictive, and stony-hearted, as she had been and was. Helen's life had dawned in the consciousness of love for this beautiful mother, whom she had worshipped with the ardent humility of a little dog. Afterwards, with a vehemence as great, she had grown to hate her. All her girlhood had been filled with struggles against her mother. Sometimes for weeks they had not spoken to each other, epochs during which, completely indifferent though she was, Mrs. Buchanan had given herself the satisfaction of smartly boxing her daughter's ears when her mute, hostile presence too much exasperated her. There had been no refuge for Helen with her father, a gloomy man, immersed in sport and study, nor in her brother Nigel, gay and pleasant though he was. When once Nigel got away to school and college, he spent as little time at home as possible. Helen was as solitary as a sea-bird, blown far inland and snared. Then came the visits to Merriston House — the cheerful, chattering houseful of happy girls, the kind father and mother, and Gerald. Gerald! From the time that he came into her life all the pictures were full of him, so full that she hardly saw herself any longer; she was only some one who watched and felt.

Her violent nature, undisciplined except by its own pride, did not submit easily to the taming processes of a wholesome family life; she dominated the girl cousins, and they only counted as chorus in the drama of her youth. It was Gerald who counted, at once, counted for everything else. She cared so much for him that, feeling her independence slipping from her, she at first quarrelled with him constantly, as far as he would let her quarrel with him. Her brooding bitterness amazed and amused him. While she stormed, he would laugh at her, gaily and ironically, and tell her that she was an absurd little savage. And, after she had burst into a frenzy of tears and fled from him, he would seek her out, find her hidden in some corner of the garden or shrubberies, and, grieved and alarmed, put his arms around her, kiss her and say: 'Look here, I'm awfully sorry. I can't bear to have you take things like this. Please make up.'

He could not bear to see her suffering, ludicrous though he thought her suffering to be. And it was this sweetness, this comprehension and tenderness, like sunlight flooding her gloomy and petrified young heart, that filled Helen with astonished bliss. She was tamed at last to the extent of laughing with Gerald at herself; and, though the force of her nature led him, the sweetness of his nature controlled her. They became the dearest of friends.

Yes, so it had always been; so it had always looked — to all the rest of the world, and to Gerald. Helen, lying on her divan, saw the pictures of comradeship filling the years. It was her consciousness of what the real meaning of the pictures was that supplied something else, something hidden and desperate that pulsed in them all. How she remembered the first time that she had drawn away when Gerald kissed her, putting up between them the shield of a lightly yet decisively accepted conventionality. They were 'growing up'; this was her justification. How she remembered what it had cost her to keep up the lightness of her smile so that he should not guess what lay beneath. Her nature was all passion, and enclosing this passion, like a steady hand held round a flame, was a fierce purity, a fierce pride. Gerald had never guessed. No one had ever guessed. It seemed to Helen that the pain of it had broken her heart in the very spring of her years; that it was only a maimed and cautious creature that the world had ever known.

She lay, and drew long quiet breaths in looking at it all. The day of reawakened memories had been like a sword in her heart, and now she seemed to draw it out slowly, and let the blood come with a sense of peace. She could even, as often, lend to the contemplation of her tragedy the bitter little grimace of mockery with which she met so much of life. She could tell herself, as often, that she had never outgrown love-sick girlhood, and that she was merely in love with Gerald's smile. Yet Gerald was all in his smile; and Gerald, it seemed, was made to be loved, all of him, helplessly and hopelessly, by unfortunate her. She felt her love as a misfortune; it was too strong and too unsatisfied to be felt in any sense as joy, though it strung her nature to a painful appreciation of joy. She saw life with a cold, appraising eye; it was like a landscape robbed of all sunlight, and, so robbed, so bleak, and so bereft, it was easy to appraise it, to see, since one could have no warmth or light, what were the next best things to have. She had missed the next best things again and again, when the moment had come for taking them; she had drawn back sick, blanched, shaken with the throes of desperate hope. Only in these last years, when next best things were no longer so plentiful, had hope really died. Her heart still beat, but it seemed to beat thinly, among all the heaped-up ashes of dead hopes. She was free to go forth into the sunless world and choose what place should be hers. She did not care much for anything that world had to give her. But she intended to choose carefully and calmly. She was aware in herself of firm, well-knit faculty, of tastes, sharp and sensitive, demanding only an opportunity to express themselves in significant and finished forms of life; and though Helen did not think of it in these terms, saying merely to herself that she wanted money and power, the background of her intention was a consciousness of capacity for power. Reflecting on this power, and on the paths to its realisation, she was led far, indeed, from any thought of Althea; and Althea was not at all in her mind as, sleepy at last, and very weary, she remembered Gerald's last words. It was the thought of Gerald that brought the thought of Althea, and of Althea's pages. Fair and empty they were, she felt sure, adorned only here and there with careful and becoming maxims. She smiled a little, not untenderly, as she thought of Althea. But, just before sinking to deeper drowsiness, and deciding that she must rouse herself and go upstairs to bed, a further consciousness came to her. The sunny day at Merriston had not, in her thoughts, brought them near to one another — Gerald, and Althea, and her; yet something significant ran through her sudden memory of it. She had moments of her race's sense of second-sight, and it never came without making her aware of a pause — a strange, forced pause — where she had to look at something, touch something, in the dark, as it were. It was there as she roused herself from her half-somnolent state; it was there in the consciousness of a turning-point in her life — in Gerald's, in Althea's. 'We may write something on Althea's pages,' was the thought with which, smiling over its inappropriateness, she went upstairs. And the fancy faded from her memory, as if it had been a bird's wing that brushed her cheek in the darkness.

CHAPTER IX.

Althea went down to Merriston House in the middle of July. Helen accompanied her to see her safely installed and to set the very torpid social ball rolling. There were not many neighbours, but Helen assembled them all. She herself could stay only a few days. She was bound, until the middle of August, in a rush of engagements, and meanwhile Althea, rather ruefully, was forced to fall back on Miss Buckston for companionship. She had always, till now, found Miss Buckston's cheerful dogmatism fortifying, and, even when it irritated her, instructive; but she had now new standards of interest, and new sources of refreshment, and, shut up with Miss Buckston for a rainy week, she felt as never before the defects of this excellent person's many qualities.

She had fires lighted, much to Miss Buckston's amusement, and sat a good deal by the blaze in the drawing-room, controlling her displeasure when Miss Buckston, dressed in muddy tweed and with a tweed cap pulled down over her brows, came striding in from a ten-mile tramp and said, pulling open all the windows, 'You are frightfully frusty in here.'

It was not 'frusty.' Althea had a scientific regard for ventilation, and a damp breeze from the garden blew in at the furthest window. She had quite enough air.

Miss Buckston was also very critical of Merriston House, and pointed out the shabbiness of the chintz and faded carpets. The garden, she said, was shamefully neglected, and she could not conceive how people could bear to let a decent place like this go to ruin. 'But he's a slack creature, Gerald Digby, I've heard.'

Althea coldly explained that Mr. Digby was too poor to live at Merriston and to keep it up. She did not herself in the least mind the shabbiness.

'Oh, I don't mind it,' said Miss Buckston. 'I only think he's done himself very well in getting you to take the place in this condition. How much do you give for it?'

Althea, more coldly, named the sum. It was moderate; Miss Buckston had to grant that, though but half-satisfied that there was no intention to 'do' her friend. 'When once you get into the hands of hard-up fashionable folk,' she said, 'it's as well to look sharp.'

Althea did not quite know what to say to this. She had never in the past opposed Miss Buckston, and it would be difficult to tell her now that she took too much upon herself. At a hint of hesitancy, she knew, Miss Buckston would pass to and fro over her like a steam-roller, nearly as noisy, and to her own mind as composedly efficient. Hesitancy or contradiction she flattened and left behind her.

She had an air of owning Bach that became peculiarly vexatious to Althea, who, in silence, but armed with new standards, was assembling her own forces and observed, in casting an eye over them, that she had heard five times as much music as Miss Buckston and might be granted the right of an opinion on it. She took satisfaction in a memory of Miss Buckston's face singing in the Bach choir — even at the time it had struck her as funny — at a concert to which Althea had gone with her some years ago in London. It was to see, for her own private delectation, a weak point in Miss Buckston's iron-clad personality to remember how very funny she could look. Among the serried ranks of singing heads hers had stood out with its rubicund energy, its air of mastery, the shining of its eye-glasses and of its large white teeth; and while she sang Miss Buckston had jerked her head rhythmically to one side and beaten time with her hand as if to encourage and direct her less competent companions. Sometimes, now, she looked almost as funny, when she sat down to the piano and gave forth a recitative.

After Bach, Woman's Suffrage was Miss Buckston's special theme, and, suspecting a new hint of uncertainty in Althea, whose conviction she had always taken for granted, she attacked her frequently and mercilessly.

'Pooh, my dear,' she would say, 'don't quote your frothy American women to me. Americans have no social conscience. That's the trouble with you all; rank individualists, every one of you. When the political attitude of the average citizen is that of the ostrich keeping his head in the sand so that he shan't see what the country's coming to, what can you expect of the women? Your arguments don't affect the suffrage question, they merely dismiss America. I shall lose my temper if you trot them out to me.' Miss Buckston never lost her temper, however; other people's opinions counted too little with her for that.

At the end of the first week Althea felt distinctly that though the country, even under these dismal climatic conditions, might be delightful if shared with some people, it was not delightful shared with Miss Buckston. She did not like walking in the rain; she was a creature of houses, cabs and carriages. The sober beauty of blotted silhouettes, and misty, rolling hills at evening when the clouds lifted over the sunset, did not appeal to her. She wished that she had stayed in London; she wished that Helen and Mr. Digby were with her; she was even glad that Aunt Julia and the girls were coming.

There was a welcome diversion afforded for her, when Aunt Julia came, by the prompt hostility that declared itself between her and Miss Buckston. Aunt Julia was not a person to allow a steam-roller to pass over her without protest, and Althea felt that she herself had been cowardly when she saw how Aunt Julia resented, for them both, Miss Buckston's methods. Miss Buckston had a manner of saying rude things in sincere unconsciousness that they could offend anybody. She herself did not take offence easily; she was, as she would have said, 'tough.' But Mrs. Pepperell had all the sensitiveness — for herself and for others — of her race, the British race, highly strung with several centuries of transplantation to an electric climate. If she was rude it was never unconsciously so. After her first talk with Miss Buckston, in which the latter, as was her wont, told her a number of unpleasant facts about America and the Americans, Mrs. Pepperell said to her niece, 'What an intolerable woman!'

'She doesn't mean it,' said Althea feebly.

'Perhaps not,' said Aunt Julia; 'but I intend that she shall see what I mean.'

Althea's feeling was of mingled discomfort and satisfaction. Her sympathies were with Aunt Julia, yet she felt a little guilty towards Miss Buckston, for whom her affection was indeed wavering. Inner loyalty having failed she did not wish outer loyalty to be suspected, and in all the combats that took place she kept in the background and only hoped to see Aunt Julia worst Miss Buckston. But the trouble was that Aunt Julia never did worst her. Even when, passing beyond the bounds of what she considered decency, she became nearly as outspoken as Miss Buckston, that lady maintained her air of cheerful yet impatient tolerance. She continued to tell them that the American wife and mother was the most narrow, the most selfish, the most complacent of all wives and mothers; and, indeed, to Miss Buckston's vigorous virginity, all wives and mothers, though sociologically necessary, belonged to a slightly inferior, more rudimentary species. The American variety, she said, were immersed in mere domesticity or social schemes and squabbles. 'Oh, they talked. I never heard so much talk in all my life as when I was over there,' said Miss Buckston; 'but I couldn't see that they got anything done with it. They had debates about health, and yet one could hardly for love or money get a window open in a train; and they had debates on the ethics of citizenship, and yet you are governed by bosses. Voluble and inefficient creatures, I call them.'

Aunt Julia, conscious of her own honourable career, with its achievements in enlightened philanthropy and its background of careful study, heard this with inexpressible ire; but when she was dragged to the execrable taste of a retaliation, and pointed to the British countryside matron, as they saw her at Merriston — a creature, said Aunt Julia, hardly credible in her complacency and narrowness, Miss Buckston rejoined with an unruffled smile: 'Ah, we'll wake them up. They've good stuff in them — good, staying stuff; and they do a lot of useful work in keeping down Radicalism and keeping up the sentiment of our imperial responsibilities and traditions. They are solid, at all events, not hollow.' And to this poor Aunt Julia, whose traditions did not allow her the retort of sheer brutality, could find no answer.

The absurd outcome of the situation was that Althea and Aunt Julia came to look for succour to the girls. The girls were able — astonishingly so, to cope with Miss Buckston. In the first place, they found her inexpressibly funny, and neither Althea nor Aunt Julia quite succeeded at that; and in the second, they rather liked her; they did not argue with her, they did not take her seriously for a moment; they only played buoyantly about her. A few months before, Althea would have been gravely disturbed by their lack of reverence; she saw it now with guilty satisfaction. Miss Buckston, among the nets they spread for her, plunged and floundered like a good-tempered bull — at first with guileless acquiescence in the game, and then with growing bewilderment. They flouted gay cloaks before her dizzy eyes, and planted ribboned darts in her quivering shoulders. Even Althea could not accuse them of aggressiveness or rudeness. They never put themselves forward; they were there already. They never twisted the tail of the British lion; they never squeezed the eagle; they were far too secure under his wings for that. The bird, indeed, had grown since Althea's youth, and could no longer be carried about as a hostile trophy. They took it for granted, gaily and kindly, that America was 'God's country,' and that all others were schools or playgrounds for her children. They Were filled with a confident faith in her future and in their own part in making that future better. And something in the faith was infectious. Even Miss Buckston felt it. Miss Buckston felt it, indeed, more than Althea, whose attitude towards her own native land had always been one of affectionate apology.

'Nice creatures,' said Miss Buckston, 'undisciplined and mannerless as they are; but that's a failing they share with our younger generation. I see more hope for your country in that type than in anything else you can show me. They are solid, and don't ape anything.'

So by degrees a species of friendship grew up between Miss Buckston and the girls, who said that she was a jolly old thing, and more fun than a goat, especially when she sang Bach. Mildred and Dorothy sang exceptionally well and were highly equipped musicians.

Althea could not have said why it was, but this progress to friendliness between her cousins and Miss Buckston made her feel, as she had felt in the Paris hotel drawing-room over a month ago, jaded and unsuccessful. So did the fact that the vicar's eldest son, a handsome young soldier with a low forehead and' a loud laugh, fell in love with Dorothy. That young men should fall in love with them was another of the pleasant things that Mildred and Dorothy took for granted. Their love affairs, frank and rather infantile, were of a very different calibre from the earnest passions that Althea had aroused — passions usually initiated by intellectual sympathy and nourished on introspection and a constant interchange of serious literature.

It was soon evident that Dorothy, though she and Captain Merton became the best of friends, had no intention of accepting him. Mrs. Merton, the vicar's wife, had at first been afraid lest she should, not having then ascertained what Mrs. Pepperell's fortune might be; but after satisfying herself on this point by a direct cross-examination of Althea, she was as much amazed as incensed when her boy told her ruefully that he had been refused three times. Althea was very indignant when she realised that Mrs. Merton, bland and determined in her latest London hat, was trying to find out whether Dorothy was a good enough match for Captain Merton, and it was pleasant to watch Mrs. Merton's subsequent discomfiture. At the same time, she felt that to follow in Mildred and Dorothy's triumphant wake was hardly what she had expected to do at Merriston House.

Other things, too, were discouraging. Helen had hardly written at all. She had sent a postcard from Scotland to say that she would have to put off coming till later in August. She had sent another, in answer to a long letter of Althea's, in which Gerald had been asked to come with her, to say that Gerald was yachting, and that she was sure he would love to come some time in the autumn, if his plans allowed it; and Althea, on reading this, felt certain that if she counted for little with Helen, she counted for nothing with Mr. Digby. Whom did she count with? That was the question that once more assailed her as she saw herself sink into insignificance beside Mildred and Dorothy. If Mildred and Dorothy counted for more than she, where was she to look for response and sympathy? And now, once again, as if in answer to these dismal questionings, came a steamer letter from Franklin Winslow Kane, announcing his immediate arrival. Althea had thought very little about Franklin in these last weeks; her mind had been filled with those foreground figures that now seemed to have become uncertain and vanishing. And it was not so much that Franklin came forward as that there was nothing else to look at; not so much that he counted, as that to count so much, in every way, for him might almost atone for counting with no one else. Physically, mentally, morally, Franklin's appreciations of her were deep; they were implied all through his letter, which was at once sober and eager. He said that he would stay at Merriston House for 'just as long as ever she would let him.' Merely to be near her was to him, separated as he was from her for so much of his life, an unspeakable boon. Franklin rarely dealt in demonstrative speeches, but, in this letter, after a half-shy prelude to his own daring, he went on to say: 'Perhaps, considering how long it's been since I saw you, you'll let me kiss your beautiful hands when we meet.'

Franklin had only once kissed her beautiful hands, years ago, on the occasion of her first touched refusal of him. She had severe scruples as to encouraging, by such graciousness, a person you didn't intend to marry; but she really thought, thrilling a little as she read the sentence, that this time, perhaps, Franklin might. Franklin himself never thrilled her; but the words he wrote renewed in her suddenly a happy self-confidence. Who, after all, was Franklin's superior in insight? Wrapped in the garment of his affection, could she not see with equanimity Helen's vagueness and Gerald's indifference? Why, when one came to look at it from the point of view of the soul, wasn't Franklin their superior in every way? It needed some moral effort to brace herself to the inquiry. She couldn't deny that Franklin hadn't their charm; but charm was a very superficial thing compared to moral beauty.

Althea could not have faced the perturbing fact that charm, to her, counted for more than goodness. She clung to her ethical valuations of life, feeling, instinctively, that only in this category lay her own significance. To abandon the obvious weights and measures was to find herself buffeted and astray in a chaotic and menacing universe. Goodness was her guide, and she could cling to it if the enchanting will-o'-the-wisp did not float into sight to beckon and bewilder her. She indignantly repudiated the conception of a social order founded on charm rather than on solid worth; yet, like other frail mortals, she found herself following what allured her nature rather than what responded to the neatly tabulated theories of her mind. It was her beliefs and her instincts that couldn't be made to tally, and in her refusal to see that they did not tally lay her danger, as now, when with an artificially simplified attitude she waited eagerly for the coming of somebody who would restore to her her own sense of significance.

Franklin Winslow Kane arrived late one afternoon, and Althea arranged that she should greet him alone. Miss Buckston, Aunt Julia, the girls, and Herbert Vaughan had driven over to a neighbouring garden-party, and Althea alleged the arrival of her old friend as a very valid excuse. She walked up and down the drawing-room, dressed in one of her prettiest dresses; the soft warmth and light of the low sun filled the air, and her heart expanded with it. She wondered if — ah, if only! — Franklin would himself be able to thrill her, and her deep expectation almost amounted to a thrill. Expectation culminated in a wave of excitement and emotion as the door opened and her faithful lover stood before her.

Franklin Winslow Kane (he signed himself more expeditiously as Franklin W. Kane) was a small, lean man. He had an air of tension, constant, yet under such perfect control, that it counted as placidity rather than as strain. His face was sallow and clean-shaven, and the features seemed neatly drawn on a flat surface rather than modelled, so discreet and so meagre were the sallies and shadows. His lips were calm and firmly closed, and had always the appearance of smiling; of his eyes one felt the bright, benignant beam rather than the shape or colour. His straight stiff hair was shorn in rather odd and rather ugly lines along his forehead and temples, and of his clothes the kindest thing to say was that they were unobtrusive. Franklin had once said of himself, with comic dispassionateness, that he looked like a cheap cigar, and the comparison was apt. He seemed to have been dried, pressed, and moulded, neatly and expeditiously, by some mechanical process that turned out thousands more just like him. A great many things, during this process, had been done to him, but they were commonplace, though complicated things, and they left him, while curiously finished, curiously undifferentiated. The hurrying streets of any large town in his native land would, one felt, be full of others like him: good-tempered, shrewd, alert, yet with an air of placidity, too, as though it were a world that required effort and vigilance of one, and yet, these conditions fulfilled, would always justify one's expectations. If differences there were in Franklin Kane, they were to be sought for, they did not present themselves; and he himself would have been the last to be conscious of them. He didn't think of himself as differentiated; he didn't desire differentiation.

He advanced now towards his beloved, after a slight hesitation, for the sunlight in which she stood as well as her own radiant appearance seemed to have dazzled him a little. Althea held out her hands, and the tears came into her eyes; it was as if she hadn't known, until then, how lonely she was. 'O Franklin, I'm so glad to see you,' she said.

He held her hands, gazing at her with a gentle yet intent rapture, and he forgot, in a daring greater than any he had ever known, to kiss them. Franklin never took anything for granted, and Althea knew that it was because he saw her tears and saw her emotion that he could ask her now, hesitatingly, yet with sudden confidence: 'Althea, it's been so long — you are so lovely — it will mean nothing to you, I know; so may I kiss you?'

Put like that, why shouldn't he? Conscience had not a qualm, and Franklin had never seemed so dear to her. She smiled a sisterly benison upon his request, and, still holding her hands, he leaned to her and kissed her. Closing her eyes she wondered intently for a moment, able, in the midst of her motion, to analyse it; for, yes, it had thrilled her. She needed to be kissed, were it only Franklin who kissed her.

They went, hand in hand, to a sofa, and there she was able to show him only the sisterly benignity that he knew so well. She questioned him sweetly about his voyage, his health, his relatives — his only near relative was a sister who taught in a college — and about their mutual friends and his work. To all he replied carefully and calmly, though looking at her delightedly while he spoke. He had a very deliberate, even way of speaking, and in certain words so broadened the a's that, almost doubled in length by this treatment, they sounded like little bleats. His 'yes' was on two notes and became a dissyllable.

After he had answered all her questions he took up the thread himself. He had tactfully relinquished her hand at a certain moment in her talk. Althea well remembered his sensitiveness to any slightest mood in herself; he was wonderfully imaginative when it came to any human relation. He did not wait for her to feel consciously that it was not quite fitting that her hand should be held for so long.

'This is a nice old place you've got, Althea,' he said, looking about. 'Homelike and welcoming. I liked the look of it as I drove up. Have you a lot of English people with you?'

'Only one; Miss Buckston, you know. Aunt Julia and the girls are here, and Herbert Vaughan, their friend. You know Herbert Vaughan; such a nice young creature; his mother is a Bostonian.'

'I know about him; I don't know him,' said Franklin, who indeed, as she reflected, would not be likely to have met the fashionable Herbert. 'And where is that attractive new friend of yours you wrote to me about — the one you took care of in Paris — the Scotch lady?'

'Helen Buchanan? She is coming; she is in Scotland now.'

'Oh, she's coming. I am to see her, I hope.'

'You are to see everybody, dear Franklin,' said Althea, smiling upon him. 'You are to stay, you know, for as long as you will.'

'That's sweet of you, Althea.' He looked at her. Her kindness still buoyed him above his wonted level. He had never allowed himself to become utterly hopeless, yet he had become almost resigned to hope deferred; a pressing, present hope grew in him now. 'But it's ambiguous, you know,' he went on, smiling back. 'If I'm to stay as long as I will, I'm never to leave you, you know.'

Hope was becoming to Franklin. Althea felt herself colouring a little under his eyes. 'You still feel that?' she said rather feebly.

'I'll always feel that.'

'It's very wonderful of you, Franklin. It makes me, sometimes, feel guilty, as though I kept you from fuller happiness.'

'You can't do that. You are the only person who can give me fuller happiness.'

'And I give you happiness, like this — even like this? — really?'

'Of course; but,' he smiled a little forcedly, 'I can't pretend it's anything like what I want. I want a great deal.'

Althea's eyes fell before the intent and gentle gaze.

'Dear Franklin — I wish — '

'You wish you could? I wonder — I wonder, Althea, if you feel a little nearer to it just now. I seem to feel, myself, that you are.'

Was she? How she wished she were. Yet the wish was mixed with fear. She said, faltering, 'Don't ask me now. I'm so glad to see you — so glad; but that's not the same thing, is it?'

'It may be on the way to it.'

'May it?' she sighed tremblingly.

There was a silence; and then, taking her hand again, he again kissed it, and holding it for an insistent moment said, 'Althea, won't you try being engaged to me?'

She said nothing, turning away her face.

'You might make a habit of loving me, you know,' he went on half whimsically. 'No one would know anything about it. It would be our secret, our little experiment. If only you'd try it. Dearest, I do love you so deeply.'

And then — how it was she did not know, but it was again Franklin's words rather than Franklin that moved her, so that he must have seen the yielding to his love, if not to him, in her face — she was in his arms, and he was kissing her and saying, 'O Althea, won't you try?'

Althea's mind whirled. She needed to be kissed; that alone was evident; for she did not draw away; but the tears came, of perplexity and pathos, and she said, 'Franklin, dear Franklin, I'll try — I mean, I'll try to be in love with you — I can't be engaged, not really engaged — but I will try.'

'Darling — you are nearer it — '

'Yes — I don't know, Franklin — I mustn't bind myself. I can't marry you unless I am in love with you — can I, Franklin?'

'Well, I don't know about that,' said Franklin, his voice a little shaken. 'You can't expect me to give you an impartial answer to that now — can you, dear? I feel as if I wanted you to marry me on the chance you'd come to love me. And you do care for me enough for this, don't you? That in itself is such an incredible gift.'

Yes, she evidently cared for him enough for this; and 'this' meant his arm about her, her hand in his, his eyes of devotion upon her, centre of his universe as she was. And 'this' had, after years of formality, incredibly indeed altered all their relation. But — to marry him — it meant all sorts of other things; it meant definitely giving up; it meant definitely taking on. What it meant taking on was Franklin's raylessness, Franklin's obscurity, Franklin's dun-colour — could a wife escape the infection? What it meant giving up was more vague, but it floated before her as the rose-coloured dream of her youth — the hero, the earnest, ardent hero, who was to light all life to rapture and significance. And, absurdly, while the drift of glamour and regret floated by, and while she sat with Franklin's arm about her, her hand in his, it seemed to shape itself for a moment into the gay, irresponsible face of Gerald Digby. Absurd, indeed; he was neither earnest nor ardent, and if he were he would never feel earnestness or ardour on her account. Franklin certainly responded, in that respect, to the requirements of her dream. Yet — ah, yet — he responded in no other. It was not enough to have eyes only for her. A hero should draw others' eyes upon him; should have rays that others could recognise. Althea was troubled, and she was also ashamed of herself, but whether because of that vision of Gerald Digby, or whether because she was allowing Franklin privileges never allowed before, she did not know. Only the profundity of reverence that beamed upon her from Franklin's eyes enabled her to regain her self-respect.

Smiling a little constrainedly, she drew her hand from his and rose. 'I mustn't bind myself,' she repeated, standing with downcast eyes before him, 'but I'll try; indeed, I'll try.'

'You want to be in love with me, if only you can manage it, don't you, dear?' he questioned; and to this she could truthfully reply, 'Yes, dear Franklin, I want to be in love with you.'

CHAPTER X.

Althea found, as she had hoped, that her whole situation was altered by the arrival of her suitor. A woman boasting the possession of even the most rayless of that species is in a very different category from the woman as mere unsought unit. As unit she sinks easily into the background, is merged with other unemphatic things, but as sought she is always in the foreground, not only in her own, but in others' eyes. Be she ever so unnoticeable, she then gains, at least, the compliment of conjecture. The significance of her personal drama has a universal interest; the issues of her situation are those that appeal forcibly to all.

Althea and her steady, sallow satellite, became the centre of a watchful circle; watchful and kindly. Even to others her charms became more apparent, as, indeed, they were more actual. To be loved and to live in the presence of the adorer is the most beautifying of circumstances. Althea bloomed under it. Her eyes became larger, sweeter, sadder; her lips softer; the mild fever of her indecision and of her sense of power burned dimly in her cheeks. As the centre of watchfulness she gained the grace of self-confidence.

Aunt Julia, observant and shrewd, smiled with half-ironic satisfaction. She had felt sure that Althea must come to this, and 'this,' she considered as on the whole fortunate for Althea. Anything, Aunt Julia thought, was better than to become a wandering old maid, and she had, moreover, the highest respect for Franklin Winslow Kane. As a suitor for one of her own girls he would, of course, have been impossible; but her girls she placed in a different category from Althea; they had the rights of youth, charm, and beauty.

The girls, for their part, though seeing Franklin as a fair object for chaff, conceived of him as wholly suitable. Though they chaffed him, they never did so to his disadvantage, and they were respectful spectators of his enterprise. They had the nicest sense of loyalty for serious situations.

And Miss Buckston was of all the most satisfactory in her attitude. Her contempt for the disillusions and impediments of marriage could not prevent her from feeling an altogether new regard for a person to whom marriage was so obviously open; moreover, she thought Mr. Kane highly interesting. She at once informed Althea that she always found American men vastly the superior in achievement and energy to the much-vaunted American woman, and Althea was not displeased. She was amused but gratified, when Miss Buckston told her what were Franklin's good qualities, and said that though he had many foolish democratic notions, he was more worth while talking to than any man she had met for a long time. She took every opportunity for talking to him about sociology, science, and international themes, and Althea even became a little irked by the frequency of these colloquies and tempted sometimes to withdraw Franklin from them; but the subtle flattery that Miss Buckston's interest in Franklin offered to herself was too acceptable for her to yield to such impulses. Yes, Franklin had a right to his air of careful elation; she had never been so near it. She had not again allowed him to kiss her — she was still rather ashamed when she remembered how often she had, on that one occasion, allowed him to kiss her; yet, in spite of her swift stepping back to discretion, she had never in all her life been so near to saying 'yes' to Franklin as during the eight or ten days after his arrival. And the fact that a third postcard from Helen expressed even further vagueness as to the chance of Gerald's being able to be with them that autumn at Merriston, added to the sense of inevitability. Althea had been for this time so absorbed in Franklin, his effect on others and on herself, that she had not felt, as she would otherwise have done, Helen's unsatisfactory attitude. Helen was at last coming, and she was fluttered at the thought of her coming, but she was far more able to cope with Helen; there was more self to do it with; she was stronger, more independent of Helen's opinion and of Helen's affection. But dimly she felt also — hardly aware she felt it — that she was a more effective self as the undecided recipient of Franklin's devotion than as his affianced wife. A rayless person, it seemed, could crown one with beams as long as one maintained one's distance from him; merged with him one shared his insignificance. To accept Franklin might be to shear them both of all the radiance they borrowed from each other.

Helen arrived on a very hot evening in mid-August. She had lost the best train, which brought one to Merriston at tea-time — Althea felt that Helen was the sort of person who would always lose the best train — and after a tedious journey, with waits and changes at hot stations, she received her friend's kisses just as the dressing-bell for dinner sounded. Helen, standing among her boxes, while Amélie hurriedly got out her evening things, looked extremely tired, and felt, Althea was sure, extremely ill-tempered. It was characteristic of Helen, she knew it intuitively, to feel ill-temper, and yet to have it so perfectly under control that it made her manner sweeter than usual. Her sense of social duty never failed her, and it did not in the least fail her now as she smiled at Althea, and, while she drank the cup of tea that had been brought to her, gave an account of her misfortunes. She had arrived in London from Scotland the night before, spent two hours of the morning in frantic shopping — the shops like ovens and the London pavements exhaling a torrid heat; had found, on getting back to Aunt Grizel's — Aunt Grizel was away — that the silly maid had muddled all her packing; then, late already, had hurled herself into a cab, and observed, half-way to the station, that the horse was on the point of collapse; had changed cabs and had arrived at the station to see her train just going out. 'So there I paced up and down like a caged, suffocating lioness for over an hour, had a loathsome lunch, and read half a dozen papers before my train started, I came third class with a weary mother and two babies, the sun beat in all the way, and I had three changes. I'm hardly fit to be seen, and not fit to speak. But, yes, I'll have a bath and come down in time for something to eat. I'd rather come down; please don't wait for me.'

They did, however, and she was very late. The windows in the drawing-room were widely open to the evening air, and the lamps had not yet been lit; and when Helen came she made Althea think a little of a beautiful grey moth, hovering vaguely in the dusk.

Captain Merton dined with them that evening, and young Harry Evans, son of a neighbouring squire; and Herbert Vaughan was still at Merriston, the masculine equivalent of Mildred and Dorothy, an exquisitely appointed youth, frank and boisterous, with charming, candid eyes, and the figure of an Adonis. These young men's eyes were fixed upon Helen as they took their places at the dinner-table, though not altogether, Althea perceived, with admiration. Helen, wherever she was, would always be centre; things and people grouped themselves about her; she made the picture, and she was the focus of interest. Why was it? Althea wondered, as, with almost a mother's wistful pleasure, she watched her friend and watched the others watch her. Pale, jaded, in her thin grey dress, haggard and hardly beautiful, Helen was full of apathetic power, and Helen was interested in nobody. It was Althea's pride to trace out reasons and to see in what Helen's subjugating quality consisted. Franklin had taken Helen in, and she herself sat at some distance from them, her heart beating fast as she wondered what Helen would think of him. She could not hear what they said, but she could see that they talked, though not eagerly. Helen had, as usual, the air of giving her attention to anything put before her. One never could tell in the least what she really thought of it. She smiled with pale lips and weary eyes upon Franklin, listened to him gravely and with concentration, and, when she did speak, it was, once or twice, with gaiety, as though he had amused and surprised her. Yet Althea felt that her thoughts were far from Franklin, far from everybody in the room. And meanwhile, of everybody in the room, it was the lean, sallow young man beside her who seemed at once the least impressed and the most interested. But that was so like Franklin; no one could outdo him in interest, and no one could outdo him in placidity. That he could examine Helen with his calm, careful eye, as though she were an object for mental and moral appraisement only; that he could see her so acutely, and yet remain so unmoved by her rarity, at once pleased and displeased Althea. It showed him as so safe, but it showed him as so narrow. She found herself thinking almost impatiently that Franklin simply had no sense of charm at all. Helen interested him, but she did not stir in him the least wistfulness or wonder, as charm should do. Miss Buckston interested him, too. And she was very sure that Franklin while liking Helen as a human creature — so he liked Miss Buckston — disapproved of her as a type. Of course, he must disapprove of her. Didn't she contradict all the things he approved of — all the laboriousness, the earnestness, the tolerant bias towards the views and feelings of the majority? And Althea felt, with a rather sharp satisfaction, that it would give her some pleasure to show Franklin that she differed from him; that she had other tastes than his, other needs — needs which Helen more than satisfied.

She had no opportunity that night for fathoming Helen's impressions of Franklin, and indeed felt that the task was a delicate one to undertake. If Helen didn't volunteer them she could hardly ask for them. Loyalty to Franklin and to the old bond between them, to say nothing of the new, made it unfit that Helen should know that her impressions of Franklin were of any weight with her friend. But the next morning Helen did not come down to breakfast, and there was no reason why, in a stroll round the garden with Franklin afterwards, she should not be point blank; the only unfairness here was that in his opinion of Helen it would not be Helen he judged, but himself.

'How do you like her, my new friend?' she asked.

Franklin was very willing to talk and had already clear impressions. The clearest was the one he put at once before her in the vernacular he had never taken the least pains to modify. 'She looks sick; I'd be worried about her if I were you. Can't you rouse her?'

'Rouse her? She is always like that. Only she was particularly tired last night.'

'A healthy young woman oughtn't to get so tired. If she's always like that she always needs rousing.'

'Don't be ridiculous, Franklin. What do you mean?'

'Why, I'm perfectly serious. I think she looks sick. She ought to take tonics and a lot of outdoor exercise.'

'Is that all that you can find to say about her?' Althea asked, half amused and half indignant.

'Why no,' Franklin replied. 'I think she's very attractive; she has a great deal of poise. Only she's half alive. I'd like to see her doing something.'

'It's enough for her to be, I think.'

'Enough for you, perhaps; but is it enough for her? She'd be a mighty lot happier if she had some work.'

'Really, Franklin, you are absurd,' said Althea laughing. 'There is room in the world, thank goodness, for other people besides people who work.'

'Oh no, there isn't; not really. The trouble with the world is that they're here and have to be taken care of; there's not room for them. It's lovely of you to care so much about her,' he went on, turning his bright gaze upon her. 'I see how you care for her. It's because of that — for her sake, you know — what it can mean to her — that I emphasise the side that needs looking after. You look after her, Althea; that'll be the best thing that can happen to her.'

With all his acuteness, how guileless he was, the dear! She saw herself 'looking after' Helen!

'You might have a great deal of influence on her,' Franklin added.

Althea struggled for a moment with her pride. She liked Franklin to have this high opinion of her ministering powers, and yet she liked even more to have the comfort of confiding in him; and she was willing to add to Helen's impressiveness at the expense of her own. 'I've no influence with her,' she said. 'I never shall have. I don't believe that any one could influence Helen.'

Franklin looked fixedly at her for some time as though probing what there must be of pain for her in this avowal. Then he said, 'That's too bad. Too bad for her, I mean. You're all right, dear. She doesn't know what she misses.'

They sat out on the lawn that afternoon in the shade of the great trees. Mildred and Dorothy, glittering in white, played lawn-tennis indefatigably with Herbert Vaughan and Captain Merton. Aunt Julia embroidered, and Miss Buckston read a review with a concentrated brow and an occasional ejaculation of disapproval. Helen was lying prone in a green linen chair; her garden hat was bent over her eyes and she seemed to doze. Franklin sat on the grass in front of Althea, just outside the radius of shadow, clasping his thin knees with his thin hands. He looked at his worst out of doors, on a lawn and under trees. He was typically civic. Even with his attempts to adapt his clothes to rural requirements, he was out of place. His shoes seemed to demand a pavement, and his thin grey coat and trousers an office stool. Althea also eyed his tie with uncertainty. He wasn't right; he didn't in the least look like Herbert Vaughan, who was elegant, or like Captain Merton, who was easy. He sat out in the sunlight, undisturbed by it, though he screwed up his features in a very unbecoming way while he talked, the sun in his eyes. In her cool green shadow, Helen now and then opened her eyes and looked at him, and Althea wished that he would not remain in so resolutely disadvantageous a situation.

'See here, Althea,' he was saying, 'if you've gone so much into this matter' — the topic was that of sweated industries — 'I don't see how you can avoid feeling responsible — making some use of all you know. I don't ask you to come home to do it, though we need you and your kind badly there, but you ought to lend a hand here.'

'I don't really think I could be of any use,' said Althea.

'With all your knowledge of political economy? Why, Miss Buckston could set you to something at once. Knowledge is always of use, isn't it, Miss Buckston?'

'Yes, if one cares enough about things to put them through,' said Miss Buckston. 'I always tell Althea that she might make herself very useful to me.'

'Exactly,' said Franklin. 'And she does care. All you need do, Althea, is to harness yourself. You mustn't drift.'

'The number of drifting American women one sees over here!' Miss Buckston ejaculated; to which Franklin cheerfully replied: 'Oh, we'll work them all in; they are of use to us in their own way, though they often don't know it. They are learning a lot; they are getting equipped. The country will get the good of it some day. Look at Althea, for instance. You might say she drifted, but she's been a hard scholar; I know it; all she needs now is to get harnessed.'

It was not lover-like talk; yet what talk, in its very impartiality, could from a lover be more gratifying? Althea again glanced at Helen, but Helen again seemed to slumber. Her face in repose had a look of discontent and sorrow, and Franklin's eyes, following her own, no doubt recognised what she did. He observed Helen for some moments before returning to the theme of efficiency.

It was a little later on that Althea's opportunity — and crisis — came. Aunt Julia had gone in and Miss Buckston suggested to Franklin that he should take a turn with her before tea. Franklin got up at once and walked away beside her, and Althea knew that his alacrity was the greater because he felt that by going with Miss Buckston he left her alone with her cherished friend. As he and Miss Buckston disappeared in the shrubberies, Helen opened her eyes and looked at them.

'How do you like Miss Buckston now that you see her at closer quarters?' Althea asked, hoping to approach the subject that preoccupied her by a circuitous method.

Helen smiled. 'One hardly likes her better at closer quarters, does one? She is like a gun going off every few moments.'

Althea smiled too; she no longer felt many qualms of loyalty on Miss Buckston's behalf.

Helen said no more, and the subject was still unapproached. 'And how do you like Mr. Kane?' Althea now felt herself forced to add.

She had not intended to use that casual tone, nearly the same tone that she had used for Miss Buckston. But she had a dimly apprehended and strongly felt wish not to forestall any verdict of Helen's; to make sure that Helen should have an open field for pronouncing her verdict candidly. Yet she was hardly prepared for the candour of Helen's reply, though in the shock that attended it she knew in a moment that she had brought it upon herself. One didn't question people about one's near friends in that casual tone.

'Funny little man,' said Helen.

After the shock of it — her worst suspicions confirmed — it was a deep qualm that Althea felt, a qualm in which she knew that something definite and final had happened to her; something sharp yet vague, all blurred by the balmy softness of the day, the sense of physical well-being, the beauty of green branches and bays of deep blue sky above. It was difficult to know, for a moment, just what had happened, for it was not as if she had ever definitely told herself that she intended to marry Franklin. The clearest contrast between the moment of revelation and that which had gone before lay in the fact that not until Helen spoke those idle, innocent words had she ever definitely told herself that she could never marry him. And there was a pang in the knowledge, and with it a drowsy lassitude, as of relief and certainty. The reason now was there; it gazed at her. Not that she couldn't have seen it for herself, but pity, loneliness, the craving for love had blinded her. Franklin was a funny little man, and that was why she could not marry him. And now, with the lassitude, the relief from long tension, came a feeling of cold and sickness.

Helen, baleful in her unconsciousness, had again closed her eyes. Althea looked at her, and she was aware of being angry with Helen. She was further aware that, since all was over for Franklin, she owed him something. She owed it to him at least to make clear to Helen that she didn't place him with Miss Buckston.

'Yes,' she said, 'Franklin is funny in his way. He is very quaint and original and simple; but he is a dear, too, you know.'

Helen did not open her eyes. 'I'm sure he is,' she acquiesced. Her placid acceptance of whatever interpretation of Mr. Kane Althea should choose to set before her, made Althea still angrier — with herself and with Helen.

'He is quite a noted scientist,' she went on, keeping her voice smooth, 'and has a very interesting new theory about atoms that's exciting a good deal of attention.'

Her voice was too successful; Helen still suspected nothing. 'Yes,' she said. 'Really.'

'You mustn't judge him from his appearance,' said Althea, smiling, for Helen had now opened her eyes and was looking dreamily at the lawn-tennis players.' His clothes are odd, of course; he doesn't know how to dress; but his eyes are fine; one sees the thinker in them.' She hoped by sacrificing Franklin's clothes to elicit some appreciation of his eyes. But Helen merely acquiesced again with: 'Yes; he doesn't know how to dress.'

'He isn't at all well off, you know,' said Althea. 'Indeed, he is quite poor. He spends most of his money on research and philanthropy.'

'Ah, well!' Helen commented, 'it's extraordinary how little difference money makes if a man knows how to dress.'

The thought of Gerald Digby went like a dart through Althea's mind. He was poor. She remembered his socks and ties, his general rightness. She wondered how much he spent on his clothes. She was silent for a moment, struggling with her trivial and with her deep discomfitures, and she saw the figures of Miss Buckston and of Franklin — both so funny, both so earnest — appear at the farther edge of the lawn engaged in strenuous converse. Helen looked at them too, kindly and indifferently. 'That would be quite an appropriate attachment, wouldn't it?' she remarked. 'They seem very much interested in each other, those two.'

Althea grew very red. Her mind knew a horrid wrench. She did not know whether it was in pride of possessorship, or shame of it, or merely in helpless loyalty that, after a pause, she said: 'Perhaps I ought to have told you, Helen, that Franklin has wanted to marry me for fifteen years. I've no intention of accepting him; but no one can judge as I can of how big and dear a person he is — in spite of his funniness.' As she spoke she remembered — it was with a gush of undiluted dismay — that to Helen she had in Paris spoken of the 'delightful' suitor, the 'only one.' Did Helen remember? And how could Helen connect that delightful 'one' with Franklin, and with her own attitude towards Franklin?

But Helen now had turned her eyes upon her, opening them — it always seemed to be with difficulty that she did it — widely. 'My dear,' she said, 'I do beg your pardon. You never gave me a hint.'

How, indeed, could the Paris memory have been one?

'There wasn't any hint to give, exactly,' said Althea, blushing more deeply and trying to prevent the tears from rising. 'I'm not in the least in love with Franklin. I never shall be.'

'No, of course not,' Helen replied, full of solicitude. 'Only, as you say, you must know him so well; — to have him talked over, quite idly and ignorantly, as I've been talking. — Really, you ought to have stopped me.'

'There was no reason for stopping you. I can see Franklin with perfect detachment. I see him just as you do, only I see so much more. His devotion to me is a rare thing; it has always made me feel unworthy.'

'Dear me, yes. Fifteen years, you say; it's quite extraordinary,' said Helen.

To Althea it seemed that Helen's candour was merciless, and revealed her to herself as uncandid, crooked, and devious. It was with a stronger wish than ever to atone to Franklin that she persisted: '*He* is extraordinary; that's what I mean about him. I am devoted to him. And my consolation is that since I can't give him love he finds my friendship the next best thing in life.'

'Really?' Helen repeated. She was silent then, evidently not considering herself privileged to ask questions; and the silence was fraught for Althea with keenest discomfort. It was only after a long pause that at last, tentatively and delicately, as though she guessed that Althea perhaps was resenting something, and perhaps wanted her to ask questions, Helen said: 'And — you don't think you can ever take him?'

'My dear Helen! How can you ask me? He isn't a man to fall in love with, is he?'

'No, certainly not,' said Helen, smiling a little constrainedly, as though her friend's vehemence struck her as slightly excessive. 'But he might, from what you tell me, be a man to marry.'

'I couldn't marry a man I was not in love with.'

'Not if he were sufficiently in love with you? Such faithful and devoted people are rare.'

'You know, Helen, that, however faithful and devoted he were, you couldn't fancy yourself marrying Franklin.'

Helen, at this turning of the tables, looked slightly disconcerted. 'Well, as you say, I hardly know him,' she suggested.

'However well you knew him, you do know that under no circumstances could you marry him.'

'No, I suppose not.'

Her look of readjustment was inflicting further and subtler wounds.

'Can't I feel in the same way?' said Althea.

Helen, a little troubled by the feeling she could not interpret in her friend's voice, hesitated before saying — as though in atonement to Mr. Kane she felt bound to put his case as favourably as possible: 'It doesn't quite follow, does it, that somebody who would suit you would suit me? We are so different, aren't we?'

'Different? How?'

'Well, I could put up with a very inferior, frivolous sort of person. You'd have higher ideas altogether.'

Althea still tried to smile. 'You mean that Franklin is too high an idea for you?'

'Far, far too high,' said Helen, smiling back.

Franklin and Miss Buckston were now approaching them, and Althea had to accept this ambiguous result of the conversation. One result, however, was not ambiguous. She seemed to see Franklin, as he came towards her over the thick sward, in a new light, a light that diminished and removed him; so that while her heart ached over him as it had never ached, it yet, strangely, was hardened towards him, and almost hostile. How had she not seen for herself, clearly and finally, that she and Helen were alike, and that whether it was that Franklin was too high, or whether it was that Franklin was merely funny — for either or for both reasons, Franklin could never be for her.

Her heart was hard and aching; but above everything else one hot feeling pulsed: Helen should not have said that he was funny and then glided to the point where she left him as too high for herself, yet not too high for her friend. She should not have withdrawn from her friend and stranded her with Franklin Winslow Kane.

CHAPTER XI.

In the course of the next few days Miss Buckston went back to her Surrey cottage, and two friends of Helen's arrived. Helen was fulfilling her promise of giving Althea all the people she wanted. Lady Pickering was widowed, young, coquettish, and pretty; Sir Charles Brewster a lively young bachelor with high eyebrows, upturned tips to his moustache, and an air of surprise and competence. They made great friends at once with Mildred, Dorothy and Herbert Vaughan, who shared in all Sir Charles's hunting and yachting interests. Lady Pickering, after a day of tennis and flirtation, would drift at night into Dorothy and Mildred's rooms to talk of dresses, and for some days wore her hair tied in a large black bow behind, reverting, however, to her usual dishevelled picturesqueness. 'One needs to look as innocent as a pony to have that bow really suit one,' she said.

Althea, in this accession of new life, again felt relegated to the background. Helen did not join in the revels, but there was no air of being relegated about her; she might have been the jaded and kindly queen before whom they were enacted. 'Dear Helen,' said Lady Pickering to Mildred and Althea, 'I can see that she's down on her luck and very bored with life. But it's always nice having her about, isn't it? Always nice to have her to look at.'

Althea felt that her guests found no such decorative uses for herself, and that they took it for granted that, with a suitor to engage her attention, she would be quite satisfied to remain outside, even if above, the gayer circle. She could not deny that her acceptance of Franklin's devotion before Helen's arrival, their air of happy withdrawal — a withdrawal that had then made them conspicuous, not negligible — absolutely justified her guests in their over-tactfulness. They still took it for granted that she and Franklin wanted to be alone together; they still left them in an isolation almost bridal; but now Althea did not want to be left alone with Franklin, and above all wished to detach herself from any bridal association; and she tormented herself with accusations concerning her former graciousness, responsible as it was for her present discomfort. She knew that she was very fond of dear Franklin, and that she always would be fond of him, but, with these accusations crowding thickly upon her, she was ill at ease and unhappy in his presence. What could she say to Franklin? 'I did, indeed, deceive myself into thinking that I might be able to marry you, and I let you see that I thought it; and then my friend's chance words showed me that I never could. What am I to think of myself, Franklin? And what can you think of me?' For though she could no longer feel pride in Franklin's love; though it had ceased, since Helen's words, to have any decorative value in her eyes, its practical value was still great; she could not think of herself as not loved by Franklin. Her world would have rocked without that foundation beneath it; and the fear that Franklin might, reading her perplexed, unstable heart, feel her a person no longer to be loved, was now an added complication.

'O Franklin, dear Franklin!' she said to him suddenly one day, turning upon him eyes enlarged by tears, 'I feel as if I were guilty towards you.'

She almost longed to put her head on his shoulder, to pour out all her grief, and be understood and comforted. Franklin had not been slow to recognise the change in his beloved's attitude towards him. He had shown no sign of grievance or reproach; he seemed quite prepared for her reaction from the moment of only dubious hope, and, though quite without humility, to find it natural, however painful to himself, that Althea should be rather bored after so much of him. But the gentle lighting of his face now showed her, too, that her reticence and withdrawal had hurt more than the new loss of hope.

'You mean,' he said, trying to smile a little as he said it, 'you mean that you've found out that you can't, dear?'

She stood, stricken by the words and their finality, and she slowly nodded, while two large tears rolled down her cheeks.

Franklin Kane controlled the signs of his own emotion, which was deep. 'That's all right, dear,' he said. 'You're not guilty of anything. You've been a little too kind — more than you can keep up, I mean. It's been beautiful of you to be kind at all and to think you might be kinder. Would you rather I went away? Perhaps it's painful to have me about just now. I've got a good many places I can go to while I'm over here, you know. You mustn't have me on your mind.'

'O Franklin!' Althea almost sobbed; 'you are an angel. Of course I want you to stay for as long as you will; of course I love to have you here.' He was an angel, indeed, she felt, and another dart of hostility towards Helen went through her — Helen, cynical, unspiritual, blind to angels.

So Franklin stayed on, and the next day another guest arrived. It was at breakfast that Althea found at her place a little note from Gerald Digby asking her very prettily if she could take him in that evening. He was in town and would start at once if she could wire that he might come. Althea controlled, as best she could, her shock of delight. He had, then, intended to come; he had not forgotten all about her. Even if she counted only in his memory as tenant, it was good, she felt it helplessly and blissfully, to count in any way with Gerald Digby. She did not analyse and hardly recog-

nised these sentiments, yet she strongly felt the need for composure, and it was only with an air of soft exhilaration that she made
the announcement over the table to Helen. 'Isn't it nice, Helen?
Mr. Digby is coming this evening.' The soft exhilaration could not
be noticeable, for everybody seemed in some degree to share it.

'Dear Gerald, how delightful!' said Lady Pickering, with, to
Althea's consciousness, too much an air of possessorship. 'Gerald
is a splendid actor, Miss Pepperell,' Sir Charles said to Dorothy.
'Miss Buchanan, you and he must do some of your best parts
together.' The girls were full of expectancy. It was Helen herself
who looked least illuminated by the news; but then, as Althea realised, to Helen Gerald must be the most matter-of-fact thing in life.

They were all sitting under the trees on the lawn when Gerald
arrived; he had not lost the best train. Every one was in white,
except Helen who wore black, and Franklin who wore grey; every
one was lolling on the grass or extended on chairs, except Aunt
Julia, erect and embroidering, and Althea who was giving her
attention to tea. It had just been poured out when Gerald came
strolling over the lawn towards them.

He carried his Panama hat doubled in his hand; he looked
exquisitely cool, and he glanced about him as he came, well
pleased, apparently, to find himself again in his old home. Althea
felt his manner of approaching them to be characteristic; it was at
once so desultory and so pleasant.

'You look like a flock of doves,' he said, as, smiling, he took
Althea's welcoming hand and surveyed the group. 'Hello, Helen,
how are you? Hello, Charlie; and how nice to find you, Frances.'

He was introduced to the others, continuing to smile with
marked approbation, Althea felt, upon Mildred and Dorothy, who
certainly looked charming, and then he dropped on the grass
beside Lady Pickering's chair.

Althea knew that if she looked like a dove, she felt like a very
fluttering one. She was much moved by this welcoming of Mr.
Digby to his home, and she wondered if the quickened beating of
her heart manifested itself in any change of glance or colour. She
soon felt, however, as she distributed teacups and looked about
her circle, that if she were visibly moved Mr. Digby would not be
aware of the fact. The fact, obviously, that he was most aware of
was Lady Pickering's presence, and he was talking to her with a
lightness and gaiety that she could presently only define, for her
own discomfort, as flirtation. Althea had had little experience of
flirting, and the little had not been personal. It had remained for
her always a rather tasteless, rather ludicrous spectacle; yet Mr.
Digby's manner of flirting, if flirting it was, was neither. It was
graceful, unemphatic, composed of playful repartee and merry

glances. It was Lady Pickering who overdid her side of the dialogue and brought to it a significance that Mr. Digby's eyes and smile disowned even while they evoked it. One of the things of which Mr. Digby had shown himself most completely unaware was Franklin Kane, who sat, as usual, just outside the circle in the sun, balancing his tea-cup on his raised knees and 'Fletcherising' a slice of cake. Gerald had glanced at him as one might glance — Althea had felt it keenly — at some nice little insect on one's path, a pleasant insect, but too small to warrant any attention beyond a casual recognition of type. But Franklin, who had a casual interest in nobody, was very much aware of the newcomer, and he gazed attentively at Gerald Digby as he had gazed at Helen on the first evening of their meeting, with less of interest perhaps, but with much the same dispassionate intentness; and Althea felt sure that he already did not approve of Gerald Digby.

She asked Helen that evening, lightly, as Helen had asked an equivalent question about Franklin and Miss Buckston, whether Mr. Digby and Lady Pickering were in love; she felt sure that they were not in love, which made the question easier.

'Oh no; not at all, I fancy,' said Helen.

'I only asked,' said Althea, 'because it seemed the obvious explanation.'

'You mean their way of flirting.'

'Yes. I suppose I'm not used to flirtation, not to such extreme flirtation. I don't like it, do you?'

'I don't know that I do; but Gerald is only a flirt through sympathy and good nature. It's Frances who leads him on; she is a flirt by temperament.'

'I'm glad of that,' said Althea. 'I'm sure he is too nice to be one by temperament.'

'After all, it's a very harmless diversion.'

'Do you think it harmless? It pains me to see a sacred thing being mimicked.'

'I hardly think it's a sacred thing Frances and Gerald are mimicking,' Helen smiled.

'It's love, isn't it?'

'Love of such a trivial order that I can't feel anything is being taken in vain.'

Helen was amused, yet touched by her friend's standards. Such distaste was not unknown to her, and Gerald's sympathetic propensities had caused her qualms with which she could not have imagined that Althea's had any analogy. Yet it was not her own taste she was considering that evening after dinner when, in walking up and down with Gerald on the gravelled terrace outside the drawing-room, she told him of Althea's standards. She felt responsible for Gerald, and that she owed it to Althea that he should not be allowed to displease her. It had struck her more than once, immersed in self-centred cogitations as she was, that Althea was altogether too much relegated.

'I wish you and Frances would not go on as you do, Gerald,' she said. 'It disturbs Althea, I am sure. She is not used to seeing people behaving like that.'

'Behaving?' asked the innocent Gerald. 'How have I been behaving?'

'Very foolishly. You have been flirting, and rather flagrantly, with Frances, ever since you came.'

'But, my dear, you know perfectly well that one can't talk to Frances without flirting with her. All conversation becomes flirtation. The most guileless glance, in meeting her eye, is transmuted, like a straight stick looking crooked when you put it into water, you know. Frances has a charmingly deviating quality that I defy the straightest of intentions to evade.'

'Are yours so straight?'

'Well — she is pretty and pleasant, and perfectly superficial, as you know. I own that I do rather like to put the stick in the water and see what happens to it.'

'Well, don't put it in too often before Althea. After all, you are all of you here because of her friendship with me, and it makes me feel guilty if I see her having a bad time because of your misbehaviour.'

'A bad time?'

'Really. She takes things hard. She said it was mimicking a sacred thing.'

'Oh! but, I say, how awfully funny, Helen. You must own that it's funny.'

'Funny, but sweet, too.'

'She is a sweet creature, of course, one can see that; and her moral approvals and disapprovals are firmly fixed, however funny; one likes that in her. I'll try to be good, if Frances will let me. She looked quite pretty this evening, Miss Jakes; only she dresses too stiffly. What's the matter? Couldn't you give her a hint? She is like a satin-box, and a woman ought to be like a flower; ought to look as if they'd bend if a breeze went over them. Now you can't imagine Miss Jakes bending; she'd have to stoop.'

Helen, in the darkness, smiled half bitterly, half affectionately. Gerald's nonsense always pleased her, even when she was most exasperated with him. She was not exasperated with Gerald in particular just now, but with everything and everybody, herself included, and the fact that he liked to flirt flagrantly with Lady Pickering did not move her more than usual. It was not a particular but a general irritation that edged her voice a little as she said, drawing her black scarf more closely round her shoulders, 'Frances must satisfy you there. Your tastes, I think, are becoming more and more dishevelled.'

But innocent Gerald answered with a coal of fire: 'No, she is too dishevelled. You satisfy my tastes there entirely; you flow, but you don't flop. Now if Miss Jakes would only try to dress like you she'd be immensely improved. You are perfect.' And he lightly touched her scarf as he spoke with a fraternal and appreciative hand.

Helen continued to smile in the darkness, but it was over an almost irresistible impulse to sob. The impulse was so strong that it frightened her, and it was with immense relief that she saw Althea's figure — her 'box-like' figure — appear in the lighted window. She did not want to talk to Althea, and she could not, just now, go on talking to Gerald. From their corner of the terrace she indicated the vaguely gazing Althea. 'There she is,' she said. 'Go and talk to her. Be nice to her. I'm tired and am going to have a stroll in the shrubberies before bed.'

She left Gerald obediently, if not eagerly, moving towards the window, and slipping into the obscurity of the shrubberies she threw back her scarf and drew long breaths. She was becoming terribly overwrought. It had been, since so long, a second nature to live two lives that any danger of their merging affected her with a dreadful feeling of disintegration. There was the life of comradeship, the secure little compartment where Gerald was at home, so at home that he could tell her she was perfect and touch her scarf with an approving hand, and from this familiar shelter she had looked for so long, with the calmest eye, upon his flirtations, and in it had heard, unmoved, his encomiums upon herself. The other life, the real life, was all outdoors in comparison; it was all her real self, passionate, untamed, desolate; it was like a bleak, wild moorland, and the social, the comrade self only a strongly built little lodge erected, through stress of wind and weather, in the midst of it. Since girlhood it had been a second nature to her to keep comradeship shut in and reality shut out. And tonight reality seemed to shake and batter at the doors.

She had come to Merriston House to rest, to drink *eau rougie* and to rest. She wanted to lapse into apathy and to recover, as far as might be, from her recent unpleasant experiments and experiences. Had she allowed herself any illusions about the experiment, the experience would have been humiliating; but Helen was not humiliated, she had not deceived herself for a moment. She had, open-eyed, been trying for the 'other things,' and she had only just missed them. She had intended to marry a very important person who much admired her. She had been almost sure that she could marry him if she wanted to, and she had found out that she couldn't. It had not been, as in her youth, her own shrinking and her own recoil at the last decisive moment. She had been resolved and unwavering; her discomfiture had been sudden and its cause the quite grotesque one of her admirer having fallen head over heels in love with a child of eighteen — a foolish, affected little child, who giggled and glanced and blushed opportunely, and who, beside these assets, had a skilful and determined mother. Without the mother to waylay, pounce, and fix, Helen did not believe that her sober, solid friend would have yielded to the momentary beguilement, and Helen herself deigned not one hint of contest; she had been resolved, but only to accept; she could never have waylaid or pounced. And now, apathetic, yet irritated, exhausted and sick at heart, she had been telling herself, as she lay in the garden-chairs at Merriston House, that it was more than probable that the time was over, even for the 'other things.' The prospect made her weary. What — with Aunt Grizel's one hundred and fifty a year — was she to do with herself in the future? What was to become of her? She didn't feel that she much cared, and yet it was all that there was left to care about, for Aunt Grizel's sake if not for her own, and she felt only fit to rest from the pressure of the question. Tonight, as she turned and wandered among the trees, she said to herself that it hadn't been a propitious time to come for rest to Merriston House. Gerald had been the last person she desired to see just now. She had never been so near to feeling danger as tonight. If Gerald were nice to her — he always was — but nice in a certain way, the way that expressed so clearly his tenderness and his dreadful, his merciful unawareness, she might break down before him and sob. This would be too horrible, and when she thought that it might happen she felt, rising with the longing for tears, an old resentment against Gerald, fierce, absurd, and unconquerable. After making the round of the lawns and looking up hard and unseeingly at the stars, she came back to the terrace. Gerald and Althea were gone, and she surmised that Gerald had not taken much trouble to be nice. She was passing along an unillumined corner when she came suddenly upon a figure seated there — so suddenly that she almost fell against it. She murmured a hasty apology as Mr. Kane rose from a chair where, with folded arms, he had been seated, apparently in contemplation of the night.

'Oh, I beg your pardon,' said Helen. 'It's so dark here. I didn't see you.'

'And I didn't hear you coming,' said Mr. Kane. 'I beg your pardon. I'm afraid you hurt your foot.'

'Not at all,' Helen assured him. She had stepped into the light from the windows and, Mr. Kane being beside her, she could see his face clearly and see that he looked very tired. She had been aware, in these days of somnolent retirement, that one other member of the party seemed, though not in her sense retired from it, to wander rather aimlessly on its outskirts. That his removal to this ambiguous limbo had been the result of her own arrival Helen had no means of knowing, since she had never seen Mr. Kane in his brief moment of hope when he and Althea had been centre and everybody else outskirts. She had found him, during her few conversations with him, so tamely funny as to be hardly odd, though his manner of speaking and the way in which his hair was cut struck her as expressing oddity to an unfortunate degree; but though only dimly aware of him, and aware mainly in this sense of amusement, she had, since Althea had informed her of his status, seen him with some compassionateness. It didn't make him less funny to her that he should have been in love with Althea for fifteen years, rather it made him more so. Helen found it difficult to take either the devotion or its object very seriously. She thought hopeless passions rather ridiculous, her own included, but Gerald she did consider a possible object of passion; and how Althea could be an object of passion for anybody, even for funny little Mr. Kane, surpassed her comprehension, so that the only way to understand the situation was to decide that Mr. Kane was incapable of passion altogether. But tonight she received a new impression; looking at Mr. Kane's face, thin, jaded, and kindly attentive to herself, it suddenly became apparent to her that whatever his feeling might be it was serious. He might not know passion, but his heart was aching, perhaps quite as fiercely as her own. She felt sorry for Mr. Kane, and her step lingered on her way to the house.

'Isn't it a lovely night,' she said, in order to say something. 'Do you like sitting in the dark? It's very restful, isn't it?'

Franklin saw the alien Miss Buchanan's eyes bent kindly and observantly upon him.

'Yes, it's very restful,' he said. 'It smooths you out and straightens you out when you get crumpled, you know, and impatient.'

'I should not imagine you as ever very impatient,' smiled Helen. 'Perhaps you do sit a great deal in the dark.'

He took her whimsical suggestion with careful humour. 'Why, no, it's not a habit of mine; and it's not a recipe that it would be a good thing to overdo, is it?'

'Why not?' she asked.

'There are worse things than impatience, aren't there?' said

Franklin. 'Gloominess, for instance. You might get gloomy if you sat out in the dark a great deal.'

It amused her a little to wonder, as they went in together, whether Mr. Kane disciplined his emotions and withdrew from restful influences before they had time to become discouraging ones. She imagined that he would have a recipe for everything.

CHAPTER XII.

It was after this little nocturnal encounter that Helen found herself watching Mr. Kane with a dim, speculative sympathy. There was nothing else of much interest to watch, as far as she was aware, for Helen's powers of observation were not sharpened by much imaginativeness. Her sympathy must be aroused for her to care to see, and just now she felt no sympathy for any one but Mr. Kane.

Gerald, flirting far less flagrantly and sketching assiduously, was in no need of sympathy; nor Althea, despite the fact that Helen felt her to be a little reserved and melancholy. Althea, on the whole, seemed placidly enough absorbed in her duties of hostess, and her state of mind, at no time much preoccupying Helen, pre-occupied her now less than ever. The person who really interested her, now that she had come to look at him and to realise that he was suffering, was Mr. Kane. He was puzzling to her, not mysti-fying; there was no element of depth or shadow about him; even his suffering — it was odd to think that a person with such a small, flat nose should suffer — even his suffering was pellucid. He puz-zled her because he was different from anything she had ever encountered, and he made her think of a page of trite phrases printed in a half-comprehended dialect. If it was puzzling that any man should be sufficiently in love with Althea to suffer over it, it was yet more puzzling that, neglected as he so obviously was by his beloved, he should show no dejection or consciousness of dimi-nution. He seemed a little aimless, it is true, but not in the least injured; and Helen, as she watched him, found herself liking Mr. Kane.

He had an air, pleasant to her, of finding no one beneath him, and at the same time he seemed as unaware of superiority — unless it were definitely moral or intellectual. A general indiscriminating goodwill was expressed in his manner towards everybody, and when he did discriminate — which was always on moral issues — his goodwill seemed unperturbed by any amount of reprobation. He remained blandly humane under the most dis-concerting circumstances. She overtook him one day in a lane holding a drunkard by the shoulder and endeavouring to steer him homeward, while he expounded to him in scientific tones the ill effects of alcohol on the system, and the remarkable results to be attained by steady self-suggestion. Mr. Kane's collar was awry and his coat dusty, almost as dusty as the drunkard's, with whom he had evidently had to grapple in raising him from the highway; and Helen, as she paused at the turning of the road which brought her upon them, heard Franklin's words:

'I've tried it myself for insomnia. I'm a nervous man, and I was in a bad way at the time; over-pressure, you know, and worry. I guess it's like that with you, too, isn't it? You get on edge. Well, there's nothing better than self-suggestion, and if you'll give it a try you'll be surprised by the results, I'm sure of it.'

Helen joined them and offered her assistance, for the bewildered proselyte seemed unable to move forward now that he was upon his feet.

'Well, if you would be so kind. Just your hand on his other shoulder, you know,' said Franklin, turning a grateful glance upon her. 'Our friend here is in trouble, you see. It's not far to the village, and what he wants is to get to bed, have a good sleep and then a wash. He'll feel a different man then.'

Helen, her hand at 'our friend's' left shoulder, helped to propel him forward, and ten minutes took them to his door, where, surrounded by a staring crowd of women and children, they delivered him into the keeping of his wife, a thin and weary person, who looked upon his benefactors with almost as much resentment as upon him.

'What he really needs, I'm afraid I think,' Helen said, as she and Mr. Kane walked away, 'is a good whipping.' She said it in order to see the effect of the ruthlessness upon her humanitarian companion.

Mr. Kane did not look shocked or grieved; he turned a cogitating glance upon her, and she saw that he diagnosed the state of mind that could make such a suggestion and could not take it seriously. He smiled, though a little gravely, in answering: 'Why, no, I don't think so; and I don't believe you think so, Miss Buchanan. What you want to give him is a hold on himself, hope, and self-respect; it wouldn't give you self-respect to be whipped, would it?'

'It might give me discretion,' said Helen, smiling back.

'We don't want human beings to have the discretion of animals; we want them to have the discretion of men,' said Franklin; 'that is, self-mastery and wisdom.'

Helen did not feel able to argue the point; indeed, it did not interest her; but she asked Mr. Kane, some days later, how his roadside friend was progressing towards the discretion of a man.

'Oh, he'll be all right,' said Franklin. 'He'll pull round. Self-suggestion will do it. It's not a bad case. He couldn't get hold of the idea at first — he's not very bright; but I found out that he'd got some very useful religious notions, and I work it in on these.'

From the housekeeper, a friend of her youth, Helen learned that in the village Mr. Kane's ministrations to Jim Betts were regarded with surprise, yet not without admiration. He was supposed to be some strange sort of foreign clergyman, not to be placed in any recognisable category. 'He's a very kind gentleman, I'm sure,' said Mrs. Fielding.

Mr. Kane was fond, Helen also observed, of entering into conversation with the servants. The butler's political views — which were guarded — he determinedly pursued, undeterred by Baines's cautious and deferential retreats. He considered the footman as a potential friend, whatever the footman might consider him. Their common manhood, in Franklin's eyes, entirely outweighed the slight, extraneous accidents of fortune — nay, these differences gave an additional interest. The footman had, no doubt, a point of view novel and valuable, if one could get at it. Franklin did not attempt to get at it by any method subversive of order or interfering with Thomas's duties; he observed all the conventions demanded by varying function. But Helen, strolling one morning before breakfast outside the dining-room windows, heard within and paused to listen to Mr. Kane's monotonous and slightly nasal tones as he shared the morning news with Thomas, who, with an air of bewildered if obedient attention, continued his avocations between the sideboard and the breakfast-table.

'Now I should say,' Franklin remarked, 'that something of that sort — Germany's doing wonders with it — could be worked here in England if you set yourselves to it.'

'Yes, sir,' said Thomas.

'Berlin has eliminated the slums, you know,' said Franklin, looking thoughtfully at Thomas over the top of the paper. 'What do you feel about it, all of you over here? It's a big question, you know, that of the housing of the poor.'

'Well, I can't say, sir,' said Thomas, compelled to a guarded opinion. 'Things do look black for the lower horders.'

'You're right, Thomas; and things will go on looking black for helpless people until they determine to help themselves, or until people who aren't helpless — like you and me — determine they shan't be so black.'

'Yes, sir.'

'Talk it over, you know. Get your friends interested in it. It's a mighty big subject, of course, that of the State and its poor, but it's wonderful what can be done by personal initiative.'

Helen entered at this point, and Thomas turned a furtive eye upon her, perhaps in appeal for protection against these unprovoked and inexplicable attacks. 'One might think the gentleman thought I had a vote and was canvassing me,' he said to Baines, condescending in this their common perplexity. And Baines replied: 'I'm sure I don't know what he's up to.'

Meanwhile Franklin, in the dining-room, folded his paper and said: 'You know, Miss Buchanan, that Thomas, though a nice fellow, is remarkably ignorant. I can't make out that there's anything of a civic or national nature that he's interested in. He doesn't seem to read anything in the papers except the racing and betting news. He doesn't seem to feel that he has any stake in this great country of yours, or any responsibility towards it. It makes me believe in manhood suffrage as I've never believed before. Our people may be politically corrupt, but at least they're interested; they're alive — alive enough to want to understand how to get the best of things — as they see best. I've rarely met an American that I couldn't get to talk; now it's almost impossible to get Thomas to talk. Yet he's a nice young fellow; he has a nice, open, intelligent face.'

'Oh yes, has he?' said Helen, who was looking over the envelopes at her place. 'I hadn't noticed his face; very pink, isn't it?'

'Yes, he has a healthy colour,' said Franklin, still meditating on Thomas's impenetrability. 'It's not that I don't perfectly understand his being uncommunicative when he's engaged in his work — it was rather tactless of me to talk to him just now, only the subject came up. I'd been talking to Baines about the Old Age Pensions yesterday. That's one of my objections to domestic service; it creates an artificial barrier between man and man; but I know that the barrier is part of the business, while the business is going on, and I've no quarrel with social convention, as such. But even when they are alone with me — and I'm referring to Baines now as much as to Thomas — they are very uncommunicative. I met Thomas on the road to the village the other day and could hardly get a word out of him till I began to talk about cricket and ask him about it.'

'He is probably a stupid boy,' said Helen, 'and you frighten him.'

'If you say that, it's an indictment on the whole system, you know,' said Franklin very gravely.

'What system?' Helen asked, opening her letters, but looking at Mr. Kane.

'The system that makes some people afraid of others,' said Franklin.

'It will always frighten inferior people to be talked to by their superiors as if they were on a level. You probably talk to Thomas about things he doesn't understand, and it bewilders him.' Helen, willing to enlighten his idealism, smiled mildly at him, glancing down at her letters as she spoke.

Mr. Kane surveyed her with his bright, steady gaze. Her simple elucidation evidently left him far from satisfied, either with her or the system. 'In essentials, Miss Buchanan,' he said, 'in the power of effort, endurance, devotion, I've no doubt that Thomas and I are equals, and that's all that ought to matter.'

The others now were coming in, and Helen only shook her head, smiling on and quite unconvinced as she said, taking her chair, and reaching out her hand to shake Althea's, 'I'm afraid the inessentials matter most, then, in human intercourse.'

From these fortuitous encounters Helen gathered the impression by degrees that though Mr. Kane might not find her satisfactory, he found her, in her incommunicativeness, quite as interesting as Thomas the footman. He spent as much time in endeavouring to probe her as he did in endeavouring to probe Baines, even more time. He would sit beside her garden-chair looking over scientific papers, making a remark now and then on their contents — contents as remote from Helen's comprehension as was the housing of the Berlin poor from Thomas's; and sometimes he would ask her a searching question, over the often frivolous answer to which he would carefully reflect.

'I gather, Miss Buchanan,' he said to her one afternoon, when they were thus together under the trees, 'I gather that the state of your health isn't good. Would it be inadmissible on my part to ask you if there is anything really serious the matter with you?'

'My state of health?' said Helen, startled. 'My health is perfectly good. Who told you it wasn't?'

'Why, nobody. But since you've been here — that's a fortnight now — I've observed that you've led an invalid's life.'

'I am lazy, that's all; and I'm in rather a bad temper,' Helen smiled; 'and it's very warm weather.'

'Well, when you're not lazy; when you're not in a bad temper; when it's cold weather — what do you do with yourself, anyway?' Franklin, now that he had fairly come to his point, folded his papers, clasped his hands around his knees and looked expectantly at her.

Helen returned his gaze for some moments in silence; then she found that she was quite willing to give Mr. Kane all he asked for — a detached sincerity. 'I can't say that I do anything,' she replied.

'Haven't you any occupation?'

'Not unless staying about with people is an occupation,' Helen suggested. 'I'm rather good at that — when I'm not too lazy and not too out of temper.'

'You don't consider society an occupation. It's only justifiable as a recreation when work's done. Every one ought to have an occupation. You're not alive at all unless you've a purpose that's organising your life in some way. Now, it strikes me,' said Franklin, eyeing her steadily, 'that you're hardly half alive.'

'Oh, dear!' Helen laughed. 'Why, pray?'

'Don't laugh at it, Miss Buchanan. It's a serious matter; the most serious matter there is. No, don't laugh; you distress me.'

'I beg your pardon,' said Helen, and she turned her head aside a little, for the laugh was not quite genuine, and she was suddenly afraid of those idiotic tears. 'Only it amuses me that any one should think me a serious matter.'

'Don't be cynical, Miss Buchanan; that's what's the trouble with you; you take refuge in cynicism rather than in thought. If you'd think about it and not try to evade it, you'd know perfectly well that there is nothing so serious to you in all the world as your own life.'

'I don't know,' said Helen, after a little pause, sobered, though still amused. 'I don't know that I feel anything very serious, except all the unpleasant things that happen, or the pleasant things that don't.'

'Well, what's more serious than suffering?' Mr. Kane inquired, and as she could really find no answer to this he went on: 'And you ought to go further; you ought to be able to take every human being seriously.'

'Do you do that?' Helen asked.

'Any one who thinks must do it; it's all a question of thinking things out. Now I've thought a good deal about you, Miss Buchanan,' Franklin continued, 'and I take you very seriously, very seriously indeed. I feel that you are very much above the average in capacity. You have a great deal in you; a great deal of power. I've been watching you very carefully, and I've come to the conclusion that you are a woman of power. That's why I take it upon myself to talk to you like this; that's why it distresses me to see you going to waste — half alive.'

Helen, her head still turned aside in her chair, looked up at the green branches above her, no longer even pretending to smile. Mr. Kane at once startled and steadied her. He made her feel vaguely ashamed of herself, and he made her feel sorry for herself, too, so that, funny as he was, his effect upon her was to soften and to calm her. Her temper felt less bad and her nerves less on edge.

'You are very kind,' she said, after a little while. 'It is very good of you to have thought about me like that. And you do think, at all events, that I am half alive. You think I have wants, even if I have no purposes.'

'Yes, that's it. Wants, not purposes; though what they are I can't find out.'

She was willing to satisfy his curiosity. 'What I want is money.'

'Well, but what do you want to do with money?' Franklin inquired, receiving the sordid avowal without a blink.

'I really don't know,' said Helen; 'to use what you call my

power, I suppose.'

'How would you use it? You haven't trained yourself for any use of it — except enjoyment — as far as I can see.'

'I think I could spend money well. I'd give the people I liked a good time.'

'You'd waste their time, and yours, you mean. Not that I object to the spending of money — if it's in the right way.'

'I think I could find the right way, if I had it.' She was speaking with quite the seriousness she had disowned. 'I hate injustice, and I hate ugliness. I think I could make things nicer if I had money.'

Franklin now was silent for some time, considering her narrowly, and since she had now looked down from the branches and back at him, their eyes met in a long encounter. 'Yes,' he said at length, 'you'd be all right — if only you weren't so wrong. If only you had a purpose — a purpose directed towards the just and the beautiful; if only instead of waiting for means to turn up, you'd created means yourself; if only you'd kept yourself disciplined and steady of aim by some sort of hard work, you'd be all right.'

Helen, extended in her chair, an embodiment of lovely aimlessness, kept her eyes fixed on him. 'But what work can I do?' she asked. She was well aware that Mr. Kane could have no practical suggestions for her case, yet she wanted to show him that she recognised it as a case, she wanted to show him that she was grateful, and she was curious besides to hear what he would suggest. 'What am I fit for? I couldn't earn a penny if I tried. I was never taught anything.'

But Mr. Kane was ready for her, as he had been ready for Jim Betts. 'It's not a question of earning that I mean,' he said, 'though it's a mighty good thing to measure yourself up against the world and find out just what your cash value is, but I'm not talking about that; it's the question of getting your faculties into some sort of working order that I'm up against. Why don't you study something systematically, something you can grind at? Biology, if you like, or political economy, or charity organisation. Begin at once. Master it.'

'Would Dante do, for a beginning?' Helen inquired, smiling rather wanly. 'I brought him down, with an Italian dictionary. Shall I master Dante?'

'I should feel more comfortable about you if it was political economy,' said Franklin, now smiling back. 'But begin with Dante, by all means. Personally I found his point of view depressing, but then I read him in a translation and never got even as far as the Purgatory. Be sure you get as far as the Paradise, Miss Buchanan, and with your dictionary.'

CHAPTER XIII.

Franklin had all his time free for sitting with Helen under the trees. Althea's self-reproach, her self-doubt and melancholy, had been effaced by the arrival of Gerald Digby, and, at that epoch of her life, did not return at all. She had no time for self-doubt or self-reproach, no time even for self-consciousness. Franklin had faded into the dimmest possible distance; she was only just aware that he was there and that Helen seemed, kindly, to let him talk a good deal to her. She could not think of Franklin, she could not think of herself, she could think of nobody but one person, for her whole being was absorbed in the thought of Gerald Digby and in the consciousness of the situation that his coming had created. From soft exhilaration she had passed to miserable depression, yet a depression far different from the stagnant melancholy of her former mood; this was a depression of frustrated feeling, not of lack of feeling, and it was accompanied by the recognition of the fact that she exceedingly disliked Lady Pickering and wished exceedingly that she would go away. And with it went a brooding sense of delight in Gerald's mere presence, a sense of delight in even the pain that his indifference inflicted upon her.

He charmed her unspeakably — his voice, his smile, his gestures — and she knew that she did not charm him in any way, and that Lady Pickering, in her very foolishness, did charm him, and the knowledge made her very grave and careful when she was with him. Delight and pain were hidden beneath this manner of careful gravity, but, as the excitement of Franklin's presence had at first done — and in how much greater degree — they subtly transformed her; made her look and speak and move with a different languor and gentleness.

Gerald himself was the first to feel a change, the first to become aware of an aroma of mystery. He had been indifferent indeed, though he had obeyed Helen and had tried not only to be very courteous but to be very nice as well. Now, finding Althea's grave eyes upon him when he sometimes yielded to Lady Pickering's allurements, finding them turned away with that look of austere mildness, he ceased to be so indifferent, he began to wonder how much the little Puritan disapproved and how much she really minded; he began to make surmises about the state of mind that could be so aloof, so gentle, and so inflexible.

He met Althea one afternoon in the garden and walked up and down with her while she filled her basket with roses. She was very gentle, and immeasurably distant. The sense of her withdrawal roused his masculine instinct of pursuit. How different she was from Frances Pickering! How charmingly different. Yes, in her elaborate little dress of embroidered lawn, with her elaborate garden hat pinned so neatly on her thick fair hair, she pleased him by the sense of contrast. There was charm in her lack of charm, attraction in her indifference. How impossible to imagine those grave eyes smiling an alluring smile — he was getting tired of alluring smiles — how impossible to imagine Miss Jakes flirting.

'It's very nice to see you here,' he said. 'I have so many nice memories about this old garden. You don't mind my cigarette?'

Althea said that she liked it.

'There is a beautiful spray, Miss Jakes. Let me reach it for you.'

'Oh, thank you so much.'

'You are fond of flowers?'

'Very fond.'

'Which are your favourites?'

'Lilies of the valley.' Althea spoke kindly, as she might have spoken to a rather importunate child; his questions, indeed, were not original.

Gerald tried to mend the tameness of the effect that he was making. 'Yes, only the florists have rather spoiled them, haven't they? My favourites are the wilder ones — honeysuckle, grass of Parnassus, bell-heather. Helen always makes me think of grass of Parnassus and bell-heather, she is so solitary and delicate and strong.' He wanted Althea to realise that his real appreciation was for types very different from Lady Pickering. She smiled kindly, as if pleased with his simile, and he went on. 'You are like pansies, white and purple pansies.'

It was then that Althea blushed. Gerald noticed it at once. Experienced flirt as he was he was quick to perceive such symptoms. And, suddenly, it occurred to him that perhaps the reason she disapproved so much was the wish — unknown to herself, poor little innocent — that some one would flirt a little with her. He felt quite sure that no one had ever flirted with Althea. Helen had told him of Mr. Kane's hopeless suit, and they had wandered in rather helpless conjecture about the outside of a case that didn't, from their experience of cases, seem to offer any possibilities of an inside. Gerald had indeed loudly laughed at the idea of Mr. Kane as a wooer and Helen had smiled, while assuring him that wooing wasn't the only test of worth. Gerald was rather inclined to think it was. He was quite sure, though, that however worthy Mr. Kane might be he had never made any one blush. He was quite sure that Mr. Kane was incapable of flirting, and it pleased him now to observe the sign of susceptibility in Althea. It was good for women, he felt sure, to be made to blush sometimes, and he promised himself that he would renew the experiment with Althea. All the same it must be very unemphatically done;

there would be something singularly graceless in venturing too far with this nice pansy, for though she might, all unaware, want to be made to blush, she would never want it to be because of his light motives.

Meanwhile Althea was in dread lest he should see her discomposure and her bliss. He did not see further than her discomposure.

They rehearsed theatricals all the next day — he, Helen, Lady Pickering, and the girls — and Lady Pickering was very naughty. Gerald, more than once, had caught Althea's eye fixed, repudiating in its calm, upon her. It had been especially repudiating when Frances, at tea, had thrown a bun at him.

'Do you know, Miss Jakes,' he said to her after dinner, when, to Lady Pickering's discomfiture, as he saw, he joined Althea on her little sofa, 'do you know, I suspect you of being dreadfully bored by all of us. We behave like a lot of children, don't we?' He was thinking of the bun.

'Indeed! I think it charming to be able to behave like a child, if one feels like one,' said Althea, coldly and mildly.

'Don't you ever feel like one? Do you always behave like a gentle muse?'

'Do I seem to behave like a muse? How tiresome I must be,' smiled Althea.

'Not tiresome, rather impressive. It's like looking up suddenly from some nocturnal *fête* — all Japanese lanterns and fireworks — and seeing the moon gazing down serenely and unseeingly upon one; it startles and sobers one a little, you know.'

'I suppose you are sober sometimes,' said Althea, continuing to smile.

'Lord, yes!' Gerald laughed. 'Really and truly, Miss Jakes, I'm only playing at being a child, you know. I'm quite a serious person. I like to look at the moon.'

And again Althea blushed. She looked down, sitting straightly in the corner of their sofa and turning her fan slowly between her fingers, and, feeling the sense of gracelessness in this too easy success, Gerald went on in a graver tone. 'I wish you would let me be serious with you sometimes, Miss Jakes; you'd see I'd quite redeem myself in your eyes.'

'Redeem yourself? From what?'

'Oh! from all your impression of my frivolity and folly. I can talk about art and literature and the condition of the labouring classes as wisely as anybody, I assure you.'

He said it so prettily that Althea had to laugh. 'But what makes you think I can?' she asked, and, delighted with the happy result of his appeal, he said that Helen had told him all about her wisdoms.

He sounded these wisdoms next day when he asked her to walk with him to the village. He told her, as they walked, of the various projects for using his life to some advantage that he had used to make — projects for improved agricultural methods and the bettering of the conditions of life in the country. Althea had read a great deal of political economy. She had, indeed, ground at it and mastered it in the manner advised by Franklin to Helen. Gerald found her quiet comments and criticisms very illuminating, not only of his theme, but of his own comparative ignorance. 'But, Miss Jakes, how did you come to understand all this?' he ejaculated; and she said, laughing a little at the impression she had made, that she had only read, gone to a few courses of lectures, and had a master for one winter in Boston. Gerald looked at her with new interest. It impressed him that an unprofessional woman should take anything so seriously. 'Have you gone into other profound things like this?' he asked; and, still laughing, Althea said that she supposed she had.

Her sympathy for those old plans of his, based on such understanding, was really inspiring. 'Ah, if only I had the money,' he sighed.

'But you wouldn't care to live in the country?' said Althea.

'There's nowhere else I really care to live. Nothing would please me so much as to spend the rest of my life at Merriston, dabbling at my painting and going in seriously for farming.'

'Why don't you do it?'

'Why, money! I've got no money. It's expensive work to educate oneself by experience, and I'm ignorant. You show me how ignorant. No; I'm afraid I'm to go on drifting, and never lead the life I best like.'

Althea was silent. She hardly knew what she was feeling, but it pressed upon her so, that she was afraid lest a breath would stir some consciousness in him. She had money, a good deal. What a pity that he had none.

'Now you,' Gerald went on, 'have all sorts of big, wise plans for life, I've no doubt. It would interest me to hear about them.'

'No; I drift too,' said Althea.

'You can't call it drifting when you read and study such a lot.'

'Oh yes, I can, when there is no real aim in the work. You should hear Mr. Kane scold me about that.'

Gerald was not interested in Mr. Kane. 'I should think, after all you've done, you might rest on your oars for a bit,' he remarked. 'It's quite enough, I should think, for a woman to know so much. If you liked to do anything, you'd do it awfully well, I'm sure.'

Ah, what would she not like to do! Help you to steer to any

port you wanted was the half-articulate cry of her heart.

'She really is an interesting little person, your Althea,' Gerald said to Helen. 'You were wrong not to find her interesting. She is so wise and calm and she knows such a lot.'

'I'm too ignorant to be interested in knowledge,' said Helen.

'It's not mere knowledge, it's the gentle temperateness and independence one feels in her.'

Helen, somehow, did not feel them, or, at all events, felt other things too much to feel them preeminently. It was part of her unselfconsciousness not to guess why Althea's relation to her had slightly changed. She could hardly have followed with comprehension the suffering instability of her friend's character, nor dream that her own power over her was so great, yet so resented; but something in their talk about Mr. Kane had made Helen uncomfortable, and she said no more now, not wishing to emphasise any negative aspect of her attitude to Althea at a time when their relation seemed to have become a little strained. And she was pleased that Gerald should talk about political economy with Althea — it was so much better than flirting with Frances Pickering.

No one, indeed, unless it were Franklin Kane, gave much conjecture to Gerald's talks with his hostess. Lady Pickering noticed; but she was vexed, rather than jealous. She couldn't imagine that Gerald felt anything but a purely intellectual interest in such talks. It was rather as if a worshipper in some highly ritualistic shrine, filled with appeals to sight and hearing, had unaccountably wandered off into a wayside chapel. Lady Pickering felt convinced that this was mere vagrant curiosity on Gerald's part. She felt convinced that he couldn't care for chapels. She was so convinced that, moved to emphatic measures, she came into the open as it were, marched processions and waved banners before him, in order to remind him what the veritable church was for a person of taste. Sometimes Gerald joined her, but sometimes he waved a friendly greeting and went into the chapel again.

So it was that Althea suddenly found herself involved in that mute and sinister warfare — an unavowed contest with another woman for possession of a man. How it could be a real contest she did not know; she felt sure that Lady Pickering did not love Gerald Digby, that she herself loved him she had not yet told herself, and that he loved neither of them was obvious. It seemed a mere struggle for supremacy, in which Lady Pickering's role was active and her own passive. For when she saw that Lady Pickering looked upon Gerald as a prey between them, that she seized, threatened and allured, she herself, full of a proud disdain, drew away, relinquished any hold, any faintest claim she had, handed

Gerald over, as it were, to his pursuer; and as she did this, coldly, gravely, proudly, she was not aware that no tactics could have been more effective. For Gerald, when he found himself pursued, and then dropped by Althea at the feet of the pursuer, became more and more averse to being seized. And what had been a gracefully amorous dialogue with Lady Pickering, became a slightly malicious discussion. 'Well, what *do* you want of me?' he seemed to demand of her, under all his grace. Lady Pickering did not want anything except to keep him, and to show Althea that she kept him. And she was willing to go to great lengths if this might be effected.

Gerald and Althea, walking one afternoon in the little wood that lay at the foot of the lawn, came upon Lady Pickering seated romantically upon a stone, her head in her hands. She said, looking up at them, with pathetic eyes of suffering, that she had wrenched her ankle and was in agony. 'I think it is sprained, perhaps broken,' she said.

Now both Althea and Gerald felt convinced that she was not in agony, and had perhaps not hurt her ankle at all. They were both a little embarrassed and a little ashamed for her.

'Take my arm, take Miss Jakes's,' said Gerald. 'We will help you back to the house.'

'Oh no. I must sit still for a little while,' said Lady Pickering.' I couldn't bear to stir yet. It must be only a wrench; yes, there, I can feel that it is a bad wrench. It's only that the pain has been so horrible, and I feel a little faint. Please sit down here for a moment, Gerald, beside me, and console me for my sufferings.'

It was really very shameless. Without a word Althea walked away.

'Miss Jakes — we'll — I'll follow in a moment,' Gerald called after her, while, irritated and at a loss, he stood over Lady Pickering. 'Have you really hurt it?' was his first inquiry, as Althea disappeared.

'Why does she go?' Lady Pickering inquired. 'I didn't mean that she was to go. Stiff, *guindée* little person. One would really think that she was jealous of me.'

'No, I don't think that one would think that at all,' Gerald returned.

Lady Pickering was pushed beyond the bounds of calculation, and when quite sincere she was really charming. 'O Gerald,' she said, looking up at him and full of roguish contrition, 'how unkind you are! And how horribly clear sighted. It's I who am jealous! Yes, I really am. I can't bear being neglected.'

'I don't see why you should,' said Gerald laughing, 'and I certainly shouldn't show such bad taste as to neglect you. So that it is jealousy, pure and simple. Is your ankle in the least hurt?'

'Really, I don't know. I did tumble a little, and then I saw you coming, and felt that I wanted to be talked to, that it was my turn.'

'What an absurd woman you are.'

'But do say that you like absurd women better than solemn ones.'

'I shall say nothing of the sort. Sometimes absurdity is delightful, and sometimes solemnity — not that I find Miss Jakes in the least solemn. It would do you a world of good to let her inform your mind a little.'

'Oh, please, I don't want to be informed, it might make my back look like that. My foot really is a little hurt, you know. Is it swollen?'

Gerald looked down, laughing, but very unsympathetic, at the perilous heel and pinched, distorted toe. 'Really, I can't say.'

'Do sit down, there is plenty of room, and tell me you aren't cross with me.'

'I'm not at all cross with you, but I'm not going to sit down beside you,' said Gerald. 'I'm going to take you and your ankle back to the house and then find Miss Jakes and go on talking.'

'You may make *me* cross,' said Lady Pickering, rising and leaning her arm on his.

'I don't believe I shall. You really respect me for my strength of character.'

'Wily creature!'

'Foolish child!' They were standing in the path, laughing at each other, far from displeased with each other, and it was fortunate that neither of them perceived among the trees Althea, passing again at a little distance, and glancing round irrepressibly to see if Gerald had indeed followed her; even Lady Pickering might have been slightly discomposed, for when Gerald said 'Foolish child!' he completed the part expected of him by lightly stooping his head and kissing her.

He then took Lady Pickering back to the house, established her in a hammock, and set off to find Althea. He knew that he had kept her waiting — if she had indeed waited. And he knew that he really was a little cross with Frances Pickering; he didn't care to carry flirtation as far as kissing.

Althea, however, was nowhere to be found. He looked in the house, heard that she had been there but had gone out again; he looked in the garden; he finally went back to the woods, an uncomfortable surmise rising; and finding her nowhere there, he strolled on into the meadows. Then, suddenly, he saw her, sitting on a rustic bench at a bend of the little brook. Her eyes were bent upon the running water, and she did not look up as he approached her. When he was beside her, her eyes met his, reluctantly and resentfully, and he was startled to observe that she had wept. His surmise returned. She must have seen him kiss Frances. Yet even then Gerald did not know why it should make Miss Jakes weep that he should behave like a donkey.

'May I sit down here?' he asked, genuinely grieved and genuinely anxious to find out what the matter was.

'Certainly,' said Althea in chilly tones.

He was a little confused. It had something to do with the kissing, he felt sure. 'Miss Jakes, I'm afraid you'll never believe me a serious person,' he said.

'Why should you be serious?' said Althea.

'You are angry with me,' Gerald remarked dismally.

'Why should I be angry?'

He raised his eyebrows, detached a bit of loosened wood from the seat, and skipped it over the water. 'Well, to find me behaving like a child again.'

'I should reserve my anger for more important matters,' said Althea. She was angry, or she hoped she was, for, far more than anger, it was misery and a passion of shame that surged in her. She knew now, and she could not hide from herself that she knew; and yet he cared so little that he had not even kept his promise; so little that he had stayed behind to kiss that most indecorous woman. If only she could make him think that it was only anger.

'Ah, but you are angry, and rather unjustly,' said Gerald. His eyes were seeking hers, rallying, pleading, perhaps laughing a little at her. 'And really, you know, you are a little unkind; I thought we were friends — what?'

She forced herself to meet those charming eyes, and then to smile back at him. It would have been absurd not to smile, but the effort was disastrous; her lips quivered; the tears ran down her cheeks. She rose, trembling and aghast. 'I am very foolish. I have such a headache. Please don't pay any attention to me — it's the heat, I think.'

She turned blindly towards the house.

The pretence of the headache was, he knew it in the flash of revelation that came to him, on a par with Frances's ankle — but with what a difference in motive! Grave, a little pale, Gerald walked silently beside her to the woods. He did not know what to say. He was a little frightened and a great deal touched.

'Mr. Digby,' Althea said, when they were among the trees again — and it hurt him to see the courage of her smile — 'you must forgive me for being so silly. It is the heat, you know; and this headache — it puts one so on edge. I didn't mean to speak as I did. Of course I'm not angry.'

He was ready to help her out with the most radiant tact. 'Of course I knew it couldn't make any real difference to you — the way I behaved. Only I don't like you to be even a little cross with me.'

'I'm not — not even a little,' she said.

'We are friends then, really friends?'

His smile sustained and reassured her. Surely he had not seen — if he could smile like that — ever so lightly, so merrily, and so gravely too. Courage came back to her. She could find a smile as light as his in replying: 'Really friends.'

CHAPTER XIV.

Gerald, after Althea had gone in, walked for some time in the garden, taking counsel with himself. The expression of his face was still half touched and half alarmed. He smoked two cigarettes and then came to the conclusion that, until he could have a talk with Helen, there was no conclusion to be come to. He never came to important conclusions unaided. He would sleep on it and then have a talk with Helen.

He sought her out next morning on the first opportunity. She was in the library writing letters. She looked, as was usual with her at early morning hours, odd to the verge of ugliness. It always took her some time to recover from the drowsy influences of the night. She was dimmed, as it were, with eyelids half awake, and small lips pouting, and she seemed at once more childlike and more worn than later in the day. Gerald looked at her with satisfaction. To his observant and appreciative eye, Helen was often at her most charming when at her ugliest.

'I've something to talk over,' he said. 'Can you give me half an hour or so?'

She answered, 'Certainly,' laying down her pen, and leaning back in her chair.

'Your letters aren't important? I may keep you for a longish time. Perhaps we might put it off till the afternoon?'

'They aren't in the least important. You may keep me as long as you like.'

'Thanks. Have a cigarette?' He offered his case, and Helen took one and lighted it at the match he held for her, and then Gerald, lighting his own, proceeded to stroll up and down the room reflecting.

'Helen,' he began, 'I've been thinking things over.' His tone was serene, yet a little inquiring. He might have been thinking over some rather uncertain investment, or the planning of a rather exacting trip abroad. Yet Helen's intuition leaped at once to deeper significances. Looking out of the window at the lawn, bleached with dew, the trees, the distant autumnal uplands, while she quietly smoked her cigarette, it was as if her sub-consciousness, aroused and vigilant, held its breath, waiting.

'You know,' said Gerald, 'what I've always really wanted to do more than anything else. As I get older, I want it more and more, and get more and more tired of my shambling sort of existence. I love this old place and I love the country. I'd like nothing so much as to be able to live here, try my hand at farming, paint a little, read a little, and get as much hunting as I could.'

Helen, blowing a ring of smoke and watching it softly hover, made no comment on these prefatory remarks.

'Well, as you know,' said Gerald, 'to do that needs money; and I've none. And you know that the only solution we could ever find was that I should marry money. And you know that I never found a woman with money whom I liked well enough.' He was not looking at Helen as he said this; his eyes were on the shabby old carpet that he was pacing. And in the pause that followed Helen did not speak. She knew — it was all that she had time to know — that her silence was expectant only, not ominous. Consciousness, now, as well as sub-consciousness, seemed rushing to the bolts and bars and windows of the little lodge of friendship, making it secure — if still it might be made secure — against the storm that gathered. She could not even wonder who Gerald had found. She had only time for the dreadful task of defence, so that no blast of reality should rush in upon them.

'Well,' said Gerald, and it was now with a little more inquiry and with less serenity, 'I think, perhaps, I've found her. I think, Helen, that your nice Althea cares about me, you know, and would have me.'

Helen sat still, and did not move her eyes from the sky and trees. There was a long white cloud in the sky, an island floating in a sea of blue. She noted its bays and peninsulas, the azure rivers that interlaced it, its soft depressions and radiant uplands. She never forgot it. She could have drawn the snowy island, from memory, for years. All her life long she had waited for this moment; all her life long she had lived with the sword of its acceptance in her heart. She had thought that she had accepted; but now the sword turned — horribly turned — round and round in her heart, and she did not know what she should do.

'Well,' Gerald repeated, standing still, and, as she knew, looking at the back of her head in a little perplexity.

Helen looked cautiously down at the cigarette she held; it still smoked languidly. She raised it to her lips and drew a whiff. Then, after that, she dared a further effort. 'Well?' she repeated.

Gerald laughed a trifle nervously. 'I asked you,' he reminded her.

She was able, testing her strength, as a tight-rope walker slides a careful foot along the rope, to go on. 'Oh, I see. And do you care about her?'

Gerald was silent for another moment, and she guessed that he had run his hand through his hair and rumpled it on end.

'She really is a little dear, isn't she?' he then said. 'You mayn't find her interesting — though I really do; and she may be like *eau rougie*; but, as you said, it's a pleasant draught to have beside one. She is gentle and wise and good, and she seems to take her place here very sweetly, doesn't she? She seems really to belong here, don't you think so?'

Helen could not answer that question. 'Do you want me to tell you whether you care for her?' she asked.

He laughed. 'I suppose I do.'

'And, on the whole, you hope I'll tell you that you do.'

'Well, yes,' he assented.

The dreadful steeling of her will at the very verge of swooning abysses gave an edge to her voice. She tried to dull it, to speak very quietly and mildly, as she said: 'I must have all the facts of the case before me, then. I confess I hadn't suspected it was a case.'

'Which means that you'd never dreamed I could fall in love with Miss Jakes.' Gerald's tone was a little rueful.

'Oh — you have fallen in love with her?'

'Why, that's just what I'm asking you!' he laughed again. 'Or, at least, not that exactly, for of course it's not a question of being in love. But I think her wise and good and gentle, and she cares for me — I think; and it seems almost like the finger of destiny — finding her here. Have you any idea how much money she has? It must be quite a lot,' said Gerald.

Helen was ready with her facts. 'A very safe three thousand a year, I believe. Not much, of course, but quite enough for what you want to do. But,' she added, after the pause in which he reflected on this sum — it was a good deal less than he had taken for granted — 'I don't think that Althea would marry you on that basis. She is very proud and very romantic. If you want her to marry you, you will have to make her feel that you care for her in herself.' It was her own pride that now steadied her pulses and steeled her nerves. She would be as fair to Gerald's case as though he were her brother; she would be too fair, perhaps. Here was the pitfall of her pride that she did not clearly see. Perhaps it was with a grim touch of retribution that she promised herself that since he could think of Althea Jakes, he most certainly should have her.

'Yes, she is proud,' said Gerald. 'That's one of the things one so likes in her. She'd never hold out a finger, however much she cared.'

'You will have to hold out both hands,' said Helen.

'You think she won't have me unless I can pretend to be in love with her? I'm afraid I can't take that on.'

'I'm glad you can't. She is too good for such usage. No,' said Helen, holding her scales steadily, 'perfect frankness is the only way. If she knows that you really care for her — even if you are not romantic — if you can make her feel that the money — though a necessity — is secondary, and wouldn't have counted at all unless you had come to care, I should say that your chances are good —

since you have reason to believe that she has fallen in love with you.'

'It's not as if I denied her anything I had to give, is it?' Gerald pondered on the point of conscience she put before him.

'You mean that you're incapable of caring more for any woman than for Althea?'

'Of course not. I care a great deal more for you,' said Gerald, again rather rueful under her probes. 'I only mean that I'm not likely to fall in love again, or anything of that sort. She can be quite secure about me. I'll be her devoted and faithful husband.'

'I think you care,' said Helen. 'I think you can make her happy.'

But Gerald now came and sat on the corner of the writing-table beside her, facing her, his back to the window. 'It's a tremendous thing to decide on, isn't it, Helen?'

She turned her eyes on him, and he looked at her with a gaze troubled and a little groping, as though he sought in her further elucidations; as though, for the first time, she had disappointed him a little.

'Is it?' she asked. 'Is marriage really a tremendous thing?'

'Well, isn't it?'

'I'm not sure. In one way, of course, it is. But people, perhaps, exaggerate the influence of their own choice on the results. You can't be sure of results, choose as carefully as you will; it's what comes after that decides them, I imagine — the devotion, the fidelity you speak of. And since you've found some one to whom you can promise those, some one wise and good and gentle, isn't that all that you need be sure of?'

Gerald continued to study her face. 'You're not pleased, Helen,' he now said. It was a curious form of torture that Helen must smile under.

'Well, it's not a case for enthusiasm, is it?' she said. 'I'm certainly not displeased.'

'You'd rather I married her than Frances Pickering?'

'Would Frances have you, too, irresistible one?'

'Oh, I don't think so; pretty sure not. She would want a lot of things I can't give. I was only wondering which you'd prefer.'

Helen heard the clamour of her own heart. Frances! Frances! She is trivial; she will not take your place: she will not count in his life at all. Althea will count; she will count more and more. She will be his habit, his *haus-frau*, the mother of his children. He is not in love with her; but he will come to love her, and there will be no place for friendship in his life. Hearing that clamour she dragged herself together, hating herself for having heard it, and answered: 'Althea, of course; she is worth three of Frances.'

Gerald gave a little sigh. 'Well, I'm glad we agree there,' he said. 'I'm glad you see that Althea is worth three of her. What I do wish is that you cared more about Althea.'

What he was telling her was that if she would care more about Althea, he would too, and she wondered if this, also, were a part of pride; should she help him to care more for Althea? A better pride sustained her; she felt the danger in these subtleties of her torment. 'I like Althea,' she said. 'I, too, think that she is wise and good and gentle. I think that she will be the best of wives, the best of wives and mothers. But, as I said, I don't feel enthusiasm; I don't feel it a case for enthusiasm.'

'Of course it's not a case for enthusiasm,' said Gerald, who was evidently eager to range himself completely with her. 'I'm fond, and I'll grow fonder; and I believe you will too. Don't you, Helen?'

'No doubt I shall,' said Helen. She got up now and tossed her cigarette into the waste-paper basket, and stood for a moment looking past Gerald's head at the snowy island, now half dissolved in blue, as though its rivers had engulfed it. They were parting, he and she, she knew it, and yet there was no word that she could say to him, no warning or appeal that she could utter. If he could see that it was the end he would, she knew, start back from his shallow project. But he did not know that it was the end and he might never know. Did he not really understand that an adoring wife could not be fitted into their friendship? His innocent unconsciousness of inevitable change made Helen's heart, in its deeper knowledge of human character, sink to a bitterness that felt like a hatred of him, and she wondered, looking forward, whether Gerald would ever miss anything, or ever know that anything was gone.

Gerald sat still looking up at her as though expecting some further suggestion, and as her eyes came back to him, she smiled to him with deliberate sweetness, showing him thus that her conclusions were all friendly. And he rose, smiling back, reassured and fortified. 'Well,' he said, 'since you approve, I suppose it's settled. I shan't ask her at once, you know. She might think it was because of what I'd guessed. I'll lead up to it for a day or two. And, Helen, you might, if you've a chance, put in a good word for me.'

'I will, if I've a chance,' said Helen.

Gerald, as if aware that he had taken up really too much of her time, now moved towards the door. But he went slowly, and at the door he paused. He turned to her smiling. 'And you give me your blessing?' he asked.

He was most endearing when he smiled so. It was a smile like a child's, that caressed and cajoled, and that saw through its own cajolery and pleaded, with a little wistfulness, that there was more than could show itself, behind. Helen knew what was behind — the sense of strangeness, the affection and the touch of fear. She had never refused that smile anything; she seemed to refuse it nothing now, as she answered with a maternal acquiescence, 'I give you my blessing, dear Gerald.'

CHAPTER XV.

It was still early. When he had left her, Helen looked at her watch; only half-past ten. She stood thinking. Should she go out, as usual, take her place in a long chair under the limes, close her eyes and pretend to sleep? No, she could not do that. Should she sit down in her room with Dante and a dictionary? No, that she would not do. Should she walk far away into the woods and lie upon the ground and weep? That would be a singularly foolish plan, and at lunch everybody would see that she had been crying. Yet it was impossible to remain here, to remain still, and thinking. She must move quickly, and make her body tired. She went to her room, pinned on her hat, drew on her gloves, and, choosing a stick as she went through the hall, passed from the grounds and through the meadow walk to a long road, climbing and winding, whose walls, at either side, seemed to hold back the billows of the woodland. The day was hot and dusty. The sky was like a blue stone, the green monotonous, the road glared white. Helen, with the superficial fretfulness of an agony controlled, said to herself that nothing more like a bad water-colour landscape could be imagined; there were the unskilful blots of heavy foliage, the sleekly painted sky, and the sunny road was like the whiteness of the paper, picked out, for shadows, in niggling cobalt. A stupid, bland, heartless day.

She walked along this road for several miles and left it to cross a crisp, grassy slope from where, standing still and turning to see, she looked down over all the country and saw, far away, the roofs of Merriston House. She stood for a long time looking down at it, the hot wind ruffling her skirts and hair. It was a heartless day and she herself felt heartless. She felt herself as something silent, swift, and raging. For now she was to taste to the full the bitter difference between the finality of personal decision and a finality imposed, fatefully and irrevocably, from without. She had thought herself prepared for this ending of hope. She had even, imagining herself hardened and indifferent, gone in advance of it and had sought to put the past under her feet and to build up a new life. But she had not been prepared; that she now knew. The imagination of the fact was not its realisation in her very blood and bones, nor the standing ready, armed for the blow, this feel of the blade between her ribs. And looking down at the only home she had ever had, in moments long, sharp, dream-like, her strength was drained from her as if by a fever, and she felt that she was changed all through and that each atom of her being was set, as it were, a little differently, making of her a new personality, through this shock of sudden hopelessness.

She felt her knees weak beneath her and she moved on slowly, away from the sun, to a lonely little wood that bordered the hilltop. In her sudden weakness she climbed the paling that enclosed it with some difficulty, wondering if she were most inconveniently going to faint, and walking blindly along a narrow path, in the sudden cool and darkness, she dropped down on the moss at the first turning of the way.

Here, at last, was beauty. The light, among the fanlike branches, looked like sea-water streaked with gold; the tall boles of the beeches were like the pillars of a temple sunken in the sea. Helen lay back, folded her arms behind her head, and stared up at the chinks of far brightness in the green roof overhead. It was like being drowned, deep beneath the surface of things. If only she could be at peace, like a drowned thing. Lying there, she longed to die, to dissolve away into the moss, the earth, the cool, green air. And feeling this, in the sudden beauty, tears, for the first time, came to her eyes. She turned over on her face, burying it in her arms and muttering in childish language, 'I'm sick of it; sick to death of it.'

As she spoke she was aware that some one was near her. A sudden footfall, a sudden pause, followed her words. She lifted her head, then she sat up. The tears had flowed and her cheeks were wet with them, but of that she was not conscious, so great was her surprise at finding Franklin Winslow Kane standing before her on the mossy path.

Mr. Kane carried his straw hat in his hand. He was very warm, his hair was untidy on his moist brow, his boots were white with dust, his trousers were turned up from them and displayed an inch or so of thin ankle encased in oatmeal-coloured socks. His tie — Helen noted the one salient detail among the many dull ones that made up a whole so incongruous with the magic scene — was of a peculiarly harsh and ugly shade of blue. He had only just climbed over a low wall near by and that was why he had come upon her so inaudibly and had, so inadvertently, been a witness of her grief.

He did not, however, show embarrassment, but looked at her with the hesitant yet sympathetic attentiveness of a vagrant dog.

Helen sat on the moss, her feet extended before her, and she returned his look from her tearful eyes, making no attempt to soften the oddity of the situation. She found, indeed, a gloomy amusement in it, and was aware of wondering what Mr. Kane, who made so much of everything, would make of their mutual predicament.

'Have you been having a long walk, too?' she asked.

He looked at her, smiling now a little, as if he wagged a

responsive tail; but he was not an ingratiating dog, only a friendly and a troubled one.

'Yes, I have,' he said. 'We have got rather a long way off, Miss Buchanan.'

'That's a comfort sometimes, isn't it,' said Helen. She took out her handkerchief and dried her eyes, drawing herself, then, into a more comfortable position against the trunk of a beech-tree.

'You'd rather I went away, wouldn't you,' said Mr. Kane; 'but let me say first that I'm very sorry to have intruded, and very sorry indeed to see that you're unhappy.'

She now felt that she did not want him to go, indeed she felt that she would rather he stayed. After the loneliness of her despair, she liked the presence of the friendly, wandering dog. It would be comforting to have it sit down beside you and to have it thud its tail when you chanced to look at it. Mr. Kane would not intrude, he would be a consolation.

'No, don't go,' she said. 'Do sit down and rest. It's frightfully hot, isn't it.'

He sat down in front of her, clasping his knees about, as was his wont, and exposing thereby not only the entire oatmeal sock, but a section of leg nearly matching it in tint.

'Well, I am rather tired,' he said. 'I've lost my way, I guess.' And, looking about him, he went on: 'Very peaceful things aren't they, the woods. Trees are very peaceful things, pacifying things, I mean.'

Helen looked up at them. 'Yes, they are peaceful. I don't know that I find them pacifying.'

His eyes came back to her and he considered her again for a moment before he said, smiling gently, 'I've been crying too.'

In the little pause that followed this announcement they continued to look at each other, and it was not so much that their eyes sounded the other's eyes as that they deepened for each other and, without effort or surprise, granted to each other the quiet avowal of complete sincerity.

'I'm very sorry that you are unhappy, too,' said Helen. She noticed now that his eyes were jaded and that all his clear, terse little face was softened and relaxed.

'Yes, I'm unhappy,' said Franklin. 'It's queer, isn't it, that we should find each other like this. I'm glad I've found you: two unhappy people are better together, I think, than alone. It eases things a little, don't you think so?'

'Perhaps it does,' said Helen. 'That is, it does if one of them is so kind and so pacifying as you are; you do remind me of the trees,' she smiled.

'Ah, well, that's very sweet of you, very sweet indeed,' said

Franklin, looking about him at the limpid green. 'It makes me feel I'm not intruding, to have you say that to me. It didn't follow, of course, because I'm glad to find you that you would be glad I'd come. You don't show it much, Miss Buchanan' — he was looking at her again — 'your crying.'

'I'm always afraid that I show it dreadfully. That's the worst of it, I don't dare indulge in it often.'

'No, you don't show it much. You sometimes look as though you had been crying when I'm sure you haven't — early in the morning, for instance.'

Helen could but smile again. 'You are very observant. You really noticed that?'

'I don't know that I'm so very observant, Miss Buchanan, but I'm interested in everybody, and I'm particularly interested in you, so that of course I notice things like that. Now you aren't particularly interested in me — though you are so kind — are you?' and again Mr. Kane smiled his weary, gentle smile.

It seemed very natural to sit under peaceful trees and talk to Mr. Kane, and it was easy to be perfectly frank with him. Helen answered his smile. 'No, I'm not. I'm quite absorbed in my own affairs. I'm interested in hardly anybody. I'm very selfish.'

'Ah, you would find that you wouldn't suffer so — in just your way, I mean — if you were less selfish,' Franklin Kane remarked.

'What other way is there?' Helen asked. 'What is your way?'

'Well, I don't know that I've found a much better one, our ways seem to have brought us to pretty much the same place, haven't they,' he almost mused. 'That's the worst of suffering, it's pretty much alike, at all times and in all ways. I'm not unselfish either, you know, a mighty long way from it. But I'm not sick of it, you know, not sick to death of it. Forgive me if I offend in repeating your words.'

'You are unselfish, I'm sure of that,' said Helen. 'And so you must have other things to live for. My life is very narrow, and when things I care about are ruined I see nothing further.'

'Things are never ruined in life, Miss Buchanan. As long as there is life there is hope and action and love. As long as you can love you can't be sick to death of it.' Mr. Kane spoke in his deliberate, monotonous tones.

Helen was silent for a little while. She was wondering; not about Mr. Kane, nor about his suffering, nor about the oddity of thus talking with him about her own. It was no more odd to talk to him than if he had been the warm-hearted dog, dowered for her benefit with speech; she was wondering about what he said and about that love to which he alluded. 'Perhaps I don't know much about love,' she said, and more to herself than to Mr. Kane.

'I've inferred that since knowing you,' said Franklin.

'I mean, of course,' Helen defined, 'the selfless love you are talking of.'

'Yes, I understand,' said Franklin. 'Now, you see, the other sort of love, the sort that makes people go away and cry in the woods — for I've been crying because I'm hopelessly in love, Miss Buchanan, and I presume that you are too — well, that sort of love can't escape ruin sometimes. That side of life may go to pieces and then there's nothing left for it but to cry. But that side isn't all life, Miss Buchanan.'

Helen did not repudiate his interpretation of her grief. She was quite willing that Mr. Kane should know why she had been crying, but she did not care to talk about that side to him. It had been always, and it would always be, she feared, all life to her. She looked sombrely before her into the green vistas.

'Of course,' Franklin went on, 'I don't know anything about your hopeless love affair. I'm only sure that your tragedy is a noble one and that you are up to it, you know — as big as it is. If it's hopeless, it's not, I'm sure, because of anything in you. It's because of fate, or circumstance, or some unworthiness in the person you care for. Now with me one of the hardest things to bear is the fact that I've nothing to blame but myself. I'm not adequate, that's the trouble; no charm, you see,' Mr. Kane again almost mused, 'no charm. Charm is the great thing, and it means more than it seems to mean, all evolution, the survival of the fittest — natural selection — is in it, when you come to think of it. If I'd had charm, personality, or, well, greatness of some sort, I'd have probably won Althea long ago. You know, of course, that it's Althea I'm in love with, and have been for years and years. Well, there it is,' Franklin was picking tall blades of grass that grew in a little tuft near by and putting them neatly together as he spoke. 'There it is, but even with the pain of just that sort of failure to bear, I don't intend that my life shall be ruined. It can't be, by the loss of that hope. I'm not good enough for Althea. I've got to accept that; natural selection rejects me,' looking up from his grass blades he smiled gravely at his companion; 'but I'm good enough for other beautiful things that need serving. And I'm good enough to go on being Althea's friend, to be of some value to her in that capacity. So my life isn't ruined, not by a long way, and I wish you'd try to feel the same about yours.'

Helen didn't feel in the least inclined to try, but she found herself deeply interested in Mr. Kane's attitude; for the first time Mr. Kane had roused her intent interest. She looked hard at him while he sat there, demonstrating to her the justice of life's dealings with him and laying one blade of grass so accurately against another, and she was wondering now about him. It was not because she thought her own feelings sacred that she preferred them to be concealed, but she saw that Mr. Kane's were no less sacred to him for being thus unconcealed. She even guessed that his revelation of feeling was less for his personal relief than for her personal benefit; that he was carrying out, in all the depths of his sincerity, a wish to comfort her, to take her out of herself. Well, he had taken her out of herself, and after having heard that morning what Althea's significance could be in the life of another man, she was curious to find what her so different significance could be in the life of this one, as alien from Gerald in type and temperament as it was possible to imagine. Why did Althea mean anything at all to Gerald, and why did she mean everything to Mr. Kane? And through what intuition of the truth had Mr. Kane come to his present hopelessness?

'Do you think women always fall in love with the adequate man, and *vice versa?*' she asked, and her eyes were gentle as they mused on him. 'Why should you say that it's because you're not adequate that Althea isn't in love with you?'

Franklin fixed his eye upon her and it had now a new light, it deepened for other problems than Helen's and his own. 'Not adequate for her — not what she wants — that's my point,' he said. 'But there are other sorts of mistakes to make, of course. If Althea falls in love with a man equipped as I'm not equipped, that does prove that I lack something that would have won her; but it doesn't prove that she's found the right man. We've got beyond natural selection when it comes to life as a whole. He may be the man for her to fall in love with, but is he the man to make her happy? That's just the question for me, Miss Buchanan, and I wish you'd help me with it.'

'Help you?' Helen rather faltered.

'Yes, please try. You must see — I see it plainly enough — that Mr. Digby is going to marry Althea.' He actually didn't add, 'If she'll have him.' Helen wondered how far his perspicacity went; had he seen what Gerald had seen, and what she had not seen at all?

'You think it's Gerald who is in love with her?' she asked.

Again Franklin's eye was on her, and she now saw in it his deep perplexity. She couldn't bear to add to it. 'I've guessed nothing,' she said. 'You must enlighten me.'

'I wasn't sure at first,' said Franklin, groping his way. 'He seemed so devoted to Lady Pickering; but for some days it's been obvious, hasn't it, that that wasn't in the least serious?'

'Not in the least.'

'I couldn't have reconciled myself,' said Franklin, 'to the idea of a man, who could take Lady Pickering seriously, marrying Althea. I can't quite reconcile myself to the idea of a man who could, well, be so devoted to Lady Pickering, marrying Althea. He's your friend, I know, Miss Buchanan, as well as your relative, but you know what I feel for Althea, and you'll forgive my saying that if I'm not big enough for her he isn't big enough either; no, upon my soul, he isn't.'

Helen's eyes dwelt on him. She knew that, with all the forces of concealment at her command, she wanted to keep from Mr. Kane the blighting irony of her own inner comments; above everything, now, she dreaded lest her irony should touch one of Mr. Kane's ideals. It was so beautiful of him to think himself not big enough for Althea, that she was well content that he should see Gerald in the same category of unfitness. Perhaps Gerald was not big enough for Althea; Gerald's bigness didn't interest Helen; the great point for her was that Mr. Kane should not guess that she considered Althea not big enough for him. 'If Gerald is the lucky man,' she said, after the pause in which she gazed at him; 'if she cares enough for Gerald to marry him, then I think he will make her happy; and that's the chief thing, isn't it?'

Mr. Kane could not deny that it was, and yet, evidently, he was not satisfied. 'I believe you'll forgive me if I go on,' he said. 'You see it's so tremendously important to me, and what I'm going to say isn't really at all offensive — I mean, people of your world and Mr. Digby's world wouldn't find it so. I'll tell you the root of my trouble, Miss Buchanan. Your friend is a poor man, isn't he, and Althea is a fairly rich woman. Can you satisfy me on this point? I can give Althea up; I must give her up; but I can hardly bear it if I'm to give her up to a mere fortune-hunter, however happy he may be able to make her.'

Helen's cheeks had coloured slightly. 'Gerald isn't a mere fortune-hunter,' she said. 'People of my world do think fortune-hunting offensive.'

'Forgive me then,' said Franklin, gazing at her, contrite but unperturbed. 'I'm very ignorant of your world. May I put it a little differently. Would Mr. Digby be likely to fall in love with a woman if she hadn't a penny?'

She had quite forgiven him. She smiled a little in answering. 'He has often fallen in love with women without a penny, but he could hardly marry a woman who hadn't one.'

'He wouldn't wish to marry Althea, then, if she had no money?'

'However much he would wish it, I don't think he would be so foolish as to do it,' said Helen.

'Can't a man worth his salt work for the woman he loves?'

'A man well worth his salt may not be trained for making money,' Helen returned. She knew the question clamouring in his heart, the question he must not ask, nor she answer: 'Is he in love with Althea?' Mr. Kane could never accept nor understand what the qualified answer to such a question would have to be, and she must leave him with his worst perplexity unsolved. But one thing she could do for him, and she hoped that it might soften a little the bitterness of his uncertainty. The sunlight suddenly had failed, and a slight wind passed among the boughs overhead. Helen got upon her feet, straightening her hat and putting back her hair. It was time to be going homewards. They went down the path and climbed over the palings, and it was on the hill-top that Helen said, looking far ahead of her, far over the now visible roofs of Merriston:

'I've known Gerald Digby all my life, and I know Althea, now, quite well. And if Gerald is to be the lucky man I'd like to say, for him, you know — and I think it ought to set your mind at rest — that I think Althea will be quite as lucky as he will be, and that I think that he is worthy of her.'

Franklin kept his eyes on her as she spoke, and though she did not meet them, her far gaze, fixed ahead, seemed in its impersonal gravity to commune with him, for his consolation, more than an answering glance would have done. She was giving him her word for something, and the very fact that she kept it impersonal, held it there before them both, made it more weighty and more final. Franklin evidently found it so. He presently heaved a sigh in which relief was mingled with acceptance — acceptance of the fact that, from her, he must expect no further relief. And presently, as they came out upon the winding road, he said: 'Thanks, that's very helpful.'

They walked on then in silence. The sun was gone and the wind blew softly; the freshness of the coming rain was in the air. Helen lifted her face to them as the first slow drops began to fall. In her heart, too, the fierceness of her pain was overcast. Something infinitely sad, yet infinitely peaceful, stilled her pulses. Infinitely sad, yet infinitely funny too. How small, how insignificant, this tangle of the whole-hearted and the half-hearted; what did it all come to, and how feel suffering as tragic when farce grimaced so close beside it? Who could take it seriously when, in life, the whole-hearted were so deceived and based their loves on such illusion? To feel the irony was to acquiesce, perhaps, and acquiescence, even if only momentary, like the lull and softness in nature, was better than the beating fierceness of rebellion. Everything was over. And here beside her went the dear ungainly dog. She turned her head and smiled at him, the raindrops on her lashes.

'You don't mind the rain, Miss Buchanan?' said Franklin, who had looked anxiously at the weather, and probably felt himself responsible for not producing an umbrella for a lady's need.

'I like it.' She continued to smile at him.

'Miss Buchanan,' said Franklin, looking at her earnestly and not smiling back, 'I want to say something. I've seemed egotistic and I've been egotistic. I've talked only about my own troubles; but I don't believe you wanted to talk about yours, did you?' Helen, smiling, slightly shook her head. 'And at the same time you've not minded my knowing that you have troubles to bear.' Again she shook her head. 'Well, that's what I thought; that's all right, then. What I wanted to say was that if ever I can help you in any way — if ever I can be of any use — will you please remember that I'm your friend.'

Helen, still looking at him, said nothing for some moments. And now, once more, a slight colour rose in her cheeks. 'I can't imagine why you should be my friend,' she said. 'I feel that I know a great deal about you; but you know nothing about me, and please believe me when I say that there's very little to know.'

Already he knew her well enough to know that the slight colour, lingering on her cheek, meant that she was moved. 'Ah, I can't believe you there,' he said. 'And at all events, whatever there is to know, I'm its friend. You don't know yourself, you see. You only know what you feel, not at all what you are.'

'Isn't that what I am?' She looked away, disquieted by this analysis of her own personality.

'By no means all,' said Franklin. 'You've hardly looked at the you that can do things — the you that can think things.'

She didn't want to look at them, poor, inert, imprisoned creatures. She looked, instead, at the quaint, unexpected, and touching thing with which she was presented — Mr. Kane's friendship. She would have liked to have told him that she was grateful and that she, too, was his friend; but such verbal definitions as these were difficult and alien to her, as alien as discussion of her own character and its capacities. It seemed to be claiming too much to claim a capacity for friendship. She didn't know whether she was anybody's friend, really — as Mr. Kane would have counted friendship. She thought him dear, she thought him good, and yet she hardly wanted him, would hardly miss him if he were not there. He touched her, more deeply than she perhaps quite knew, and yet she seemed to have nothing for him. So she gave up any explicit declaration, only turning her eyes on him and smiling at him again through her rain dimmed lashes, as they went down the winding road together.

CHAPTER XVI.

It was Althea who, during the next few days, while Gerald with the greatest tact and composure made his approaches, was most unconscious of what was approaching her. Everybody else now saw quite clearly what Gerald's intentions were. Althea was dazed; she did not know what the bright object that had come so overpoweringly into her life wanted of her. She had feared — sickeningly — with a stiffening of her whole nature to resistance, that he wanted to flirt with her as well as with Lady Pickering. Then she had seen that he wasn't going to flirt, that he was going to be her friend, and then — this in the two or three days that followed Gerald's talk with Helen — that he was going to be a dear one. She had only adjusted her mind to this grave joy and wondered, with all the perplexity of her own now recognised love, whether it could prove more than a very tremulous joy, when the final revelation came upon her. It came, and it was still unexpected, one afternoon when she and Gerald sat in the drawing-room together. It was very warm, and they had come into the cooler house after tea to look at a book that Gerald wanted to show her. It had proved to be not much of a book after all, and even while standing with him in the library, while he turned the musty leaves for her and pointed out the funny old illustrations he had been telling her of, Althea had felt that the book was only a pretext for getting her away to himself. He had led her back to the drawing-room and he had said, 'Don't let's go out again, it's much nicer here. Please sit here and talk to me.'

It was just the hour, just such an afternoon as that on which poor Franklin had arrived; Althea thought of that as she and Gerald sat down on the same little sofa where she and Franklin had sat. And, in a swift flash of association, she remembered that Franklin had wanted to kiss her, and had kissed her. They had left Franklin under the limes with Helen; he had been reading something to Helen out of a pamphlet, and Helen had looked, though rather sleepy, kindly acquiescent; but the memory of the past could do no more than stir a faint pity for the present Franklin; she was wishing — and it seemed the most irresistible longing of all her life — that Gerald Digby wanted to kiss her too. The memory and the wish threw her thoughts into confusion, but she was still able to maintain her calm, to smile at him and say, 'Certainly, let us talk.'

'But not about politics and philanthropy today,' said Gerald, who leaned his elbow on his knee and looked quietly yet intently at her; 'I want to talk about ourselves, if I may.'

'Do let us talk about ourselves,' said Althea.

'Well, I don't believe that what I'm going to say will surprise you. I'm sure you've seen how much I've come to care about you,' said Gerald.

Althea kept her eyes fixed calmly upon him; her self-command was great, even in the midst of an overpowering hope.

'I know that we are real friends,' she returned, smiling.

Her calm, her cool, sweet smile, like the light in the shaded room, were very pleasing to Gerald. 'Ah, yes, but that was only a step, you see,' he smiled back. He did not let her guess his full confidence, he took all the steps one after the other in their proper order. He couldn't give her romance, but he could give her every grace, and her calm made him feel, happily and securely, that grace would quite content her.

'You must see,' he went on, still with his eyes on hers, 'that it's more than that. You must see that you are dearer than that.' And then he brought out his simple question, 'Will you be my wife?'

Althea sat still and her mind whirled. Until then she had been unprepared. Her own feeling, the feeling that she had refused for days to look at, had been so strong that she had only known its strength and its danger to her pride; she had had no time to wonder about Gerald's feeling. And now, in its freedom, her feeling was so joyous that she could know only its joy. She was dear to him. He asked her to marry him. It seemed enough, more than enough, to make joy a permanent thing in her life. She had not imagined it possible to marry a man who did not woo and urge, who did not make her feel the ardour of his love. But, now, breathlessly, she found that reality was quite different from her imagination and yet so blissful that she could feel nothing wanting in it. And she could say nothing. She looked at him with her large eyes, gravely, and touched, a little abashed by their gaze, he took her hand, kissed it, and murmured, 'Please say you'll have me.'

'Do you love me?' Althea breathed out; it was not that she questioned or hesitated; the words came to her lips in answer to the situation rather than in questioning of him. And it was hardly a shock; it was, in a subtle way, a further realisation of exquisiteness, when the situation, in his reply, defined itself as a reality still further removed from her imagination of what such a situation should be.

Holding her hand, his gay brown eyes upon her, he said, after only the very slightest pause, 'Miss Jakes, I'm not a romantic person, you see that; you see the sort of person I am. I can't make pretty speeches, not when I'm serious, as I am now. When I make pretty speeches, I'm only flirting. I like you. I respect you. I've watched you here in my old home and I've thought, "If only she would make it home again." I've thought that you'd help me to make a new life. I want to come and live here, with you, and do the things I told you about — the things that needed money.'

His eyes were on hers, so quietly and so gravely, now, that they seemed to hold from her all ugly little interpretations; he trusted her with the true one, he trusted her not to see it as ugly. 'You see, I'm not romantic,' he went on, 'and I can only tell you the truth. I couldn't have thought of marrying you if you hadn't had money, but I needn't tell you that, if you'd had millions, I wouldn't have thought of marrying you unless I cared for you. So there it is, quite clear and simple. I think I can make you happy; will you make me happy?'

It was exquisite, the trust, the truth, the quiet gravity, and yet there was pain in the exquisiteness. She could not look at it yet distinctly for it seemed part of the beauty. It was rarer, more dignified, this wooing, than commonplace protestations of devotion. It was a large and beautiful life he opened to her and he needed her to make it real. They needed each other. Yet — here the pain hovered — they needed each other so differently. To her, he was the large and beautiful life; to him, she was only a part of it, and a means to it. But she could not look at pain. Pride was mounting in her, pride in him, her beloved and her possession. Before all the world, henceforth, he would be hers. And the greatness of that pride cast out lesser ones. He had discriminated, been carefully sincere; her sincerity did not need to be careful, it was an unqualified gift she had to make him. 'I love you,' she said. 'I will make it your home.'

And again Gerald was touched and a little confused. He kissed her hand and then, her eyes of mute avowal drawing him, he leaned to her and kissed her cheek. He felt it difficult to answer such a speech, and all that he found to say at last was, 'You will make me romantic, dear Althea.'

That evening he sought Helen out again; but he need not have come with his news, for it was none. Althea's blissful preoccupation and his gaiety had all the evening proclaimed the happy event. But he had to talk to Helen, and finding her on the terrace, he drew her hand through his arm and paced to and fro with her. She was silent, and, suddenly and oddly, he found it difficult to say anything. 'Well,' he ventured at last.

'Well,' Helen echoed in the darkness.

'It's all settled,' said Gerald.

'Yes,' said Helen.

'And I'm very happy.'

'I am so glad.'

'And she is really a great dear. Anything more generously sweet I've never encountered.'

'I'm so glad,' Helen repeated.

There seemed little more to say, but, before they went in, he squeezed her hand and added: 'If it hadn't been for you, I'd never have met her. Dear Helen, I have to thank you for my good fortune. I've always had to thank you for the nice things that have happened to me.'

But to this Helen demurred, though smiling apparently, as she answered, going in, 'Oh no, I don't think you have this to thank me for.'

After they had gone upstairs, Althea came to Helen's room, and putting her arms around her she hid her face on her shoulder. She was too happy to feel any sense of shyness. It was Helen who was shy. So shy that the tears rose to her eyes as she stood there, embraced. And, strangely, she felt, with all her disquiet at being so held by Althea, that the tears were not only for shyness, but for her friend. Althea's happiness touched her. It seemed greater than her situation warranted. Helen could not see the situation as rapturous. It was not such a tempered, such a reasonable joy that she could have accepted, had it been her part to accept or to decline. And, held by Althea, hot, shrinking, sorry, she was aware of another anger against Gerald.

'My dear Althea, I know. I do so heartily congratulate you and Gerald,' she said.

'He told you, dear Helen?'

'Yes, he told me, but of course I saw.'

'I feel now as if you were my sister,' said Althea, tightening her arms. 'We will always be very near each other, Helen. It is so beautiful to think that you brought us together, isn't it?'

Helen was forced to put the distasteful cup to her lips. 'Yes indeed,' she said.

'He is so dear, so wonderful,' said Althea. 'There is so much more in him than he knows himself. I want him to be a great man, Helen. I believe he can be, don't you?'

'I've never thought of Gerald as great,' Helen replied, trying to smile.

'Ah, well, wait; you will see! I suppose it is only a woman in love with a man who sees all his capacities. We will live here, and in London.' Althea, while she spoke her guileless assurance, raised her head and threw back her unbound hair, looking her full trust into Helen's eyes. 'I wouldn't care to live for more than half the year in the country, and it wouldn't be good for Gerald. I want to do so much, Helen, to make so many people happy, if I can. And, Helen dear,' she smiled now through her tears, 'if only you could be one of them; if only this could mean in some way a new opening in your life, too. One can never tell; happiness is such an infectious thing; if you are a great deal with two very happy people, you may catch the habit. I can't bear to think that you aren't happy, rare and lovely person that you are. I told Gerald so today. I said to him that I felt life hadn't given you any of the joy we all so need. Helen, dear, you must find your fairy-prince. You must, you shall fall in love, too.'

Helen controlled her face and gulped on. 'That's not so easily managed,' she remarked. 'I've seen a good many fairy-princes in my life, and either I haven't melted their hearts, or they haven't melted mine. We can't all draw lucky numbers, you know; there are not enough to go round.'

'As if anybody wouldn't fall in love with you, if you gave them the chance,' said Althea. 'You *are* the lucky number.'

Althea felt next day a certain tameness in the public reception of her news. She had not intended the news to be public yet for some time. Franklin's presence seemed to make an announcement something of an indelicacy, but, whether through her responsibility or whether through Gerald's, or whether through the obviousness of the situation, she found that everybody knew. It could not make commonplace to her her own inner joy, but she saw that to Aunt Julia, to the girls, to Lady Pickering, and Sir Charles, her position was commonplace. She was, to them, a nice American who was being married as much because she had money as because she was nice.

Aunt Julia voiced this aspect to her on the first opportunity, drawing her away after breakfast to walk with her along the terrace while she said, very gravely, 'Althea, dear, do you really think you'll be happy living in England?'

'Happier than anywhere else in the world,' said Althea.

'I didn't realise that you felt so completely expatriated.'

'England has always seemed very homelike to me, and this already is more of a home to me than any I have known for years,' said Althea, looking up at Merriston House.

'Poor child!' said Aunt Julia, 'what a comment on your rootless life. You must forgive me, Althea,' she went on in a lower voice, 'but I feel myself in a mother's place to you, and I do very much want to ask you to consider more carefully before you make things final. Mr. Digby is a charming man; but how little you have seen of him. I beg you to wait for a year before you marry.'

'I'm afraid I can't gratify you, Aunt Julia. I certainly can't ask Gerald to wait for a year.'

'My dear, why not!' Aunt Julia did not repress.

Althea went on calmly. 'It is true, of course, that we are not in love like two children, with no thought of responsibility or larger claims. You see, one outgrows that rather naïve American idea about marriage. Mine is, if you like, a *mariage de convenance*, in the sense that Gerald is a poor man and cannot marry unless he marries money. And I am proud to have the power to help him to build up a large and dignified life, and we don't intend to postpone our marriage when we know, trust, and love each other as we do.'

'A large life, my dear,' said Aunt Julia. 'Don't deceive yourself into thinking that. One needs a far larger fortune than your tiny one, nowadays, if one is to build up a large life. What I fear more than anything is that you don't in the least realise what English country life is all the year round. Imagine, if you can, your winters here.'

'I shan't spend many winters here,' said Althea smiling. She did not divulge her vague, bright plans to Aunt Julia, but they filled the future for her; she saw the London drawing-room where, when Gerald was in Parliament, she would gather delightful people together. Among such people, Lady Blair, Miss Buckston, her friends in Devonshire, and of Grimshaw Rectory, seemed hardly more than onlookers; they did not fit into the pictures of her new life.

And if they did not fit, what of Franklin? Even in old unsophisticated pictures of a *salon* he had been a figure adjusted with some difficulty. It had, in days that seemed immeasurably remote — days when she had wondered whether she could marry Franklin — it had been difficult to see herself introducing him with any sense of achievement to Lady Blair or to the Collings, and she knew now, clearly, why: in Lady Blair's drawing-room, as in Devonshire and at Grimshaw Rectory, Franklin would have looked a funny little man. How much more funny in the new setting. What would he do in it? What was it to mean to him? What would any setting mean to Franklin in which he was to see her as no longer needing him? For, and this was the worst of it, and in spite of happiness Althea felt it as a pang indeed, she no longer needed Franklin; and knowing this she longed at once to avoid and to atone to him.

She found him after her walk with Aunt Julia sitting behind a newspaper in the library. Franklin always read the newspapers every morning, and it struck Althea as particularly touching that this good habit should be persevered in under his present circumstances. She was so much touched by Franklin, the habit of old intimacy was so strong, that her own essential change of heart seemed effaced by the uprising of feeling for him. 'O Franklin!' she said. He had risen as she entered, and he stood looking at her with a smile. It seemed to receive her, to forgive, to understand. Almost weeping, she went to him with outstretched hands, faltering, 'I am so happy, and I am so sorry, dear Franklin. Oh, forgive me if I have hurt your life.'

He looked at her, no longer smiling, very gravely, holding her hands, and she knew that he was not thinking of his life, but of hers. And, with a further pang, she remembered that the last time they had stood so — she and Franklin — she had given him more hope for his life than ever before in all their histories. He must remember, too, and he must feel her unworthy in remembering, and even though she did not need Franklin, she could not bear him to think her unworthy. 'Forgive me,' she repeated. And the tears rose to her eyes. 'I've been so tossed, so unstable. I haven't known. I only know now, you see, dear Franklin. I've really fallen in love at last. Can you ever forgive me?'

'For not having fallen in love with me?' he asked gently.

'No, dear,' she answered, forced into complete sincerity. What was it in Franklin that compelled sincerity, and made it so easy to be sincere? There, at least, was a quality for which one would always need him. 'No, not for that, but for having thought that I might, perhaps, fall in love with you. It is the hope I gave you that must make this seem so sudden and so cruel.'

He had not felt her cruel, but he had felt something that was now giving his eyes their melancholy directness of gaze. He was looking at his Althea; he was not judging her; but he was wishing that she had been able to think of him a little more as mere friend, a little more as the man who, after all, had loved her all these years; wishing that she had not so completely forgotten him, so completely relegated and put him away when her new life was coming to her. But he understood, he did not judge, and he answered, 'I don't think you've been cruel, Althea dear, though it's been rather cruel of fortune, if you like, to arrange it in just this way. As for hurting my life, you've been the most beautiful thing in it.'

Something in his voice, final acceptance, final resignation, as though, seeing her go for ever, he bowed his head in silence, filled her with intolerable sadness. Was it that she wanted still to need him, or was it that she could not bear the thought that he might, some day, no longer need her?

The sense of an end of things, chill and penetrating like an autumnal wind, made all life seem bleak and grey for the moment. 'But, Franklin, you will always be my friend. That is not changed,' she said. 'Please tell me that nothing of that side of things is changed, dear Franklin.'

And now that sincerity in him, that truth-seeing and truth-speaking quality that was his power, became suddenly direful. For though he looked at her ever so gently and ever so tenderly, his eyes pierced her. And, helplessly, he placed the truth before them both, saying: 'I'll always be your friend, of course, dear Althea. You'll always be the most beautiful thing I've had in my life; but what can I be in yours? I don't belong over here, you know. I'll not be in your life any longer. How can it not be changed? How will you stay my friend, dear Althea?'

The tears rolled down her cheeks. That he should see, and accept, and still love her, made him seem dearer than ever before, while, in her heart, she knew that he spoke the truth. 'Don't — don't, dear Franklin,' she pleaded. 'You will be often with us. Don't talk as if it were at an end. How could our friendship have an end? Don't let me think that you are leaving me.'

He smiled a little, but it was a valorous smile. 'I'll never leave you in that way.'

'Don't speak, then, as if I were leaving you.'

But Franklin, though he smiled the valorous smile, couldn't give her a consolation not his to give. Did he see clearly, and for the first time, that he had always counted for her as a solace, a substitute for the things he couldn't be, and that now, when these things had come to her, he counted really for nothing at all? If he did see it, he didn't resent it; he would understand that, too, even though it left him with no foothold in her life. But he couldn't pretend — to give her comfort — that she needed him any longer. 'I want to count for anything you'll let me count for,' he said; 'but — it isn't your fault, dear — I don't think I will ever count for much, now; I don't see how I can. If that's being left, I guess I am left.'

She gazed at him, and all that she had to offer was her longing that the truth were not the truth, and for the moment of silent confrontation her pain was so great that its pressure brought an involuntary cry — protest or presage — it felt like both. 'You will — you will count — for much more, dear Franklin.'

She didn't know that it was the truth; his seemed to be the final truth; but it came, and it had to be said, and he could accept it as her confession and her atonement.

CHAPTER XVII.

Franklin was gone and Sir Charles was gone, and Lady Pickering soon followed, not in the least discomfited by the unexpected turn of events. Lady Pickering could hardly have borne to suspect that Gerald preferred to flirt with Miss Jakes rather than with herself; that he preferred to marry her was nothing of an affront. Althea herself was very soon to return to America for a month with Aunt Julia and the girls, settle business matters and see old friends before turning her face, this time for good, to the country that was now to be her home.

Franklin was gone, and Gerald and Helen were left, and all that Gerald more and more meant, all that was bright and alien too — the things of joy and the things of adjustment and of wonder — effaced poor Franklin while it emphasised those painful truths that he had seen and shown her and that she had only been able to protest against. The thought of Franklin came hardly at all, though the truths he had put before her lingered in a haunting sense of disappointment with herself; she had failed Franklin in deeper, more subtle ways than in the mere shattering of his hopes.

Althea had never been a good business woman; her affairs were taken care of for her in Boston by wise and careful cousins; but she found that Gerald, in spite of his air of irresponsibility, was a very good business man, and it was he who pointed out to her, with cheerful and affectionate frankness, that her fortune was not as large as she, with her heretofore unexacting demands on it, had imagined. It was only when Althea took for granted that it could suffice for much larger, new demands, that Gerald pointed out the facts of limitation; to himself, he made this clear and sweet, the facts were amply sufficient; there was more than enough for his sober wants. But Althea, sitting over the papers with him in the library, and looking rather vague and wistful, realised that if Gerald's wants were to be the chief consideration many of her own must, indeed, go unsatisfied. Gerald evidently took it perfectly for granted that her wants would be his. Looking up at the flat and faded portraits of bygone Digbys, while this last one, his charming eyes lifted so brightly and so intelligently upon her, made things clear, looking up, over his head, at these ancestors of her affianced, Althea saw in their aspect of happy composure that they, too, had always taken it for granted that their wives' wants were just that — just their own wants. She couldn't — not at first — lucidly articulate to herself any marked divergence between her wants and Gerald's; she, too, wanted to see Merriston House restored and made again into a home for Digbys; but Merriston

House had been seen by her as a means, not as an end. She had seen it as a centre to a larger life; he saw it as a boundary beyond which they could not care to stray. After the golden bliss of the first days of her new life there, as Gerald's promised wife, there came for her a pause of rather perplexed reaction in this sense of limits, this sense of being placed in a position that she must keep, this strange sense of slow but sure metamorphosis into one of a succession of Mrs. Digbys whose wants were their husbands'.

'Yes, yes, I quite see, dear,' she said at intervals, while Gerald explained to her what it cost to keep up even such a small place. 'What a pity that those stocks of mine you were telling me about don't yield more. It isn't much we have, is it?'

'I think it's a great deal,' laughed Gerald. 'It's quite enough to be very happy on. And, first and foremost, when it's a question of happiness, and since you are so dear and generous, I shall be able to hunt at last and keep my own horses. I'm sick of being dependent on my friends for a mount now and then. Not that you'll have much sympathy with that particular form of happiness, I know,' he added, smiling, as he put his hand on her shoulder and scanned the next document.

Althea was silent for a moment. She hardly knew what the odd shock that went through her meant; then she recognised that it was fear. To see it as that gave her courage; at all events, love Gerald as she did, she would not be a coward for love of him. The effort was in her voice, making it tremulous, as she said: 'But, Gerald, you know I don't like hunting; you know I think it cruel.'

He looked at her; he smiled. 'So do I, you nice dear.'

'But you won't pain me by doing it — you will give it up?'

It was now his turn to look really a little frightened. 'But it's in my blood and bones, the joy of it, Althea. You wouldn't, seriously, ask me to give it up for a whim?'

'Oh, it isn't a whim.'

'A theory, then.'

'I think you ought to give it up for a theory like that one. Yes, I even think that you ought to give it up to please me.'

'But why shouldn't you give up your theory to please me?' He had turned his eyes on his papers now, and was feigning to scan them.

'It is a question of right and wrong to me.'

Gerald was silent for a moment. He was not irritated, she saw that; not angry. He quite recognised her point, and he didn't like her the less for holding to it; but he recognised his own point just as clearly, and, after the little pause, she found that he was resolute in holding to it.

'I'm afraid I can't give it up — even to please you, dear,' he said.

Althea sat looking down at the papers that lay on the table; she saw them through tears of helpless pain. There was nothing to be done and nothing to be said. She could not tell him that, since he did not love her sufficiently to give up a pleasure for her sake, she must give him up; nor could she tell him that he must not use her money for pleasures that she considered wrong. But it was this second impossible retort — the first, evidently, did not cross his mind — that was occupying Gerald. He was not slow in seeing delicacies, though he was slow indeed in seeing what might have been solemnities. The position couldn't strike him as solemn; he couldn't conceive that a woman might break off her engagement for such a cause; but he did see his own position of beneficiary as delicate.

His next words showed it: 'Of course I won't hunt here, if you really say not. I could go away to hunt. The difficulty is that we want to keep horses, don't we? and if I have a hunter it will be rather funny never to use him at home.'

Althea saw that it would be rather funny. 'If you have a hunter I would far rather you hunted here than that you went away to hunt.'

'Perhaps you'd rather I had a horse that couldn't hunt. The hunter would be your gift, of course. I could just go on depending on my friends for a mount, though that would look funny, too, wouldn't it?'

'If you will hunt, I want to give you your hunter.'

'In a sense it will be using your money to do something you disapprove of.' Gerald was smiling at her as though he felt that he was bringing her round to reasonableness. 'Perhaps that's ugly.'

'Please don't speak of the money; mine is yours.'

'That makes me seem all the dingier, I know,' said Gerald, half ruefully, yet still smiling at her. 'I do wish I could give it up, just to please you, but really I can't. You must just shut your eyes and pretend I'm not a brute.'

After this little encounter, which left its mark on Althea's heart, she felt that Gerald ought to be the more willing to yield in other things and to enter into her projects. 'Don't you think, dear,' she said to him a day or two after, when they were walking together, 'don't you think that you ought soon to be thinking of a seat in Parliament? That will be such a large, worthy life for you.'

Gerald, as they walked, was looking from right to left, happily, possessively, over the fields and woods. He brought his attention to her suggestion with a little effort, and then he laughed. 'Good gracious, no! I've no political views.'

'But oughtn't you to have them?'

'You shall provide me with them, dear.'

'Gladly; and will you use them?'

'Not in Parliament,' laughed Gerald.

'But seriously, dear, I hope you will think of it.'

He turned gay, protesting, and now astonished eyes upon her. 'But I can't think of it seriously. Old Battersby is a member for these parts, and his seat is as firm as a rock.'

'Can't you find another seat?'

'But, my dear, even if I had any leaning that way, which I haven't, where am I to find the time and money?'

'Give less time and money to hunting,' she could not repress.

But, over the sinking of her heart, she kept her voice light, and Gerald, all unsuspecting, answered, as if it were a harmless jest they were bandying, 'What a horrid score! But, yes, it's quite true; I want my time for hunting and farming and studying a bit, and then you mustn't forget that I enjoy dabbling at my painting in my spare moments and have the company of my wise and charming Althea to cultivate. I've quite enough to fill my time with.'

She was baffled, perplexed, and hurt. Her thoughts fixed with some irony on his painting. Dabble at it indeed. Gerald had shown her some of his sketches and they had hardly seemed to Althea to merit more than that description. Her own tastes had grown up securely framed by books and lectures. Her speciality was early Italian art. She liked pictures of Madonnas surrounded by exquisite accessories — all of which she accurately remembered. She didn't at all care for Japanese prints, and Gerald's sketches looked to her rather like Japanese prints. She really didn't imagine that he intended her to take them seriously, and when he had brought them out and shown them to her she had said, 'Pretty, very pretty indeed, dear; really you have talent, I'm sure of it. With hard work, under a good master, you might have become quite a painter.' She had then seen the little look of discomfiture on Gerald's face, though he laughed good-humouredly as he put away his sketches, saying to Helen, who was present, 'I'm put in my place, you see.'

Althea had hastened to add, 'But, dear, really I think them very pretty. They show quite a direct, simple feeling for colour. Don't they, Helen? Don't you feel with me that they are very pretty?'

Helen had said that she knew nothing about pictures, but liked Gerald's very much.

It was hard now to be asked to accept this vagrant artistry instead of the large, political life she had seen for him. And what of the London drawing-room?

'You must keep in touch with people, Gerald,' she said. 'You mustn't sink into the country squire for ever.'

'Oh, but that's just what I want to sink into,' said Gerald. 'Don't bother about people, though, dear. We can have plenty of people to stay with us, and go about a bit ourselves.'

'But we must be in London for part of the year,' said Althea.

'Oh, you will run up now and then for a week whenever you like,' said Gerald.

'A week! How can one keep in touch with what is going on in a week? Can't we take a little house there? One of those nice little old houses in Westminster, for example?'

'A house, my dear! Why, you don't want to leave Merriston, do you? What would become of Merriston if we had a house in London — and of all our plans? We really couldn't manage that, dear — we really couldn't afford it.'

Yes, she saw the life very distinctly, now; that of the former Mrs. Digbys — that of cheerful squiress and wise helpmate. And, charmed though she was with her lover, Althea was not charmed with that prospect. She promised herself that things should turn out rather differently. What was uncomfortable already was to find that her promises were becoming vague and tentative. There was a new sense of bondage. Bliss was in it, but the bonds began to chafe.

CHAPTER XVIII.

On a chill day in late October, Franklin Winslow Kane walked slowly down a narrow street near Eaton Square examining the numbers on the doors as he passed. He held his umbrella open over his shoulder, for propitiation rather than for shelter, since the white fog had not yet formed into a drizzle. His trousers were turned up, and his feet, wisely, for the streets were wet and slimy, encased in neat galoshes. After a little puzzling at the end of the street, where the numbers became confusing, he found the house he sought on the other side — a narrow house, painted grey, a shining knocker upon its bright green door, and rows of evenly clipped box in each window. Franklin picked his way over the road and rang the bell. This was his first stay in London since his departure from Merriston in August. He had been in Oxford, in Cambridge, in Birmingham, and Edinburgh. He had made friends and found many interests. The sense of scientific links between his own country and England had much enlarged his consciousness of world-citizenship. He had ceased altogether to feel like a tourist, he had almost ceased to feel like an alien; how could he feel so when he had come to know so many people who had exactly his own interests? This wider scope of understanding sympathy was the main enlargement that had come to him, at least it was the main enlargement for his own consciousness. Another enlargement there was, but it seemed purely personal and occupied his thoughts far less.

He waited now upon the doorstep of old Miss Buchanan's London house, and he had come there to call upon young Miss Buchanan. The memory of Helen's unobtrusive, wonderfully understanding kindness to him during his last days at Merriston, remained for him as the only bright spot in a desolate blankness. He had not seen her again. She had been paying visits, but she had written in return to a note of inquiry from Cambridge, to say that she was settled, now, in London for a long time and that she would be delighted to see him on the day he suggested — that of his arrival in town.

He was ushered by the most staid, most crisp of parlour-maids, not into Helen's own little sanctum downstairs, but into the drawing-room. It was a narrow room, running to the back of the house where a long window showed a ghostly tree in the fog outside, and it was very much crowded with over-large furniture gathered together from Miss Buchanan's past. There were chintz-covered chairs and sofas that one had to make one's way around, and there were cabinets filled with china, and there were tables with reviews and book-cutters laid out on them. And it was the most cheerful of rooms; three canaries sang loudly in a spacious gilt cage that stood in a window, the tea-table was laid before the fire, and the leaping firelight played on the massive form of the black cat, dozing in his basket, on the gilt of the canaries' cage, on the china in the cabinets, the polished surface of the chintz, and the copper kettle on the tea-table.

Franklin stood and looked about him, highly interested. He liked to think that Helen had such a comfortable refuge to fall back upon, though by the time that old Miss Buchanan appeared he had reflected that so much comfort might be just the impediment that had prevented her from taking to her wings as he felt persuaded she could and should do. Old Miss Buchanan interested him even more than her room. She was a firm, ample woman of over sixty, with plentiful grey hair brushed back uncompromisingly from her brow, tight lips, small, attentive eyes with projecting eyebrows over them, and an expression at once of reticence and cordiality. She wore a black dress of an old-fashioned cut, and round her neck was a heavy gold chain and a large gold locket.

Helen would be in directly, she said, and expected him.

Franklin saw at once that she took him for granted, and that she was probably in the habit of taking all Helen's acquaintances for granted, and of making them comfortable until Helen came and took them off her hands. She had, he inferred, many interests of her own, and did not waste much conjecture on stray callers. Franklin was quite content to count as a stray caller, and he had always conjecture enough for two in any encounter. He talked away in his even, deliberate tones, while they drank tea and ate the hottest of muffins that stood in a covered dish on a brass tripod before the fire, and, while they talked, Miss Buchanan shot rather sharper glances at him from under her eyebrows.

'So you were at Merriston with Helen's Miss Jakes,' she said, placing him. 'It made a match, that party, didn't it? Quite a good thing for Gerald Digby, too, I hear. Miss Jakes is soon to be back, Helen tells me.'

'Next week,' said Franklin.

'And the wedding for November.'

'So I'm told.'

'You've known Miss Jakes for some time?'

'For almost all my life,' said Franklin, with his calm and candid smile.

'Oh, old friends, then. You come from Boston, too, perhaps?'

'Well, I come from the suburbs, in the first place, but I've been in the hub itself for a long time now,' said Franklin. 'Yes, I'm a very old friend of Miss Jakes's. I'm very much attached to her.'

'Ah, and are you pleased with the match?'

'It seems to please Althea, and that's the main thing. I think Mr. Digby will make her happy; yes, I'm pleased.'

'Yes,' said Miss Buchanan meditatively. 'Yes, I suppose Gerald Digby will make a pleasant husband. He's a pleasant creature. I've always considered him very selfish, I confess; but women seem to fall in love with selfish men.'

Franklin received this ambiguous assurance with a moment or so of silence, and then remarked that marriage might make Mr. Digby less selfish.

'You mean,' said Miss Buchanan, 'that she's selfish too, and won't let him have it all his own way?'

Franklin did not mean that at all. 'Life with a high-minded, true-hearted woman sometimes alters a man,' he commented.

'Oh, she's that, is she?' said Miss Buchanan. 'I've not met her yet, you see. Well, I don't know that I've much expectation of seeing Gerald Digby alter. But he's a pleasant creature, as I said, and I don't think he's a man to make any woman unhappy. In any case your friend is probably better off married to a pleasant, selfish man than not married at all,' and Miss Buchanan smiled a tight, kindly smile. 'I don't like this modern plan of not getting married. I want all the nice young women I know to get married, and the sooner the better; it gives them less time to fuss over their feelings.'

'Well, it's better to fuss before than after, isn't it?' Franklin inquired.

'Fussing after doesn't do much harm,' said Miss Buchanan, 'and there's not so much time for fussing then. It's fussing before that leaves so many of the nicest girls old maids. My niece Helen is the nicest girl I know, and I sometimes think she'll never marry now. It vexes me very much,' said Miss Buchanan.

'She's a very nice girl,' said Franklin. 'And she's a very noble woman. But she doesn't know it; she doesn't know her own capacities. I'm very much attached to your niece, Miss Buchanan.'

Miss Buchanan shot him another glance and then laughed. 'Well, we can shake hands over that,' she remarked. 'So am I. And you are quite right; she is a fine creature and she's never had a chance.'

'Ah, that's just my point,' said Franklin gravely. 'She ought to have a chance; it ought to be made for her, if she can't make it for herself. And she's too big a person for that commonplace solution of yours, Miss Buchanan. You're of the old ideas, I see; you don't think of women as separate individuals, with their own worth and identity. You think of them as borrowing worth and identity from some man. Now that may be good enough for the nice girl who's only a nice girl, but it's not good enough for your niece, not good enough for a noble woman. I'd ask a happy marriage for her, of course, but I'd ask a great deal more. She ought to put herself to some work, develop herself, find herself all round.'

Miss Buchanan, while Franklin delivered himself of these convictions, leaned back in her chair, her arms crossed on her bosom, and observed him with amused intentness. When he had done, she thus continued to observe him for some moments of silence. 'No, I'm of the old ideas,' she said at last. 'I don't want work for Helen, or development, or anything of that sort. I want happiness and the normal life. I don't care about women doing things, in that sense, unless they've nothing better to do. If Helen were married to a man of position and ability she would have quite enough to occupy her. Women like Helen are made to hold and decorate great positions; it's the ugly, the insignificant women, who can do the work of the world.'

Franklin heard her with a cheerful, unmoved countenance, and after a moment of reflection observed, 'Well, that seems to me mighty hard on the women who aren't ugly and insignificant — mighty hard,' and as Miss Buchanan looked mystified, he was going on to demonstrate to her that to do the work of the world was every human creature's highest privilege, when Helen entered.

Franklin, as he rose and saw his friend again, had a new impression of her and a rather perturbing one. Little versed as he was in the lore of the world — the world in Miss Buchanan's sense — he felt that Helen, perhaps, expressed what Miss Buchanan could not prove. It was true, her lovely, recondite personality seemed to flash it before him, she didn't fit easily into his theories of efficiency and self-development by effort. Effort — other people's effort — seemed to have done long ago all that was necessary for her. She was developed, she was finished, she seemed to belong to quite another order of things from that which he believed in, to an order framed for her production, as it were, and justified, perhaps, by her mere existence. She was like a flower, and ought a flower to be asked to do more than to show itself and bloom in silence?

Franklin hardly formulated these heresies; they hovered, only, as a sort of atmosphere that had its charm and yet its sadness too, and that seemed, in charm and sadness, to be part of Helen Buchanan's very being.

She had taken his hand and was looking at him with those eyes of distant kindness — so kind and yet so distant — and she said in the voice that was so sincere and so decisive, a voice sweet and cold as a mountain brook, that she was very glad to see him again.

Yes, she was like a flower, a flower removed immeasurably from his world; a flower in a crystal vase, set on a high and precious cabinet, and to be approached only over stretches of shining floor. What had he to do with, or to think of, such a young woman who, though poverty-stricken, looked like a princess, and who, though smiling, had at her heart, he knew, a despair of life?

'I'm very glad indeed to see you,' he said gravely, despite himself, and scanning her face; 'it seems a very long time.'

'Does that mean that you have been doing a great deal?'

'Yes; and I suppose it means that I've missed you a great deal, too,' said Franklin. 'I got into the habit of you at Merriston; I feel it's queer not to find you in a chair under a tree every day.'

'I know,' said Helen; 'one gets so used to people at country houses; it's seeing them at breakfast that does it, I think. It was nice under that tree, wasn't it? and how lazy I was. I'm much more energetic now; I've got to the Purgatory, with the dictionary. Am I to have a fresh pot of tea to myself, kind Aunt Grizel? You see how I am spoiled, Mr. Kane.'

She had drawn off her gloves and tossed aside her long, soft coat — that looked like nobody else's coat — and, thin and black and idle, she sat in a low chair by the fire, and put out her hand for her cup. 'I've been to a musical,' she said. And she told them how she had been wedged into a corner for an interminable sonata and hadn't been able to get away. 'I tried to, once, but my hostess saw me and made a most ominous hiss at me; every one's eye was turned on me, and I sank back again, covered with shame and confusion.'

Then she questioned him, and Franklin told her about his interesting little tour, and the men he had met and the work they were doing. 'Splendid work, I can tell you,' said Franklin, 'and you have splendid men. It's been a great time for me; it's done me a lot of good. I feel as if I'd got hold of England; it's almost like being at home when you find so many splendid people interested in the things that interest you.'

And presently, after a little pause, in which he contemplated the fire, he added, lifting his eyes to Helen and smiling over the further idea: 'And see here, I'm forgetting another thing that's happened to me since I saw you.'

'Something nice, I hope.'

'Well, that depends on how one looks at it,' said Franklin, considering. 'I can't say that it pleases me; it rather oppresses me, in fact. But I'm going to get even with it, though that will take thought — thought and training.'

'It sounds as though you were going to be a jockey.'

'No, I'm not going to be a jockey,' said Franklin. 'It's more solemn than you think. What do you say to this? I'm a millionaire; I'm a multi-millionaire. If that isn't solemn I don't know what is.'

Miss Grizel Buchanan put down the long golf-stocking she was knitting, and, over her spectacles, fixed her eyes on the strange young man who had delayed till now the telling of this piece of news. She examined him. In all her experience she had never come across anything like him. Helen gave a little exclamation.

'My dear Mr. Kane, I do congratulate you,' she said.

'Why?' asked Franklin.

'Why, it's glorious news,' said Helen.

'I don't know about that,' said Franklin. 'I'm not a glorious person. The mere fact of being a millionaire isn't glorious; it may be lamentable.'

'The mere fact of power is glorious. What shall you do?' asked Helen, gazing thoughtfully at him as though to see in him all the far, new possibilities.

'Well, I shall do as much as I can for my own science of physics — that is rather glorious, I own. I shall be able to help the first-rate men to get at all sorts of problems, perhaps. Yes, that is rather glorious.'

'And won't you build model villages and buy a castle and marry a princess?'

'I don't like castles and I don't know anything about princesses,' said Franklin, smiling. 'As for philanthropy, I'll let people wiser than I am at it think out plans for doing good with the money. I'll devote myself to doing what I know something about. I do know something about physics, and I believe I can do something in that direction.'

'You take your good fortune very calmly, Mr. Kane,' Miss Grizel now observed. 'How long have you known about it?'

'Well, I heard a week ago, and news has been piling in ever since. I'm fairly snowed up with cables,' said Franklin. 'It's an old uncle of mine — my mother's brother — who's left it to me. He always liked me; we were always great friends. He went out west and built railroads and made a fortune — honestly, too; the money is clean — as clean as you can get it nowadays, that is to say. I couldn't take it if it wasn't. The only thing to do with money that isn't clean is to hand it over to the people it's been wrongfully taken from — to the nation, you know. It's a pity that isn't done; it would be a lot better than building universities and hospitals with it — though it's a problem; yes, I know it's a problem.' Franklin seemed today rather oppressed with a sense of problems. He gave this one up after a thoughtful survey of the fire, and went on: 'He was a fine old fellow, my uncle; I didn't see him often, but we sometimes wrote, and he used to like to hear how I was getting on in my work. He didn't know much about it; I don't think he ever got over thinking that atoms were a sort of bug,' Franklin smiled, unaware of his listeners' surprise; 'but he seemed to like to hear, so I always told him everything I'd time to write about. It made me sad to hear he'd gone; but it was a fine life, yes, it was a mighty big, fine, useful life,' said Franklin Kane, looking thoughtfully into the fire. And while he looked, musing over his memories, Miss Buchanan and her niece exchanged glances. 'This is a very odd creature, and a very nice one,' Miss Grizel's glance said; and Helen's replied, with playful eyebrows and tender lips, 'Isn't he a funny dear?'

'Now, see here,' said Franklin, looking up from his appreciative retrospect and coming back to the present and its possibilities, 'now that I've got all this money, you must let me spend a little of it on having good times. You must let me take you to plays and concerts — anything you've time for; and I hope, Miss Buchanan,' said Franklin, turning his bright gaze upon the older lady, 'that I can persuade you to come too.'

Helen said that she would be delighted, and Miss Grizel avowed herself a devoted playgoer, and Franklin, taking out his notebook, inscribed their willingness to do a play on Wednesday night. 'Now,' he said, scanning its pages, 'Althea lands on Friday and Mr. Digby goes to meet her, I suppose. They must come in, too; we'll all have fun together.'

'Gerald can't meet her,' said Helen; 'he has an engagement in the country, and doesn't get back to London till Saturday. It's an old standing engagement for a ball. I'm to welcome Althea back to London for him.'

Franklin paused, his notebook in his hand, and looked over it at Helen. He seemed taken aback, though at once he mastered his surprise. 'Oh, is that so?' was his only comment. Then he added, after a moment's reflection: 'Well, I guess I'll run up and meet her myself, then. I've always met and seen her off in America, and we'll keep up the old custom on this side.'

'That would be very nice of you,' said Helen. 'Of course she has that invaluable Amélie to look after her, and, of course, Gerald knew that she would be all right, or he would have managed it.'

'Of course,' said Franklin. 'And we'll keep up the old custom.'

That evening there arrived for Miss Buchanan and her niece two large boxes — one for Miss Grizel, containing carnations and roses, and one for Helen containing violets. Also, for the younger lady, was a smaller — yet still a large box — of intricately packed and very sophisticated sweets. Upon them Mr. Kane had laid a card which read: 'I don't approve of them, but I'm sending them in the hope that you do.' Another box for Miss Grizel contained fresh groundsel and chickweed for her canaries.

CHAPTER XIX.

Althea was an excellent sailor and her voyage back to England was as smooth and as swift as money could make it. She had been seen off by many affectionate friends, and, since leaving America, the literature, the flowers and the fruit with which they had provided her had helped to pass the hours, tedious at best on shipboard. Two other friends, not so near, but very pleasant — they were New York people — were also making the voyage, but as they were all very seasick, intercourse with them consisted mainly in looking in upon them as they lay, mute and enduring, within their berths, and cheering them with the latest reports of progress. Althea looked in upon them frequently, and she read all her books, and much of her time, besides, had been spent in long, formless meditations — her eyes fixed on the rippled, grey expanse of the Atlantic while she lay encased in furs on her deck chair. These meditations were not precisely melancholy, it was rather a brooding sense of vague perplexity that filled the dreamlike hours. She had left her native land, and she was speeding towards her lover and towards her new life; there might have been exhilaration as well as melancholy in these facts. But though she was not melancholy, she was not exhilarated. It was a confused regret that came over her in remembering Boston, and it was a confused expectancy that filled her when she looked forward to Gerald. Gerald had written to her punctually once a week while she had been in America, short, but very vivid, very interesting and affectionate letters. They told her about what he was doing, what he was reading, the people he saw and his projects for their new life together. He took it for granted that this was what she wanted, and of course it was what she wanted, only — and it was here that the confused regrets arose in remembering Boston — the letters received there, where she was so much of a centre and so little of a satellite, had seemed, in some way, lacking in certain elements that Boston supplied, but that Merriston House, she more and more distinctly saw, would never offer. She was, for her own little circle, quite important in Boston. At Merriston House she would be important only as Gerald Digby's wife and as the mistress of his home, and that indeed — this was another slightly confusing fact — would not be great importance. Even in Boston, she had felt, her importance was still entirely personal; she had gained none from her coming marriage. Her friends were perfectly accustomed to the thought of coronets and ancient estates in connection with foreign alliances, and Althea was a little vexed in feeling that they really did not appreciate at its full value the significance of a simple English gentleman with a small country seat.

'I suppose you'll live quite quietly, Althea, dear,' more than one old friend had said, with an approbation not altogether grateful to her. 'Your aunt tells me that it's such a nice little place, your future home. I'm so glad you are not making a great worldly match.' Althea had no wish to make a great worldly match, but she did not care that her friends should see her upon such an over-emphatically sober background.

The report of Gerald's charm had been the really luminous fact in her new situation, and it had been most generously spread by Aunt Julia. Althea had felt warmed by the compensatory brightness it cast about her. Althea Jakes was not going to make a great match, but she was, and everybody knew it, going to marry a 'perfectly charming' man. This, after all, was to be crowned with beams. It was upon the thought of that charm that she dwelt when the long meditations became oppressively confused. She might be giving up certain things — symbolised by the books, the fruit, the flowers, that testified to her importance in Boston; she might be going to accept certain difficulties and certain disappointments, but the firm ground on which she stood was the fact that Gerald was charming. At moments she felt herself yearn towards that charm; it was a reviving radiance in which she must steep her rather numbed and rather weary being. To see his eyes, to see his smile, to hear his voice that made her think of bells and breezes, would be enough to banish wistfulness, or, at all events, to put it in its proper place as merely temporary and negligible.

Althea's heart beat fast as the shores of Ireland stole softly into sight on a pearly horizon, and it really fluttered, like that of any love-sick girl, when her packet of letters was brought to her at Queenstown. In Gerald's she would feel the central rays coming out to greet her. But when she had read Gerald's letter it was as if a blank curtain had fallen before her, shutting out all rays. He was not coming to meet her at Liverpool. The sharpness of her dismay was like a box on the ear, and it brought tears to her eyes and anger to her heart. Yes, actually, with no contrition, or consciousness of the need for it, he said quite gaily and simply that he would see her in London on Saturday; he had a ball in the country for Friday night. He offered not the least apology. He was perfectly unaware of guilt. And it was this innocence that, after the first anger, filled poor Althea with fear. What did it bode for the future? Meanwhile there was the humiliating fact to face that she, the cherished and appreciated Althea, who had never returned to America without at least three devoted friends to welcome her, was to land on the dismal Liverpool docks and find no lover to greet her there. What would Mrs. Peel and Sally Arlington think when they saw her so bereft? It was the realisation of what they would think, the memory of the American wonder at the Englishman's traditional indifference to what the American woman considered her due in careful chivalry, that roused her pride to the necessity of self-preservation. Mrs. Peel and Sally, at all events, should not imagine her to be either angry or surprised. She would show them the untroubled matter-of-fact of the English wife. And she succeeded admirably in this. When Miss Arlington, sitting up and dressed at last, said, in Mrs. Peel's cabin, where, leaning on Althea's arm, she had feebly crept to tea, 'And what fun, Althea, to think that we shall see him tomorrow morning,' Althea opened candidly surprised eyes: 'See him? Who, dear?'

'Why, Mr. Digby, of course. Who else could be him?' said Miss Arlington.

'But he isn't coming to Liverpool,' said Althea blandly.

'Not coming to meet you?' Only tact controlled the amazement in Miss Arlington's question.

'Didn't you know? Gerald is a very busy man; he has had a long-standing engagement for this week, and besides I shouldn't have liked him to come. I'd far rather meet comfortably in London, where I shall see him the first thing on Saturday. And then you'll see him too.'

She only wished that she could really feel, what she showed them — such calm, such reasonableness, and such detachment.

It was with a gloomy eye that she surveyed the Liverpool docks in the bleak dawn next morning, seated in her chair, Amélie beside her, a competent Atlas, bearing a complicated assortment of bags, rugs, and wraps. No, she had nothing to hope from these inhospitable shores; no welcoming eyes were there to greet hers. It was difficult not to cry as she watched the ugly docks draw near and saw the rows of ugly human faces upturned upon it — peculiarly ugly in colour the human face at this hour of the morning. Then, suddenly, Amélie made a little exclamation and observed in dispassionate yet approving tones, 'Tiens; et voilà Monsieur Frankline.'

'Who? Where?' Althea rose in her chair.

'Mais oui; c'est bien Monsieur Frankline,' Amélie pointed. 'Voilà ce qui est gentil, par exemple,' and by this comment of Amélie's Althea knew that Gerald's absence was observed and judged. She got out of her chair, yet with a strange reluctance. It was not pleasure that she felt; it was, rather, a fuller realisation of pain. Going to the railing she looked down at the wharf. Yes, there was Franklin's pale buff-coloured countenance raised to hers, serene and smiling. He waved his hat. Althea was only able not to look dismayed and miserable in waving back. That Franklin should care enough to come; that Gerald should care too little.

But she drew herself together to smile brightly down upon her faithful lover. Franklin — Franklin above all — must not guess what she was feeling.

'Well,' were his first words, as she came down the gangway, 'I thought we'd keep up our old American habits.' The words, she felt, were very tactful; they made things easier for her; they even comforted her a little. One mustn't be too hard on Gerald if it was an American habit.

'It *is* a nice one,' she said, grasping Franklin's hand. 'I must make Gerald acquire it.'

'Why don't you keep it for me?' smiled Franklin. She felt, as he piloted her to the Customs, that either his tact or his ingenuousness was sublime. She leaned on it, whichever it was.

'Have you seen Gerald?' she asked, as they stood beside her marshalled array of boxes. 'He seemed very fit and happy in the letters I had at Queenstown.'

'No, I've not seen him yet,' smiled Franklin, looking about to catch the eye of an official.

'Then' — was on the tip of Althea's tongue — 'how did you know I was not going to be met?' She checked the revealing question, and Franklin's next remark — whether tactful or ingenuous in its appropriateness she once more could not tell — answered it: 'I've been seeing a good deal of Miss Buchanan; she told me Mr. Digby wouldn't be able to come up here.'

'Oh — Helen!' Althea was thankful to be able to pass from the theme of Gerald and his inabilities. 'So you have been seeing her. Have you been long in London? Have you seen her often?'

'I got to London last Monday, and I've seen her as often as she could let me. We're very good friends, you know,' said Franklin.

She didn't know at all, and she found the information rather bewildering. At Merriston her own situation had far too deeply absorbed her to leave her much attention for other people's. She had only noticed that Helen had been kind to Franklin. She suspected that it was now his ingenuousness that idealised Helen's tolerant kindness. But though her superior sophistication made a little touch of irony unavoidable, it was overwhelmed in the warm sense of gratitude.

Everything was in readiness for her; her corner seat in the train, facing the engine; a foot-warmer; the latest magazines, and a box of fruit. How it all brought back Boston — dear Boston — and the reviving consciousness of imaginative affection. And how it brought back Franklin. Well, everybody ought to be his good friend, even if they weren't so in reality.

'You didn't suppose I'd forget you liked muscatels?' inquired Franklin, with a mild and unreproachful gentleness when she exclaimed over the nectarines and grapes. 'Now, please, sit back and let me put this rug around you; it's chilly, and you look rather pale.' He then went off and looked out for her friends and for Amélie. Mrs. Peel and Sally, when they arrived with him, showed more than the general warmth of compatriots in a foreign land. They knew Franklin but slightly, and he could but have counted with them as one of Althea's former suitors; but now, she saw it, he took his place in their eyes as the devoted friend, and, as the journey went on, counted for more and more in his own right. Sally and Mrs. Peel evidently thought Franklin a dear. Althea thought so too, her eyes dwelling on him with wistful observation. There was no charm; there never had been charm; but the thought of charm sickened her a little just now. What she rested in was this affection, this kindness, this constant devotion that had never failed her in the greatest or the littlest things. And though it was not to see him change into a different creature, not to see him move on into a different category — as he had changed and moved in the eyes of the Miss Buchanans — he did gain in significance when, after a little while, he informed them of the new fact in his life — the fact of millions. They were Americans of an old stock, and millions meant to them very external and slightly suspicious things — things associated with rawness and low ideals; but they couldn't associate Franklin with low ideals. They exclaimed with interest and sympathy over his adventure, and they felt nothing funny in his projects for benefiting physics. They all understood each other; they took light things — like millions — lightly, and grave things — like ideals and responsibilities — gravely. And, ah yes, there it was — Althea turning her head to look at the speeding landscape of autumnal pearl and gold, thought, over her sense of smothered tears — they knew what things were really serious. They couldn't mistake the apparent for the real triviality; they knew that some symbols of affection — trifling as they might be — were almost necessary. But then they understood affection. It was at this point that her sore heart sank to a leaden depression. Affection — cherishing, forestalling, imaginative affection — there was no lack of it, she was sure of that, in this beautiful England of pearl and gold which, in its melancholy, its sweetness, its breathing out of memories immemorial, so penetrated and possessed her; but was there not a terrible lack of it in the England that was to be hers, and where she was to make her home?

CHAPTER XX.

It was four days after Althea's arrival in London that Gerald stood in Helen's sitting-room and confronted her — smoking her cigarette in her low chair — as he had confronted her that summer on her return from Paris. Gerald looked rather absent and he looked rather worried, and Helen, who had observed these facts the moment he came in, was able to observe them for some time while he stood there before her, not looking at her, looking at nothing in particular, his eyes turning vaguely from the mist-enveloped trees outside to the flowers on the writing-table, and his eyebrows, always very expressive, knitting themselves a little or lifting as if in the attempt to dispel recurrent and oppressive pre-occupations. It would have been natural in their free intercourse that, after a certain lapse of time, Helen should ask him what the matter was, helping him often, with the mere question, to recog-nise that something was the matter. But today she said nothing, and it was her silence instead of her questioning that made Gerald aware that he was standing there expecting to have his state of mind probed and then elucidated. It added a little to his sense of perplexity that Helen should be silent, and it was with a slight irri-tation that he turned and kicked a log before saying — 'I'm rather bothered, Helen.'

'What is it?' said Helen. 'Money?' This had often been a bother to them both.

Half turned from her, he shook his head. 'No, not money; that's all right now, thanks to Althea.'

'Well?' Helen questioned.

He faced her again, a little quizzical, a little confused and at a loss. 'I suppose it's Althea herself.'

'Oh!' said Helen. She said it with a perceptible, though very mild change of tone; but Gerald, in his preoccupation, did not notice the change.

'You've seen her several times since she came back?' he asked.

'Yes, twice; I lunched with her and these American friends of hers yesterday,' said Helen.

'Well, I've seen her three times,' said Gerald. 'I went to her, as you know, directly I got back to London on Saturday; I cut my visit at the Fanshawes two days shorter on purpose. I saw her on Sunday, and I'm just come from her now. No one could say that I didn't show her every attention, could they?' It hardly seemed a question, and Helen did not answer it. 'I don't think she's quite pleased with me,' Gerald then brought out.

Still silent, Helen looked at him thoughtfully, but her gaze gave him no clue.

'Can you imagine why not?' he asked.

She reflected, then she said that she couldn't.

'Well,' said Gerald, 'I think it's because I didn't go to meet her at Liverpool; from something she said, I think it's that. But I never dreamed she'd mind, you know. And, really, I ask you, Helen, is it reasonable to expect a man to give up a long-standing engagement and take that dreary journey up to that dreary place — I've never seen the Liverpool docks, but I can imagine them at six o'clock in the morning — is it reasonable, I say, to expect that of any man? It wasn't as if I wasn't to see her the next day.'

Again Helen carefully considered. 'I suppose she found the docks very dreary — at six o'clock,' she suggested.

'But surely that's not a reason for wanting me to find them dreary too,' Gerald laughed rather impatiently. 'I'd have had to go up to Liverpool on Thursday and spend the night there; do you realise that?'

Helen went on with the theme of the docks: 'I suppose she wouldn't have found them so dreary if you'd been on them; and I suppose she expected you not to find them dreary for the same reason.'

Gerald contemplated this lucid statement of the case. 'Has she talked to you about it?' he asked.

'Not a word. Althea is very proud. If you have hurt her it is the last thing that she would talk about.'

'I know she's proud and romantic, and a perfect dear, of course; but do you really think it a ground for complaint? I mean — would you have felt hurt in a similar case?'

'I? No, I don't suppose so; but Althea, I think, is used to a great deal of consideration.'

'But, by Jove, Helen, I'm not inconsiderate!'

'Not considerate, in the way Althea is used to.'

'Ah, that's just it,' said Gerald, as if, now, they had reached the centre of his difficulty; 'and I can't pretend to be, either. I can't pretend to be like Mr. Kane. Imagine that quaint little fellow going up to meet her. You must own it's rather grotesque — rather taste-less, too, I think, under the circumstances.'

'They are very old friends.'

'Well, but after all, he's Althea's rejected suitor.'

'It wasn't as a suitor, it was as a friend he went. The fact that she rejected him doesn't make him any less her friend, or any less solicitous about her.'

'It makes me look silly, her rejected suitor showing more solic-itude than I do — unless it makes him look silly; I rather feel it's that way. But, apart from that, about Althea, I'm really bothered. It's all right, of course; I've brought her round. I laughed at her a little and teased her a little, and told her not to be a dear little goose, you know. But, Helen, deuce take it! the trouble is — ' Again Gerald turned and kicked the log, and then, his hands on the mantelpiece, he gazed with frowning intentness into the flames. 'She takes it all so much more seriously than I do,' so he finally brought out his distress; 'so much more seriously than I can, you know. It's all right, of course; only one doesn't know quite how to get on.' And now, turning to Helen, he found her eyes on his, and her silence became significant to him. There was no response in her eyes; they were veiled, mute; they observed him; they told him nothing. And he had a sense, new to him and quite inexpressibly painful, of being shut out. 'I may go on talking to you — about everything — as I have always done, Helen?' he said. It was hardly a question; he couldn't really dream that there was anything not to be talked out with Helen. But there was. Gerald received one of the ugliest shocks of his life when Helen said to him in her careful voice: 'You may not talk about Althea to me; not about her feeling for you — or yours for her.'

There was a pause after this, and then Gerald got out: 'I say — Helen!' on a long breath, staring at her. 'You mean — ' he stammered a little.

'That you owe it to Althea — just because we had to talk her over once, before you were sure that you wanted to make her your wife — not to discuss her feelings or her relation to you with anybody, now that she is to be your wife. I should think you would see that for yourself, Gerald. I should think you would see that Althea would not marry you if she thought that you were capable of talking her over with me.'

Gerald had flushed deeply and vividly. 'But Helen — with *you*!' he murmured. It was a helpless appeal, a helpless protest. His whole life seemed to rise up and confront her with the contrast between their reality — his relation and hers — and the relative triviality of this new episode in his life. And there was his error, and there her inexorable opposition; the episode was one no longer; he must not treat it as trivial, a matter for mutual musings and conjectures. His 'With you!' shook Helen's heart; but, looking past him and hard at the fire, she only moved her head in slow, slight, and final negation.

Gerald was silent for a long time, and she knew that he was gazing at her as a dog gazes when some inexorable and inexplicable refusal turns its world to emptiness. And with her pain for his pain came the rising of old anger and old irony against him; for whose fault was it that even the bitter joy of perfect freedom was cut off? Who had been so blind as not to see that a wife must, in common loyalty, bring circumspection and a careful drawing of

limits? Who was it who, in his folly, had not known that his impulsive acquiescence, his idle acceptance of the established comfort
and order held out to him, had cut away half of their friendship?
Absurd for Gerald, now, to feel reproach and injury. For when he
spoke again it was, though in careful tones, with uncontrollable
reproach. 'You know, Helen, I never expected this. I don't know
that I'd have been able to face this — ' He checked himself; already
he had learned something of what was required of him. 'It's like
poisoning part of my life for me.'

Helen did not allow the bitter smile to curl her lips; her inner
rejoinder answered him with: 'Whose fault is it that all my life is
poisoned?'

'After all,' said Gerald, and now with a tremor in his voice, 'an
old friend — a friend like you — a more than sister — is nearer
than any new claims.' She had never heard Gerald's voice break
before — for anything to do with her, at least — and she felt that
her cheek whitened in hearing it; but she was able to answer in the
same even tones: 'I don't think so. No one can be near enough to
talk about your wife with you.'

He then turned his back and looked for a long time into the
fire. She guessed that there were tears in his eyes, and that he was
fighting with anger, pain, and amazement, and the knowledge
filled her with cruel joy and with a torturing pity. She longed to tell
him that she hated him, and she longed to put her arms around
him and to comfort him — comfort him because he was going to
marry some one else, and must be loyal to the woman preferred as
wife. It was she, however, who first recovered herself. She got up
and pinched a withered flower from the fine azalea that Franklin
Kane had sent her the day before, and, dropping it into the waste-
paper basket, she said at last, very resolutely, 'Come, Gerald, don't
be silly.'

He showed her now the face of a miserable, sulky boy, and
Helen, smiling at him, went on: 'We have a great many other subjects of conversation, you will recollect. We can still talk about all
the things we used to talk about. Sit down, and don't look like that,
or I shall be angry with you.'

She knew her power over him; it was able to deceive him as to
their real situation, and this was to have obeyed pity, not anger.
Half unwillingly he smiled a little, and, rubbing his hand through
his hair and sinking into a chair, he said: 'Laugh at me if you feel
like it; I'm ill-used.'

'Terribly ill-used, indeed,' said Helen. 'I shall go on laughing
at you while you are so ridiculous. Now tell me about the ball at
the Fanshawes, and who was there, and who was the prettiest
woman in the room.'

CHAPTER XXI.

Althea had intended to fix the time of her marriage for the end of November; but, not knowing quite why, she felt on her return to England that she would prefer a slightly more distant date. It might be foolish to give oneself more time for uneasy meditation, yet it might be wise to give oneself more time for feeling the charm. The charm certainly worked. While Gerald opened his innocent, yet so intelligent eyes, rallied her on her dejection, called her a dear little goose, and kissed her in saying it, she had known that however much he might hurt her she was helplessly in love with him. In telling him that she would marry him just before Christmas — they were to have their Christmas in the Riviera — she didn't intend that he should be given more opportunities for hurting her, but more opportunities for charming her. Helplessly as she might love, her heart was a tremulously careful one; it could not rush recklessly to a goal nor see the goal clearly when pain intervened. It was not now actual pain or doubt it had to meet, but it was that mist of confusion, wonder, and wistfulness; it needed to be dispersed, and Gerald, she felt sure, would disperse it. Gerald, after a questioning lift of his eyebrows, acquiesced very cheerfully in the postponement. After all, they really didn't know each other very well; they would shake down into each other's ways all the more quickly, after marriage, for the wisdom gained by a longer engagement. He expressed these reasonable resignations to Althea, who smiled a little wanly over them.

She was now involved in the rush of new impressions. They were very crowded. She was to have but a fortnight of London and then, accompanied by Mrs. Peel and Sally, to go to Merriston for another fortnight or so before coming back to London for final preparations. Gerald was to be at Merriston for part of the time, and Miss Harriet Robinson was coming over from Paris to sustain and guide her through the last throes of her trousseau. Already every post brought solemn letters from Miss Robinson filled with detailed questionings as to the ordering of *lingerie*. So it was really in this fortnight of London that she must gain her clearest impression of what her new environment was to be; there would be no time later on.

There were two groups of impressions that she felt herself, rather breathlessly, observing; one group was made by Helen and Franklin and herself, and one by Gerald's friends and relatives, with Gerald himself as a bright though uncertain centre to it.

Gerald's friends and relations were all very nice to her and all very charming people. She had never, she thought, met so many people at once to whom the term might be applied. Their way of dressing, their way of talking, their way of taking you, themselves, and everything so easily, seemed as nearly perfect, as an example of human achievement, as could well be. Life passed among them would assuredly be a life of gliding along a sunny, unruffled stream. If there were dark things or troubled things to deal with, they were kept well below the shining surface; on the surface one always glided. It was charming, indeed, and yet Althea looked a little dizzily from side to side, as if at familiar but unattainable shores, and wondered if some solid foothold on solid earth were not preferable. She wondered if she would not rather walk than glide, and under the gliding she caught glimpses, now and then, of her own dark wonders. They were all very nice to her; but it was as Gerald's wife that they were nice to her; she herself counted for nothing with them. They were frivolous people for the most part, though some among them were serious, and often the most frivolous were those from whom she would have expected gravity, and the serious those whom, on a first meeting, she had thought perturbingly frivolous. Some of the political friends — one who was in the Cabinet, for instance — seemed to think more about hunting and bridge than about their functions in the State; while an aunt of Gerald's, still young and very pretty, wrote articles on philosophy and was ardently interested in ethical societies, in spite of the fact that she rouged her cheeks, wore clothes so fashionable as to look recondite, and had a reputation perfectly presentable for social uses, but not exempt from private whispers. Althea caught such whispers with particular perturbation. The question of morals was one that she had imagined herself to face with a cosmopolitan tolerance; but she now realised that to live among people whose code, in this respect, seemed one of manners only, was a very different thing from reading about them or seeing them from afar, as it were, in foreign countries. Gerald's friends and relatives were anything rather than Bohemian, and most of them were flawlessly respectable; but they were also anything but unworldly; they were very worldly, and, from the implied point of view of all of them, what didn't come out in the world it didn't concern anybody to recognise — except in whispers. It all resolved itself, in the case of people one disapproved of, into a faculty for being nice to them without really having anything to do with them; and to poor Althea this was a difficult task to undertake; social life, in her experience, was more involved in the life of the affections and matched it more nearly. She found, when the fortnight was over, that she was glad, very glad, to get away to Merriston. The comparative solitude would do her good, she felt, and in it, above all, the charm would perhaps work more restoringly than in London. She had been, through everything, more aware than of any new impression that the old one held firm; but, in that breathless fortnight, she found that the charm, persistently, would not be to her what she had hoped it might be. It did not revive her; it did not lift and glorify her; rather it subjugated her and held her helpless and in thrall. She was not crowned with beams; rather, it seemed to her in moments of dizzy insight, dragged at chariot wheels. And more than once her pride revolted as she was whirled along.

It was at Merriston, installed, apparently, so happily with her friends, that the second group of impressions became clearer for her than it had been in London, when she had herself made part of it — the group that had to do with Helen, Franklin, and herself. In London, among all the wider confusions, this smaller but more intense one had not struck her as it did seeing it from a distance. Perhaps it had been because Franklin, among all that glided, had been the raft she stood upon, that, in his company, she had not felt to the full how changed was their relation. His devotion to her was unchanged; of that she was sure. Franklin had not altered; it was she who had altered, and she had now to look at him from the new angle where her own choice had placed her. Seen from this angle it was clear that Franklin could no longer offer just the same devotion, however truly he might feel it; she had barred that out; and it was also clear that he would continue to offer the devotion that she had left it open to him to offer; but here came the strange confusion — this devotion, this remnant, this all that could still be given, hardly differed in practice from the friendship now so frankly bestowed upon Helen as well as upon herself; and, for a further strangeness, Franklin, whom she had helplessly seen as passing from her life, no longer counting in it, was not gone at all; he was there, indeed, as never before, with the background of his sudden millions to give him significance. Franklin was, indeed, as firmly ensconced in this new life that she had entered as he chose to be, and did he not, as a matter of fact, count in it for more than she did? If it was confusing to look at Franklin from the angle of her own withdrawal, what was it to see him altered, for the world, from drab to rose-colour and to see that people were running after him? This fantastic result of wealth, Althea, after a stare or two, was able to accept with other ironic acceptations; it was not indeed London's vision of Franklin that altered him for her, though it confused her; no, what had altered him more than anything she could have thought possible, was Helen's new seeing of him. Helen, she knew quite well, still saw Franklin, pleasantly and clearly, as drab-colour, still, it was probable, saw him as funny; but it was evident that Helen had come to feel fond of him, if anything so detached could be called fondness. He could hardly count for anything with her — after all, who did? — but she liked him, she liked him very much, and it amused her to watch him adjust himself to his new conditions. She took him about with her in London and showed him things and people, ironically smiling, no doubt, and guarding even while she exposed. And Helen wouldn't do this unless she had come to see something more than drab-colour and oddity, and whatever the more might be it was not the millions. No, sitting in the drawing-room at Merriston, with its memories of the two emotional climaxes of her life, Althea, with a sinking heart, felt sure that she had lost something, and that she only knew it lost from seeing that Helen had found it. It had been through Helen's blindness to the qualities in Franklin which, timidly, tentatively, she had put before her, that his worth had grown dim to herself; this was the cutting fact that Althea tried to edge away from, but that her sincerity forced her again and again to examine. It was through Helen's appreciation that she now saw more in Franklin than she had ever seen before. If he was funny he was also original, full of his own underivative flavour; if he was drab-colour, he was also beautiful. Althea recalled the benignity of Helen's eyes as they dwelt upon him, her smile, startled, almost touched, when some quaint, telling phrase revealed him suddenly as an unconscious torch-bearer in a dusky, self-deceiving world. Helen and Franklin were akin in that; they elicited, they radiated truth, and Althea recalled, too, how their eyes would sometimes meet in silence when they both saw the same truth simultaneously. Not that Helen's truth was often Franklin's; they were as alien as ever in their outlook, of this Althea was convinced; but though the outlook was so different, the faculty of sight was the same in both — clear, unperturbed, and profoundly independent. They were neither of them dusky or self-deceived. And what was she? Sitting in the drawing-room at Merriston and thinking it all over, Althea asked herself the question while her heart sank to a deeper dejection. Not only had she lost Franklin; she had lost herself. She embarked on the dangerous and often demoralising search for a definite, recognisable personality — something to lean on with security, a standard and a prop. With growing dismay she could find only a sorry little group of shivering hopes and shaken adages. What was she? Only a well-educated nonentity with, for all coherence and purpose in life, a knowledge of art and literature and a helpless feeling for charm. Poor Althea was rapidly sinking to the nightmare stage of introspection; she saw, fitfully, not restoringly, that it was nightmare, and dragging herself away from these miserable dissections, fixed her eyes on something not herself, on the thing that, after all, gave her, even to the nightmare vision, purpose and meaning. If it were only that, let her, at all events, cling to it; the helpless feeling for charm must then shape her path. Gerald was coming, and to be subjugated was, after all, better than to disintegrate.

She drove down to meet him in the little brougham that was now established in the stables. It was a wet, chilly day. Althea, wrapped in furs, leaned in a corner and looked with an unseeing gaze at the dripping hedgerows and grey sky. She fastened herself in anticipation on the approaching brightness. Ah, to warm herself at the light of his untroubled, unquestioning, unexacting being, to find herself in him. If he would love her and charm her, that, after all, was enough to give her a self.

He was a little late, and Althea did not feel willing to face a public meeting on the platform. She remained sitting in her corner, listening for the sound of the approaching train. When it had arrived, she heard Gerald's voice before she saw him, and the sound thrilled through her deliciously. He was talking to a neighbour, and he paused for some moments to chat with him. Then his head appeared at the window, little drops of rain on his crisp hair, his eyes smiling, yet, as she saw in a moment, less at her in particular than at the home-coming of which she was a part. 'Yes,' he turned to the porter to say, 'the portmanteau outside, the dressing-case in here.' The door was opened and he stepped in beside her. 'Hello, Althea!' He smiled at her again, while he drew a handful of silver from his pocket and picked out a sixpence for the porter. 'Here; all right.' The brougham rolled briskly out of the station yard. They were in the long up-hill lanes. 'Well, how are you, dear?' he asked.

Althea was trembling, but she was controlling herself; she had all the pain and none of the advantage of the impulsive, emotional woman; consciousness of longing made instinctive appeal impossible. 'Very well, thank you,' she smiled, as quietly as he.

'What a beastly day!' said Gerald, looking out. 'You can't imagine London. It's like breathing in a wet blanket. The clean air is a comfort, at all events.'

'Yes,' smiled Althea.

'Old Morty Finch is coming down in time for dinner,' Gerald went on. 'I met him on my way to the station and asked him. Such a good fellow — you remember him? He won't be too many, will he?'

'Indeed no.'

Gerald leaned back, drew the rug up about his knees, and folded his arms, looking at her, still with his generally contented smile. 'And your guests are happy? You're enjoying yourself? Miss Arlington plays the violin, you said. I'm looking forward to hearing her — and seeing her again, too; she is such a very pretty girl.'

'Isn't she?' said Althea. And now, as they rolled on between the dripping hedges, she knew that the trembling of hope and fear was gone, and that a sudden misery, like that of the earth and sky, had settled upon her. He had not kissed her. He did not even take her hand. Oh, why did he not kiss her? why did he not know that she wanted love and comfort? Only her pride controlled the cry.

Gerald looked out of the window and seemed to find everything very pleasant. 'I went to the play last night,' he said. 'Kane took a party of us — Helen, Miss Buchanan, Lord Compton, and Molly Fanshawe. What a good sort he is, Kane; a real character.'

'You didn't get at him at all in the summer, did you?' said Althea, in her deadened voice.

'No,' said Gerald reflectively, 'not at all; and I don't think that I get much more at him now, you know; but I see more what's in him; he is so extraordinarily kind and he takes his money so nicely. And, O Lord! how he is being run after! He really has millions, you know; the mothers are all at his traces trying to track him down, and he is as cheerful and as unconcerned as you please.' Gerald suddenly smiled round at her again. 'I say, Althea, don't you regret him sometimes? It would have been a glorious match, you know.'

Althea felt herself growing pale. 'Regret him!' she said, and, for her, almost violently, the opportunity was an outlet for her wretchedness; 'I can't conceive how a man's money can make any difference. I couldn't have married Franklin if he'd been a king!'

'Oh, my dear!' said Gerald, startled; 'I didn't mean it seriously, of course.'

'It seems to me,' said Althea, trying to control her labouring breath, 'that over here you take nothing quite so seriously as that — great matches, I mean, and money.'

Gerald was silent for a moment; then, in a very courteous voice he said: 'Have I offended you in any way, Althea?'

Tears stood in her eyes; she turned away her head to hide them. 'Yes, you have,' she said, and the sound of her voice shocked her, it so contradicted the crying out of her disappointed heart.

But though Gerald was blind on occasions that did not seem to him to warrant any close attention, he was clear-sighted on those that did. He understood that something was amiss; and though her exclamation had, indeed, made him angry for a moment, he was now sorry; he felt that she was unhappy, and he couldn't bear people to be unhappy. 'I've done something that displeases you,' he said, taking her hand and leaning forward to look into her eyes, half pleading and half rallying her in the way she knew so well. 'Do forgive me.'

She longed to put her head on his shoulder and sob: 'I wanted you to love me'; but that would have been to abase herself too much; yet the tears fell as she answered, trying to smile: 'It was only that you hurt me; even in jest I cannot bear to have you say that I could have been so sordid.'

He pressed her hand. 'I was only in fun, of course. Please forgive me.'

She knew, with all his gay solicitude, his gentle self-reproach, that she had angered and perplexed him, that she made him feel a little at a loss with her talk of sordidness, that, perhaps, she wearied him. And, seeing this, she was frightened — frightened, and angry that she should be afraid. But fear predominated, and she forced herself to smile at him and to talk with him during the long drive, as though nothing had happened.

CHAPTER XXII.

Some days after Gerald had gone to Merriston, Franklin Kane received a little note from old Miss Buchanan. Helen, too, had gone to the country until Monday, as she had told Franklin when he had asked her to see some pictures with him on Saturday. Franklin had felt a little bereft, especially since, hoping for her on Saturday, he had himself refused an invitation. But he did not miss that; the invitations that poured in upon him, like a swelling river, were sources of cheerful amusement to him. He, too, was acquiring his little ironies and knew why they poured in. It was not the big house-party where he would have been a fish out of water — even though in no sense a fish landed — that he missed; he missed Helen; and he wouldn't think of going to see pictures without her. It was, therefore, pleasant to read Miss Buchanan's hospitable suggestion that he should drop in that afternoon for a cup of tea and to keep an old woman company. He was very glad indeed to keep Miss Buchanan company. She interested him greatly; he had not yet in the least made out what was her object in life, whether she had gained or missed it, and whether, indeed, she had ever had one to gain or miss. People who went thus unpiloted through life filled him with wonder and conjecture.

He found Miss Buchanan as he had found her on the occasion of his first visit to the little house in Belgravia. Her acute and rugged face showed not much greater softening for this now wonted guest — showed, rather, a greater acuteness; but any one who knew Miss Buchanan would know from its expression that she liked Franklin Kane. 'Well,' she said, as he drew his chair to the opposite side of the tea-table — very cosy it was, the fire shining upon them, and the canaries trilling intermittently — 'Well, here we are, abandoned. We'll make the best of it, won't we?'

Franklin said that under the circumstances he couldn't feel at all abandoned. 'Nor do I,' said Miss Buchanan, filling the tea-pot. 'You and I get on very well together, I consider.' Franklin thought so too.

'I hope we may go on with it,' said Miss Buchanan, leaning back in her chair while the tea drew. 'I hope we are going to keep you over here. You've given up any definite idea of going back, I suppose.'

Franklin was startled by this confident assurance. His definite idea in coming over had been, of course, to go back at the end of the autumn, unless, indeed, a certain cherished hope were fulfilled, in which case Althea should have decided on any movements. He had hardly, till this moment, contemplated his own intentions, and now that he did so he found that he had been guided by none that were definable. It was not because he had suddenly grown rich and, in his funny way, the fashion, that he thus stayed on in London, working hard, it is true, and allowing no new developments to interfere with his work, yet making no plans and setting no goal before himself. To live as he had been living for the past weeks was, indeed, in a sense, to drift. There was nothing Franklin disapproved of more than of drifting; therefore he was startled when Miss Buchanan's remarks brought him to this realisation. 'Well, upon my word, Miss Buchanan,' he said, 'I hadn't thought about it. No — of course not — of course, I've not given up the idea of going back. I shall go back before very long. But things have turned up, you see. There is Althea's wedding — I must be at that — and there's Miss Helen. I want to see as much of her as I can before I go home, get my friendship firmly established, you know.'

Miss Buchanan now poured out the tea and handed Franklin his cup. 'I shouldn't think about going yet, then,' she observed. 'London is an admirable place for the sort of work you are interested in, and I entirely sympathise with your wish to see as much as you can of Helen.' She added, after a little pause in which Franklin, still further startled to self-contemplation, wondered whether it was work, Althea's wedding, or Helen who had most kept him in London, — 'I'm troubled about Helen; she's not looking at all well; hasn't been feeling well all the summer. I trace it to that attack of influenza she had in Paris when she met Miss Jakes.'

Franklin's thoughts were turned from himself. He looked grave. 'I'm afraid she's delicate,' he said.

'There is nothing sickly about her, but she is fragile,' said Miss Buchanan. 'She can't stand wear and tear. It might kill her.'

Franklin looked even graver. The thought of his friend killed by wear and tear was inexpressibly painful to him. He remembered — he would never forget — the day in the woods, Helen's 'I'm sick to death of it.' That Helen had a secret sorrow, and that it was preying upon her, he felt sure, and there was pride for him in the thought that he could help her there; he could help her to hide it; even her aunt didn't know that she was sick to death of it. 'What do you suggest might be done?' he now inquired. 'Do you think she goes out too much? Perhaps a rest-cure.'

'No; I don't think she over-tires herself; she doesn't go out nearly as much as she used to. There is nothing to cure and nothing to rest from. It isn't so much now; I'm here now to make things possible for her. It's after I'm gone. I'm an old woman; I'm devoted to my niece, and I don't see what's to become of her when

I'm dead.'

If Franklin had been startled before, he was shocked now. He had never given much thought to the economic basis of Helen's life, taking it for granted that though she would like more money, she had, and always would have, quite enough to live on happily. The idea of an insecure future for her had never entered his head. He now knew that, for all his theories of the independence of women, it was quite intolerable to contemplate an insecure future for Helen. Some women might have it in them to secure them-selves — she was not one of them. She was a flower in a vase; if the vase were taken away the flower would simply lie where it fell and wither. He had put down his tea-cup while Miss Buchanan spoke, and he sat gazing at her. 'Isn't Miss Helen provided for?' he asked.

'Yes, in a sense she is,' said Miss Buchanan, who, after drinking her tea, did not go on to her muffin, but still leaned back with folded arms, her deep-set, small grey eyes fixed on Franklin's face. 'I've seen to that as best I could; but one can't save much out of a small annuity. Helen, after my death, will have an income of £150 a year. It isn't enough. You have only to look at Helen to see that it isn't enough. She's not fit to scrape and manage on that.'

Franklin repeated the sum thoughtfully. 'Well, no, perhaps not,' he half thought, only half agreed; 'not leading the kind of life she does now. If she could only work at something as well; bring in a little more like that.' But Miss Buchanan interrupted him.

'Nonsense, my dear man; what work is there — work that will bring in money — for a decorative, untrained idler like Helen? And what time would she have left to live the only life she's fit to lead if she had to make money? I'm not worried about bare life for Helen; I'm worried about what kind of life it's to be. Helen was brought up to be an idler and to make a good marriage — like most girls of her class — and she hasn't made it, and she's not likely to make it now.'

'One hundred and fifty pounds isn't enough,' said Franklin, still thoughtfully, 'for a decorative idler.'

'That's just it,' Miss Buchanan acquiesced; and she went on after a moment, 'I'm willing to call Helen a decorative idler if we are talking of purely economic weights and measures; thank goodness there are other standards, and we are not likely to see them eliminated from civilised society for many a generation. For many a generation, I trust, there'll be people in the world who don't earn their keep, as one may say, and yet who are more worth while keeping than most of the people who do. To my mind Helen is such a person. I'd like to tell you a little about her life, Mr. Kane.'

'I should be very much obliged if you would,' Franklin mur-mured, his thin little face taking on an expression of most intense concentration. 'It would be a great privilege. You know what I feel about Miss Helen.'

'Yes; it's because I know what you feel about her that I want to tell you,' said Miss Grizel. 'Not that it's anything startling, or anything you wouldn't have supposed for yourself; but it illustrates my point, I think, very well, my point that Helen is the type of person we can't afford to let go under. Has Helen ever spoken to you about her mother?'

'Never,' said Franklin, his intent face expressing an almost ritualistic receptivity.

'Well, she's a poor creature,' said Miss Buchanan, 'a poor, rubbishy creature; the most selfish and reckless woman I know. I warned my brother how it would turn out from the first; but he was infatuated and had his way, and a wretched way it turned out. She made him miserable, and she made the children miserable, and she nearly ruined him with her extravagance; he and I together managed to put things straight, and see to it that Nigel should come into a property not too much encumbered and that Helen should inherit a little sum, enough to keep her going — a little more it was, as a matter of fact, than what I'll be able to leave her. Well, when my brother died, she was of age and she came into her modest fortune; for a young girl, with me to back her up, it wasn't bad. She had hardly seen her mother for three years — they'd always been at daggers drawn — when one day, up in Scotland, when she was with her brother — it was before Nigel married — who should appear but Daisy. She had travelled up there in desperate haste to throw herself on her children's mercy. She was in terrible straits. She had got into debt — cards and racing — and she was frightfully involved with some horror of a man. Her honour was wrecked unless she could pay her debts and extricate herself. Well, she found no mercy in Nigel; he refused to give her a farthing. It was Helen who stripped herself of every penny she possessed and saved her. I don't know whether she touched Helen's pity, or whether it was mere family pride; the thought of the horror of a man was probably a strong motive too. All Helen ever said about it to me was, "How could I bear to see her like that?" So, she ruined herself. Of course after that it was more than ever necessary that she should marry. I hadn't begun to save for her, and there was nothing else for her to look to. Of course I expected her to marry at once; she was altogether the most charming girl of her day. But there is the trouble; she never did. She refused two most brilliant offers, one after the other, and hosts of minor ones. There was some streak of girlish romance in her, I suppose. I wish I could have been more on the spot and put on pressure. But it was difficult to be on the spot. Helen never told me about her offers until long after; and pressure with her wouldn't come to much. Of course I didn't respect her the less for her foolishness. But, dear me, dear me,' said Miss Buchanan, turning her eyes on the fire, 'what a pity it has all been, what a pity it is, to see her wasted.'

Franklin listened to this strange tale, dealing with matters to him particularly strange, such as gambling, dishonoured mothers, horrors of men and mercenary marriages. It all struck him as very dreadful; it all sank into him; but it didn't oppress him in its strangeness; no outside fact, however dreadful, ever oppressed Franklin. What did oppress him was the thought of Helen in it all. This oppressed him very much.

Miss Buchanan continued to look into the fire for a little while after she had finished her story, and then, bringing her eyes back to Franklin's countenance, she looked at him keenly and steadily. 'And now, Mr. Kane,' she said, 'you are perhaps asking yourself why I tell you all this?'

Franklin was not asking it at all, and he answered with earnest sincerity: 'Why, no; I think I ought to be told. I want to be told everything about my friends that I may hear. I'm glad to know this, because it makes me feel more than ever what a fine woman Miss Helen is, and I'm sorry, because she's wasted, as you say. I only wish,' said Franklin, and the intensity of cogitation deepened on his face, 'I only wish that one could think out some plan to give her a chance.'

'I wish one could,' said Miss Buchanan. And without any change of voice she added: 'I want you to marry her, Mr. Kane.'

Franklin sat perfectly still and turned his eyes on her with no apparent altering of expression, unless the arrested stillness of his look was alteration. His eyes and Miss Buchanan's plunged deep into each other's, held each other's for a long time. Then, slowly, deeply, Franklin flushed.

'But, Miss Buchanan,' he said, pausing between his sentences, for he did not see his way, 'I'm in love with another woman — that is — ' and for a longer pause his way became quite invisible — 'I've been in love with another woman for years.'

'You mean Miss Jakes,' said Miss Buchanan. 'Helen told me about it. But does that interfere? Helen isn't likely to be in love with you or to expect you to be in love with her. And the woman you've loved for years is going to marry some one else. It's not as if you had any hope.'

There was pain for Franklin in this reasonable speech, but he could not see clearly where it lay; curiously, it did not seem to centre on that hopelessness as regarded Althea. He could see nothing clearly, and there was no time for self-examination. 'No,' he agreed. 'No, that's true. It's not as if I had any hope.'

'I think Helen worthy of any man alive,' said Miss Buchanan, 'and yet, under the strange circumstances, I know that what I'm asking of you is an act of chivalry. I want to see Helen safe, and I think she would be safe with you.'

Franklin flushed still more deeply. 'Yes, I think she would,' he said. He paused then, again, trying to think, and what he found first was a discomfort in the way she had put it. 'It wouldn't be an act of chivalry,' he said. 'Don't think that. I care for Miss Helen too much for that. It's all the other way round, you know. I mean' — he brought out — 'I don't believe she'd think of taking me.'

Miss Grizel's eyes were on him, and it may have been their gaze that made him feel the discomfort. She seemed to be seeing something that evaded him. 'I don't look like a husband for a decorative idler, do I, Miss Buchanan?' he tried to smile.

Her eyes, with their probing keenness, smiled back. 'You mayn't look like one, but you are one, with your millions,' she said. 'And I believe Helen might think of taking you. She has had plenty of time to outgrow youthful dreams. She's tired. She wants ease and security. She needs a husband, and she doesn't need a lover at all. She would get power, and you would get a charming wife — a woman, moreover, whom you care for and respect — as she does you; and you would get a home and children. I imagine that you care for children. Decorative idler though she is, Helen would make an excellent mother.'

'Yes, I care very much for children,' Franklin murmured, not confused — pained, rather, by this unveiling of his inner sanctities.

'Of course,' Miss Buchanan went on, 'you wouldn't want Helen to live out of England. Of course you would make generous settlements and give her her proper establishments here. I want Helen to be safe; but I don't want safety for her at the price of extinction.'

Obviously, Franklin could see that very clearly, whatever else was dim, he was the vase for the lovely flower. That was his use and his supreme significance in Miss Buchanan's eyes. And the lovely flower was to be left on its high stand where all the world could see it; what other use was there for it? He quite saw Miss Buchanan's point, and the strange thing was, in spite of all the struggling of confused pain and perplexity in him, that here he, too, was clear; with no sense of inner protest he could make it his point too. He wanted Helen to stay in her vase; he didn't want to take her off the high stand. He had not time now to seek for consistency with his principles, his principles must stretch, that was all; they must stretch far enough to take in Helen and her stand; once they had done that he felt that there might be more to say and that he should be able to say it; he felt sure that he should say nothing that Helen would not like; even if she disagreed, she would always smile at him.

'No,' he said, 'it wouldn't do for her to live anywhere but in England.'

'Well, then, what do you say to it?' asked Miss Buchanan. She had rather the manner of a powerful chancellor negotiating for the marriage of a princess.

'Why,' Franklin replied, smiling very gravely, 'I say yes. But I can't think that Miss Helen will.'

'Try your chances,' said Miss Buchanan. She reached across the table and shook his hand. 'I like you, Mr. Kane,' she said. 'I think you are a good man; and, don't forget, in spite of my world-liness, that if I weren't sure of that, all your millions wouldn't have made me think of you for Helen.'

CHAPTER XXIII.

Helen returned to town on Monday afternoon, and, on going to her room, found two notes there. One from Gerald said that he was staying on for another week at Merriston, the other from Franklin said that he would take his chances of finding her in at 5.30 that afternoon. Helen only glanced at Franklin's note and then dropped it into the fire; at Gerald's she looked long and attentively. She always, familiar as they were, studied any letter of Gerald's that she received; they seemed, the slightest of them, to have something of himself; the small crisp writing was charming to her, and the very way he had of affixing his stamps in not quite the same way that most people affixed theirs, ridiculously endeared even his envelopes. She turned the note over in her fingers as she stood before the fire, seeing all that it meant to him — how little! — and all that it meant to her, and she laid it for a moment against her cheek before tearing it across and putting it, too, into the fire. Aunt Grizel was gone out and had left word that she would not be in till dinner-time. Helen looked idly at the clock and decided that she would take a lazy afternoon, have tea at home, and await Franklin.

When he arrived he found her reading before the fire in the little room where she did not often receive him; it was usually in the drawing-room that they met. Helen wore a black tea-gown, transparent and flowing, the same gown, indeed, remodelled to more domestic uses, in which Althea had first seen her. She looked pale and very thin.

Franklin, too, was aware of feeling pale; he thought that he had felt pale ever since his talk with Miss Buchanan on Saturday. He had not yet come to any decision about the motives that had made him acquiesce in her proposal; he only knew that, whatever they were, they were not those merely reasonable ones that she had put before him. A charming wife, a home and children; these were not enough, and Franklin knew it, to have brought him here today on his strange errand; nor was it an act of chivalry; nor was it pity and sympathy for his friend. All these, no doubt, made some small part of it; but they far from covered the case; they would have left him as calm and as rational as, he knew, he looked; but since he did not feel calm and rational he knew that the case was covered by very different motives. What they were he could not clearly see; but he felt that something was happening to him and that it was taking him far out of his normal course. Even his love for Althea had not taken him out of his course; it had never been incalculable; it had been the ground he walked on, the goal he worked towards; what was happening now was like a current, swift and unfathomable, that was bearing him he knew not where.

Helen smiled at him and, turning in her chair to look up at him, gave him her hand. 'You look tired,' she said. 'You'll have some tea?'

'I've been looking up some things at the British Museum,' said Franklin, 'and I had a glass of milk and a bun; the bun was very satisfying, though I can't say that it was very satisfactory; I guess I shan't want anything else for some hours yet.'

'A bun? What made you have a bun?' said Helen, laughing.

'Well, it seemed to go with the place, somehow,' said Franklin.

'I can imagine that it might; I've only been there once; very large and very indigestible I found it, and most depressing. Yes, I see that it might make a bun seem suitable.'

'Ah, but it's a very wonderful place, you know,' Franklin said. 'I should have expected you to go oftener; you care about beauty.'

'Not beauty in a museum. I don't like museums. The mummies were what impressed me most, after the Elgin marbles, and everything there seemed like a mummy — dead and desecrated. Well, what have you been doing besides eating buns at the British Museum? Has London been working you very hard?'

'I've not seen much of London while you've been away,' said Franklin, who had drawn a chair to the other side of the fire. 'I think that you are London to me, and when you are out of it it doesn't seem to mean much — beyond museums and work.'

'Come, what of all your scientific friends?'

'They don't mean London; they mean science,' said Franklin, smiling back at her. She always made him feel happy for himself, and at ease, even when he was feeling unhappy for her; and just now he was feeling strangely, deeply unhappy for her. It wasn't humility, in the usual sense, that showed his coming offer to him as so inadequate; he did not think of himself as unworthy; but he did think of himself as incongruous; and that this fine, sad, subtle creature should be brought, from merely reasonable motives, to taking the incongruous intimately into her life made him more unhappy for her than usual. He wished he wasn't so incongruous; he wished he had something besides friendship and millions; he wished, almost, that his case was hopeless and that friendship and millions would not gain her. Yet, under these wishes, which made his face look tired and jaded, was another feeling; it was too self-less to be called a wish; rather it was a wonder, deep and melancholy, as to what was being done to him, and what would be done, as an end of it all. That something had been done he knew; it was because of Helen — that was one thing at last seen clearly — that he had not, long ago, left London.

'Science is perfectly impersonal, perfectly cosmopolitan, you know,' he went on. 'Now you are intensely personal and intensely local.'

'I don't think of myself as London, then, if I'm local,' said Helen, her eyes on the fire. 'I think of myself as Scotland, in the moorlands, on a bleak, grey day, when the heather is over and there's a touch of winter in the wind. You don't know the real me.'

'I'd like to,' said Franklin, quietly and unemphatically.

They sat for a little while in silence, and Helen, so unconscious of what was approaching her, seemed in no haste to break it. She was capable of sitting thus in silent musing, her cheek on her hand, her eyes on the fire, for half an hour with Mr. Kane beside her.

Franklin was reflecting. It wouldn't do to put it to her as her need; it must be put to her as his; as his reasonable need for the castle, the princess, the charming wife, the home, and children. And it must be that need only, the need of the dry, matter-of-fact friend who could give her a little and to whom she could give much. To hint at other needs — if other needs there were — would not be in keeping with the spirit of the transaction, and would, no doubt, endanger it. He well remembered old Miss Buchanan's hint; it was as a husband that Helen might contemplate him, not as a lover. 'Miss Buchanan,' he said at last, 'you don't consider that love, romantic love, is necessary in marriage, do you? I've gathered more than once from remarks of yours that that point of view is rather childish to you.'

Helen turned her eyes on him with the look of kindly scrutiny to which he was accustomed. She had felt, in these last weeks, that London might be having some unforeseen effect on Franklin Kane; she thought of him as very clear and very fixed, yet of such a guilelessly open nature as well, that new experience might impress too sharply the candid tablets of his mind. She did not like to think of any alteration in Franklin. She wanted him to remain a changeless type, tolerant of alteration, but in itself inalterable. 'To tell you the truth, I used to think so,' she said, 'for myself, I mean. And I hope that you will always think so.'

'Why?' asked Franklin.

'I want you to go on believing always in the things that other people give up — the nice, beautiful things.'

'Well, that's just my point; can't marriage without romantic love be nice and beautiful?'

'Well, can it?' Helen smiled.

Franklin appeared conscientiously to ponder. 'I've a high ideal of marriage,' he said. 'I think it's the happiest state for men and women; celibacy is abnormal, isn't it?'

'Yes, I suppose it is,' Helen acquiesced, smiling on.

'A mercenary or a worldly marriage is a poor thing; it can't bring the right sort of growth,' Franklin went on. 'I'm not thinking of anything sordid or self-seeking, except in the sense that self-development is self-seeking. I'm thinking of conditions when a man and woman, without romantic love, might find the best chances of development. Even without romantic love, marriage may mean fine and noble things, mayn't it? a home, you know, and shared, widened interests, and children,' said poor Franklin, 'and the mutual help of two natures that understand and respect each other.'

'Yes, of course,' said Helen, as he paused, fixing his eyes upon her; 'it may certainly mean all that, the more surely, perhaps, for having begun without romance.'

'You agree?'

She smiled now at his insistence. 'Of course I agree.'

'You think it might mean happiness?'

'Of course; if they are both sensible people and if neither expects romance of the other; that's a very important point.'

Franklin again paused, his eyes on hers. With a little effort he now pursued. 'You know of my romance, Miss Buchanan, and you know that it's over, except as a beautiful and sacred memory. You know that I don't intend to let a memory warp my life. It may seem sudden to you, and I ask your pardon if it's too sudden; but I want to marry; I want a home, and children, and the companionship of some one I care for and respect, very deeply. Therefore, Miss Buchanan,' he spoke on, turning a little paler, but with the same deliberate steadiness, 'I ask you if you will marry me.'

While Franklin spoke, it had crossed Helen's mind that perhaps he had determined to follow her suggestion — buy a castle and find a princess to put in it; it had crossed her mind that he might be going to ask her advice on this momentous step — she was used to giving advice on such momentous steps; but when he brought out his final sentence she was so astonished that she rose from her chair and stood before him. She became very white, and, with the strained look that then came to them, her eyes opened widely. And she gazed down at Franklin Winslow Kane while, in three flashes, searing and swift, like running leaps of lightning, three thoughts traversed her mind: Gerald — All that money — A child. It was in this last thought that she seemed, then, to fall crumblingly, like a burnt-out thing reduced to powder. A child. What would it look like, a child of hers and Franklin Kane's? How spare and poor and insignificant were his face and form. Could she love a child who had a nose like that — a neat, flat, sallow little nose? A spasm, half of laughter, half of sobbing, caught her breath.

'I've startled you,' said Franklin, who still sat in his chair looking up at her. 'Please forgive me.'

A further thought came to her now, one that she could utter, was able to utter. 'I couldn't live in America. Yes, you did startle me. But I am much honoured.'

'Thank you,' said Franklin. 'I needn't say how much I should consider myself honoured if you would accept my proposal.' He rose now, but it was to move a little further away from her, and, taking up an ornament from the mantelpiece, he examined it while he said: 'As for America, I quite see that; that's what I was really thinking of in what I was saying about London. You are London, and it wouldn't do to take you away from it. I shouldn't think of taking you away. What I would ask you to do would be to take me in. Since being over here, this time, and seeing some of the real life of the country — what it's working towards, what it needs and means — and, moreover, taking into consideration the character of my own work, I should feel perfectly justified in making a compromise between my patriotism and my — my affection for you. Some day you might perhaps find that you'd like to pay us a visit, over there; I think you'd find it interesting, and it wouldn't, of course, be my America that you'd see, not the serious and unfashionable America; it would be a very different America from that that you'd find waiting to welcome you. So that what I should suggest — and feel justified in suggesting — would be that I spent three months alternately in England and America; I should in that way get half a year of home life and half a year of my own country, and be able, perhaps, to be something of a link between the English and American scientific worlds. As for our life here' — Franklin remembered old Miss Buchanan's words — 'you should have your own establishments and,' he lifted his eyes to hers, now, and smiled a little, 'pursue the just and the beautiful under the most favourable conditions.'

Helen, when he smiled so at her, turned from him and sank again into her chair. She leaned her elbow on the arm and put her hand over her eyes. A languor of great weariness went over her, the languor of the burnt-out thing floating in the air like a drift of ashes.

Here, at last, in her hand, however strange the conditions, was the power she had determined to live for. She could, with Franklin's millions, mould circumstances to her will, and Franklin would be no more of an odd impediment than the husbands of many women who married for money — less of an impediment, indeed, than most, for — though it could only be for his money — she liked him, she was very fond of him, dear, good, and exquisite little man. Impossible little man she, no doubt, would once have thought him — impossible as husband, not as friend; but so many millions made all the difference in possibility. Franklin was now as possible as any prince, though, she wondered with the cold languor, could a prince have a nose like that?

Franklin was possible, and it was in her hand, the power, the high security; yet she felt that it would be in weariness rather than in strength that the hand would close. It must close, must it not? If she refused Franklin what, after all, was left to her, what was left in herself or in her life that could say no to him? Nothing; nothing at all, no hope, no desire, no faith in herself or in life. If it came to that, the clearest embodiment of faith and life she knew sat opposite to her waiting for an answer. He was good; she was fond of him; he had millions; what could it be but yes? Yet, while her mind sank, like a feather floating downwards in still air, to final, inevitable acquiescence, while the little clock ticked with a fine, insect-like note, and the flames made a soft flutter like the noise of shaken silk, a blackness of chaotic suffering rose suddenly in her, and her thoughts were whirled far away. In flashes, dear and terrible, she saw it — her ruined youth. It rose in dim symbolic pictures, the moorland where melancholy birds cried and circled, where the rain fell and the wind called with a passionate cadence among the hills. To marry Franklin Kane — would it not be to abandon the past; would it not be to desecrate it and make it hers no longer? Was not the solitary moorland better, the anguish and despair better than the smug, warm, sane life of purpose and endeavour? If she was too tired, too indifferent, if she acquiesced, if she married Franklin Kane, would she forget that the reallest thing in her life had not been its sanity, and its purpose, but its wild, its secret, its broken-hearted love? Surely the hateful wisdom of the daily fact would not efface the memory so that, with years, she would come to smile over it as one smiles at distant childish griefs? Surely not. Yet the presage of it passed bleakly over her soul. Life was so reasonable. And there it sat in the person of Franklin Winslow Kane; life, wise, kind, commonplace, and inexorably given to the fact, to the present, to the future that the present built, inexorably oblivious of the past. Her tragic, rebel heart cried out against it, but her mind whispered with a hateful calm that life conquered tragedy.

Let it be so, then. She faced it. In the very fact of submission to life her tragedy would live on; the tragedy — and this she would never forget — would be to feel it no longer. She would be life's captive, not its soldier, and she would keep to the end the captive's bitter heart. She knew, as she put down her hand at last and looked at Franklin Kane, that it was to be acquiescence, unless he could not accept her terms. She was ready, ironically, wearily ready for life; but it must be on her own terms. There must be no loophole for misunderstanding between her and her friend — if she were to marry him. Only by the clearest recognition of what she owed him could her pride be kept intact; and she owed him cold, cruel candour. 'Do you understand, I wonder,' she said to him, and in a voice that he had never heard from her before, the voice, he knew, of the real self, 'how different I am from what you think a human being should be? Do you realise that, if I marry you, it will be because you have money — because you have a great deal of money — and only for that? I like you, I respect you; I would be a loyal wife to you, but if you weren't rich — and very rich — I should not think of marrying you.'

Franklin received this information with an unmoved visage, and after a pause in which they contemplated each other deeply, he replied: 'All right.'

'That isn't all,' said Helen. 'You are very good — an idealist. You think me — even in this frankness of mine — far nicer than I am. I have no ideals — none at all. I want to be independent and to have power to do what I please. As for justice and beauty — it's too kind of you to remember so accurately some careless words of mine.'

Franklin remained unperturbed, unless the quality of intent and thoughtful pity in his face were perturbation. 'You don't know how nice you are,' he remarked, 'and that's the nicest thing about you. You are the honestest woman I've met, and you seem to me about the most unhappy. I guessed that. Well, we won't talk about unhappiness, will we? I don't believe that talking about it does much good. If you'll marry me, we'll see if we can't live it down somehow. As for ideals, I'll trust you in doing what you like with your money; it will be yours, you know. I shall make half my property over to you for good; then if I disapprove of what you do with it, you'll at all events be free to go on pleasing yourself and displeasing me. I won't be able to prevent you by force from doing what I think wrong any more than you will me. You'll take your own responsibility, and I'll take mine. And I don't believe we shall quarrel much about it,' said Franklin, smiling at her.

Tears rose to Helen's eyes. Franklin Kane, since she had become his friend, often touched her; something in him now smote upon her heart; it was so gentle, so beautiful, and so sad.

'My dear friend,' she said, 'you will be marrying a hard, a selfish, and a broken-hearted woman who will bring you nothing.'

'All right,' said Franklin again.

'I won't do you any good.'

'You won't do me any harm.'

'You want me to marry you, even if I'm not to do you any good?'

He nodded, looking brightly and intently at her.

She rose now and stood beside him. With all the strange new sense of unity between them there was a stronger sense of formality, and that seemed best expressed by their clasp of hands over what, apparently, was an agreement. 'You understand, you are sure you understand,' said Helen.

'What I want to understand is that you are going to marry me,' said Franklin.

'I will marry you,' Helen said.

And now, rather breathlessly, as if after a race hardly won, Franklin answered: 'Well, I guess you can leave the rest to me.'

CHAPTER XXIV.

Gerald had decided to stay on for another week at Merriston and to come up to town with Althea, and she fancied that the reason for his decision was that he found Sally Arlington such very good company. Sally played the violin exceedingly well and looked like an exceedingly lovely muse while she played, and Gerald, who was very fond of music, also expressed more than once to Althea his admiration of Miss Arlington's appearance. There was nothing in Gerald's demeanour towards Sally to arouse a hint of jealousy; at least there would not have been had Althea been his wife. But she was not yet his wife, and he treated her — this was the fact that the week was driving home — as though she were, and as though with wifely tolerance she perfectly understood his admiring pretty young women who looked like muses and played the violin. She was not yet his wife; this was the fact, she repeated it over her hidden misery, that Gerald did not enough realise. She was not his wife, and she did not like to see him admiring other young women and behaving towards herself as though she were a comprehending and devoted spouse, who found pleasure in providing them for his delectation. She knew that she could trust Gerald, that not for a moment would he permit himself a flirtation, and not for a moment fail to discriminate between admiration of the newcomer and devotion to herself; yet that the admiration had been sufficient to keep him on at Merriston, while the devotion took for granted the right to all sorts of marital neglects, was the fact that rankled. It did more than rankle; it burned with all the other burnings. Althea had, at all events, been dragged from her mood of introspection. She had lost the sense of nonentity. She was conscious of a passionate, protesting self that cried out for justice. Who was Gerald, after all, to take things so for granted? Why should he be so sure of her? He was not her husband. She was his betrothed, not his wife, and more, much more was due to a betrothed than he seemed to imagine. It was not so that another man would have treated her; it was not so that Franklin would have handled his good fortune. Her heart, bereft and starving, cried out for Franklin and for the love that had never failed, even while, under and above everything, was her love for Gerald, and the cold fear lest he should guess what was in her heart, should be angry with her and turn away. It was this fear that gave her self-mastery. She acted the part that Gerald took for granted; she was the tolerant, devoted wife. Yet even so she guessed that Gerald had still his instinct of something amiss. He, too, with all his grace, all his deference and sweetness, was guarded. And once or twice when they were alone together an embarrassed silence had fallen between them.

Mrs. Peel and Sally left on Saturday, and on Saturday afternoon Miss Harriet Robinson was to arrive from Paris, to spend the Sunday, to travel up to town with Althea and Gerald on Monday, and to remain there with Althea until her marriage. Saturday morning, therefore, after the departure of Mrs. Peel and Sally, would be empty, and when she and Gerald met, just before the rather bustled breakfast, Althea suggested to him that a walk together when her guests were gone would be nice, and Gerald had genially acquiesced. A little packet of letters lay beside Gerald's plate and a larger one by Althea's, hers mainly from America as she saw, fat, friendly letters, bearing the Boston postmark; a thin note from Franklin in London also, fixing some festivity for the coming week no doubt; but Sally and Mrs. Peel engaged her attention, and she postponed the reading until after they were gone. She observed, however, in Gerald's demeanour during the meal, a curious irritability and preoccupation. He ate next to nothing, drank his cup of coffee with an air of unconsciousness, and got up and strolled away at the first opportunity, not reappearing until Mrs. Peel and Sally were making their farewells in the hall. He and Althea stood to see them drive off, and then, since she was ready for the walk, they went out together.

It was a damp day, but without rain. A white fog hung closely and thickly over the country, and lay like a clogging, woollen substance among the scattered gold and russets of the now almost leafless trees.

Gerald walked beside Althea in silence, his hands in his pockets. Althea, too, was silent, and in her breast was an oppression like that of the day — a dense, dull, clogging fear. They had walked for quite ten minutes, and had left the avenue and were upon the high road when Gerald said suddenly, 'I've had some news this morning.'

It was a relief to hear that there was some cause for his silence unconnected with her own inadequacy. But anger rose with the relief; it must be some serious cause to excuse him.

'Have you? It's not bad, I hope,' she said, hoping that it was.

'Bad? No; I don't suppose it's bad. It's very odd, though,' said Gerald. He then put his hand in his breast-pocket and drew out a letter. Althea saw that the writing on the envelope was Helen's. 'You may read it,' said Gerald.

The relief was now merged in something else. Althea's heart seemed standing still. It began to thump heavily as she opened the letter and read what Helen wrote:

'DEAR GERALD, — I have some surprising news for you; but I

hardly think that you will be more surprised than I was. I am going to marry Mr. Kane. I accepted him some days ago, but have been getting used to the idea since then, and you are the first person, after Aunt Grizel, who knows. It will be announced next week and we shall probably be married very soon after you and Althea. I hope that both our ventures will bring us much happiness. The more I see of Mr. Kane, the more I realise how fortunate I am. — Yours affectionately,

    'HELEN.'

Althea gazed at these words. Then she turned her eyes and gazed at Gerald, who was not looking at her but straight before him. Her first clear thought was that if he had received a shock it could not be comparable to that which she now felt. It could not be that the letter had fallen on his heart like a sword, severing it. Althea's heart seemed cleft in twain. Gerald — Franklin — it seemed to pulse, horribly divided and horribly bleeding. Looking still at Gerald's face, pallid, absorbed, far from any thought of her, anger surged up in her, and not now against Gerald only, but against Franklin, who had failed her, against Helen, who, it seemed, did not win love, yet won something that took people to her and bound them to her. Then she remembered her unread letters, and remembered that Franklin could not have let this news come to her from another than himself. She drew out his letter and read it. It, too, was short.

'DEAREST ALTHEA, — I know how glad you'll be to hear that happiness, though of a different sort, has come to me. Any sort of happiness was, for so many years, connected with you, dear Althea, that it's very strange to me to realise that there can be another happiness; though this one is connected with you, too, and that makes me gladder. Helen, your dear friend, has consented to marry me, and the fact of her being your dear friend makes her even dearer to me. So that I must thank you for your part in this wonderful new opening in my life, as well as for all the other lovely things you've always meant to me. — Your friend,

    'FRANKLIN.'

Althea's hand dropped. She stared before her. She did not offer the letter to Gerald. 'It's incredible,' she said, while, in the heavy mist, they walked along the road.

Gerald still said nothing. He held his head high, and gazed before him too, as if intent on difficult and evasive thoughts.

'I could not have believed it of Helen,' said Althea after a little pause.

At this he started and looked round at her. 'Believed? What? What is that you say?' His voice was sharp, as though she had struck him on the raw.

Althea steadied her own voice; she wished to strike him on the raw, and accurately; she could only do that by hiding from him her own great dismay. 'I could not have believed that Helen would marry a man merely for his money.' She did not believe that Helen was to marry Franklin merely for his money. If only she could have believed it; but the bleeding heart throbbed: 'Lost — lost — lost.' It was not money that Helen had seen and accepted; it was something that she herself had been too blind and weak to see. In Helen's discovery she helplessly partook. He *was* of value, then. He, whom she had not found good enough for her, was good enough for Helen. And this man — this affianced husband of hers — ah, his value she well knew; she was not blind to it — that was the sickening knowledge; she knew his value and it was not hers, not her possession, as Franklin's love and all that Franklin was had been. Gerald possessed her; she seemed to have no part in him; how little, his next words showed.

'What right have you to say she's taking him merely for his money?' Gerald demanded in his tense, vibrant voice.

Ah, how he made her suffer with his hateful unconsciousness of her pain — the male unconsciousness that rouses woman's conscious cruelty.

'I know Helen. She has always been quite frank about her mercenary ideas. She always told me she would marry a man for his money.'

'Then why do you say it's incredible that she is going to?'

Why, indeed? but Althea held her lash. 'I did not believe, even of her, that she would marry a man she considered so completely insignificant, so completely negligible — a man she described to me as a funny little man. There are limits, even to Helen's insensitiveness, I should have imagined.'

She had discovered the raw. Gerald was breathing hard.

'That must have been at first — when she didn't know him. They became great friends; everybody saw that Helen had become very fond of him; I never knew her to be so fond of anybody. You are merely angry because a man who used to be in love with you has fallen in love with another woman.'

So he, too, could lash. 'How dare you, Gerald!' she said.

At her voice he paused, and there, in the wet road, they stood and looked at each other.

What Althea then saw in his face plunged her into the nightmare abyss of nothingness. What had she left? He did not love her — he did not even care for her. She had lost the real love, and this brightness that she clung to darkened for her. He looked at her, steadily, gloomily, ashamed of what she had made him say, yet too sunken in his own pain, too indifferent to hers, to unsay it. And in her dispossession she did not dare make manifest the severance that she saw. He did not care for her, but she could not tell him so; she could not tell him to go. With horrid sickness of heart she made a feint that hid her knowledge.

'What you say is not true. Franklin does not love her. I know him through and through. I am the great love of his life; even in his letter to me, here, he tells me that I am.'

'Well, since you've thrown him over, he can console himself, I hope.'

'You do not understand, Gerald. I am disappointed — in both my friends. It is an ugly thing that has happened. You feel it so; and so do I.'

He turned and began to walk on again. And still it lay with her to speak the words that would make truth manifest. She could not utter them; she could not, now, think. All that she knew was the dense, suffocating fear.

Suddenly she stopped, put her hands on her heart, then covered her eyes. 'I am ill; I feel very ill,' she said. It was true. She did feel very ill. She went to the bank at the side of the road and sank down on it. Gerald had supported her; she had dimly been aware of the bitter joy of feeling his arm around her, and the joy of it slid away like a snake, leaving poison behind. He stood above her, alarmed and pitying.

'Althea — shall I go and get some one? I am so awfully sorry — so frightfully sorry,' he repeated.

She shook her head, sitting there, her face in her hands and her elbows on her knees. And in her great weakness an unbelievable thing happened to her. She began to cry piteously, and she sobbed: 'O Gerald — don't be unkind to me! don't be cruel! don't hurt me! O Gerald — love me — please love me!' The barriers of her pride, of her thought, were down, and, like the flowing of blood from an open wound, the truth gushed forth.

For a moment Gerald was absolutely silent. It was a tense, a stricken silence, and she felt in it something of the horror that the showing of a fatal wound might give. Then he knelt beside her; he took her hand; he put his arm around her. 'Althea, what a brute — what a brute I've been. Forgive me.' It was for something else than his harsh words that he was asking her forgiveness. He passed hurriedly from that further, that inevitable hurt. 'I can't tell you how — I mean I'm so completely sorry. You see, I was so taken aback — so cut up, you know. I could think of nothing else. She is such an old friend — my nearest friend. I never imagined her marrying, somehow; it was like hearing that she was going away for ever. And what you said made me angry.' Even he, with all his compunction, could but come back to the truth.

And, helpless, she could but lean on his pity, his sheer human pity.

'I know. He was my nearest friend too. For all my life I've been first with him. I was cut up too. I am sorry — I spoke so.'

'Poor girl — poor dear. Here, take my arm. Here. Now, you do feel better.'

She was on her feet, her hand drawn through his arm, her face turned from him and still bathed in tears.

They walked back slowly along the road. They were silent. From time to time she knew that he looked at her with solicitude; but she could not return his look. The memory of her own words was with her, a strange, new, menacing fact in life. She had said them, and they had altered everything. Henceforth she depended on his pity, on his loyalty, on his sense of duty to a task undertaken. Their bond was recognised as an unequal one. Once or twice, in the dull chaos of her mind, a flicker of pride rose up. Could she not emulate Helen? Helen was to marry a man who did not love her. Helen was to marry rationally, with open eyes, a man who was her friend. But Helen did not love the man who did not love her. She was not his thrall. She gained, she did not lose, her freedom.

CHAPTER XXV.

A week was gone since Helen had given her consent to Franklin, and again she was in her little sitting-room and again waiting, though not for Franklin. Franklin had been with her all the morning; and he had been constantly with her through the week, and she had found the closer companionship, until today, strangely easy. Franklin's very lacks endeared him to her. It was wonderful to see any one so devoid of any glamour, of any adventitious aid from nature, who yet so beamed. This beaming quality was, for Helen, his chief characteristic. There was certainly no brilliancy in Franklin's light; it was hardly a ray and it emitted never a sparkle; but it was a mild, diffused effulgence, and she always felt more peaceful and restored for coming within its radius.

It had wrapped her around all the week, and it had remained so unchanged that their relation, too, had seemed unchanged and her friend only a little nearer, a little more solicitous. They had gone about together; they had taken walks in the parks; they had made plans while strolling beside the banks of the Serpentine or leaning on the bridge in St. James's Park, to watch the ducks being fed. Already she and Franklin and the deeply triumphant Aunt Grizel had gone on a journey down to the country to look at a beautiful old house in order to see if it would do as one of Helen's 'establishments.' Already Franklin had brought her a milky string of perfect pearls, saying mildly, as he had said of the box of sweets, 'I don't approve of them, but I hope you do.' And on her finger was Franklin's ring, a noble emerald that they had selected together.

Helen had been pleased to feel in herself a capacity for satisfaction in these possessions, actual and potential. She liked to look at the great blot of green on her hand and to see the string of pearls sliding to her waist. She liked to ponder on the Jacobean house with its splendid rise of park and fall of sward. She didn't at all dislike it, either, when Franklin, as calmly possessed as ever with a clear sense of his duties, discussed with her the larger and more impersonal uses of their fortune. She found that she had ideas for him there; that the thinking and active self, so long inert, could be roused to very good purpose; that it was interesting, and very interesting, to plan, with millions at one's disposal, for the furtherance of the just and the beautiful. And she found, too, in spite of her warnings to Franklin, that though she might be a hard, a selfish, and a broken-hearted woman, she was a woman with a very definite idea of her own responsibilities. It did not suit her at all to be the mere passive receiver; it did not suit her to be greedy.

She turned her mind at once, carefully and consistently, to Franklin's interests. She found atoms and kinetics rather confusing at first, but Franklin's delighted and deliberate elucidations made a light for her that promised by degrees to illuminate these dark subjects. Yes; already life had taken hold of her and, ironically, yet not unwillingly, she followed it along the appointed path. Yesterday, however, and today, especially, a complication, subtle yet emphatic, had stolen upon her consciousness.

All the week long, in spite of something mastered and controlled in his bearing, she had seen that he was happy, and though not imaginative as to Franklin's past, she had guessed that he had never in all his life been so happy, and that never had life so taken hold of him. He enjoyed the pearls, he enjoyed the emerald, he enjoyed the Jacobean house and going over it with her and Aunt Grizel; above all he enjoyed herself as a thinking and acting being, the turning of her attention to atoms, her grave, steady penetration of his life. And in this happiness the something controlled and mastered had melted more and more; she had intended that it should melt. She had guessed at the pain, the anxiety for her that had underlain the dear little man's imperturbability, and she had determined that as far as in her lay Franklin should think her happy, should think that, at all events, she was serene and without qualms or misgivings. And she had accomplished this. It was as if she saw him breathing more deeply, more easily; as if, with a long sigh of relief, he smiled at her and said, with a new accent of confidence: 'All right.' And then, after the sigh of relief, she saw that he became too happy. It was only yesterday that she began to see it; it was today that she had clearly seen that Franklin had fallen in love with her.

It wasn't that, in any blindness to what she meant, he came nearer and made mistakes. He did not come a step nearer, and, in his happiness, his unconscious happiness, he was further from the possibility of mistakes than before. He did not draw near. He stood and gazed. Men had loved Helen before, yet, she felt it, no man had loved her as Franklin did. She could not have analysed the difference between his love and that of other men, yet she felt it dimly. Franklin stood and gazed; but it was not at charm or beauty that he gazed; whether he was really deeply aware of them she could not tell; the only words she could find with which to express her predicament and its cause sounded silly to her, but she could find no others. Franklin was gazing at her soul. She couldn't imagine what he found to fix him in it; he had certainly said that she was the honestest woman he had known; she gloomily made out that she was, she supposed, 'straight'; she liked clear, firm things, and she liked to keep a bargain. It didn't seem to her a very arresting array of virtues; but then — no, she couldn't settle Franklin's case so glibly as that; if it wasn't what she might have of charm that he had fallen in love with, it wasn't what she might have of virtue either. Perhaps one's soul hadn't much to do with either charm or virtue. And, after all, whatever it was, he was gazing at it, rapt, smiling, grave, in the lover's trance. He saw her, and only her. And she saw him, and a great many other things besides.

The immediate hope that came to her was that Franklin, perhaps, might really never know just what had happened to him. If he never recognised it, it might never become explicit; it might be managed; it could of course be managed in any case; but how she should hate having him made conscious of pain. If he never said to himself, and far less to her, that he had fallen in love with her, he might not really suffer in the strange, ill-adjusted union before them. She did not think that he had yet said it to himself; but she feared that he was hovering on the verge of self-recognition. His very guilelessness in the realm of the emotions exposed him to her, and with her perplexity went a yearning of pity as she witnessed the soft, the hesitant, the delicate unfolding.

For more had come than the tranced gaze. That morning, writing notes, with Franklin beside her, her hand had inadvertently touched his once or twice in taking the papers from him, and Helen then had seen that Franklin blushed. Twice, also, looking up, she had found his eyes fixed on her with the lover's dwelling tenderness, and both times he had quickly averted his glance in a manner very new in him.

Helen had pondered deeply in the moments before his departure. Franklin had never kissed her; the time would come when he must kiss her. The time would come when a kiss of farewell or greeting must, however rare, be a facile, marital custom. How would Franklin — trembling on that verge of a self-recognition that might make a chaos of his life — how and when would he initiate that custom? How could it be initiated by him at all unless with an emotion that would not only reveal him to himself, but make it known to him that he was revealed to her. The revelation, if it came, must come gradually; they must both have time to get used to it, she to having a husband she did not love in love with her; he to loving a wife who would never love him back. She shrank from the thought of emotional revelations. It was her part to initiate and to make a kiss an easy thing. Yet she found, sitting there, writing the last notes, with Franklin beside her, that it was not an easy thing to contemplate. The thought of her own cowardice spurred her on. When Franklin rose at last, gave her his hand, said that he'd come back that evening, Helen rose too, resolved. 'Good-bye,' she said. 'Don't forget the tickets for that concert.'

'No, indeed,' said Franklin.

'And I think, don't you? that we might put the announcement in the papers tomorrow. Aunt Grizel wants, I am sure, to see me safely Morning Posted.'

'So do I,' smiled Franklin.

Helen was summoning her courage. 'Good-bye,' she repeated, and now she smiled with a new sweetness. 'I think we ought to kiss each other good-bye, don't you? We are such an old engaged couple.'

Resolved, and firm in her resolve, though knowing commotion of soul, she leaned to him and kissed his forehead and turned her cheek to him. Franklin had kept her hand, and in the pause, where she did not see his face, she felt his tighten on it; but he did not kiss her. Smiling a little nervously, she raised her head and looked at him. He was gazing at her with a shaken, stricken look.

'You must kiss me good-bye,' said Helen, speaking as she would have spoken to a departing child. 'Why, we have no right to be put in the *Morning Post* unless we've given each other a kiss.'

And, really like the child, Franklin said: 'Must I?'

He kissed her then, gently, and spoke no further word. But she knew, when he had gone, and when thinking over the meaning of his face as it only came to her when the daze of her own daring faded and left her able to think, that she had hardly helped Franklin over a difficulty; she had made him aware of it rather; she had shown him what his task must be. And it could not reassure her, for Franklin, that his face, after that stricken moment, and with a wonderful swiftness of delicacy, had promised her that it should be accomplished. It promised her that there should be no emotions, or, if there were, that they should be mastered ones; it promised her that she should see nothing in him to make her feel that she was refusing anything, nothing to make her feel that she was giving pain by a refusal. It seemed to say that he knew, now, at last, what the burden was that he laid upon her and that it should be as light as he could make it. It did not show her that he saw his own burden; but Helen saw it for him. She, too, made herself promises as she stood after his departure, taking a long breath over her discovery; she was not afraid in looking forward. All that she was afraid of — and it was of this that she was thinking as she now stood leaning her arm upon the mantelshelf and looking into the fire, — all that she was afraid of was of looking back. It was for Gerald that she was waiting and it was Gerald's note that hung from her hand against her knee, and since that note had come, not long after Franklin had left her, her thoughts had been centred on the coming interview. Gerald had not written to her from the country; she had expected to have an answer to her announcement that morning, but none had come. This note had been brought by hand, and it said that if he could not find her at four would she kindly name some other hour when he might do so. She had answered that he would find her, and it was now five minutes to the hour.

Gerald's note had not said much more, and yet, in the little it did say, it had contrived to be tense and cool. It seemed to intimate that he reserved a great deal to say to her, and that, perhaps more, he reserved a great deal to think and not to say. It was a note that had startled her and that then had filled her with a bitterness of heart greater than any she had ever known. For that she would not accept, not that tone from Gerald. That it should be Gerald — Gerald of all the people in the world — to adopt that tone to her! The exceeding irony of it brought a laugh to her lips. She was on edge. Her strength had only just taken her through the morning and its revelations, there was none left now for patience and evasion. Gerald must be careful, was the thought that followed the laugh.

CHAPTER XXVI.

She heard the door-bell ring, and then his quick step. It did not seem to her this afternoon that she had to master the disquiet of heart that his coming always brought. It was something steeled and hostile that waited for him.

When he had entered and stood before her she saw that he intended to be careful, to be very careful, and the recognition of that attitude in him gave further bitterness to her cold, her fierce revolt. What right had he to that bright formal smile, that chill pressure of her fingers, that air of crisp cheerfulness, as of one injured but willing, magnanimously, to conceal his hurt? What right — good heavens! — had Gerald to feel injured? She almost laughed again as she looked at him and at this unveiling of his sublime self-centredness. He expected to find his world just as he would have it, his cushion at his head and his footstool at his feet, the wife in her place fulfilling her comely duties, the spinster friend in hers, administering balms and counsels; the wife at Merriston House, and the spinster friend in the little sitting-room where, for so many years, he had come to her with all his moods and misfortunes. She felt that her eyes fixed themselves on him with a cold menace as he stood there on the other side of the fire and, putting his foot on the fender, looked first at her and then down at the flames. His very silence was full of the sense of injury; but she knew that hers was the compelling silence and that she could force him to be the first to speak. And so it was that presently he said:

'Well, Helen, this is great news.'

'Yes, isn't it?' she answered. 'It has been a year of news, hasn't it?'

He stared, courteously blank, and something in her was pleased to observe that he looked silly with his affectation of blandness.

'I beg your pardon?'

'You had your great event, and I, now, have mine.'

'Ah yes, I see.'

'It's all rather queer when one comes to think of it,' said Helen. 'Althea, my new friend — whom I told you of here, only a few months ago — and her friend. How important they have become to us, and how little, last summer, we could have dreamed of it.' She, too, was speaking artificially, and was aware of it; but she was well aware that Gerald didn't find that she looked silly. She had every advantage over the friend who came with his pretended calm and his badly hidden rancour. And since he stood silent, looking at the fire, she added, mildly and cheerfully: 'I am so glad for your happiness, Gerald, and I hope that you are glad for mine.'

He looked up at her now, and she could not read the look; it hid something — or else it sought for something hidden; and in its oddity — which reminded her of a blind animal dazedly seeking its path — it so nearly touched her that, with a revulsion from any hint of weakening pity for him, it made her bitterness against him greater than before.

'I'm afraid I can't say I'm glad, Helen,' he replied. 'I'm too amazed, still, to feel anything except' — he seemed to grope for a word and then to give it up — 'amazement.'

'I was surprised myself,' said Helen. 'I had not much hope left of anything so fortunate happening to me.'

'You feel it, then, so fortunate?'

'Don't you think that it is — to marry millions,' Helen asked, smiling, 'and to have found such a good man to care for me?'

'I think it is he who is fortunate,' said Gerald, after a moment.

'Thank you; perhaps we both are fortunate.'

Once more there was a long silence and then, suddenly, Gerald flung away, thrusting his hands in his pockets and stopping before the window, his back turned to her. 'I can't stand this,' he declared.

'What can't you stand?'

'You don't love this man. He doesn't love you.'

'What is that to you?' asked Helen.

'I can't think it of you; I can't bear to think it.'

'What is it to you?' she repeated, in a deadened voice.

'Why do you say that?' he took her up with controlled fury. 'How couldn't it but be a great deal to me? Haven't you been a great deal — for all our lives nearly? Do you mean that you're going to kick me out completely — because you are going to marry? What does it mean to me? I wish it could mean something to you of what it does to me. To give yourself — you — you — to a man who doesn't love you — whom you don't love — for money. Oh, I know we've always talked of that sort of thing as if it were possible — and perhaps it is — for a man. But when it comes to a woman — a woman one has cared for — looked up to — as I have to you — it's a different matter. One expects a different standard.'

'What standard do you expect from me?' asked Helen. There were tears, but tears of rage, in her voice.

'You know,' said Gerald, who also was struggling with an emotion that, rising, overcame his control, 'you know what I think of you — what I expect of you. A great match — a great man — something fitting for you — one could accept that; but this little American nonentity, this little American — barely a gentleman — whom you'd never have looked at if he hadn't money — a man who will make you ridiculous, a man who can't have a thought or feeling in common with you — it's not fit — it's not worthy; it smirches you; it's debasing.'

He had not turned to look at her while he spoke, perhaps did not dare to look. He knew that his anger, his more than anger, had no warrant, and that the words in which it cloaked itself — though he believed in all he said — were unjustifiable. But it was more than anger, and it must speak, must plead, must protest. He had no right to say these things, perhaps, but Helen should understand the more beneath, should understand that he was lost, bewildered, miserable; if Helen did not understand, what was to become of him? And now she stood there behind him, not speaking, not answering him, so that he was almost frightened and murmured on, half inaudibly: 'It's a wrong you do — to me — to our friendship, as well as to yourself.'

Helen now spoke, and the tone of her voice arrested his attention even before the meaning of her words reached him. It was a tone that he had never heard from her, and it was not so much that it made him feel that he had lost her as that it made him feel — strangely and penetratingly — that he had never known her.

'You say all this to me, Gerald, you who in all these years have never taken the trouble to wonder or think about me at all — except how I might amuse you or advise you, or help you.' These were Helen's words. 'Why should I go on considering you, who have never considered me?'

It was so sudden, so amazing, and so cruel that, turning to her, he literally stared, open-eyed and open-mouthed. 'I don't know what you mean, Helen,' he said.

'Of course you don't,' she continued in her measured voice, 'of course you don't know what I mean; you never have. I don't blame you; you are not imaginative, and all my life I've taken care that you should know very little of what I meant. The only bit of me that you've known has been the bit that has always been at your service. There is a good deal more of me than that.'

'But — what have you meant?' he stammered, almost in tears.

Her face, white and cold, was bent on him, and in her little pause she seemed to deliberate — not on what he should be told, that was fixed — but on how to tell it; and for this she found finally short and simple words.

'Can't you guess, even now, when at last I've become desperate and indifferent?' she said. 'Can't you see, even now, that I've always loved you?'

They confronted each other in a long moment of revelation and avowal. It grew like a great distance between them, the distance of all the years through which she had suffered and he been blind. Gerald saw it like a chasm, dark with time, with secrecy, with his intolerable stupidity. He gazed at her across it, and in her face, her strange, strong, fragile, weary face, he saw it all, at last. Yes, she had loved him all her life, and he had never seen it.

She had moved, in speaking to him, away from her place near the fire, and he now went to it, and put his arms on the mantel-piece and hid his face upon them. 'Fool — fool that I am!' he uttered softly. He stood so, his face hidden from her, and his words seemed to release some bond in Helen's heart. The worst of the bitterness against him passed away. The tragedy, after all, was not his fault, but Fate's, and to suggest that he was accountable was to be grotesquely stupid. That he had not loved her was the tragedy; that he had never seen was, in reality, the tragedy's allevi-ation. Absurd to blame poor Gerald for not seeing. When she spoke again it was in an altered voice.

'No, you're not,' she said, and she seemed with him to con-template the chasm and to make it clear for him — she had always made things clear for him, and there was now, with all the melan-choly, a peacefulness in sharing with him this, their last, situation. Never before had they talked over one so strange, and never again would they talk over any other so near; to speak at last was to make it, in its very nearness, immeasurably remote, to put it away, from both their lives, for ever. 'No, you're not; I shouldn't have said that you were not imaginative; I shouldn't have said that you had never considered me; you have — you have been the best of friends; I was letting myself be cruel. It's only that *I'm* not a fool. A woman who isn't can always keep a man from imagining; it's the one thing that even a stupid woman can do. And my whole nature has been moulded by the instinct for concealment.' She looked round mechanically for a seat while she spoke; she felt horribly tired; and she sank on a straight, high chair near the writing-table. Here, leaning forward, her arms resting on her knees, her hands clasped and hanging, she went on, looking before her. 'I want to tell you about it now. There are things to confess. I haven't been a nice woman in it all; I've not taken it as a nice woman would. I've hated you for not loving me. I've hated you for not wanting anything more from me and for your contentment with what I gave you, and for caring as much as you did, too, for being fonder of me than of any one else in the world, and yet never caring more. Of course I understood; it was a little comfort to my pride to under-stand. Even if I'd been the sort of woman you would have fallen in love with, I was too near. I had to make myself too near; that was my shield. I had to give you everything you wanted because that was the sure way to hide from you that I had so much more to give.

And for years I went on hoping — not that you would see — I should have lost everything then — but that, of yourself, you would want more.'

Gerald had lifted his head, but his hand still hid his eyes. 'Helen, dear Helen,' he said, and she did not understand his voice — it was pain, but more than pain; 'why were you so cruel? why were you so proud? If you'd only let me see; if you'd only given me a hint. Don't you know it only needed that?'

She paused over his question for so long that he put down his hand and looked at her, and her eyes, meeting his unfalteringly, widened with a strained, suffering look.

'It's kind of you to say so,' she said. 'And I know you believe it now; you are so fond of me, and so sorry for this horrid tale I inflict on you, that you have to believe it. And of course it may be true. Perhaps it did only need that.'

They had both now looked away again, Gerald gazing unseeingly into the mirror, Helen at the opposite wall. 'It may be true,' she repeated. 'I had only, perhaps, to be instinctive — to withdraw — to hide — create the little mysteries that appeal to men's senses and imaginations. I had only to put aside my pride and to shut my eyes on my horrible, hard, lucid self-consciousness, let instinct guide me, be a mere woman, and you might have been in love with me. It's true. I used often to think it, too. I used often to think that I might make you fall in love with me if I could stop being your friend. But, don't you see, I knew myself far too well. I *was* too proud. I didn't want you if you only wanted me because I'd lured you and appealed to your senses and imagination. I didn't want you unless you wanted me for the big and not for the little things of love. I couldn't pretend that I had something to hide — I know perfectly how it is done — the air of evasion, of wistfulness — all the innocent hypocrisies women make use of; but I couldn't. I didn't want you like that. There was nothing for it but to look straight at you and pretend, not that there was anything to hide, but that there was nothing.'

Again, his eyes meeting hers, she looked, indeed, straight at him and smiled a little; for there was, indeed, nothing now to hide; and she went on quietly, 'You see now, how I've been feeling for these last months, when everything has gone, at last, completely. I'd determined, long ago, to give up hope and marry some one else. But I didn't know till this autumn, when you decided to marry Althea, I didn't know till then how much hope there was still left to be killed. When a thing like that has been killed, you see, one hasn't much feeling left for the rest of life. I don't care enough, one way or the other, not to marry as I'm doing. There is still one's life to live, and one may as well make what seems the best of it. I've not succeeded, you see, in marrying your great man, and I've fallen back very thankfully on my dear, good Franklin, who is not, let me tell you, a nonentity in my eyes; I'm fonder of him than of any one I've ever known except yourself. And it was too much, just the one touch too much, to have you come to me today with reproaches and an air of injury. But, at the same time, I ask your pardon for having spoken to you like that — as though you'd done *me* a wrong. And if I've been too cruel, if the memory rankles and makes you uncomfortable, you must keep away from me as long as you like. It won't be for ever, I'm sure. In spite of everything I'm sure that we shall always be friends.'

She got up now, knowing in her exhaustion that she was near tears, and she found her cigarette-case on the writing-table; it was an automatic relapse to the customary. She felt that everything, indeed, was over, and that the sooner one relapsed on every-day trivialities the better.

Gerald watched her light the cigarette, the pulsing little flicker of yellow flame illuminating her cheek and hair as she stood half turned from him. She was near him and he had but one step to take to her. He was almost unaware of motive. What he did was nearly as automatic, as inevitable, as her search for the cigarette. He was beside her and he put his arms around her and took the cigarette from her hand. Then, folding her to him, he hid his face against her hair.

It was, then, not excitement he felt so much as the envelopment of a great, a beautiful necessity. So great, so beautiful, in its peace and accomplishment, that it was as if he had stood there holding Helen for an eternity, and as if all the miserable years that had separated them were looked down at serenely from some far height.

And Helen had stood absolutely still. When she spoke he heard in her voice an amazement too great for anger. It was almost gentle in its astonishment. 'Gerald,' she said, 'I am not in need of consolation.'

Foolish Helen, he thought, breathing quietly in the warm dusk of her hair; foolish dear one, to speak from that realm of abolished time.

'I'm not consoling you,' he said.

She was again silent for a moment and he felt that her heart was throbbing hard; its shocks went through him. 'Let me go,' she said.

He kissed her hair, holding her closer.

Helen, starting violently, thrust him away with all her strength, and though blissfully aware only of his own interpretation, Gerald half released her, keeping her only by his clasp of her wrists.

His kiss had confirmed her incredible suspicion. 'You insult me!' she said. 'And after what I told you! What intolerable assumption! What intolerable arrogance! What baseness!'

Her eyes seemed to burn their eyelids; her face was transformed in its wild, blanched indignation.

'But I love you,' said Gerald, and he looked at her with a candour of conviction too deep for pleading.

'You love me!' Helen repeated. She could have wept for sheer fury and humiliation had not her scornful concentration on him been too intent to admit the flooding image of herself — mocked and abased by this travesty — which might have brought the fears. 'I think that you are mad.'

'But I do love you,' Gerald reiterated. 'I've been mad, if you like; but I'm quite sane now.'

'You are a simpleton,' was Helen's reply; she could find no other word for his fatuity.

'Be as cruel as you like; I know I deserve it,' said Gerald. 'You imagine I'm punishing you?'

'I don't imagine anything, or see anything, Helen, except that we love each other and that you've got to marry me.'

Helen looked deeply into his eyes, deeply and, he saw it at last, implacably. 'If your last chance hadn't been gone, can you believe that I would ever have told you? Your last chance is gone. I will never marry you.' And hearing steps outside, she twisted her hands from his, saying, 'Think of appearances, please. Here is Franklin.'

CHAPTER XXVII.

Gerald was standing at the window looking out when Franklin entered, and Helen, in the place where he had left her, met the gaze of her affianced with a firm and sombre look. There was a moment of silence while Franklin stood near the door, turning a hesitant glance from Gerald's back to Helen's face, and then Helen said, 'Gerald and I have been quarrelling.'

Franklin, feeling his way, tried to smile. 'Well, that's too bad,' he said. He looked at her for another silent moment before adding, 'Do you want to go on? Am I in the way?'

'No, I don't want to go on, and you are very welcome,' Helen answered. Her eyes were fixed on Franklin and she wondered at her own self-command, for, in his eyes, so troubled and so kindly, she seemed to see mutual memories; the memory of herself lying in the wood and saying 'I'm sick to death of it'; the memory of herself standing here and saying to him 'I'm a broken-hearted woman.' And she knew that Franklin was seeing in her face the same memories, and that, with his intuitive insight where things of the heart were concerned, he was linking them with the silent figure at the window.

'I suppose,' he said, going to the fire and standing before it, his back to the others, 'I suppose I can't help to elucidate things a little.'

'No, I think they are quite clear,' said Helen, 'or, at all events, you put an end to them by staying; especially' — and she fixed her gaze on the figure at the window — 'as Gerald is going now.'

But Gerald did not move and Franklin presently remarked, 'Sometimes, you know, a third person can see things in another way and help things out. If you could just, for instance, talk the matter over quietly, before me, as a sort of adviser, you know. That might help. It's a pity for old friends to quarrel.'

Gerald turned from the window at this. He had come down from the heights and knew that he had risen there too lightly, and that the tangles of lower realities must be unravelled before he could be free to mount again — Helen with him. He knew, at last, that he had made Helen very angry and that it might take some time to disentangle things; but the radiance of the heights was with him still, and if, to Helen's eye, he looked fatuous, to Franklin, seeing his face now, for the first time, he looked radiant.

'Helen,' he said, smiling gravely at her, 'what Kane says is very sensible. He is the one person in the world one could have such things out before. Let's have them out; let's put the case to him and he shall be umpire.'

Helen bent her ironic and implacable gaze upon him and

remained silent.

'You think I've no right to put it before him, I suppose.'

'You most certainly have no right. And you would gain nothing by it. What I told you just now was true.'

'I can't accept that.'

'Then you are absurd.'

'Very well, I am absurd, then. But there's one thing I have a right to tell Kane,' Gerald went on, unsmiling now. 'I owe it to him to tell him. He'll think badly of me, I know; but that can't be helped. We've all got into a dreadful muddle and the only way out of it is to be frank. So I must tell you, Kane, that Althea and I have found out that we have made a mistake; we can't hit it off. I'm not the man to make her happy and she feels it, I'm sure she feels it. It's only for my sake, I know, that she hasn't broken off long ago. You are in love with Althea, and I am in love with Helen; so there it is. I'm only saying what we are all seeing.' Gerald spoke gravely, yet at the same time with a certain blitheness, as though he took it for granted, for Franklin as well as for himself, that he thus made both their paths clear and left any hazardous element in their situations the same for both. Would Althea have Franklin and would Helen have him? This was really all that now needed elucidation.

A heavy silence followed his words. In the silence the impression that came to Gerald was as if one threw reconnoitring pebbles into a well, expecting a swift response of shallowness, and heard instead, after a wondering pause, the hollow reverberations of sombre, undreamed-of depths. Franklin's eyes were on him and Helen's eyes were on him, and he knew that in both their eyes he had proved himself once more, to say the least of it, absurd.

'Mr. Digby,' said Franklin Kane, and his voice was so strange that it sounded indeed like the fall of the stone in far-off darkness, 'perhaps you are saying what we all see; but perhaps we don't all see the same things in the same way; perhaps,' Franklin went on, finding his way, 'you don't even see some things at all.'

Gerald had flushed. 'I know I'm behaving caddishly. I've no right to say anything until I see Althea.'

'Well, perhaps not,' Franklin conceded.

'But, you know,' said Gerald, groping too, 'it's not as if it were really sudden — the Althea side of it, I mean. We've not hit it off at all. I've disappointed her frightfully; it will be a relief to her, I know — to hear' — Gerald stammered a little — 'that I see now, as clearly as she does, that we couldn't be happy together. Of course,' and he grew still more red, 'it will be she who throws me over. And — I think I'd better go to her at once.'

'Wait, Gerald,' said Helen.

He paused in his precipitate dash to the door. Only her gaze, till now, had told of the chaos within her; but when Gerald said that he was going to Althea, she found words. 'Wait a moment. I don't think that you understand. I don't think, as Franklin says, that you see some things at all. Do you realise what you are doing?'

Gerald stood, his hand on the door knob, and looked at her. 'Yes; I realise it perfectly.'

'Do you realise that it will not change me and that I think you are behaving outrageously?'

'Even if it won't change you I'd have to do it now. I can't marry another woman when I'm in love with you.'

'Can't you? When you know that you can never marry me?'

'Even if I know that,' said Gerald, staring at her and, with his deepening sense of complications, looking, for him, almost stern.

'Well, know it; once for all.'

'That you won't ever forgive me?' Gerald questioned.

'Put it like that if you like to,' she answered.

Gerald turned again to go, and it was now Franklin who checked him.

'Mr. Digby — wait,' he said; 'Helen — wait.' He had been looking at them both while they interchanged their hostilities, and yet, though watching them, he had been absent, as though he were watching something else even more. 'What I mean, what I want to say, is this — ' he rather stammered. 'Don't please go to Althea directly. I'm to go to her this evening. She asked me to come and see her at six.' He pulled out his watch. 'It's five now. Will you wait? Will you wait till this evening, please?'

Gerald again had deeply flushed. 'Of course, if you ask it. Only I do feel that I ought to see her, you know,' he paused, perplexed. Then, as he looked at Franklin Kane, something came to him. The cloud of his oppression seemed to pass from his face and it was once more illuminated, not with blitheness, but with recognition. He saw, he thought he saw, the way Franklin opened for them all. And his words expressed the dazzled relief of that vision. 'I see,' he said, gazing on at Franklin, 'yes, I see. Yes, if you can manage that it will be splendid of you, Kane.' Flooded with the hope of swift elucidation he seized the other's hand while he went on. 'It's been such a dreadful mess. Do forgive me. You must; you will, won't you? It may mean happiness for you, even though Helen says it can't for me. I do wish you all good fortune. And — I'll be at my club until I hear from you. And I can't say how I thank you.' With this, incoherently and rapidly pronounced, Gerald was gone and Franklin and Helen were left standing before each other.

For a long time they did not speak, but Franklin's silence seemed caused by no embarrassment. He still looked perplexed, but, through his perplexity, he looked intent, as though tracing in greater and greater clearness the path before him — the path that Gerald had seen that he was opening and that might, Gerald had said, mean happiness to them all. It was Helen watching him who felt a cruel embarrassment. She saw Franklin sacrificed and she saw herself unable to save him. It would not save him to tell him again that she would never marry Gerald. Franklin knew, too clearly for any evasion, that Althea's was the desperate case, the case for succour. She, Helen, could be thrown over — for they couldn't evade that aspect — and suffer never a scratch; but for Althea to throw over Gerald meant that in doing it she must tear her heart to pieces.

And she could not save Franklin by telling him that she had divined his love for her; that would give him all the more reason for ridding her of a husband who hadn't kept to the spirit of their contract. No, the only way to have saved him would have been to love him and to make him know and feel it; and this was the only thing she could not do for Franklin.

She took refuge in her nearest feeling, that of scorn for Gerald. 'It's unforgivable of Gerald,' she said.

Franklin's eyes — they had a deepened, ravaged look, but they were still calm — probed hers, all their intentness now for her. 'Why, no,' he said, after a moment, 'I don't see that.'

Helen, turning away, had dropped into her chair, leaning her forehead on her hand. 'I shall never forgive him,' she said.

Franklin, on the other side of the fire, stood thinking, thinking so hard that he was not allowing himself to feel. He was thinking so hard of Helen that he was unconscious how the question he now asked might affect himself. 'You do love him, Helen? It's him you've always loved?'

'Always,' she said.

'And he's found it out — only today.'

'He didn't find it out; I told him. He came to reproach me for my engagement.'

Franklin turned it over. 'But what he has found out, then, is that he loves you.'

'So he imagines. It's not a valuable gift, as you see, Gerald's love.'

Again Franklin paused and she knew that, for her sake, he was weighing the value of Gerald's love. And he found in answer to what she said his former words: 'Why, no, I don't see that,' he said.

'I'm afraid it's all I do see,' Helen replied.

He looked down upon her and after a silence he asked: 'May I say something?'

She nodded, resting her face in her hands.

'You're wrong, you know,' said Franklin. 'Not wrong in feeling this way now; I don't believe you can help that; but in deciding to go on feeling it. You mustn't talk about final decisions.'

'But they are made.'

'They can't be made in life. Life unmakes them, I mean, unless you set yourself against it and ruin things that might be mended.'

'I'm afraid I can't take things as you do,' said Helen. 'Some things are ruined from the very beginning.'

'Well, I don't know about that,' said Franklin; 'at all events some things aren't. And you're wrong about this thing, I'm sure of it. You're hard and you're proud, and you set yourself against life and won't let it work on you. The only way to get anything worth while out of life is to be humble with it and be willing to let it lead you, I do assure you, Helen.'

Suddenly, her face hidden in her hands, she began to cry.

'He is spoiled for me. Everything is spoiled for me,' she sobbed. 'I'd rather be proud and miserable than humiliated. Who wants a joy that is spoiled? Some things can't be joys if they come too late.'

She wept, and in the silence between them knew only her own sorrow and the bitterness of the desecration that had been wrought in her own love. Then, dimly, through her tears, she heard Franklin's voice, and heard that it trembled.

'I think they can, Helen,' he said. 'I think it's wonderful the way joy can grow if we don't set ourselves against life. I'm going to try to make it grow' — how his poor voice trembled, she was drawn from her own grief in hearing it — 'and I wish I could leave you believing that you were going to try too.'

She put down her hands and lifted her strange, tear-stained face.

'You are going to Althea.'

'Yes,' said Franklin, and he smiled gently at her.

'You are going to ask her to marry you before she can know that Gerald is giving her up.'

He paused for a moment. 'I'm going to see if she needs me.'

Helen gazed at him. She couldn't see joy growing, but she saw a determination that, in its sudden strength, was almost a joy.

'And — if she doesn't need you, Franklin?'

'Ah, well,' said Franklin, continuing to smile rather fixedly, 'I've stood that, you see, for a good many years.'

Helen rose and came beside him. 'Franklin,' she said, and she took his hand, 'if she doesn't have you — you'll come back.'

'Come back?' he questioned, and she saw that all his hardly held fortitude was shaken by his wonder.

'To me,' said Helen. 'You'll marry me, if Althea won't have you. Even if she does — I'm not going to marry Gerald. So don't go to her with any mistaken ideas about me.'

He was very pale, holding her hand fast, as it held his. 'You mean — you hate him so much — for never having seen — that you'll go through with it — to punish him.'

She shook her head. 'No, I'm not so bad as that. It won't be for revenge. It will be for you — and for myself, too; because I'd rather have it so; I'd rather have you, Franklin, than the ruined thing.'

She knew that it was final and supreme temptation that she put before him, and she held it there resolved, so that if there were one chance for him he should have it. She knew that she would stand by what she said. Franklin was her pride and Gerald her humiliation; she would never accept humiliation; and though she could see Franklin go without a qualm, she could, she saw it clearly, have a welcome for him nearly as deep as love's, if he came back to her. And what she hoped, quite selflessly, was that the temptation would suffice; that he would not go to Althea. She looked into his face, and she saw that he was tormented.

'But, Helen,' he said, 'the man you love loves you; doesn't that settle everything?'

She shook her head again. 'It settles nothing. I told you that I was a woman with a broken heart. It's not mended; it never can be mended.'

'But, Helen,' he said, and a pitiful smile of supplication dawned on his ravaged little face, 'that's where you're so wrong. You've got to let it soften and then it will have to mend. It's the hard hearts that get broken.'

'Well, mine is hard.'

'Let it melt, Helen,' he pleaded with her, 'please let it melt. Please let yourself be happy, dear Helen.'

But still she shook her head, looking deeply at him, and in the negation, in the look, it was as if she held her cup of magic steadily before him. She was there, for him, if he would have her. She kept him to his word for his sake; but she kept him to his word for hers, too. Yes, he saw that though it was for his sake, it was not for his alone — there was the final magic — that her eyes met his in that long, clear look. It was the nearest he would ever come to Helen; it was the most she could ever do for him; and, with a pang, deep and piercing, he felt all that it meant, and felt his love of her avowed in his own eyes, and recognised, received in hers. Helplessly, now, he looked at her, his lips pressed together so that they should not show their trembling, and only a little muscle in his cheek quivering irrepressibly. And he faltered: 'Helen — you could never love me back.'

'Not in that way,' said Helen. She was grave and clear; she had not a hesitation. 'But that way is ruined and over for me. I could live for you, though. I could make it worth your while.'

He looked, and he could say nothing. Against his need of Helen he must measure Althea's need of him. He must measure, too — ah, cruel perplexity — the chance for Helen's happiness. She was unhesitating; but how could she know herself so inflexible, how could she know that the hard heart might not melt? For the sake of Helen's happiness he must measure not only Gerald's need of her against his own and Gerald's power against his own mere pitifulness, but he must wonder, in an agony of sudden surmise, which, in the long-run, could give her most, the loved or the unloved man. In all his life no moment had ever equalled this in its fulness, and its intensity, and its pain. It thundered, it rushed, it darkened — like the moment of death by drowning and like the great river that bears away the drowning man. Memories flashed in it, broken and vivid — of Althea's eyes and Helen's smile; Althea so appealing, Helen so strong; and, incongruous in its remoteness, a memory of the bleak, shabby little street in a Boston suburb, the small wooden house painted brown, where he was born, where scanty nasturtiums flowered on the fence in summer, and in winter, by the light of a lamp with a ground glass shade, his mother's face, careful, worn, and gentle, bent over the family mending. Where, indeed, had the river borne him, and what had been done to him?

Helen's voice came to him, and Helen's face reshaped itself — a strange and lovely beacon over the engulfing waters. She saw his torment and she understood. 'Go to her if you must,' she said; 'and I know that you must. But don't go with mistaken ideas. Remember what I tell you. Nothing is changed — for me, or in me. If Althea doesn't want you back — or if Althea does want you back — I shall be waiting.' And, seeing his extremity, Helen, grave and clear, filled her cup of magic to the brim. As she had said that morning, she said now — but with what a difference: 'Kiss me good-bye, Franklin.'

He could not move towards her; he could not kiss her; but, smiling more tenderly than he could have thought Helen would ever smile, she put her arms around him and drew his rapt, transfigured face to hers. And holding him tenderly, she kissed him and said: 'Whatever happens — you've had the best of me.'

CHAPTER XXVIII.

Althea, since the misty walk with Gerald, had been plunged in a pit of mental confusion. She swung from accepted abasement to the desperate thought of the magnanimity in such abasement; she dropped from this fragile foothold to burning resentment, and, seeing where resentment must lead her, she turned again and clasped, with tight-closed eyes, the love that, looked upon, could not be held without humiliation. Self-doubt and self-analysis had brought her to this state of pitiful chaos. The only self left seemed centred in her love; if she did not give up Gerald, what was left her but accepted abasement? If she let him go, it would be to own to herself that she had failed to hold him, to see herself as a nonentity. Yet, to go on clinging, what would that show? Only with closed eyes could she cling. To open them for the merest glimmer was to see that she was, indeed, nothing, if she had not strength to relinquish a man who did not any longer, in any sense, wish to make her his wife. With closed eyes one might imagine that it was strength that clung; with open eyes one saw that it was weakness.

Miss Harriet Robinson, all alert gaiety and appreciation, had arrived at Merriston on Saturday, had talked all through Sunday, and had come up to London with Althea and Gerald on Monday morning. Gerald had gone to a smoking-carriage, and Althea had hardly exchanged a word with him. She and Miss Robinson went to a little hotel in Mayfair, a hotel supposed to atone for its costliness and shabbiness by some peculiar emanation of British comfort. Americans of an earnest, if luxurious type, congregated there and found a satisfactory local flavour in worn chintzes and uneven passages. Lady Blair had kindly pressed Althea to stay with her in South Kensington and be married from her house; but even a week ago, when this plan had been suggested, Althea had shrunk from it. It had seemed, even then, too decisive. Once beneath Lady Blair's quasi-maternal roof one would be propelled, like a labelled parcel, resistlessly to the altar. Even then Althea had felt that the little hotel in Mayfair, with its transient guests and impersonal atmosphere, offered further breathing space for indefiniteness.

She was thankful indeed for breathing space as, on the afternoon of her arrival, she sat sunken in a large chair and felt, as one relief, that she would not see Miss Robinson again until evening. It had been tormenting, all the journey up, to tear herself from her own sick thoughts and to answer Miss Robinson's unsuspecting comments and suggestions.

Miss Robinson was as complacent and as beaming as though she had herself 'settled' Althea. She richly embroidered the themes, now so remote, that had once occupied poor Althea's imagination — house-parties at Merriston; hostess-ship on a large scale in London; Gerald's seat in Parliament taken as a matter-of-course. Althea, feeling the intolerable irony, had attempted vague qualifications; Gerald did not care for politics; she herself preferred a quieter life; they probably could not afford a town house. But to such disclaimers Miss Robinson opposed the brightness of her faith in her friend's capacities. 'Ah, my dear, it's your very reticence, your very quietness, that will tell. Once settled — I've always felt it of you — you will make your place — and your place can only be a big one. My only regret is that you won't get your wedding-dress in Paris — oh yes, I know that they have immensely improved over here; but, for cut and *cachet*, Paris is still the only place.'

This had all been tormenting, and Miss Buckston's presence at lunch had been something of a refuge — Miss Buckston, far more interested in her Bach choir practice than in Althea's plans, and lending but a preoccupied attention to Miss Robinson's matrimonial talk. Miss Buckston, at a glance, had dismissed Miss Robinson as frothy and shallow. They were both gone now, thank goodness. Lady Blair would not descend upon her till next morning, and Sally and Mrs. Peel were not due in London until the end of the week. Althea sat, her head leaning back, her eyes closed, and wondered whether Gerald would come and see her. He had parted from her at the station, and the memory of his face, courteous, gentle, yet so unseeing, made her feel like weeping piteously. She spent the afternoon in the chair, her eyes closed and an electric excitement of expectancy tingling through her, and Gerald did not come. He did not come that evening, and the evening passed like a phantasmagoria — the dinner in the sober little dining-room, Miss Robinson, richly dressed, opposite her; and the hours in her drawing-room afterwards, she and Miss Robinson on either side of the fire, quietly conversing. And next morning there was no word from him. It was then, as she lay in bed and felt the tears, though she did not sob, roll down over her cheeks upon the pillow, that sudden strength came with sudden revolt. A revulsion against her suffering and the cause of it went through her, and she seemed to shake off a torpor, an obsession, and to re-enter some moral heritage from which, for months, her helpless love had shut her out.

Lying there, her cheeks still wet but her eyes now stern and steady, she felt herself sustained, as if by sudden wings, at a vertiginous height from which she looked down upon herself and upon her love. What had it been, that love? what was it but passion pure and simple, the craving feminine thing, enmeshed in charm. To a woman of her training, her tradition, must not a love that could finally satisfy her nature, its deeps and heights, be a far other love; a love of spirit rather than of flesh? What was all the pain that had warped her for so long but the inevitable retribution for her backsliding? Old adages came to her, aerial Emersonian faiths. Why, one was bound and fettered if feeling was to rule one and not mind. Friendship, deep, spiritual congeniality, was the real basis for marriage, not the enchantment of the heart and senses. She had been weak and dazzled; she had followed the will-o'-the-wisp — and see, see the bog where it had led her.

She saw it now, still sustained above it and looking down. Her love for Gerald was not a high thing; it called out no greatness in her; appealed to none; there was no spiritual congeniality between them. In the region of her soul he was, and would always remain, a stranger.

Sure of this at last, she rose and wrote to Franklin, swiftly and urgently. She did not clearly know what she wanted of him; but she felt, like a flame of faith within her, that he, and he only, could sustain her at her height. He was her spiritual affinity; he was her wings. Merely to see him, merely to steep herself in the radiance of his love and sympathy, would be to recover power, poise, personality, and independence. It was a goal she flew towards, though she saw it but in dizzy glimpses, and as if through vast hallucinations of space.

She told Franklin to come at six. She gave herself one more day; for what she could not have said. A lightness of head seemed to swim over her, and a loss of breath, when she tried to see more clearly the goal, or what might still capture and keep her from it.

She told Amélie that she had a bad headache and would spend the day on her sofa, denying herself to Lady Blair; and all day long she lay there with tingling nerves and a heavily beating heart — poor heart, what was happening to it in its depths she could not tell — and Gerald did not write or come.

At tea-time Miss Robinson could not be avoided. She tip-toed in and sat beside her sofa commenting compassionately on her pallor. 'I do so beg you to go straight to bed, dear,' she said. 'Let me give you some sal volatile; there is nothing better for a headache.'

But Althea, smiling heroically, said that she must stay up to see Franklin Kane. 'He wants to see me, and will be here at six. After he is gone I will go to bed.' She did not know why she should thus arrange facts a little for Miss Robinson; but all her nature was stretched on its impulse towards safety, and it was automatically that she adjusted facts to that end. After the first great moment of enfranchisement and soaring, it was like relapsing to some subconscious function of the organism — digestion or circulation —

that did things for one if one didn't interfere with it. Her mind no longer directed her course except in this transformed and subsidiary guise; it had become part of the machinery of self-preservation.

'You really are an angel, my dear,' said Miss Robinson. 'You oughtn't to allow your devotees to *accaparer* you like this. You will wear yourself out.'

Althea, with a smile still more heroic, said that dear Franklin could never wear her out; and Miss Robinson, not to be undeceived, shook her head, while retiring to make room for the indiscreet friend.

When she was gone, Althea got up and took her place in the chintz chair where she had waited for so long yesterday.

Outside, a foggy day closed to almost opaque obscurity. The fire burned brightly, there were candles on the mantelpiece and a lamp on the table, yet the encompassing darkness seemed to have entered the room. After the aerial heights of the morning it was now at a corresponding depth, as if sunken to the ocean-bed, that she seemed to sit and wait, and feel, in a trance-like pause, deep, essential forces working. And she remembered the sunny day in Paris, and the other hotel drawing-room where, empty and aimless, she had sat, only six months ago. How much had come to her since then; through how much hope and life had she lived, to what heights been lifted, to what depths struck down. And now, once more she sat, bereft of everything, and waiting for she knew not what.

Franklin appeared almost to the moment. Althea had not seen him since leaving London some weeks before, and at the first glance he seemed to her in some way different. She had only time to think, fleetingly, of all that had happened to Franklin since she had last seen him, all the strange, new things that Helen must have meant to him; and the thought, fleeting though it was, made more urgent the impulse that pressed her on. For, after all, the second glance showed him as so much the same, the same to the unbecomingness of his clothes, the flatness of his features, the general effect of decision and placidity that he always, predominatingly, gave.

It was on Franklin's sameness that she leaned. It was Franklin's sameness that was her goal; she trusted it like the ground beneath her feet. She went to him and put out her hands. 'Dear Franklin,' she said, 'I am so glad to see you.'

He took her hands and held them while he looked into her eyes. The face she lifted to him was a woeful one, in spite of the steadying of its pale lips to a smile. It was not enfranchisement and the sustained height that he saw — it was fear and desolation; they looked at him out of her large, sad eyes and they were like an uttered cry. He saw her need, worse still, he saw her trust; and yet, ah yet, his hope, his unacknowledged hope, the hope which Helen's magic had poured into his veins, pulsed in him. He saw her need, but as he looked, full of compassion and solicitude, he was hoping that her need was not of him.

Suddenly Althea burst into sobs. She leaned her face against his shoulder, her hands still held in his, and she wept out: 'O Franklin, I had to send for you — you are my only friend — I am so unhappy, so unhappy.' Franklin put an arm around her, still holding her hand, and he slightly patted her back as she leaned upon him. 'Poor Althea, poor dear,' he said.

'Oh, what shall I do, Franklin?' she whispered.

'Tell me all about it,' said Franklin. 'Tell me what's the matter.'

She paused for a moment, and in the pause her thoughts, released for that one instant from their place of servitude, scurried through the inner confusion. His tone, the quietness, kindness, rationality of it, seemed to demand reason, not impulse, from her, the order of truth and not the chaos of feeling. But pain and fear had worked for too long upon her, and she did not know what truth was. All she knew was that he was near, and tender and compassionate, and to know that seemed to be knowing at last that here was the real love, the love of spirit from which she had turned to lower things. Impulse, not insincere, surged up, and moved by it alone she sobbed on, 'O Franklin, I have made a mistake, a horrible, horrible mistake. It's killing me. I can't go on. I don't love him, Franklin — I don't love Gerald — I can't marry him. And how can I tell him? How can I break faith with him?'

Franklin stood very still, his hand clasping hers, the other ceasing its rhythmic, consolatory movement. He held her, this woman whom he had loved for so many years, and over her bent head he looked before him at the frivolous and ugly wall-paper, a chaos of festooned chrysanthemums on a bright pink ground. He gazed at the chrysanthemums, and he wondered, with a direful pang, whether Althea were consciously lying to him.

She sobbed on: 'Even in the first week, I knew that something was wrong. Of course I was in love — but it was only that — there was nothing else except being in love. Doubts gnawed at me from the first; I couldn't bear to accept them; I hoped on and on. Only in this last week I've seen that I can't — I can't marry him. Oh — ' and the wail was again repeated, 'what shall I do, Franklin?'

He spoke at last, and in the disarray of her sobbing and darkened condition — her face pressed against him, her ears full of the sound of her own labouring breath — she could not know to the full how strange his voice was, though she felt strangeness and caught her breath to listen.

'Don't take it like this, Althea,' he said. 'It's not so bad as all this. It can all be made right. You must just tell him the truth and set him free.'

And now there was a strange silence. He was waiting, and she was waiting too; she stilled her breath and he stilled his; all each heard was the beating of his and her own heart. And the silence, to Althea, was full of a new and formless fear, and to Franklin of an acceptation sad beyond all the sadnesses of his life. Even before Althea spoke, and while the sweet, the rapturous, the impossible hope softly died away, he knew in his heart, emptied of magic, that it was he Althea needed.

She spoke at last, in a changed and trembling voice; it pierced him, for he felt the new fear in it: 'How can I tell him the truth, Franklin?' she said. 'How can I tell you the truth? How can I say that I turned from the real thing, the deepest, most beautiful thing in my life — and hurt it, broke it, put it aside, so blind, so terribly blind I was — and took the unreal thing? How can I ever forgive myself — but, O Franklin, much, much more, how can you ever forgive me?' her voice wailed up, claiming him supremely.

She believed it to be the truth, and he saw that she believed it. He saw, sadly, clearly, that among all the twistings and deviations of her predicament, one thing held firm for her, so firm that it had given her this new faith in herself — her faith in his supreme devotion. And he saw that he owed it to her. He had given it to her, he had made it her possession, to trust to as she trusted to the ground under her feet, ever since they were boy and girl together. Six months ago it would have been with joy, and with joy only, that he would have received her, and have received the gift of her bruised, uncertain heart. Six months — why only a week ago he would have thought that it could only be with joy.

So now he found his voice and he knew that it was nearly his old voice for her, and he said, in answer to that despairing statement that wailed for contradiction: 'Oh no, Althea, dear. Oh no, you haven't wrecked our lives.'

'But you are bound now,' she hardly audibly faltered. 'You have another life opening before you. You can't come back now.'

'No, Althea,' Franklin repeated, and he stroked her shoulder again. 'I can come back, if you want me. And you do want me, don't you, dear? You will let me try to make you happy?'

She put back her head to look at him, her poor face, tear-stained, her eyes wild with their suffering, and he saw the new fear in them, the formless fear. 'O Franklin,' she said, and the question was indeed a strange one to be asked by her of him: 'do you love me?'

And now, pierced by his pity, Franklin could rise to all she needed of him. The old faith sustained him, too. One didn't love some one for all one's life like that, to be left quite dispossessed. Many things were changed, but many still held firm; and though, deep in his heart, sick with its relinquishment, Helen's words seemed to whisper, 'Some things can't be joys when they come too late,' he could answer himself as he had answered her, putting away the irony and scepticism of disenchantment — 'It's wonderful the way joy can grow,' and draw strength for himself and for his poor Althea from that act of affirmation.

'Why, of course I love you, Althea, dear,' he said. 'How can you ask me that? I've always loved you, haven't I? You knew I did, didn't you, or else you wouldn't have sent? You knew I wasn't bound if you were free. I understand it all.' And smiling at her so that she should forget for ever that she had had a new fear, he added, 'And see here, dear, you mustn't delay a moment in letting Gerald know. Come, write him a note now, and I'll have it sent to his club so that he shall hear right away.'

CHAPTER XXIX.

Helen woke next morning after unbroken, heavy slumbers, with a mind as vague and empty as a young child's. All night long she had been dreaming strange, dreary dreams of her youth. There had been no pain in them, or fear, only a sad lassitude, as of one who, beaten and weary, looks back from a far distance at pain and fear outlived. And lying in her bed, inert and placid, she felt as if she had been in a great battle, and that after the annihilation of anæsthetics she had waked to find herself with limbs gone and wounds bandaged, passive and acquiescent, in a world from which all large issues had been eliminated for ever.

It was the emptiest kind of life on which her eyes opened so quietly this morning. She was not even to be life's captive. The little note which had come to her last night from Franklin and now lay beside her bed had told her that. He had told her that Althea had taken him back, and he had only added, 'Thank you, dear Helen, for all that you have given me and all that you were willing to give.'

In the overpowering sense of sadness that had been the last of the day's great emotions Helen had found no mitigation of relief for her own escape. That she had escaped made only an added bitterness. And even sadness seemed to be a memory this morning, and the relief that came, profound and almost sweet, was in the sense of having passed away from feeling. She had felt too much; though, had life been in her with which to think or feel, she could have wept over Franklin.

Sometimes she closed her eyes, too much at peace for a smile; sometimes she looked quietly about her familiar little room, above Aunt Grizel's, and showing from its windows only a view of the sky and of the chimney-pots opposite, a room oddly empty of associations and links; no photographs, few books, few pictures; only the vase of flowers she liked always to have near her; her old Bible and prayer-book and hymnal, battered by years rather than by use, for religion held no part at all in Helen's life; and two faded prints of seventeenth-century battleships, sailing in gallant squadrons on a silvery sea. These had hung in Helen's schoolroom, and she had always been fond of them. The room was symbolic of her life, so insignificant in every outer contact, so centred, in her significant self, on its one deep preoccupation. But there was no preoccupation now. Gerald's image passed before her and meant nothing more than the other things she looked at, while her mind drifted like an aimless butterfly from the flowers and the prints to the pretty old mirror — a gift of Gerald's — and hovered over the graceful feminine objects scattered upon the chairs and tables. The thought of Gerald stirred nothing more than a mild wonder. What a strange thing, her whole life hanging on this man, coloured, moulded by him. What did such a feeling mean? and what had she really wanted of Gerald more than he had given? She wanted nothing now.

It was with an effort — a painful, dragging effort — that she roused herself to talk to Aunt Grizel, who appeared at the same time as her breakfast. Not that she needed to act placidity and acquiescence before Aunt Grizel; she felt them too deeply to need to act; the pain, perhaps, came from having nothing else with which to meet her.

Aunt Grizel was amazed, distressed, nearly indignant; she only was not indignant because of a pity that perplexed even while it soothed her. She, too, had had a letter from Franklin that morning, and only that morning had heard of the broken engagement and of how Franklin faced it. She did not offer to show Helen Franklin's letter, which she held in her hand, emphasising her perplexity by doubling it over and slapping her palm with it. 'She sent for him, then.' It was on Althea that she longed to discharge her smothered anger.

Helen was ready for her; to have to be so ready was part of the pain. 'Well, in a sense perhaps, it was all she could do, wasn't it? when she found that she couldn't go on with Gerald, and really wanted Franklin at last.'

'Rather late in the day to come to that conclusion when Mr. Kane was engaged to another woman.'

'Well — he was engaged to another woman only because Althea wouldn't have him.'

'Oh! — Ah!' Aunt Grizel was non-committal on this point. 'She lets him seem to jilt you.'

'Perhaps she does.' Helen's placidity was profound.

'I know Mr. Kane, he wouldn't have been willing to do that unless pressure had been brought to bear.'

'Pressure was, I suppose; the pressure of his own feeling and of Althea's unhappiness. He saw that his chance had come and he had to take it. He couldn't go on and marry me, could he, Aunt Grizel? when he saw the chance had come for him to take,' said Helen reasonably.

'Well,' said Aunt Grizel, 'the main point isn't, of course, what the people who know of your engagement will think — we don't mind that. What we want to decide on is what we think ourselves. I keep my own counsel, for I know you'd rather I did, and you keep yours. But what about this money? He writes to me that he wants me to take over from him quite a little fortune, so that when I die I can leave you about a thousand a year. He has thought it out; it isn't too much and it isn't too little. He is altogether a remarkable man; his tact never fails him. Of course it's nothing compared with what he wanted to do for you; but at the same time it's so much that, to put it brutally, you get for nothing the safety I wanted you to marry him to get.'

Helen's delicate and weary head now turned on its pillow to look at Aunt Grizel. They looked at each other for some time in silence, and in the silence they took counsel together. After the interchange Helen could say, smiling a little, 'We mustn't put it brutally; that is the one thing we must never do. Not only for his sake,' she wanted Aunt Grizel to see it clearly, 'but for mine.'

'How shall we put it, then? It's hardly a possible thing to accept, yet, if he hadn't believed you would let him make you safe, would he have gone back to Miss Jakes? One sees his point.'

'We mustn't put it brutally, because it isn't true,' said Helen, ignoring this last inference. 'I couldn't let you take it for me unless I cared very much for him; and I care so much that I can't take it.'

Aunt Grizel was silent for another moment. 'I see: it's because it's all you can do for him now.'

'All that he can do for me, now,' Helen just corrected her.

'Wasn't it all he ever could do, and more? He makes you safe — of course it's not what I wanted for you, but it's part of it — he makes you safe and he removes himself.'

Aunt Grizel saw the truth so clearly that Helen could allow her to seem brutal. 'It's only because we could both do a good deal for each other that doing this is possible,' she said.

She then roused herself to pour out her coffee and butter her toast, and Miss Buchanan sat in silence beside her, tapping Franklin Winslow Kane's letter on her palm from time to time. And at last she brought out her final decision. 'When I write to him and tell him that I accept, I shall tell him too, that I'm sorry.'

'Sorry? For what?' Helen did not quite follow her.

'That it's all he can do now,' said Aunt Grizel; 'that he is removing himself.'

It was her tribute to Franklin, and Helen, even for the sake of all the delicate appearances, couldn't protest against such a tribute. She was glad that Franklin was to know, from Aunt Grizel, that he, himself, was regretted. So that she said, 'Yes; I'm glad you can tell him that.'

It was at this moment of complete understanding that the maid came in and said that Mr. Digby was downstairs and wanted to see Miss Helen. He would wait as long as she liked. There was then a little pause, and Aunt Grizel saw a greater weariness pass over her niece's face.

'Very well,' she spoke for her to the maid. 'Tell Mr. Digby that some one will be with him directly,' and, as the door closed: 'You're not fit to see him this morning, Helen,' she said; 'not fit to pour balms into his wounds. Let me do it for you.'

Helen lay gazing before her, and she was still silent. She did not know what she wanted; but she did know that she did not want to see Gerald. The thought of seeing him was intolerable. 'Will you pour balms?' she said. 'I'm afraid you are not too sorry for Gerald.'

'Well, to tell you the truth, I'm not,' said Aunt Grizel, smiling a little grimly. 'He takes things too easily, and I confess that it does rather please me to see him, for once in his life, "get left." He needed to "get left."'

'Well, you won't tell him that, if I let you go to him instead of me? You will be nice to him?'

'Oh, I'll be nice enough. I'll condole with him.'

'Tell him,' said Helen, as Aunt Grizel moved resolutely to the door, 'that I can't see anybody; not for a long time. I shall go away, I think.'

CHAPTER XXX.

Miss Grizel had known Gerald all his life, and yet she was not intimate with him, and during the years that Helen had lived with her she had come to feel a certain irritation against him. Her robust and caustic nature had known no touch of jealousy for the place he held in Helen's life. It was dispassionately that she observed, and resented on Helen's account, the exacting closeness of a friendship with a man who, she considered, was not worth so much time and attention. She suspected nothing of the hidden realities of Helen's feeling, yet she did suspect, acutely, that, had it not been for Gerald, Helen might have had more time for other things. It was Gerald who monopolised and took for granted. He came, and Helen was always ready. Miss Grizel had not liked Gerald to be so assured. She was pleased, now, in going downstairs, that Gerald Digby should find, for once, and at a moment of real need, that Helen could not see him.

He was standing before the fire, his eyes on the door, and as she looked at him Miss Grizel experienced a certain softening of mood. She decided that she had, to some extent, misjudged Gerald; he had, then, capacity for caring deeply. Miss Jakes's defection had knocked him about badly. There was kindness in her voice as she said: 'Good morning,' and gave him her hand.

But Gerald was not thinking of her or of her kindness. 'Where is Helen?' he asked, shaking and then automatically retaining her hand.

'You can't see Helen today,' said Miss Grizel, a little nettled by the open indifference. 'She is not at all well. This whole affair, as you may imagine, has been singularly painful for her to go through. She asks me to tell you that she can see nobody for a long time. We are going away; we are going to the Riviera,' said Miss Grizel, making the resolve on the spot.

Gerald held her hand and looked at her with a feverish unseeing gaze. 'I must see Helen,' he said.

'My dear Gerald,' Miss Grizel disengaged her hand and went to a chair, 'this really isn't an occasion for musts. Helen has had a shock as well as you, and you certainly shan't see her.'

'Does she say I shan't?'

Miss Grizel's smile was again grim. 'She says you shan't, and so do I. She's not fit to see anybody.'

Gerald looked at her for another moment and then turned to the writing-table. 'I beg your pardon; I don't mean to be rude. Only I really must see her. Do you mind my writing a line? Will you have it taken to her?'

'Certainly,' said Miss Grizel, compressing her lips.

Gerald sat down and wrote, quickly, yet carefully, pausing between the sentences and fixing the same unseeing gaze on the garden. He then rose and gave the note to Miss Grizel, who, ringing, gave it to the maid, after which she and Gerald remained sitting on opposite sides of the room in absolute silence for quite a long while.

Gerald's note had been short. 'Don't be so unspeakably cruel,' it ran, without preamble. 'You know, don't you, that it has all turned out perfectly? Althea has thrown me over and taken Kane. I've made them happy at all events. As for us — O Helen, you must see me. I can't wait. I can't wait for an hour. I beseech you to come. Only let me see you. — GERALD.'

To this appeal the maid presently brought the answer, which Gerald, oblivious of Miss Grizel's scrutiny, tore open and read.

'Don't make me despise you, Gerald. You come because of what I told you yesterday, and I told you because it was over, so that you insult me by coming. You must believe me when I say that it is over, and until you can meet me as if you had forgotten, I cannot see you. I will not see you now. I do not want to see you. — HELEN.'

He read this, and Miss Grizel saw the blood surge into his face. He leaned back in his chair, crumpled Helen's note in his fingers, and looked out of the window. Again Miss Grizel was sorry for him, though with her sympathy there mingled satisfaction. Presently Gerald looked at her, and it was as if he were, at last, aware of her. He looked for a long time, and suddenly, like some one spent and indifferent, he said, offering his explanation: 'You see — I'm in love with Helen — and she won't have me.'

Miss Grizel gasped and gazed. 'In love with Helen? You?' she repeated. The gold locket on her ample bosom had risen with her astounded breath.

'Yes,' said Gerald, 'and she won't have me.'

'But Miss Jakes?' said Miss Grizel.

'She is in love with Kane, and Kane with her — as he always has been, you know. They are all right. Everything is all right, except Helen.'

A queer illumination began to shoot across Miss Grizel's stupor.

'Perhaps you told Helen that you loved her before Miss Jakes threw you over. Perhaps you told Mr. Kane that Miss Jakes loved him before she threw you over. Perhaps it's you who have upset the apple-cart.'

'I suppose it is,' said Gerald, gloomily, but without contrition. 'I thought it would bring things right to have the facts out. It has brought them right — for Althea and Kane; they will be perfectly happy together.'

This simplicity, in the face of her own deep knowledge — the knowledge she had built on in sending for Franklin Kane a week ago — roused a ruthless ire in Miss Grizel. 'I'm afraid that you've let your own wishes sadly deceive you,' she said. 'I must tell you, since you evidently don't know it, that Mr. Kane is in love with Helen; deeply in love with her. From what I understand of the situation you have sacrificed him to your own feeling, and perhaps sacrificed Miss Jakes too; but I don't go into that.'

It was now Gerald's turn to gaze and gasp; he did not gasp, however; he only gazed — gazed with a gaze no longer inward and unseeing. He was, at last, seeing everything. He fell back on the one most evident thing he saw, and had from the beginning seen. 'But Helen — she could never have loved him. Such a marriage would be unfit for Helen. I'm not excusing myself. I see I've been an unpardonable fool in one way.'

Miss Grizel's ire increased. 'Unfit for Helen? Why, pray? He would have given her the position of a princess — in our funny modern sense. I intended, and I made the marriage. I saw he'd fallen in love with her — dear little man — though at the time he didn't know it himself. And since then I've had the satisfaction — one of the greatest of my life — of seeing how happy I had made both of them. It was obvious, touchingly so, that he was desperately in love with Helen. Yes, Gerald, don't come to me for sympathy and help. You've wrecked a thing I had set my heart on. You've wrecked Mr. Kane, and my opinion is that you've wrecked Helen too.'

Gerald, who had become very pale, kept his eyes on her, and he went back to his one foothold in a rocking world. 'Helen could never have loved him.'

Miss Grizel shook her hand impatiently above her knee. 'Love! Love! What do you all mean with your love, I'd like to know? What's this sudden love of yours for Helen, you who, until yesterday, were willing to marry another woman for her money — or were you in love with her too? What's Miss Jakes's love of Mr. Kane, who, until a week ago, thought herself in love with you? And you may well ask me what is Mr. Kane's love of Helen, who, until a week ago, thought himself in love with Miss Jakes? But there I answer you that he is the only one of you who seems to me to know what love is. One can respect his feeling; it means more than himself and his own emotions. It means something solid and dependable. Helen recognised it, and Helen's feeling for him — though it certainly wasn't love in your foolish sense — was something that she valued more than anything you can have to offer her. And I repeat, though I'm sorry to pain you, that it is clear to me that you have wrecked her life as well as Mr. Kane's.'

Miss Grizel had had her say. She stood up, her lips compressed, her eyes weighty with their hard, good sense. And Gerald rose, too. He was at a disadvantage, and an unfair one, but he did not think of that. He thought, with stupefaction, of what he had done in this room the day before to Franklin and to Helen. In the depths of his heart he couldn't wish it undone, for he couldn't conceive of himself now as married to Althea, nor could he, in spite of Miss Grizel's demonstrations, conceive of Helen as married to Franklin Kane. But with all the depths of his heart he wished what he had done, done differently. And although he couldn't conceive of Helen as married to Franklin Kane, although he couldn't accept Miss Grizel's account of her state as final, nor believe her really wrecked — since, after all, she loved him, not Franklin — he could clearly conceive from Miss Grizel's words that by doing it as he had, he had wrecked many things and endangered many. What these things were her words only showed him confusedly, and his clearest impulse now was to see just what they were, to see just what he had done. Miss Grizel couldn't show him, for Miss Grizel didn't know the facts; Helen would not show him, she refused to see him; his mind leaped at once, as he rose and stood looking rather dazedly about before going, to Franklin Kane. Kane, as he had said yesterday, was the one person in the world before whom one could have such things out. Even though he had wrecked Kane, Kane was still the only person he could turn to. And since he had wrecked him in his ignorance he felt that now, in his enlightenment, he owed him something infinitely delicate and infinitely deep in the way of apology.

'Well, thank you,' he said, grasping Miss Grizel's hand. 'You had to say it, and it had to be said. Good-bye.'

Miss Grizel, not displeased with his fashion of taking her chastisement, returned his grasp. 'Yes,' she said, 'you couldn't go on as you were. But all the same, I'm sorry for you.'

'Oh,' Gerald smiled a little. 'I don't suppose you've much left for me, and no wonder.'

'Oh yes, I've plenty left for you,' said Miss Grizel. And, in thinking over his expression as he had left her, the smile, its self-mockery, yet its lack of bitterness, his courage, and yet the frankness of his disarray, she felt that she liked Gerald more than she had ever liked him.

CHAPTER XXXI.

'Why, yes, of course I can see you. Do sit down.' Franklin spoke gravely, scanning his visitor's face while he moved piles of pamphlets from a chair and pushed aside the books and papers spread before him on the table.

Gerald had found him, after a fruitless morning call, at his lodgings in Clarges Street, and Franklin, in the dim little sitting-room, had risen from the work that, for hours, had given him a feeling of anchorage — not too secure — in a world where many of his bearings were painfully confused. Seeing him so occupied, Gerald, in the doorway, had hesitated: 'Am I interrupting you? Shall I come another time? I want very much to see you, if I may.' And Franklin had replied with his quick reassurance, too kindly for coldness, yet too grave for cordiality.

Gerald sat down at the other side of the table and glanced at the array of papers spread upon it. They gave him a further sense of being beyond his depth. It was like seeing suddenly the whole bulk of some ocean craft, of which before one had noticed only the sociable and very insignificant decks and riggings, lifted, for one's scientific edification, in its docks. All the laborious, under-lying meaning of Franklin's life was symbolised in these neat papers and heavy books. Gerald tried to remember, with only par-tial success, what Franklin's professional interests were; people's professional interests had rarely engaged his attention. It was queer to realise that the greater part of Franklin Kane's life was something entirely alien from his own imagination, and Gerald felt, as we have said, beyond his depth in realising it. Yet the fact of a significance he had no power of gauging did not disconcert him; he was quite willing to swim as best he could and even to splash grotesquely; quite willing to show Franklin Kane that he was very helpless and very ignorant, and could only appeal for mercy.

'Please be patient with me if I make mistakes,' he said. 'I prob-ably shall make mistakes; please bear with me.'

Franklin, laying one pamphlet on another, did not reply to this, keeping only his clear, kind gaze responsively on the other's face.

'In the first place,' said Gerald, looking down and reaching out for a thick blue pencil which he seemed to examine while he spoke, 'I must ask your pardon. I made a terrible fool of myself yesterday afternoon. As you said, there were so many things I didn't see. I do see them now.'

He lifted his eyes from the pencil, and Franklin, after meeting them for a moment, said gently: 'Well, there isn't much good in looking at them, is there? As for asking my pardon — you couldn't have helped not knowing those things.'

'Perhaps I ought to have guessed them, but I didn't. I was able to play the fool in perfect good faith.'

'Well, I don't know about that; I don't know that you played the fool,' said Franklin.

'My second point is this,' said Gerald. 'Of course I'm not going to pretend anything. You know that I love Helen and that I believe she loves me, and that for that reason I've a right to seem silly and fatuous and do my best to get her. I quite see what you must both of you have thought of me yesterday. I quite see that she couldn't stand my blindness — to all you meant and felt, you know, and then my imagining that everything could be patched up between her and me. She wants me to feel my folly to the full, and no wonder. But that sort of bitterness would have to go down where people love — wouldn't it? it's something that can be got over. But that's what I want to ask you; perhaps I'm more of a fool than I yet know; perhaps what her aunt tells me is true; perhaps I've wrecked Helen as well as wrecked you. It's a very queer question to ask — and you must forgive me — no one can answer it but you, except Helen, and Helen won't see me. Do you really think I have wrecked her?'

Everybody seemed to be asking this question of poor Franklin. He gave it his attention in this, its new application, and before answering, he asked:

'What's happened since I saw you?'

Gerald informed him of the events of the morning.

'I suppose,' said Franklin, reflecting, 'that you shouldn't have gone so soon. You ought to have given her more time to adjust herself. It looked a little too sure, didn't it? as if you felt that now that you'd scttlcd mattcrs satisfactorily you could come and claim her.'

'I know now what it looked like,' said Gerald; 'but, you see, I didn't know this morning. And I was sure, I am sure,' he said, fixing his charming eyes sadly and candidly upon Franklin, 'that Helen and I belong to one another.'

Franklin continued to reflect. 'Well, yes, I understand that,' he said. 'But how can you make her feel it? Why weren't you sure long ago?'

'Oh, you ask me again why I was a fool,' said Gerald gloomily, 'and I can only reply that Helen was too clever. After all, falling in love is suddenly seeing something and wanting something, isn't it? Well, Helen never let me see and never let me want.'

'Yes, that's just the trouble. She's let you see, so that you do want, now. But that can't be very satisfactory to her, can it?' said Franklin, with all his impartiality.

'Of course it can't!' said Gerald, with further gloom. 'And don't, please, imagine that I'm idiotic enough to think myself satisfactory. My only point is that I belong to her, unsatisfactory as I am, and that, unless I've really wrecked her, and myself — I must be able to make her feel that it's her point too; that other things can't really count, finally, beside it. Have I wrecked her?' Gerald repeated. 'I mean, would she have been really happier with you? Forgive me for asking you such a question.'

Franklin again resumed his occupation of laying the pamphlets of one pile neatly upon those of the other. He had all his air of impartial reflection, yet his hand trembled a little, and Gerald, noticing this, murmured again, turning away his eyes: 'Forgive me. Please understand. I must know what I've done.'

'You see,' said Franklin, after a further silence, while he continued to transfer the pamphlets; 'quite apart from my own feelings — which do, I suppose, make it a difficult question to answer — I really don't know how to answer, because what I feel is that the answer depends on you. I mean,' said Franklin, glancing up, 'do you love her most, or do I? And even beyond that — because, of course, the man who loved her least might make her happiest if she loved him — have you got it in you to give her life? Have you got it in you to give her something beyond yourself to live for? Helen doesn't love me, she never could have loved me, and I believe, with you, that she loves you; but even so it's quite possible that in the long-run I might have made her happier than you can, unless you have — in yourself — more to make her happy with.'

Gerald gazed at Franklin, and Franklin gazed back at him. In Gerald's face a flush slowly mounted, a vivid flush, sensitive and suffering as a young girl's. And as if Franklin had borne a mild but effulgent light into the innermost chambers of his heart, and made self-contemplation for the first time in his life, perhaps, real to him, he said in a gentle voice: 'I'm afraid you're making me hopeless. I'm afraid I've nothing to give Helen — beyond myself. I'm a worthless fellow, really, you know. I've never made anything of myself or taken anything seriously at all. So how can Helen take me seriously? Yes, I see it, and I've robbed her of everything. Only,' said Gerald, leaning forward with his elbows on the table and his forehead on his hands, while he tried to think it out, 'it is serious, now, you know. It's really serious at last. I would try to give her something beyond myself and to make things worth while for her — I see what you mean; but I don't believe I shall ever be able to make her believe it now.'

They sat thus for a long time in silence — Gerald with his head leant on his hands, Franklin looking at him quietly and thoughtfully. And as a result of long reflection, he said at last: 'If she loves you still, you won't have to try to make her believe it. I'd like to believe it, and so would you; but if Helen loves you, she'll take you for yourself, of course. The question is, does she love you? Does she love you enough, I mean, to want to mend and grow again? Perhaps it's that way you've wrecked her; perhaps it's withered her — going on for all these years caring, while you didn't see and want.'

From behind his hands Gerald made a vague sound of acquiescent distress. 'What shall I do?' he then articulated. 'She won't see me. She says she won't see me until I can meet her as if I'd forgotten. It isn't with Helen the sort of thing it would mean with most women. She's not saving her dignity by threats and punishments she won't hold to. Helen always means what she says — horribly.'

Franklin contemplated the bent head. Gerald's thick hair, disordered by the long, fine fingers that ran up into it; Gerald's attitude sitting there, miserable, yet not undignified, helpless, yet not humble; Gerald's whole personality, its unused strength, its secure sweetness, affected him strangely. He didn't feel near Gerald as he had, in a sense, felt near Helen. They were aliens, and would remain so; but he felt tenderly towards him. And, even while it inflicted a steady, probing wound to recognise it, he recognised, profoundly, sadly, and finally, that Gerald and Helen did belong to each other, by an affinity deeper than moral standards and immeasurable by the test of happiness. Helen had been right to love him all her life. He felt as if he, from his distance, loved him, for himself, and because he was loveable. And he wanted Helen to take Gerald. He was sure, now, that he wanted it.

'See here,' he said, in his voice of mild, fraternal deliberation, 'I don't know whether it will do much good, but we'll try it. Helen has a very real feeling for me, you know; Helen likes me and thinks of me as a true friend. I'm certainly not satisfactory to her,' and Franklin smiled a little; 'but all the same she's very fond of me; she'd do a lot to please me; I'm sure of it. So how would it be if I wrote to her and put things to her, you know?'

Gerald raised his head and looked over the table across the piled pamphlets at Franklin. For a long time he looked at him, and presently Franklin saw that tears had mounted to his eyes. The emotion that he felt to be so unusual, communicated itself to him. He really hadn't known till he saw Gerald Digby's eyes fill with tears what his own emotion was. It surged up in him suddenly, blotting out Gerald's face, overpowering the long resistance of his trained control; and it was with an intolerable sense of loss and desolation that, knowing that he loved Gerald and that Gerald's tears were a warrant for his loveableness and for the workings of fate against himself, he put his head down on his arms and, not sobbing, not weeping, yet overcome, he let the waves of his sorrow meet over him.

He did not know, then, what he thought or felt. All that he was conscious of was the terrible submerging of will and thought and the engulfing sense of desolation; and all that he seemed to hear was the sound of his own heart beating the one lovely and agonising word: 'Helen — Helen — Helen!'

He was aware at last, dimly, that Gerald had moved, had come round the table, and was leaning on it beside him. Then Gerald put his hand on Franklin's hand. The touch drew him up out of his depths. He raised his head, keeping his face hidden, and he clasped Gerald's hand for a moment. Then Gerald said brokenly: 'You mustn't write. You mustn't do anything for me. You must let me take my own chances — and if I've none left, it will be what I deserve.'

These words, like air breathed in after long suffocation under water, cleared Franklin's mind. He shook his head, and he found Gerald's hand again while he said, able now, as the light grew upon him, to think:

'I want to write. I want you to have all the chances you can.'

'I don't deserve them,' said Gerald.

'I don't know about that,' said Franklin, 'I don't know about that at all. And besides' — and now he found something of his old whimsicality to help his final argument — 'let's say, if you'd rather, that Helen deserves them. Let's say that it's for Helen's sake that I want you to have every chance.'

CHAPTER XXXII.

Helen received Franklin's letter by the first post next morning. She read it in bed, where she had remained ever since parting from him, lying there with closed eyes in the drowsy apathy that had fallen upon her.

'DEAR HELEN,' — Franklin wrote, and something in the writing pained her even before she read the words — 'Gerald Digby has been with me here. Your aunt has been telling him things. He knows that I care for you and what it all meant yesterday. It has been a very painful experience for him, as you may imagine, and the way he took it made me like him very much. It's because of that that I'm writing to you now. The thing that tormented me most was the idea that, perhaps, with all my deficiencies, I could give you more than he could. I hadn't a very high opinion of him, you know. I felt you might be safer with me. But now, from what I've seen, I'm sure that he is the man for you. I understand how you could have loved him for all your life. He's not as big as you are, nor as strong; he hasn't your character; but you'll make him grow — and no one else can, for he loves you with his whole heart, and he's a broken man.

'Dear Helen, I know what it feels like now. You're withered and burnt out. It's lasted too long to be felt any longer and you believe it's dead. But it isn't dead, Helen; I'm sure it isn't. Things like that don't die unless something else comes and takes their place. It's withered, but it will grow again. See him; be kind to him, and you'll find out. And even if you can't find out yet, even if you think it's all over, look at it this way. You know our talk about marriage and how you were willing to marry me, not loving me; well, look at it this way, for his sake, and for mine. He needs you more than anything; he'll be nothing, or less and less, without you; with you he'll be more and more. Think of his life. You've got responsibility for that, Helen; you've let him depend on you always — and you've got responsibility, too, for what's happened now. You told him — I'm not blaming you — I understand — I think you were right; but you changed things for him and made him see what he hadn't seen before; nothing can ever be the same for him again; you mustn't forget that; your friendship is spoiled for him, after what you've done. So at the very least you can feel sorry for him and feel like a mother to him, and marry him for that — as lots of women do.

'Now I'm going to be very egotistical, but you'll know why. Think of my life, dear Helen. We won't hide from what

we know. We know that I love you and that to give you up —
even if, in a way, I had to — was the greatest sacrifice of my life.
Now, what I put to you is this: Is it going to be for nothing — I
mean for nothing where you are concerned? If I'm to think of
you going on alone with your heart getting harder and drier
every year, and everything tender and trustful dying out of
you — I don't see how I can bear it.

'So what I ask you is to try to be happy; what I ask you is to
try to make him happy; just look at it like that; try to make him
happy and to help him to grow to be a fine, big person, and
then you'll find out that you are growing, too, in all sorts of
ways you never dreamed of.

'When you get this, write to him and tell him that he may
come. And when he is with you, be kind to him. Oh — my dear
Helen — I do beg it of you. Put it like this — be kind to me and
try. —
Your affectionate
FRANKLIN.'

When Helen had read this letter she did not weep, but she felt
as if some hurt, almost deeper than she could endure, was being
inflicted on her. It had begun with the first sight of Franklin's
letter; the writing of it had looked like hard, steady breathing over
some heart-arresting pain. Franklin's suffering flowed into her
from every gentle, careful sentence; and to Helen, so unaware, till
now, of any one's suffering but her own, this sharing of Franklin's
was an experience new and overpowering. No tears came, while
she held the letter and looked before her intently, and it was not as
if her heart softened; but it seemed to widen, as if some greatness,
irresistible and grave, forced a way into it. It widened to Franklin,
to the thought of Franklin and to Franklin's suffering; its sorrow
and its compassion were for Franklin; and as it received and
enshrined him, it shut Gerald out. There was no room for Gerald
in her heart.

She would do part of what Franklin asked of her, of course.
She would see Gerald; she would be kind to him; she would even
try to feel for him. But the effort was easy because she was so sure
that it would be fruitless. For Gerald, she was withered and burnt
out. If she were to 'grow' — dear, funny phrases, even in her
extremity, Helen could smile over them; even though she loved
dear Franklin and enshrined him, his phrases would always seem
funny to her — but if she were to grow it must be for Franklin, and
in a different way from what he asked. She would indeed try not to
become harder and drier; she would try to make of her life something not too alien from his ideal for her; she would try to pursue
the just and the beautiful. But to rekindle the burnt-out fires of

her love was a miracle that even Franklin's love and Franklin's suffering could not perform, and as for marrying Gerald in order to be a mother to him, she did not feel it possible, even for Franklin's sake, to assume that travesty.

It was at five o'clock that she asked Gerald to come and see her. She went down to him in her sitting-room, when, on the stroke of the clock, he was announced. She felt that it required no effort to meet him, beyond the forcing of her weariness.

Gerald was standing before the fire, and in looking at him, as she entered and closed the door, she was aware of a little sense of surprise. She had not expected to find him, since the crash of Aunt Grizel's revelations, as fatuous as the day before yesterday; nor had she expected the boyish sulkiness of that day's earlier mood. She expected change and the signs of discomfort and distress. It was this haggard brightness for which she was unprepared. He looked as if he hadn't slept or eaten, and under jaded eyelids his eyes had the sparkling fever of insomnia.

Helen felt that she could thoroughly carry out the first of Franklin's requests; she could be kind and she could be sorry; yes, Gerald was very unhappy; it was strange to think of, and pitiful.

'Have you had any tea?' she asked him, giving him her hand, which he pressed mechanically.

'No, thanks,' said Gerald.

'Do have some. You look hungry.'

'I'm not hungry, thanks.' He was neither hostile nor pleading; he only kept his eyes fixed on her with bright watchfulness, rather as a patient's eyes watch the doctor who is to pronounce a verdict, and Helen, with all her kindness, felt a little irked and ill at ease before his gaze.

'You've heard from Kane?' Gerald said, after a pause. Helen had taken her usual place in the low chair.

'Yes, this morning.'

'And that's why you sent for me?'

'Yes,' said Helen, 'he asked me to.'

Gerald looked down into the fire. 'I can't tell you what I think of him. You can't care to hear, of course. You know what I've done to him, and that must make you feel that I'm not the person to talk about him. But I've never met any one so good.'

'He is good. I'm glad to hear you say it. He is the best person I've ever met, too,' said Helen. 'As for what you did to him, you didn't know what you were doing.'

'I don't think that stupidity is any excuse. I ought to have felt he couldn't be near you like that, and not love you. I robbed him of you, didn't I? If it hadn't been for what I did, you would have married him, all the same — in spite of what you told me, I mean.'

Helen had coloured a little, and after a pause in which she thought over his words she said: 'Yes, of course I would have married him all the same. But it was really I, in what I told you, who brought it upon myself and upon Franklin.'

For a little while there was silence and then Gerald said, delicately, yet with a directness that showed he took for granted in her a detached candour equal to his own: 'I think I asked it stupidly. I suppose the thing I can't even yet realise is that, in a way, I robbed you too. I've robbed you of everything, haven't I, Helen?'

'Not of everything,' said Helen, glad really of the small consolation she could offer him. 'Not of financial safety, as it happens. It will make you less unhappy to hear, so I must tell you, Franklin is arranging things with Aunt Grizel so that when she dies I shall come into quite a nice little bit of money. I shall have no more sordid worries. In that way you mustn't have me on your conscience.'

Gerald's eyes were on her and they took in this fact of her safety with no commotion; it was but one — and a lesser — among the many strange facts he had had to take in. And he forced himself to look squarely at what he had conceived to be the final impossibility as he asked: 'And — in other ways? — Could you have fallen in love with him, Helen?'

It was so bad, so inconceivably bad a thing to face, that his relief was like a joy when Helen answered. 'No, I could never have fallen in love with dear Franklin. But I cared for him very much, the more, no doubt, from having ceased to care about love. I felt that he was the best person, the truest, the dearest, I had ever known, and that we would make a success of our life together.'

'Yes, yes, of course,' Gerald hastened past her qualifications to the one liberating fact. 'Two people like you would have had to. But you didn't love him; you couldn't have come to love him. I haven't robbed you of a man you could have loved.'

She saw his immense relief. The joy of it was in his eyes and voice; and the thought of Franklin, of what she had not been able to do for Franklin, made it bitter to her that because she had not been able to save Franklin, Gerald should find relief.

'You couldn't have robbed me of him if there'd been any chance of that,' she said. 'If there had been any chance of my loving Franklin I would never have let him go. Don't be glad, don't show me that you are glad — because I didn't love him.'

'I can't help being glad, Helen,' he said.

She leaned her head on her hand, covering her eyes. While he was there, showing her that he was glad because she had not loved Franklin, she could not be kind, nor even just to him.

'Helen,' he said, 'I know what you are feeling; but will you listen to me?' She answered that she would listen to anything he had to say, and her voice had the leaden tone of impersonal charity.

'Helen,' Gerald said, 'I know how I've blundered. I see everything. But, with it all, seeing it all, I don't think that you are fair to me. I don't think it is fair if you can't see that I couldn't have thought of all these other possibilities — after what you'd told me — the other day. How could I think of anything, then, but the one thing — that you loved me and that I loved you, and that, of course, I must set my mistake right at once, set Althea free and come to you? I was very simple and very stupid; but I don't think it's fair not to see that I couldn't believe you'd really repulse me, finally, if you loved me.'

'You ought to have believed it,' Helen said, still with her covered eyes. 'That is what is most simple, most stupid in you. You ought to have felt — and you ought to feel now — that to a woman who could tell you what I did, everything is over.'

'But, Helen, that's my point,' ever so carefully and patiently he insisted. 'How can it be over when I love you — if you still love me?'

She put down her hand now and looked up at him and she saw his hope; not yet dead; sick, wounded, perplexed, but, in his care and patience, vigilant. And it was with a sad wonder for the truth of her own words, that she said, looking up at the face dear beyond all telling for so many years, 'I don't want you, Gerald. I don't want your love. I'm not blaming you. I am fair to you. I see that you couldn't help it, and that it was my fault really. But you are asking for something that isn't there any longer.'

'You mean,' said Gerald, he was very pale, 'that I've won no rights; you don't want a man who has won no rights.'

'There are no rights to win, Gerald.'

'Because of what I've done to him?'

'Perhaps; but I don't think it's that.'

'Because of what I've done to you — not seeing — all our lives?'

'Perhaps, Gerald. I don't know. I can't tell you, for I don't know myself. I don't think anything has been killed. I think something is dead that's been dying by inches for years. Don't press me any more. Accept the truth. It's all over. I don't want you any longer.'

Helen had risen while she spoke and kept her eyes on Gerald's in speaking. Until this moment, for all his pain and perplexity, he had not lost hope. He had been amazed and helpless and full of fear, but he had not believed, not really believed, that she was lost to him. Now, she saw it in his eyes, he did believe; and as the patient, hearing his sentence, gazes dumb and stricken, facing death, so he gazed at her, seeing irrevocability in her unmoved face. And, accepting his doom, sheer childishness overcame him. As Franklin the day before had felt, so he now felt, the intolerableness of his woe; and, as with Franklin, the waves closed over his head. Helen was so near him that it was but a stumbling step that brought her within his arms; but it was not with the lover's supplication that he clung to her; he clung, hiding his face on her breast, like a child to its mother, broken-hearted, bewildered, reproachful. And, bursting into tears, he sobbed: 'How cruel you are! how cruel! It is your pride — you've the heart of a stone! If I'd loved you for years and told you and made you know you loved me back — could I have treated you like this — and cast you off — and stopped loving you, because you'd never seen before? O Helen, how can you — how can you!'

After a moment Helen spoke, angrily, because she was astounded, and because, for the first time in her life, she was frightened, beyond her depth, helpless in the waves of emotion that lifted her like great encompassing billows. 'Gerald, don't. Gerald, it is absurd of you. Gerald, don't cry.' She had never seen him cry.

He heard her dimly, and the words were the cruel ones he expected. The sense of her cruelty filled him, and the dividing sense that she, who was so cruel, was still his only refuge, his only consolation.

'What have I done, I'd like to know, that you should treat me like this? If you loved me before — all those years — why should you stop now, because I love you? why should you stop because of telling me?'

Again Helen's voice came to him after a pause, and it seemed now to grope, stupefied and uncertain, for answers to his absurdity. 'How can one argue, Gerald, like this; perhaps it was because I told you? Perhaps — '

He took her up, not waiting to hear her surmises. 'How can one get over a thing like that, all in a moment? How can it die like that? You're not over it, not really. It is all pride, and you are punishing me for what I couldn't help, and punishing yourself too, for no one will ever love you as I do. O Helen — I can't believe it's dead. Don't you know that no one will ever love you as I do? Can't you see how happy we could have been together? It's so *silly* of you not to see. Yes, you are silly as well as cruel.' He shook her while he held her, while he buried his face and cried — cried, literally, like a baby.

She stood still, enfolded but not enfolding, and now she said nothing for a long time, while her eyes, with their strained look of pain, gazed widely, and as if in astonishment, before her; and he, knowing only the silence, the unresponsive silence, continued to sob his protestation, his reproach, with a helplessness and vehemence ridiculous and heart-rending.

Then, slowly, as if compelled, Helen put her arms around him, and, dully, like a creature hypnotised to action strange to its whole nature, she said once more, and in a different voice: 'Don't cry, Gerald.' But she, too, was crying. She tried to control her sobs; but they broke from her, strange and difficult, like the sobs of the hypnotised creature waking from its trance to confused and painful consciousness, and, resting her forehead on his shoulder, she repeated dully, between her sobs: 'Don't cry.'

He was not crying any longer. Her weeping had stilled his in an instant, and she went on, between her broken breaths: 'How absurd — oh, how absurd. Sit down here — yes — keep your head so, if you must, you foolish, foolish child.'

He held her, hearing her sobs, feeling them lift her breast, and, in all his great astonishment, like a smile, the memory of the other day stole over him, the stillness, the accomplishment, the blissful peace, the lifting to a serene eternity of space. To remember it now was like seeing the sky from a nest, and in the sweet darkness of sudden security he murmured: '*You* are the foolish child.'

'How can I believe you love me?' said Helen.

'How can you not?'

They sat side by side, her arms around him and his head upon her breast. 'It was only because I told you — '

'Well — isn't that reason enough?'

'How can it be reason enough for me?'

'How can it not? You've spent your whole life hiding from me; when I saw you, why, of course, I fell in love at once. O Helen — dear, dear Helen!'

'When you saw my love.'

'Wasn't that seeing you?'

They spoke in whispers, and their hearts were not in their words. He raised his head and looked at her, and he smiled at her now with the smile of the beautiful necessity. 'How you've frightened me,' he said. 'Don't be proud. Even if it did need your cleverness to show me that, too. I mean — you've given me everything — always — and why shouldn't you have given me the chance to see you — and to know what you are to me? How you frightened me. You are not proud any longer. You love me.'

She was not proud any longer. She loved him. Vaguely, in the bewilderment of her strange, her blissful humility, among the great billows of life that encompassed and lifted her, it seemed with enormous heart-beats, Helen remembered Franklin's words. 'Let it melt — please let it melt, dear Helen.' But it had needed the inarticulate, the instinctive, to pierce to the depths of life. Gerald's tears, his head so boyishly pressed against her, his arms so childishly clinging, had told her what her heart might have been dead to for ever if, with reason and self-command, he had tried to put it into words.

She looked at him, through her tears, and she knew him dearer to her in this resurrection than if her heart had never died to him; and, as he smiled at her, she, too, smiled back, tremblingly.

CHAPTER XXXIII.

Althea had not seen Gerald after the day that they came up from Merriston together. The breaking of their engagement was duly announced, and, with his little note to her, thanking her for her frankness and wishing her every happiness, Gerald and all things connected with him seemed to pass out of her life. She saw no more of the frivolous relations who were really serious, nor of the serious ones who were really frivolous. She did not even see Helen. Helen's engagement to Franklin had never been formally announced, and few, beyond her circle of nearest friends, knew of it; the fact that Franklin had now returned to his first love was not one that could, at the moment, be made appropriately public. But, of course, Helen had had to be told, not only that Franklin had gone from her, but that he had come back to Althea, and Althea wondered deeply how this news had been imparted. She had not felt strength to impart it herself. When she asked Franklin, very tentatively, about it, he said: 'That's all right, dear. I've explained. Helen perfectly understands.'

That it was all right seemed demonstrated by the little note, kind and sympathetic, that Helen wrote to her, saying that she did understand, perfectly, and was so glad for her and for Franklin, and that it was such a good thing when people found out mistakes in time. There was not a trace of grievance; Helen seemed to relinquish a good which, she recognised, had only been hers because Althea hadn't wanted it. And this was natural; how could one show one's grievance in such a case? Helen, above all, would never show it; and Althea was at once oppressed, and at the same time oddly sustained by the thought that she had, all inevitably, done her friend an injury. She lay awake at night, turning over in her mind Helen's present plight and framing loving plans for the future. She took refuge in such plans from a sense of having come to an end of things. To think of Helen, and of what, with their wealth, she and Franklin could do for Helen, seemed, really, her strongest hold on life. It was the brightest thing that she had to look forward to, and she looked forward to it with complete self-effacement. She saw the beautiful Italian villa where Helen should be the fitting centre, the English house where Helen, rather than she, should entertain. She felt that she asked nothing more for herself. She was safe, if one liked to put it so, and in that safety she felt not only her ambitions, but even any personal desires, extinguished. Her desire, now, was to unite with Franklin in making the proper background for Helen. But at the moment these projects were unrealisable; taste, as well as circumstance, required a pause, a lull. It was a relief — so many things were a relief, so few things more than merely that — to know that Helen was in the country somewhere, and would not be back for ten days or a fortnight.

Meanwhile, Miss Harriet Robinson, very grave but very staunch, sustained Althea through all the outward difficulties of her *volte-face*. Miss Robinson, of course, had had to be told of the reason for the *volte-face*, the fact that Althea had found, after all, that she cared more for Franklin Winslow Kane. It was in regard to the breaking of her engagement that Miss Robinson was staunch and grave; in regard to the new engagement, Althea saw that, though still staunch, she was much disturbed. Miss Robinson found Franklin hard to place, and found it hard to understand why Althea had turned from Gerald Digby to him. Franklin's millions didn't count for much with Miss Robinson, nor could she suspect them of counting for anything, where marriage was concerned, with her friend. She had not, indeed, a high opinion of the millionaire type of her compatriots. Her standards were birth and fashion, and poor Franklin could not be said to embody either of these claims. His mitigating qualities could hardly shine for Miss Robinson, who, accustomed to continually seeing and frequently evading the drab, dry, utilitarian species of her country-people, could not be expected to find in him the flavour of oddity and significance that his English acquaintance prized. Franklin didn't make any effort to place himself more favourably. He was very gentle and very attentive, and he followed all Althea's directions as to clothes and behaviour with careful literalness; but even barbered and tailored by the best that London had to offer, he seemed to sink inevitably into the discreetly effaced position that the American husband so often assumes behind his more brilliant mate, and Althea might have been more aware of this had she not been so sunken in an encompassing consciousness of her own obliteration. She felt herself nearer Franklin there, and the sense of relief and safety came most to her when she could feel herself near Franklin. It didn't disturb her, standing by him in the background, that Miss Robinson should not appreciate him. After all, deeper than anything, was the knowledge that Helen had appreciated him. Recede as far as he would from the gross foreground places, Helen's choice of him, Helen's love — for after a fashion, Helen must have loved him — gave him a final and unquestionable value. It was in this assurance of Helen's choice that she found a refuge when questionings and wonders came to drag her down to suffering again. There were many things that menaced the lull of safety, things she could not bear yet to look at. The sense of her own abandonment to weak and disingenuous impulses was one; another shadowed her unstable peace more darkly. Had Helen really minded losing Franklin — apart from his money? What had his value really been to her? What was she feeling and doing now? What was Gerald doing and feeling, and what did they both think or suspect of her? The answer to some of these questionings came to her from an unsuspected quarter. It was on a morning of chill mists and pale sunlight that Althea, free of Miss Robinson, walked down Grosvenor Street towards the park. She liked to go into the park on such mornings, when Miss Robinson left her free, and sit on a bench and abandon herself to remote, impersonal dreams. It was just as she entered Berkeley Square that she met Mrs. Mallison, that aunt of Gerald's who had struck her, some weeks ago, as so disconcerting, with her skilfully preserved prettiness and her ethical and metaphysical aspirations. This lady, furred to her ears, was taking out two small black pomeranians for an airing. She wore long pearl ear-rings, and her narrow, melancholy face was delicately rouged and powdered. Althea's colour rose painfully; she had seen none of Gerald's relatives since the severance. Mrs. Mallison, however, showed no embarrassment. She stopped at once and took Althea's hand and gazed tenderly upon her. Her manner had always afflicted Althea, with its intimations of some deep, mystical understanding.

'My dear, I'm so glad — to meet you, you know. How nice, how right you've been.' Mrs. Mallison murmured her words rather than spoke them and could pronounce none of her r's. 'I'm so glad to be able to tell you so. You're walking? Come with me, then; I'm just taking the dogs round the square. Do you love dogs too? I am sure you must. You have the eyes of the dog-lover. I don't know how I could live without mine; they understand when no one else does. I didn't write, because I think letters are such soulless things, don't you? They are the tombs of the spirit — little tombs for failed things — too often. I've thought of you, and felt for you — so much; but I couldn't write. And now I must tell you that I agree with you with all my heart. Love's the *only* thing in life, isn't it?' Mrs. Mallison smiled, pressing Althea's arm affectionately. Althea remembered to have heard that Mrs. Mallison had made a most determined *mariage de convenance* and had sought love in other directions; but, summoning what good grace she could, she answered that she, too, considered love the only thing.

'You didn't love him enough, and you found it out in time, and you told him. How brave; how right. And then — am I too indiscreet? but I know you feel we are friends — you found you loved some one else; the reality came and showed you the unreality. That enchanting Mr. Kane — oh, I felt it the moment I looked at him — there was an affinity between us, our souls understood each other. And so deliciously rich you'll be, not that money makes any difference, does it? but it is nice to be able to do things for the people one loves.'

Althea struggled in a maze of discomfort. Behind Mrs. Mallison's caressing intonations was something that perplexed her. What did Mrs. Mallison know, and what did she guess? She was aware, evidently, of her own engagement to Franklin and, no doubt, of Franklin's engagement to Helen and its breaking off. What did she know about the cause of that breaking off? Her troubled cogitations got no further, for Mrs. Mallison went on:

'And how happily it has all turned out — all round — hasn't it? How horrid for you and Mr. Kane, if it hadn't; not that you'd have had anything to reproach yourselves with — really — I know — because love *is* the only thing; but if Helen and Gerald had just been left *plantés là*, it would have been harder, wouldn't it? I've been staying with them at the same house in the country and it's quite obvious what's happened. You knew from the first, no doubt; but of course they are saying nothing, just as you and Mr. Kane are saying nothing. They didn't tell me, but I guessed at once. And the first thing I thought was: Oh — how happy — how perfect this makes it for Miss Jakes and Mr. Kane. They've *all* found out in time.'

Althea grew cold. She commanded her voice. 'Helen? Gerald?' she said. 'Haven't you mistaken? They've always been the nearest friends.'

'Oh no — no,' smiled Mrs. Mallison, with even greater brightness and gentleness, 'I never mistake these things; an affair of the heart is the one thing that I always see. Helen, perhaps, could hide it from me; she is a woman and can hide things — Helen is cold too — I am never very sure of Helen's heart — of course I love her dearly, every one must who knows her; but she is cold, unawakened, the type that holds out the cheek, not the type that kisses. I confess that I love most the reckless, loving type; and I believe that you and I are unlike Helen there — we kiss, we don't hold out the cheek. But, no, I never would have guessed from Helen. It was Gerald who gave them both away. Poor, dear Gerald, never have I beheld such a transfigured being — he is radiantly in love, quite radiantly; it's too pretty to see him.'

The vision of Gerald, radiantly in love, flashed horridly for Althea. It was dim, yet bright, scintillating darkly; she could only imagine it in similes; she had never seen anything that could visualise it for her. The insufferable dogs, like tethered bubbles, bounded before them, constantly impeding their progress. Althea was thankful for the excuse afforded her by the tangling of her feet in the string to pause and stoop; she felt that her rigid face must betray her. She stooped for a long moment and hoped that her flush would cover her rigidity. It was when she raised herself that she saw suddenly in Mrs. Mallison's face something that gave her more than a suspicion. She didn't suspect her of cruelty or vulgar vengeance — Gerald's aunt was quite without rancour on the score of her jilting of him; but she did suspect, and more than suspect her — it was like the unendurable probing of a wound to feel it — of idle yet implacable curiosity, and of a curiosity edged, perhaps, with idle malice. She summoned all her strength. She smiled and shook her head a little. 'Faithless Gerald! So soon,' she said. 'He is consoled quickly. No, I never guessed anything at all.'

Mrs. Mallison had again passed her arm through hers and again pressed it. 'It *is* soon, isn't it? A sort of *chassé-croisé*. But how strange and fortunate that it should be soon — I know you feel that too.'

'Oh yes, of course, I feel it; it is an immense relief. But they ought to have told me,' Althea smiled.

'I wonder at that too,' said Mrs. Mallison. 'It is rather bad of them, I think, when they must know what it would mean to you of joy. When did it happen, do you suppose?'

Althea wondered. Wonders were devouring her.

'It happened with you quite suddenly, didn't it?' said Mrs. Mallison, who breathed the soft fragrance of her solicitude into Althea's face as she leaned her head near and pressed her arm closely.

'Quite suddenly,' Althea replied, 'that is, with me it was sudden. Franklin, of course, has loved me for a great many years.'

'So he was faithless too, for his little time?'

Althea's brain whirled. 'Faithless? Franklin?'

'I mean, while he made his mistake — while he thought he was in love with Helen.'

'It wasn't a question of that. It was to be a match of reason, and friendship — everybody knew,' Althea stammered.

'*Was* it?' said Mrs. Mallison with deep interest. 'I see, like yours and Gerald's.'

'Oh — ' Althea was not able in her headlong course to do more than glance at the implications that whizzed past. 'Gerald and I made the mistake, I think; we believed ourselves in love.'

'*Did* you?' Mrs. Mallison repeated her tone of affectionate and brooding interest. 'What a strange thing the human heart is, isn't it?'

'Very, very strange.'

'How dear and frank of you to see it all as you do. And there are no more mistakes now,' said Mrs. Mallison. 'No one is reasonable and every one is radiant.'

'Every one is radiant and reasonable too, I hope,' said Althea. Her head still whirled as she heard herself analysing for Mrs. Mallison's correction these sanctities of her life. Odious, intolerable, insolent woman! She could have burst into tears as she walked beside her, held by her, while her hateful dogs, shrilly barking, bounded buoyantly around them.

'It's dear of you too, to tell me all about it,' said Mrs. Mallison. 'Have you seen Helen yet? She is just back.'

'No, I've not seen her.'

'You will meet? I am sure you will still be friends — two such real people as you are.'

'Of course we shall meet. Helen is one of my dearest friends.'

'I see. It is so beautiful when people can rise above things. You make me very happy. Don't tell Helen what I've told you,' Mrs. Mallison with gentle gaiety warned her. 'I knew — in case you hadn't heard — that it would relieve you so intensely to hear that she and Gerald were happy, in spite of what you had to do to them. But it would make Helen cross with me if she knew I'd told you when she hadn't. I'm rather afraid of Helen, aren't you? I'm sure she'll give Gerald dreadful scoldings sometimes. Poor, dear Gerald!' Mrs. Mallison laughed reminiscently. 'Never have I beheld such a transfigured being. I didn't think he had it in him to be in love to such an extent. Oh, it was all in his face — his eyes — when he looked at her.'

Yes, malicious, malicious to the point of vulgarity; that was Althea's thought as, like an arrow released from long tension, she sped away, the turn of the square once made and Mrs. Mallison and her dogs once more received into the small house in an adjacent street. Tears were in Althea's eyes, hot tears, of fury, of humiliation, and — oh, it flooded over her — of bitterest sorrow and yearning. Gerald, radiant Gerald — lost to her for ever; not even lost; never possessed. And into the sorrow and humiliation, poisonous suspicions crept. When did it happen? Where was she? What had been done to her? She must see; she must know. She hailed a hansom and was driven to old Miss Buchanan's house in Belgravia.

CHAPTER XXXIV.

Helen was sitting at her writing-table before the window, and the morning light fell on her gracefully disordered hair and gracefully shabby shoulders. The aspect of her back struck on Althea's bitter, breathless mood. There was no effort made for anything with Helen. She was the sort of person who would get things without seeking for them and be things without caring to be them. She had taken what she wanted, when she wanted it; first Franklin, and then — and perhaps it had been before Franklin had failed her, perhaps it had been before she, Althea, had failed Gerald — she had taken Gerald. Althea's mind, reeling, yet strangely lucid after the shock of the last great injury, was also aware, in the moment of her entrance, of many other injuries, old ones, small ones, yet, in their summing up — and everything seemed to be summed up now in the cruel revelation — as intolerable as the new and great one. More strongly than ever before she was aware that Helen was hard, that there was nothing in her soft or tentative or afraid; and the realisation, though it was not new, came with an added bitterness this morning. It did not weaken her, however; on the contrary, it nerved her to self-protection. If Helen was hard, she would not, today, show herself soft. It was she who must assume the air of success, and of rueful yet helpless possessorship. These impressions and resolutions occupied but an instant. Helen rose and came to her, and what Althea saw in her face armed her resolutions with hostility. Helen's face confirmed what Mrs. Mallison had said. It was not resentful, not ironically calm. A solicitous interest, even a sort of benignity, was in her bright gaze. Helen was hard; she did not really care at all; but she was kind, kinder than ever before; and Althea found this kindness intolerable.

'Dear Helen,' she said, 'I'm so glad to see you. I had to come at once when I heard that you were back. You don't mind seeing me?'

'Not a bit,' said Helen, who had taken her hand. 'Why should I?'

'I was afraid that perhaps you might not want to — for a long time.'

'We aren't so foolish as that,' said Helen smiling.

'No, that is what I hoped you would feel too. We have been in the hands of fate, haven't we, Helen? I've seemed weak and disloyal, I know — to you and to Gerald; but I think it was only seeming. When I found out my mistake I couldn't go on. And then the rest all followed — inevitably.'

Helen had continued to hold her hand while she spoke, and

she continued to gaze at her for another moment before, pressing it, she let it fall and said: 'Of course you couldn't go on.'

Helen was as resolved — Althea saw that clearly — to act her part of unresentful kindness as she to act hers of innocent remorse. And the swordthrust in the sight was to suspect that had Helen been in reality the dispossessed and not the secretly triumphant, she might have been as kind and as unresentful.

'It's all been a dreadful mistake,' Althea said, going to a chair and loosening her furs. 'From the very beginning I felt doubt. From the very beginning I felt that Gerald and I did not really make each other happy. And I believe that you wondered about it too.'

Helen had resumed her seat at the writing-table, sitting turned from it, her hand hanging over the back of the chair, her long legs crossed, and she faced her friend with that bright yet softened gaze, interested, alert, but too benign, too contented, to search or question closely. She was evidently quite willing that Althea should think what she chose, and, this was becoming evident, she intended to help her to think it. So after a little pause she answered, 'I did wonder, rather; it didn't seem to me that you and Gerald were really suited.'

'And you felt, didn't you,' Althea urged, 'that it was only because I had been so blind, and had not seen where my heart really was, you know, that your engagement was possible? I was so afraid you'd think we'd been faithless to you — Franklin and I; but, when I stopped being blind — '

'Of course,' Helen helped her on, nodding and smiling gravely, 'of course you took him back. I don't think you were either of you faithless, and you mustn't have me a bit on your minds; it was startling, of course; but I'm not heart-broken,' Helen assured her.

Oh, there was no malice here; it was something far worse to bear, this wish to lift every shadow and smooth every path. Althea's eyes fixed themselves hard on her friend. Her head swam a little and some of her sustaining lucidity left her.

'I was so afraid,' she said, 'that you, perhaps, cared for Franklin — had come to care so much, I mean — that it might have been hard for you to forgive. I can't tell you the relief it is — '

'To see that I didn't care so much as that?' Helen smiled brightly, though with a brightness, now, slightly wary, as though with all her efforts to slide and not to press, she felt the ice cracking a little under her feet, and as though some care might be necessary if she were to skate safely away. 'Don't have that in the least on your mind, it was what you always disapproved of, you know, an arrangement of convenience. Franklin and I both understood perfectly. You know how mercenary I am — though I told you, I remember, that I couldn't think of marrying anybody I didn't like. I liked Franklin, more than I can say; but it was never a question of love.'

In Althea's ears, also, the ice seemed now to crack ominously. 'You mean,' she said, 'that you wouldn't have thought of marrying Franklin if it hadn't been for his money?'

There was nothing for Helen but to skate straight ahead. 'No, I don't suppose I should.'

'But you had become the greatest friends.'

She was aware that she must seem to be trying, strangely, incredibly, to prove to Helen that she had been in love with Franklin; to prove to her that she had no right not to resent anything; no right to find forgiveness so easy. But there was no time now to stop.

'Of course we became the greatest friends,' Helen said, and it was as if with relief for the outlet. She was bewildered, and did not know where they were going. 'I don't need to tell you what I think of Franklin. He is the dearest and best of men, and you are the luckiest of women to have won him.'

'Ah,' uncontrollably Althea rose to her feet with almost the cry, 'I see; you think me lucky to have won a man who, in himself, without money, wasn't good enough for you. Thank you.'

For a long moment — and in it they both recognised that the crash had come, and that they were struggling in dark, cold water — Helen was silent. She kept her eyes on Althea and she did not move. Then, while she still looked steadily upon her, a slow colour rose in her cheeks. It was helplessly, burningly, that she blushed, and Althea saw that she blushed as much for anger as for shame, and that the shame was for her.

She did not need Helen's blush to show her what she had done, what desecration she had wrought. Her own blood beat upwards in hot surges and tears rushed into her eyes. She covered her face with her hands and dropped again into her chair, sobbing.

Helen did not help her out. She got up and went to the mantelpiece and looked down at the fire for some moments. And at last she spoke, 'I didn't mean that either. I think that Franklin is too good for either of us.'

'Good!' wept Althea. 'He is an angel. Do you suppose I don't see that? But why should I pretend when you don't. I'm not in love with Franklin. I'm unworthy of him — more unworthy of him than you were — but I'm not in love with him, even though he is an angel. So don't tell me that I am lucky. I am a most miserable woman.' And she wept on, indifferent now to any revelations.

Presently she heard Helen's voice. It was harder than she had ever known it. 'May I say something? It's for his sake — more than for yours. What I advise you to do is not to bother so much about love. You couldn't stick to Gerald because you weren't loved enough; and you're doubting your feeling for Franklin, now, because you can't love him enough. Give it all up. Follow my second-rate example. Be glad that you're marrying an angel and that he has all that money. And do remember that though you're not getting what you want, you are getting a good deal and he is getting nothing, so try to play the game and to see if you can't make it up to him; see if you can't make him happy.'

Althea's sobbing had now ceased, though she kept her face still covered. Bitter sadness, too deep now for resentment, was in her silence, a silence in which she accepted what Helen's words had of truth. The sadness was to see at last to the full, that she had no place in Helen's life. There was no love, there was hardly liking, behind Helen's words. And so it had been from the very first, ever since she had loved and Helen accepted; ever since she had gone forth carrying gifts, and Helen had stood still and been vaguely aware that homage was being offered. It had, from the very beginning, been this; Helen, hard, self-centred, insensible, so that anything appealing or uncertain was bound to be shattered against her. And was not this indifference to offered love a wrong done to it, something that all life cried out against? Had not weakness and fear and the clinging appeal of immaturity their rights, so that the strong heart that was closed to them, that did not go out to them in tenderness and succour, was the dull, the lesser heart? Dimly she knew, not exculpating herself, not judging her beautiful Helen, that though she had, in her efforts towards happiness, pitifully failed, there was failure too in being blind, in being unconscious of any effort to be made. The more trivial, the meaner aspect of her grief was merged in a fundamental sincerity.

'What you say is true,' she said, 'for I know that I am a poor creature. I know that I give Franklin nothing, and take everything from him. But it is easy for you to talk of what is wise and strong, Helen, and to tell me what I ought to do and feel. You have everything. You have the man who loves you and the man you love. It is easy for you to be clear and hard and see other people's faults. I know — I know about you and Gerald.'

Helen turned to her. Althea had dropped her hands. She did not look at her friend, but, with tear-disfigured eyes, out of the window; and there was a desolate dignity in her aspect. For the first time in their unequal intercourse they were on an equal footing. Helen was aware of Althea, and, in a vague flash, for self-contemplation was difficult to her, she was aware of some of the things that Althea saw: the lack of tenderness; the lack of imagination; the indifference to all that did not come within the circle of her own tastes and affections. It was just as Franklin had said, and Gerald, and now Althea; her heart was hard. And she was sorry, though she did not know what she was to do; for though she was sorry for Althea her heart did not soften for her as it had softened for Franklin, and for the thought of Franklin — too good for them all, sacrificed to them all. It was the thought of the cruelty of nature, making of Franklin, with all his wealth of love, a creature never to be desired, that gave to her vision of life, and of all this strange predicament in which life had involved them, an ironic colour incompatible with the warmth of trust and tenderness which Franklin had felt lacking in her. She was ironic, she was hard, and she must make the best of it. But it was in a gentle voice that, looking at her friend's melancholy head, she asked: 'Who told you that?'

'Mrs. Mallison,' said Althea. 'I've been a hypocrite to you all the morning.'

'And I have been an odious prig to you. That ass of a Kitty Mallison. I had not intended any one to know for months.' Even in her discomfiture Helen retained her tact. She did not say 'we.'

'For my sake, I suppose?'

'Oh no! why for yours?' Helen was determined that Althea should be hurt no further. If pity for Franklin had edged her voice, pity for Althea must keep from her the blighting knowledge of Franklin's sacrifice.

'It was we who were left, wasn't it — Gerald and I? I don't want us to appear before people's eyes at once as consolation prizes to each other.'

Althea now turned a sombre gaze upon her. 'He couldn't be that to you, since you've never loved Franklin; and I know that you are not that to him; Gerald didn't need to be consoled for losing me. He did need to be consoled when he heard that you were marrying Franklin. I remember the day that your letter came — the letter that said you were engaged. That really ended things for us.' Her lip trembled. 'It is easy for you to say that I didn't stick to Gerald because he didn't love me enough. How could I have stuck to some one who, I see it well enough now, was beginning to love some one else?'

Helen contemplated her and the truths she put before her. 'Try to forgive me,' she said.

'There's nothing to forgive,' said Althea, rising. 'You told me the truth, and what I had said was so despicable that I deserved to have it told to me. All the mistakes are mine. I've wanted things that I've no right to; I suppose it's that. You and I weren't made for each other, just as Gerald and I weren't, and it's all only my mistake and my misfortune — for wanting and loving people who couldn't want or love me. I see it all at last, and it's all over. Good-bye, Helen.' She put out her hand.

'Oh, but don't — don't — ' Helen clasped her hand, strangely shaken by impulses of pity and self-reproach that yet left her helpless before her friend's sincerity. 'Don't say you are going to give me up,' she finished, and tears stood in her eyes.

'I'm afraid I must give up all sorts of things,' said Althea, smiling desolately. 'If we hadn't got so near, we might have gone on. I'm afraid when people aren't made for each other they can't get so near without its breaking them. Good-bye. I shall try to be worthy of Franklin. I shall try to make him happy.'

CHAPTER XXXV.

She drove back to her hotel. She felt very tired. The world she gazed at seemed vast and alien, a world in which she had no place. The truth had come to her and she looked at it curiously, almost indifferently. London flowed past her, long tides of purpose to right and left. The trees in Green Park were softly blurred on the chill, white sky. She looked at the trees and sky and at the far lift of Piccadilly, blackened with traffic, and, at the faces that went by, as if it were all a vast cinematograph and she the idlest of spectators. And it was here that love had first come to her, and here that despair had come. Now both were over and she accepted her defeat.

She thought, when the hotel was reached, and as she went upstairs, that she would go to bed and try to sleep. But when she entered her little sitting-room she found Franklin there waiting for her. He had been reading the newspapers before the fire and had risen quickly on hearing her step. It was as if she had forgotten Franklin all this time.

She stood by the door that she had closed, and gazed at him. It was without will, or hope, or feeling that she gazed, as if he were a part only of that alien world she had looked at, and this outward seeing was relentless. A meagre, commonplace, almost comic little man. She saw behind him his trite and colourless antecedents; she saw before him — and her — the future, trite and colourless too, but for the extraneous glitter of the millions that surrounded him as incongruously as a halo would have done. He was an angel, of course; he was good; but he was only that; there were no varieties, no graces, no mysteries. His very interests were as meagre as his personality; he had hardly a taste, except the taste for doing his best. Books, music, pictures — all the great world of beauty and intellect that the world of goodness and workaday virtues existed, perhaps, only to make possible — its finer, more ethereal super-structure — only counted for Franklin as recreations, relaxations, things half humorously accepted as one accepts a glass of lem-onade on a hot day. Not only was he without charm, but he was unaware of charm; he didn't see it or feel it or need it. And she, who had seen and felt, she who had known Gerald and Helen, must be satisfied with this. It was this that she must strive to be worthy of. She was unworthy, and she knew it; but that accepta-tion was only part of the horror of defeat. And the soulless gaze with which she looked at him oddly chiselled her pallid face. She was like a dumb, classic mask, too impersonal for tragedy. Her lips were parted in their speechlessness and her eyes vacant of thought.

Then, after that soulless seeing, she realised that she had

frightened Franklin. He came to her. 'Dear — what is the matter?' he asked.

He came so near that she looked into his eyes. She looked deeply, for a long time, in silence. And while she looked, while Franklin's hands gently found and held hers, life came to her with dreadful pain again. She felt, rather than knew — and with a long shudder — that the world was vast; she felt and feared it as vast and alien. She felt that she was alone, and the loneliness was a terror, beating upon her. And she felt — no longer seeing anything but the deeps of Franklin's eyes — that he was her only refuge; and closing her own eyes she stumbled towards him and he received her in his arms.

They sat on the sofa, and Franklin clasped her while she wept, and she seemed to re-enter childhood where all that she wanted was to cry her heart out and have gentle arms around her while she confessed every wrong-doing that had made a barrier be-tween herself and her mother's heart. 'O Franklin,' she sobbed, 'I'm so unhappy!'

He said nothing, soothing her as a mother might have done.

'Franklin, I loved him!' she sobbed. 'It was real: it was the reallest thing that ever happened to me. I only sent for you because I knew that he didn't love me. I loved him too much to go on if he didn't love me. What I have suffered, Franklin. And now he is going to marry Helen. He loves Helen. And I am not worthy of you.'

'Poor child,' said Franklin. He pressed his lips to her hair.

'You know, Franklin?'

'Yes, I know, dear.'

'I am not worthy of you,' Althea repeated. 'I have been weak and selfish. I've used you — to hide from myself — because I was too frightened to stand alone and give up things.'

'Well, you shan't stand alone any more,' said Franklin.

'But, Franklin — dear — kind Franklin — why should you marry me? I don't love you — not as I loved him. I only wanted you because I was afraid. I must tell you all the truth. I only want you now, and cling to you like this, because I am afraid, because I can't go on alone and have nothing to live for.'

'You'll have me now, dear,' said Franklin. 'You'll try that, won't you, and perhaps you'll find it more worth while than you think.'

Something more now than fear and loneliness and penitence was piercing her. His voice: poor Franklin's voice. What had she done to him? What had they all done to him among them? And dimly, like the memory of a dream, yet sharply, too, as such memory may be sharp, there drifted for Althea the formless fear that hovered — formless yet urgent — when Franklin had come to her in her desperate need. It hovered, and it seemed to shape itself, as if through delicate curves of smoke, into Helen's face — Helen's eyes and smile. Helen, charm embodied; Helen, all the things that Franklin could never be; all the things she had believed till now, Franklin could never feel or need. What did she know of Franklin? so the fear whispered softly. What had Helen done to Franklin? What had it meant to Franklin, that strange mingling with magic?

She could never ask. She could never know. It would hover and whisper always, the fear that had yet its beauty. It humbled her and it lifted Franklin. He was more than she had believed. She had believed him all hers, to take; but it was he who had given himself to her, and there was an inmost shrine — ah, was there not? — that was not his to give. And pity, deep pity, and sadness immeasurable for a loss not hers alone, was in her as she sobbed: 'Ah, it is only because you are sorry for me. I have killed all the rest. You are not in love with me any longer — poor — poor Franklin — and everything is spoiled.'

But Franklin could show her that he had seen the fear, and yet that life was not spoiled by shrines in each heart from which the other was shut out. It was difficult to know how to say it; difficult to tell her that some truth she saw and yet that there was more truth for them both — plenty of truth, as he would have said, for them both to live on. And though it took him a little while to find the words, he did find them at last, completely, for her and for himself, saying gently, while he held her, 'No, it isn't, dear. It's not spoiled. It's not the same — for either of us — is it? — but it isn't spoiled. We've taken nothing from each other; some things weren't ours, that's all. And even if you don't much want to marry me, you must please have me, now; because I want to marry you. I want to live for you so much that by degrees, I feel sure of it, you'll want to live for me, too. We must live for each other; we've got each other. Isn't that enough, Althea?'

'Is it — *is* it enough?' she sobbed.

'I guess it is,' said Franklin.

His voice was sane and sweet, even if it was sad. It seemed the voice of life. Althea closed her eyes and let it fold her round. Only with Franklin could she find consolation in her defeat, or strength to live without the happiness that had failed her. Only Franklin could console her for having to take Franklin. Was that really all that it came to? No, she felt it growing, as they sat in silence, her sobs quieting, her head on his shoulder; it came to more. But she saw nothing clearly after the hateful, soulless seeing. The only clear thing was that it was good to be with Franklin.

THE END

www.ingramcontent.com/pod-product-compliance
Lightning Source LLC
Chambersburg PA
CBHW050521260626
47157CB00004B/1423